Praise for Sarah Bird's

ABOVE THE EAST CHINA SEA

"Engaging, haunting, and illuminating. . . . A unique tale of friendship that defies time and space. . . . Poignant and deeply memorable." —*The Daily Beast*

"Compelling. . . . Bird deftly captures the unique, era-appropriate voice of each girl. . . . Revelations are at once heartbreaking and uplifting, and reinforce an Okinawan expression uttered by many of Bird's unforgettable characters: 'Nuchi du takara.' Life is the treasure." —*The Seattle Times*

"A moving dual coming-of-age story." —*Marie Claire*

"This is the rare tome that has the goods for both popular and critical acclaim at the highest level. . . . After this book, Bird should be a literary household name." —*The Dallas Morning News*

"Revelatory." —*Reader's Digest*

"Gripping. . . . This tale of how women and girls survive bloody times manages its happy ending without offering easy answers—quite a feat for such an entertaining read." —*The Austin Chronicle*

"To my mind, Bird is the finest living Texas novelist, and *Above the East China Sea* showcases all of her gifts in spades—her unmistakable voice displays warmth, wit, and that rare variety of irreverence that possesses real heart." —Robert Leleux, *The Texas Observer*

Sarah Bird

ABOVE THE EAST CHINA SEA

Sarah Bird, winner of the 2014 Texas Writer Award and a Barnes & Noble Discover Great Writers pick, is the author of eight other novels, including *The Yokota Officers Club*. She grew up on air force bases around the world and now makes her home in Austin, Texas. She is a columnist for *Texas Monthly* and has contributed to other magazines, including *O, The Oprah Magazine*; *The New York Times Magazine*; *Salon*; and *Real Simple*.

sarahbirdbooks.com

ABOVE THE
EAST CHINA SEA

A NOVEL BY

SARAH BIRD

VINTAGE BOOKS
A Division of Random House LLC
New York

FIRST VINTAGE BOOKS EDITION, APRIL 2015

The Library of Congress has cataloged the Knopf edition as follows:
Bird, Sarah.
Above the East China Sea : a novel / by Sarah Bird. — First Edition.
pages cm
1. Daughters—Fiction. 2. Orphans—Fiction.
3. Okinawa Island (Japan)—Fiction. I. Title.
PS3552.I74A425 2014 813'.54—dc23 2013024336

Vintage Books Trade Paperback ISBN: 978-1-101-87386-1
eBook ISBN: 978-0-385-35012-9

Book design by Maggie Hinders
Maps by Christy Krames

www.vintagebooks.com

Printed in the United States of America
10 9 8 7 6 5 4 3 2 1

To the people of Okinawa,

who have learned the only lesson war has to teach:

Nuchi du takara.

Children, I'm singing you the story of Miyako
the beautiful, the blue, the deepening indigo,
and the red soil made from crushed bodies
that lay down their genealogy of bones.

Their spirits are whispering to you: all of this is what is.

—from "The Ocean of the Dead" by Yonaha Mikio

CONTENTS

MAPS · x

_____

PART I
UNKEH *The First Day*
Welcoming the Dead Home · 1

PART II
NAKANUHI *The Middle Day*
Celebrating with the Dead · 143

PART III
UKUI *The Third and Final Day* · 233

PART IV
UKUI *The Last Night*
The Dead Are Escorted Back to Their World · 263

_____

ACKNOWLEDGMENTS · 319

JAPANESE EMPIRE, 1943

SOUTHERN OKINAWA

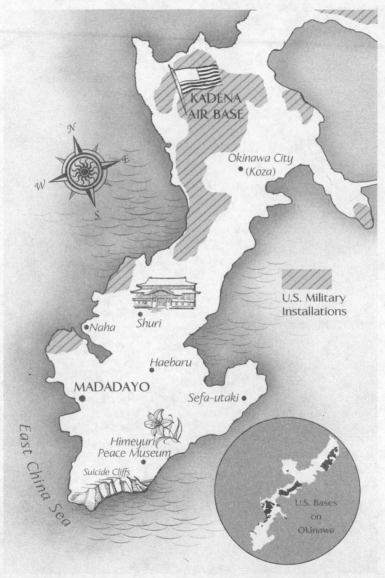

KADENA
AIR BASE

Okinawa City
(Koza)

N

E

W

S

U.S. Military
Installations

Shuri

Naha

Haebaru

MADADAYO

Sefa-utaki

Himeyuri
Peace Museum

Suicide Cliffs

East China Sea

U.S. Bases
on
Okinawa

PART I

UNKEH THE FIRST DAY

Welcoming the Dead Home

· ONE ·

The choking black smoke from the fires raging below rises up, trying to claim me and my child. I climb higher. I must hurry. I must
do what has to be done before the sun rises. The black stone tears at my
skin. I ignore the cuts and drag us up and onto the top of the cliff.

At the summit, I rise on trembling legs. The hundred thousand spirits who've gone before greet us with cries of joy, happy as a flock of
crows at sunset hailing the returned. I see them floating all around. I
see the women, the young girls, their kimonos fluttering above their
heads like tattered banners as they plummet through the air. I see the
emperor's soldiers, emaciated young men, caps flying straight up off
their heads as they hurtle down, toward the sea.

They had no choice but to jump. And, now, we have none. The soldiers, either Japanese or American, will kill us as soon as the sun rises.
We cannot die such a violent death. If we do, we will be condemned to
haunt this place forever and never be reunited with our clan. I won't
permit my child to endure such a cruel fate.

Though night still covers the carnage, I don't need to see the black of
charred ruins or the dun of mud mixed with corpses, which is all that
remains of my mutilated island. A breeze from the East China Sea lifts
sweat-dampened hair from the back of my neck. It carries with it the
stench of death from a place where not a single leaf of green hope has
survived.

I close my eyes and remember Okinawa as it was on the day before
everything changed. I see the colors of paradise. The pink of the baby

piglets. The gold of the trunks of our bamboo grove. The purple of my mother's sweet potatoes. The yellow of the flowers on the sea hibiscus hedge that lined the path leading to our house. The red of the blossoms on the *deigo* tree, blazing as though the side of the mountain were on fire. The colors sparkle against a background of infinite green. Leaf, vine, grass. Above and below are blue. The ocean is the blue of jewels. The sky is the blue of softness. All I can give my unborn child now is the blue of sky, the blue of a water death. I hope that I am carrying a son. Life is too hard for a daughter. A sister. A mother. Death will be even harder.

The stones I fill the leather satchel strapped across my chest with are so heavy I can barely stagger forward to the edge of the cliff. But they have to weigh enough to pull us down under the sea and keep us there. We can't join the hundreds of other suicides who have washed ashore, their corpses swelling even now on the beach far below. My child and I must sleep beneath the waves until the moment chosen by the *kami* arrives. That is the obligation I must fulfill.

My toes, the soles of my broad, sturdy Okinawan feet, grip the black rock. They cling like dumb animals to life even when only death remains. They beg, saying, "Tamiko, please, Tamiko, our fifteen short years on this earth have not been enough." My feet want to run again through the grass. They want to dance with such grace that I win the love of a handsome boy. They want to carry me home to my mother. To my sister, my Hatsuko.

Though I thought my heart had hardened to a rock, it aches now with missing my family, Hatsuko most of all. I shake away such weakness. I am fifteen. Old enough to know that a mother does what she must for her child in this life and, more important, in the next. I pray to our ancestors, to all the *kami-sama*. To the ones who've gone before, to the gods of hearth and field, altar and forest, to all the spirits who control our destinies. I beg them to help us, to let my child and me enter the next world and be reunited with my family. With our family.

I wrap my arms tight around my belly and step off the cliff. It is easy. The easiest thing I've had to do since the Americans invaded. The *kami* cradle us, just as I cradle my child. Still, when we land, the sea is hard as concrete. The salt water floods my mouth, throat, lungs. There is a moment of pain, of clawing struggle when I am certain I've made a terrible mistake. Then it vanishes and I let the stones drag us down, farther and farther under the waves, until the new-risen sun far overhead shrinks away to a pearl that shimmers briefly before it is lost forever in darkness.

Our wait begins.

· TWO ·

*J*ump? Or don't jump?

The question rattles around inside my head like a handful of BBs in a metal coffee can. Versions of it have been clanging around in there for the past three months, ever since I found out about Codie: *Take the pills? Don't take the pills? Run the exhaust hose in through the car window? Kick back with a bottle of Percocet, a few beers, and watch as many episodes of* True Blood *as it takes?*

I go back and forth. Good days. Bad days. The past week, since my mom's been gone on TDY, has been good. It's always easier when she's not around. Actually, they say that most suicides happen when the person is feeling better. I believe it. When you can't drag yourself out of bed, it's hard to get up the energy to even stick a fork in a wall socket. Mom's temporary duty assignment is over in two days. That gives me forty-eight hours to make up my mind.

A hundred and fifty feet straight down, at the base of the cliffs I'm standing on top of, the waves churn white against some spiked rocks stabbing up above the water. That's where I'd land. Death would be instantaneous. That's a plus. Put that one in the "pro" column.

I hold my arms out and a muggy breeze off the East China Sea lofts the hair up off the back of my sweaty neck. In spite of the steam-bath humidity, I still feel like a dried-up leaf, all withered and brown from not being attached to anything, anywhere, in such a long time. It seems like the slightest gust of wind should be enough to blow me off this cliff and out of this life forever.

I'm terminally sick of not being able to decide. Of being trapped in this cycle of what my mom would call "fiddle-fucking around." Indecision is something they cut out of her in NCO Leadership School. They recently changed the name to the Warrior Leader Course. My mom, though, she never needed a title to tell her what to become. "Shit or get off the pot" has always been her mantra. That and "Get 'er done." She regularly surprises people because she sounds so country but looks so Asian. She's half Okinawan, which is why I stupidly thought that transferring here would be like returning to some magical ancestral homeland where we would instantly be treated like family. Didn't quite turn out that way. To say the least.

I experiment with tipping forward. My weight shifts onto the balls of my feet, and my stomach drops worse than if I'd already taken the leap and landed hard. That's part of the test. Maybe if I push myself this close to the edge, I'll smoke out a deeply hidden reason for going on living. And maybe psychedelic rainbows and sparkling unicorns will fly out of my ass and I'll love life again. I'd be open to that.

I take it up a notch. I close my eyes, raise my arms higher, and sag into the wind. The instant I do, I am filled with a weird sense of being watched. But not by a bunch of pervs egging someone perched at the edge of a high-rise to do it, to jump. It's more like someone, a lot of someones, are out there, waiting, inviting me to join them. And Codie is with them. I feel her presence. She is waiting for us to be together again. And all I have to do is let go.

I am tilting forward, about to let gravity take me, when two ropy arms clamp on to me from behind.

"Hey, Luz." Kirby Kernshaw's greeting is an air-rifle puff of beer breath against my neck. "Whatcha doin', Tiger Woods?"

I open my eyes. Clouds again cover the moon. I inhale once, twice, and shift from being a body on the spiked rocks far below back to being Luz James, new girl at a new base, hanging out with her latest group of Quasis, the semistranger, friendesque beings that I meet at a new assignment, then just about, almost, but not quite, get to know right before we're transferred again.

"Tiger Woods, where you been, girl?"

"Hey, Lucky Charms."

Kirby is Lucky Charms for his red hair. A tall, lanky, demented leprechaun of a lad who's been held back at school a few times, Kirby Kernshaw is one of those gingers whose freckles blend into his lips.

I'm Tiger Woods, since it's easy shorthand for "part Okinawan–part Filipina–part Missouri redneck–part miscellaneous." You know, your basic caramel person. "Uh, Kirby, you want to stop grinding your stiffy into my butt?"

He laughs, but doesn't turn me loose.

"Kirbs, for serious, get your hand off my boob." He removes it. "And the one on my crotch?"

Lucky Charms isn't so much saving as humping me. He lets go and lurches away, muttering, "Girl, how can someone so hot be so cold."

Kirby must have been dispatched on a beer run for our nightly party going on right now so far down the long trail winding along the side of the cliff that the bonfire on the beach looks like the glowing ember of a match tip.

Kirby grabs the handles of the red-and-white Igloo cooler beside him, hoists it up, then leans back with the weight braced against his thighs. "A little help, girlfriend."

"Sure."

I grip the rear handle of the heavy cooler with both hands, and Kirby leads me down the series of switchbacks zigzagging across the steep face of the cliffs that ring the shore. Bottles and ice clank from side to side as we inch our way along the ant trail. I've still got two days left. That's plenty of time to "get 'er done" before Mom gets back. Okinawa, with its riptides and venomous *habu* vipers, unexploded ordnance left over from World War II and pill-happy base doctors, is one giant suicide op waiting to happen.

No doubt after I do it, they'll assign someone from Family Advocacy to investigate, to determine my "state of mind" at the time of my death, since suicide is such a high-priority thing now because more soldiers are killing themselves than are dying in combat. They already did a study and found out that almost none of the soldiers who killed themselves had an "intact family" to go home to. Also, they practically never seemed suicidal. Those facts haunt me; they pertain.

It's important to me not to seem suicidal. When Family Advocacy investigates after I do it and they ask the Quasis, "How did Luz James seem to you?" I can't have any of them talking about what a droopy-assed loser I was. I want them to say, "Luz? Luz James? No, she seemed perfectly fine." Maybe add, "She was always so full of life," and pretend to be all broken up. The girls especially, even the ones who didn't know me at all, since that will give them a good reason to cry and show how sensitive they are.

I'm concentrating so hard on making myself full of life and the opposite of suicidal that when Kirby sways, it knocks me off balance, and I bump into the cliff. The razor-sharp black rock scrapes my ankle. The cut will get infected, since every cut gets infected on Okinawa. The island is encircled by one of the world's great coral reefs. I watched a YouTube video that showed how coral is composed of billions of tiny polyps that form themselves into fantastical shapes—antlers, fans, brains—in these amazing purples and yellows and reds. When the polyps die, they leave their skeletons and the tiny limestone tombs they've built around themselves behind. So, dead polyp skeletons, that's what's in the cut.

"Hey, Tiger Woods?" Kirby grunts back at me. "Why are you so late? It's after twenty hundred hours."

"If you mean eight o'clock, Kirby, say eight o'clock."

"You're such a civilian, Luz."

"Only a Gung Ho would even think that that's an insult."

"You callin' me a gun ho?"

I start to tell him about how Codie called the freaks who were genetically engineered to be military brats Gung Hos. I see her doing her imitation of a typical Gung Ho, jumping around all excited, going, "I love moving! It gives me a chance to reinvent myself!" like they're Lady Gaga with the whole world just waiting to see the latest incarnation. After a lifetime of our mom and the U.S. Air Force uprooting us every other year or so, Codie and I were so anti–Gung Ho that we even developed mental blocks about decoding the twenty-four-hour clock. It meant that we occasionally committed the worst brat sin of all: being late. But to us, being late was a lot better than being a Gung Ho.

I'm doing it again. I'm relating everything back to Codie.

"Loozer," Kirby repeats, "why'd you call me a gun ho?"

"Never mind, Kirb. It's nothing." Suddenly very, very tired, I dump my end of the cooler down onto the trail. "Brew thirty," I say, popping the cooler open. I ice-fish for a beer, hook a tall silver one, and reel it in. The cold feels good against my hot hand, lips, going down my throat. My thirst leaves, but not what I didn't want to think about: *Codie was not a Gung Ho.* She wasn't. That's why it doesn't make sense. Why what happened could never have happened.

· THREE ·

Are you there?

    For a moment, before I awake, I think the distant voice belongs to Hatsuko, and joy floods my being: My sister has come for us. I never doubted that she would.

It's not Aunt Hatsuko, Mother; it's me.

My child. His voice grows stronger as we both awaken.

How long have we slept?

A year? A decade? A century?

I don't know.

Mother, am I going to be born now? Is that why we awoke?

No.

I can't lie. Curled up as he is beneath the place where my heart once was, my child knows all the thoughts and memories that I allow to enter my mind. Which is why I must carefully monitor what I think so he will never know the worst.

Are we going home then? To your family in Madadayo? Will Aunt Hatsuko be waiting to greet us in the shade of the veranda? Will she offer us cool wheat tea sweetened with barley sugar and beni imo *cakes as purple as the tang fish?*

Yes, your aunt Hatsuko and all the rest of our family will be there. We will be together. I promise you, no matter what the cost, we will be reunited with our clan.

Are they waiting for us in the next world?

Yes.

But first we must be found and buried, right?

Yes, I say, though he already knows that answer. He knows everything I know, all the rules that govern this life and those that determine who will be admitted to the next. He also knows my ignorance, the parts I don't understand. And those voids frighten him.

How will we be found down here so far beneath the sea?

That is not for you to concern yourself with. The kami will find a way.

Will we become fiidama, *like the one who drowned your brother and stole his corpse?*

When had I allowed such a sad memory to enter our minds?

Yes.

Are we waiting here until we can lure a swimmer out to us, then steal his spirit and use his corpse to gain entrance to the next world?

There is no other way left to us.

Mother?

Call me by our Okinawan word for mother.

Yes, Anmā. Anmā, I miss the eels.

I remember the moray eels that gathered after we jumped. They were a great source of amusement for us. My son liked the ones that were mossy and green as old logs. I preferred those speckled brown and white like giraffes. Neither of us liked the ones with mad, spinning eyes, or those with only murky gray spots for eyes.

They all had blubbery lips that parted to reveal dagger-tipped teeth that tore at our flesh and released a rain of particles that lured a rainbow of fish to us in colors dazzling as hand-blown glass. So many different sorts of fish. Fish with scales of yellow, purple, silver, green. Clouds of fish that flashed a neon blue brighter than the lights of Naha. Fish with blue teeth and green lips. Fish striped black and white like prisoners. Fish that never tired of chasing one another about in endless games of tag. Our favorites, though, were the ones that floated stupefied in front of us, as if they had forgotten how to swim.

When all our flesh was gone, the eels and fish, and, finally, even the marine worms, stopped visiting, and we waited. And slept. And now my son is awake and asking questions that I am obliged to find answers for.

Anmā, we are so far from the surface down here. How will we ever steal a stranger's spirit so that we might take over his corpse and find our way to the next world, where our munchū *waits for us?*

When it is time, the kami will show us the way to our clan.

It must be time now. Why else would we have awakened?

We shall soon learn why.

But we must do something.

What? We are no longer of the living, and we certainly are not yet kami-sama. *We are trapped between worlds. The only power we have is to wait.*

Then, while we wait, tell me once more everything you know about the next world.

I told my son what his grandmother had told me: that in that other realm, the air shimmered like lapis lazuli and was perfumed by the scent of lilies and pineapples. That every one of the 2,046 ancestors of our *munchū* for ten generations into the past would meet there after death to feast on pigs' ears in vinegar, sweet potato in green-tea sauce, stir-fried bitter melon, and pork stewed in squid's ink, all washed down with cool wheat tea sweetened with black sugar for the children and millet brandy for the adults. That we would dance beneath the vast roof of a banyan tree while our legendary great-great-great-grandfather Ryō plucked tunes from his *sanshin*. That the timid dwarf deer, the emerald frog, the long-haired mouse, and the orchid leaf butterfly would all emerge from hiding to marvel at the beauty of our arm movements, the liveliness of our steps. That we would frolic there with the fairies and fauns who inhabit that other world and be reunited with our mothers, fathers, aunts, uncles, grandparents, and great-grandparents beyond remembering.

I told him of the sweetest promise the other realm held for me: I would be reunited with my sister. Hatsuko and I would be together once more.

Will there be sword fights?

That my child loved best my memories of the sword fights I used to have with my boy cousins, Shinsei and Uei, made me certain that he, too, was a boy. So I assured him that of course in the next world there would be sword fights. This excited him. There had been no real weapons on our island since they were confiscated by the Japanese invaders in 1609, so my cousins and I used to arm ourselves with the straightest boughs we could pluck from the screw pine trees and slash at one another like the valiant samurai our ancestors had been.

And spiders?

Second only to sword fights, he liked memories about the times when we children, the capering herd of us, would capture banana spiders bigger than a man's hand and stage grand battles with them.

And the hills?

He never tired of my memories of sliding down hills of grass. I assured him that in that place where all the best memories are forever real, we would never need worry about vipers hiding beneath the silvery blades. No *habus* or mosquitoes, gnats or lice exist where the evenings last an eternity and ocean breezes are always blowing, gentle and cool.

We will be there soon.

As the months or years or decades, I know not which, passed, I made this vow again and again to my son, promising him that we had not been abandoned for all eternity at the bottom of the East China Sea. That even now my sister was begging the *kami* to intercede on our behalf. Yet, eventually, despair found me, and I feared that we had, indeed, been forgotten. I could accept that my father, mother, and brothers had all ceased imploring the *kami* to save us, but Hatsuko? Hatsuko would never abandon me. I now cling to the hope that she is still visiting *yutas*, the women the spirits speak through. That she simply has not found the right one yet.

It galls me that I can do nothing to help Hatsuko rescue us from this netherworld and send us on to the shimmering place. Until I join my ancestors, I'm not *kami-sama* like them, so I don't have the power to inflict suffering on the living to remind them of their obligations to us. I can't even summon a swarm of biting flies, as Old Jug, my great-great-grandmother Uto Kokuba, once did during the worst of the invasion, when she expressed her displeasure at me for almost giving up on life. I can do nothing, except wait for the *kami* to send us a stranger.

I study my brother's story endlessly, picking it apart to find the clues I need to save my child from this watery limbo. In our village, my oldest brother, Ichirō, was known as Forest Orchid Boy, because his scent alone was said to drive girls mad. Ichirō was funny, smart, strong, and so handsome that the *juris* in the Tsuji pleasure quarter never charged him their usual rate of five yen for the privilege of making love to them. All the maidens in the village dreamed of marrying him, but none captured his fancy until Nobuko, a distant cousin of the Jiriya family, arrived to work at her uncle's factory, where she was put to work stripping fibers from the pandanus plant to weave into panama hats. From the first moment Ichirō set eyes on Nobuko, he was crazed with love for her, and she for him.

For months they met in secret, stealing away to lie together upon cool beds of leathery ferns beside the crystalline waters of the Oigama River. Ichirō's joy abounded when he learned his lover was carrying his *ashibingwa*, his love child, and they planned to be married. Nobuko's uncle, however, flew into a rage at such an idea, since he had already arranged an advantageous union between Nobuko and his largest exporter, Mr. Inafuku. The deal had been struck; glasses of *awamori* had already been shared. The uncle would not endure the humiliation of his niece's disobedience, and immediately sent Nobuku away to marry the exporter and live imprisoned behind the stone walls that surrounded his grand house in Naha.

Ichirō's spirit left his body then, and our mother exhausted herself doing all she could to lure it back. She took him to the secluded grove of acacia trees, where he had bidden Nobuko farewell, dropped to her knees facing the direction of home, placed her hands together, bowed her head, and prayed to her son's spirit, begging his *mabui* to please come home. Then, holding out leafy canes of bamboo on either side to keep her son's spirit from straying, she guided him home.

Sadly, Ichirō's spirit did not accompany them. *Anmā* kept trying to entice it back by forcing her son to eat sweets, rubbing scented oil on his arms, and sweeping the air around him with bundles of burning tobacco leaves from her patch, but nothing worked. The light was gone from her firstborn's eyes as surely as from the eyes of one of the fat pigs she butchered on special occasions to make her delicious pork miso. Ichirō cared for nothing, which was why on Ukui, the third and last day of the Obon festival, he made the terrible announcement that he would go swimming.

Though the waves that day were gentle enough to rock a baby's cradle, we all went wide-eyed with fear. Everyone knew that on the third and last day of Obon, the spirits of the drowned whose remains were lost at sea tried everything within their power to lure one of the living to his death so that the displaced souls might find a home in the corpse.

At the beach that evening we all saw what we feared most. *Fiidama*, the hazy phosphorescent fireballs that are a sure sign of the presence of an uneasy spirit, danced in terrible clusters above the waves. As tears streamed down her face, Mother tried to hold Ichirō back. She pleaded with her son, telling him what she would tell me years later: *Nuchi du takara*. Life is the treasure. But he forced her to let him go. His spirit had already left his body, and his life had stopped being a treasure. Mother wept as her brave, handsome child swam out so far that we could barely see his dark head bobbing up and down among the waves.

We watched in horror from the shore as the eerie glow of a *fiidama* shining with a particularly bright and steady green luminescence targeted Ichirō. It followed him as he swam away from us, wobbling over the black dot of his head like a jellyfish swaying in an ocean current. Our mother wailed out her grief, for she knew that some lost spirit who'd never had a proper burial—some fisherman who'd drowned in a storm, or merchant who'd fallen overboard off a trading vessel, or even one of the brave warriors who'd defended the island against the Japanese invaders—waited to claim her son's body. In the twilight, the *fiidama* pulsed with a deep, murderous glow that reflected red on the waves. And then it vanished and our brother was gone.

When his corpse washed ashore, we placed it in our family tomb and observed all the proper funeral rituals, but we knew we were honoring a stranger who did not belong with us. Mother grieved terribly that her son's body, his chance to spend eternity with his clan, had been stolen. Over the years, though she never specifically wished for Ichirō's displaced spirit to claim a stranger's body, as his had been claimed, she did go frequently to the place where he had disappeared to pray that, if such a thing were to happen, her son would find his way to our family's *munchū*. More than anything, she wanted her oldest son to be waiting for her with our clan's departed in the next world.

Had our mother been more specific in her prayers, I might now know how to become a *fiidama* myself and how to lure a stranger our way. But since she gave no instructions on this score, I am powerless, and I ache with a ferocity unknown to the living for what was promised in my mother's stories. For sweet potatoes in green-tea sauce, the scent of lilies and pineapples, but most of all, I yearn for Hatsuko. Near the end, when thirst and hunger were knives twisting ceaselessly within us, I believed that my ruined body was the cause of all my suffering. Here I have learned that pain is not sharpened by flesh; it is blunted. With no body there is no way to partition off suffering. It is a curse, yet it gives me an advantage over any of the living, who never see clearly until their eyes are closed forever. They are blind to the injustice of love withheld from the unlovely and lavished on the lovely, who, with their consolations of lovely, long necks and shiny, straight hair, need it so much less. They don't see how their foolish desires drive them to crawl over one another like crabs in a bucket fighting for a small circle of blue when the whole sky waits above.

And now, though I don't yet know why the *kami* have awakened us, I must make myself ready to use my advantage. I concentrate. I put doubt and despair aside and hone my desire. I fletch it like a samurai's arrowhead. I pull it back taut in the bow until it quivers, and I wait. The rules of destiny are harsh, but to save my child's soul, I have accepted them. The *kami-sama* will send to us someone who hovers between the living and the dead, as Ichirō once did, as my child and I do now. And when that person arrives, I shall be ready and will release the arrow of my yearning straight into his heart.

· FOUR ·

On the beach a driftwood bonfire shimmies in the offshore breeze. When I get close enough that the cave-drawing figures clustered around the fire turn into actual humans, I slap something resembling a smile on my face.

"Luz! Luz! Luz and brews!" A baboon-troop hoot of greeting goes up when they spot us. Well, not us so much as Kirby's sloshing Igloo.

DaQuane Green lopes our way, and asks Kirby, "What the hell took you so long, son?" Tonight DQ's sporting a fade with a topknot of glossy curls. In a burst of speed, a figure breaks away from the others, darts ahead of DaQuane, and reaches the cooler first. It's Jake Furusato. Jake is the reigning prince of Smokinawa, leader of the kids who are either full or part Oki and part American and attached in some permanent way to the base. The Smokinawans are perfectly fluent in both languages and cultures. I wait for Jake to take my end of the cooler, but he messes with me, pretending to take the handle, then pulling his hand away.

"Jake, quit being a douche."

He grins, grabs the handle, brushes up against me, doesn't move.

It's been this way since the first second we set eyes on each other, Jake always finding excuses to touch me in semijokey ways. I guess that if there's one thing that would keep me interested in Okinawa, it would be Jake Furusato. But he's not a possibility, since he has an attached-at-the-hip-girlfriend, Christy Medoruma. I check the group gathered around the fire to see whether Christy is over there shooting daggers my way. She's not; Jake only gets playa with me when she's not around. In fact, none of Jake's crew of Smokinawans is in attendance tonight. An empty Orion can flashes in the firelight as it arcs into the flames, sending sparks flying into the dark night.

"Dude!" Jake protests, as he leans away from the burning shower. In the light from the fire, his skin is the color of apple jelly and his eyes are two slashes of calligraphy angling into his high cheeks. He reminds me so much of Ashkii Begay, this really good-looking Navajo guy I was crushed out on at my last school, that it's eerie.

As I head toward the fire, my flip-flops pelt gritty sand against my calves with each step. I met most of the beach crew three months ago, right after my mom and I arrived at the beginning of summer. Summer is high season for PCSing—permanent change of station—when the air force shuffles the deck and, for its own random reasons, moves about a third of its personnel to yet another random spot on the globe. Which is why Kadena was having an event to welcome incoming "military teens." It was held at the Kadena Teen Center Millennium: "Where Being a Teen Has Never Been So Much Fun!" Representatives from the crafts shop, gamers' club, archery range, and bowling league spoke about their groups and services. Then the director of the center, a staff sergeant with an Adam's apple like a hatchet blade sliding up and down in his throat, told us "military teens" that joining one of the groups he ran was the best way to integrate ourselves "into the community of your choice and to find others with shared interests."

Turned out that even better than throwing pots or playing "World of Warcraft" for getting integrated into the community of *my* choice was the interest me and Kirby's crew shared in getting high. Which, thanks to my mom's endless supply of benzodiazepines, I was when I went to the meeting. It was no big trick for us—the glassy and red of eye, the inappropriate of mirth, the flattened of affect, the bad of attitude—to recognize one another at that first meeting. It was even easier to sneak out of said meeting when the director told us to "break out"—an unfortunate choice of words for a guy whose cheeks were spangled with lavender acne—into our "interest groups."

My interest group broke out into the area behind the Teen Center. That's when Kirby said, "Welcome to Smokinawa," passed around a handful of one-hitters that looked like cigarettes from a distance, and we all smoked up. Then DaQuane volunteered that he knew a GI who'd buy liquor for us at the Class Six. Someone else, maybe me, had a sampler platter of pharmaceuticals. And boom. It was party time there, "Where Being a *High* Teen Has Never Been So Much Fun!"

The next night, we adjourned to Kirby's cove, and that's when I met Jake. He'd been surfing with his boys, and his black hair was wild and bushy and all spiked out from the salt water and humidity. A sleeveless T showed off his excellent surfer's tan and shoulders. From the second Jake noticed me, he kept looking my way. When Christy and her friends left to pee, he came over.

"*Hai-sai, mensorei,*" he said.

"Hi sie to you too," I answered.

"Sorry, I thought you were part Oki."

"I am. My grandmother was born here."

"Cool."

There was a silence and, out of nervousness, I threw in that, on my dad's side, I was also part German, African American, Irish, and Filipina. I didn't mention that my mom's father was a Missouri redneck.

"So, your name, Luz, it comes from the Philippines?"

I smiled, impressed that he could pronounce my name. Looz. Not Luss. "Yeah, it was my dad's mother's name." I didn't add that my name was pretty much the last thing my parents collaborated on, since my dad was gone before my first birthday. What did my mother expect, marrying her Kali martial arts teacher? A long *harmonious* relationship?

"Means 'light,' right?"

"Indeed it does. You get the bonus points."

He tipped his head to the side, either to study me or because he knew that his eyes and lips looked amazing from that angle. "There's something different about you, Light."

"Different how?"

"I don't know. You're not like most base kids."

"I guess that's a compliment."

"It is. I like your necklace." Jake slid his fingers against my collarbone as he lifted up the opal pendant I always wear. "Your boyfriend back in the States give you this?" He was playing playa with me and we both knew it wasn't for real. Or was only as real as I wanted to make it.

"No. No boyfriend back in the States."

Rubbing the opal gently between his fingers, he asked, "Is it true what they say about you?"

"I don't know. What do they say?" His eyes—larger, rounder than Japanese eyes—tilted up into perfect paisleys.

"That your mom is head of base police."

"It's true."

"So should I try to get on your good side, so she won't bust me?"

"That's funny."

"Why?"

"Because being on my good side would actually increase your chances of her busting you."

"Jake, I'm back!" Christy, standing off with her friends, called out. She looked pure Okinawan, but, eyes popping and head bobbing with ghetto exasperation, she sounded and acted pure American high school girl. Pure *jealous* American high school girl.

Jake continued cradling the opal, until Christy called again. Then, very slowly, he glided the backs of his fingernails against my skin as he slid the pendant back into place. "Pretty," he said, walking away.

For the next three months, although Kirby and the rest of us were at the cove almost every night, Jake and his crew of surfing Smokinawans only showed up sporadically, and when he did Christy never left his side. But whether he talked to me or not, there would always be a moment when he'd catch my eye, tap the spot below his throat where my opal necklace would have hung on him, then point to me and mouth the word "pretty." The necklace was the last thing Codie gave me. If she was here, we'd have spent hours dissecting the meaning of Jake's touches and smiles. But she's not, and without her, it's obvious that there is nothing between Jake Furusato and me to dissect. And nothing to hold me on Okinawa.

· FIVE ·

I make my way closer to the fire. A bonfire in August on a subtropical island makes the air feel chewable. But it's necessary for keeping mosquitoes at bay and for giving us a focal point. Focal points are very important for bands of nomads like me and the Quasis, with our CGI ability to constantly splinter and then reconstitute on a spot halfway around the world.

"Hey, Kirby," Wynn O'Dell yells. Wynn—one of those V-shaped guys who loves lifting weights a little too much and who you always suspect might have a Confederate flag hung in his bedroom—holds up a bottle of Cuervo Gold. "Look what I got for you, man." Wynn waves the bottle around like it's a piece of bacon and he's calling a dog. Which is pretty much how Kirby reacts.

Lucky Charms bounds over and Wynn snatches it out of his reach. Kirby fakes going left and grabs the Cuervo away when Wynn falls for the feint. Kirby hoists his prize aloft and the bottle turns to a scepter of gold in the light from the fire. Standing there next to Jake and my other new Quasi-friends laughing at what a goof Kirby is, I almost think I can do this for a while longer. Maybe I could live on the beach, exist on crabs and seaweed, and never go home. Never have to see my mother again, and it would all be bearable.

"James!" Jacey Bosfeld, an all-American blue-eyed Barbie doll with shiny curtains of palomino blond hair hanging on either side of her face, who has about three more years of being cute before all her curves go convex, yells at me. "Get your ass over here, bitch."

I hopscotch over the tangle of bodies. Jacey pats a spot on the sand next to her. I drop the small woven shoulder bag that carries my ID card onto it and sink down into the yummy chemical cloud of vanilla-musk lotion and coconut-mint conditioner Jace always exudes. Here on this sixty-mile-long island Jacey uses her artificially scarce, high-demand blond American-girl status for the benefit of all by sharing the tributes from her stream of well-provisioned boyfriends. Her current smooch nugget, Airman Basic Zavie Plutino, the Italian Shetland, a handsome, if spectacularly short GI, hands me the crafty little vaporizer he cobbled together from a lightbulb, a bottle cap, and some rubber tubing. He heats up the crafty bit of herb within until ghostly trails of smoke dance around the bulb, begging me to Hoover them down. Which I do.

Jake watches me. We have one of our eye moments. He doesn't seem to be mooning for the missing Christy Medoruma.

"All right!" Kirby throws his arms open wide and looks out at the waves, studying them like he's Captain Jack Sparrow about to put a spyglass up to his eye. "This might be the night. Eee-yaaah, the shipment just might come in tonight." He nods, waits for someone to ask him about "the shipment."

When no one does, he gets all grumpy and barks at me, "Tiger Woods, you ought not be hogging that." He means the vaporizer. Which I am not hogging. "Gonna be wishing you'd shared more with ol' Cousin Kirb when the shipment comes in."

Jacey holds her hand out for the vaporizer. "Kirby, you been talking shit about this mysterious 'shipment' every night for the past week."

"Yeah, well, this night just might be different." He nods in a way that's supposed to be thoughtful but just makes him look like a sleepy turtle. "*Very* different."

"How?" I ask. "Are you *not* gonna pass out and *not* wake up the next day covered with sand-flea bites?" I have to riff. It's expected. It's what I do.

"And *not* with a couple of all y'all bitches pregnant. *That'd* be different, yo."

"Seriously, Kirby," I say to possibly the *least* gangsta human on earth, "does this mean that you've actually found a girl who meets your exacting standards?"

Kirby nails me with a look that warns me not to go on. He really should know better.

"You know," I finish, "female *and* has a pulse." *Full of life.*

DaQuane hoots and raises a fist for me to bump.

"When did he add female to the list of requirements?" Jake asks.

"Be that way." Kirby pouts. "I'll just take your comments to mean that you're not interested in the shipment."

Jake waves away the vaporizer Jacey holds out to him, shakes his head. "Lucky Charms, you talk more shit than Mexican radio."

"Call me Lucky Charms one more time, Jackie Chan," Kirby warns, "and you are definitely off the list."

"Why?" I ask, just for something to say. "You're always calling me Tiger Woods."

"Uh, *gomen nasai*, Luz, that I referred to you as a megasuccessful champion billionaire, famous for having so many people want to hook up with you. Him," he corrects himself.

I don't really care whether Kirby wants to hook up with me or if he calls me Tiger Woods, any more than he really cares if I call him Lucky Charms. Or Jake cares if we call him Jackie Chan. Or, for that matter, than Jacey Bosfeld would care if I dubbed her Snow White. Her boyfriend, though, Zavie Plutino from somewhere back east in Rhode Island or New Jersey, one of those states with no air force bases, Zavie would no doubt be highly offended if I started calling him Guido.

Why? Because Zavie is not one of us. He's not a military kid. Xavier Plutino enlisted at eighteen. Of course, it was my big sister, Codie, who explained that military kids enlisted at birth. This world, the United States military, is all we've ever known, and way more than almost any other, it is a color-blind world. Intriguing racial mixes, yummy caramel people like me and DaQuane and half the other kids out here, are the norm. Now, rank, that's different. No one's going to joke about rank. Codie maintained that rank is our race. That we're not racists, but we *are* rankists.

And that's why every single one of us knows that Wynn O'Dell's dad is a full-bird colonel. And that Jacey Bosfeld and Kirby Kernshaw's dads are both staff sergeants. That Jake's father is a civilian but permanently attached to Kadena in a way no one is quite sure about, but that doesn't really matter, since civilian is civilian and therefore outside of our visible color spectrum. And they all know that my mom is a master sergeant and, most pertinent of all, that she's the new NCOIC of Dependent Security for the base police. That she works out of the Death Star, Security Forces HQ, and could get any of their families transferred with one OSI investigation. When the Quasis found out who my mom was, they were nervous until they realized that I only talk to her when absolutely necessary. Besides, since I do all the shit they do, there's no chance I'd narc anyone out. But none of that matters. Not tonight. Not with the Cuervo and the bulb of dancing smoke being passed around a beach fire spiraling golden sparks high up into a sky as dark as tar.

"Hey," Kirby says, "I might have gotten the shipment today." He's been teasing us all summer with hints about a shipment of some new designer drug he was supposed to be getting, and we're all burned out on hearing about it. When no one says anything, Kirby huddles around the bottle of Cuervo and collapses on the sand, where he goes into a sulk, all sad and deflated. Lying on the sand, his back to us, working on the Cuervo, he's silent for a long time. Then he starts sighing. The fifth or sixth time he heaves a giant one, I crumble and ask, "Shipment of what, Kirby?"

He sits up. The backs of his bare arms are covered in sand. A dried piece of seaweed clings to his hair like a tribal decoration. "Oh just a little safe, totally legal, totally awesome high."

Jacey unsuctions herself from Zavie's face and demands, "What awesome high?"

"Oh, *now* you're interested. *Now* you're all, 'Oh, Kirby, you're so interesting. Oh, Kirby, tell me more.'"

Jacey shrugs. "No, I'm not. Don't tell me. I don't care."

"Okay, bath salts. Everyone back in the world is doing it."

Jake shakes his head like he can't believe what he just heard. "Kernshaw, we talked about this. Okay, buddy? Remember what I said?"

"The shit's legal, dude."

"Maybe. Technically," Jake says. "In a few states back in the world. But we ain't in the world, are we, 'dude'?"

"Hay-sus, Jackie Chan, who died and made you my CO?"

The Cuervo and the vaporizer make their way to me and I lose what little interest I had in Kirby's babbling. Zavie torches the glass; I take a hit and wash it down with tequila. As the liquor and smoke unfreeze my insides enough that I can inhale most of a full breath, I dig my toes into the sand, burrowing them toward the cool damp below. Far out beyond the shallow waters ringing the cove where wading-pool waves lap at the shore, beyond the coral reef that encircles and protects the island with its underwater graveyard of antlers, fans, and brains, the big rollers crash and send plumes of mist rising high into the foggy moonlight.

Zavie leans over and blows smoke into Jacey's mouth. She tips toward him until they form a cozy triangle of reciprocal lust.

Wynn starts a thumb war with Jake that quickly escalates until they're both up and exploding sharp percussive blasts of exhalations as they swing roundhouse kicks at each other. Muscle-bound Wynn is a clown show, a galumphing sheepdog of clueless goodwill. Jake, on the other hand, compact and explosive, moves with the coil-and-release lethality of a leopard. He knows how to deliver—or, more important, to pull—such surgically precise strikes that it's obvious he could destroy poor Wynn if he wanted to. I'm so distracted that for a few seconds I forget and I'm just here, on the beach, laughing with friends at a couple of guys cuffing each other around like bear cubs.

Then a breeze whips in off the water, carrying the smell of the sea so strongly that I'm back in Hawaii that last time Codie and I were together, all happy and snorkeling and everything. To stop remembering what came after, I intercept the bottle of Cuervo and switch from swigs to chugs. Given a choice between remembering or passing out, I'll pick passing out every time.

But the Cuervo fails to keep me rooted in the present and I'm hurtled back to the moment when the end began.

· SIX ·

Mother, do you feel something?
    Yes.
What is it? Is it the kami?
It must be.
For the first time since we jumped, I feel a powerful vibration that grows stronger, then weakens, fading in and out like Father's short-wave radio when he tried to tune in Tokyo for news about the war.
    Mother, I'm frightened. Are the kami *about to end our existence? Will we become nothing?*
    No, I will never allow that to happen.
    Then what is it? Anmā, I'm scared. It hurts. I want it to stop. I want to be nothing again.

Stop! Never think that! We are being saved. The kami are just waking us up so we will be ready.

For what?

They're sending one of the living to us.

How? None of the living can dive all the way down here.

The kami have their ways.

I know! They will finally turn us into fiidama so we can dance on the waves and steal the body of the one they send to us, won't they?

How would I know?

Mother, the vibrations are fading. Have the kami forgotten us again?

No, but sometimes the living do not want to know what the kami desire of them.

But the kami are more powerful than the living, aren't they?

Of course they are. Still, the living, they will try to drown out the kami's message by dulling their senses. But they never succeed, because the kami have a secret weapon that the living can never escape.

What is that, Anmā?

Memory.

· SEVEN ·

Kirby throws an old lawn chair that had washed up on the beach onto the fire. The stink of melting plastic makes everyone jump up and, cursing him for the idiot he is, move away from the toxic fumes. I move too, but not because the smoke—or much of anything else—bothers me, since I'm not even really on the beach anymore. I'm back at Kirtland Air Force Base in Albuquerque, where we were stationed before transferring here. It's a year and four months ago, and I'm enduring the last few weeks of my sophomore year, and Codie her senior year, at Pueblo Heights High. That evening, the one when everything changed, the two of us were sitting on the patio in the backyard of our base house, working our way through a four-pack of Bacardi Breezers.

Mom was pulling a double shift because of a security alert on the flight line. An electrical storm sizzled through the black sky, and Codie and I were competing for who could spot the longest streak of lightning when she suddenly went quiet.

After the silence had gone on too long, I called out, "On your three o'clock," claiming a spectacular artery. "That's a winner. What's my prize?"

I expected Codie to protest and say her last lightning strike was longer. Or to tell me that I *had* won, and my prize was ten trays of Pueblo Heights High's cafeteria signature dish, Road Kill Enchiladas. Anything, because Codie hated, hay-*ted*, to lose. Instead, in a weirdly flat voice, she said, "I enlisted."

Certain that I'd misunderstood, I made a blinky face at my sister for so long that she asked, "Caboose? Did you hear me?"

Luz the Caboose. I got the nickname because I was always following her around. Codie was the one who led, who knew where we were going. But this? The military? Our whole lives the military had been the thing we both wanted to escape. The thing that made our parents such hard-asses that it was punishment loving them. I waited for her to tell me, "All I said was that 'I insisted.'" Or, "I am twisted." Or, "Iron lisped." Any of those phrases would have made more sense than "I enlisted." I would, in fact, have been less surprised if my sister had told me she was a hermaphrodite and that I'd have to learn to love her as a brother. Then I realized: Codie was messing with me.

I humphed out a dry laugh, since this wasn't really funny, and said, "Right. You enlisted."

Looking down at the bottle she was carefully picking the label off of, she pressed her lovely, full lips together and nodded. "Yeah, I did."

"You're serious?"

"As syphilis. Signed the papers and everything."

"You enlisted?" I kept saying the word, still hoping it might have another meaning that I was unaware of.

"Air force. Security Forces."

"An air bear? Like Mom?"

"Pretty much. I leave right after graduation."

Less than two weeks away. "No," I stated flatly, trying to convey how unacceptable this was.

"Well, actually, yes."

"Does Mom know?"

"Yeah."

Of all that was incomprehensible about my sister's announcement, that was the worst of it. That our mother knew before me. That she knew and hadn't stopped her. But it was worse than that. "She signed for you, didn't she?"

Codie shrugged. "Had to." She wouldn't turn eighteen until the end of June.

"And you didn't tell me? Neither of you told me?" I could not think of another time when my sister and mom had had a secret. Codie and I were the ones who always kept secrets—from our mother.

"I knew you weren't going to be happy."

"No, Codie, I'm not happy. I'm really, really not happy."

A whole Mount Olympus of lightning bolts streaked the sky, but neither of us claimed any of them.

Our entire lives, Codie and I, always moving to another base, another state, another country, we had been like those diving beetles who can live underwater because they take a bubble of air from the surface with them. Codie was my bubble of air. No matter what hostile environment the air force thrust us into, as long as I had Codie, I could breathe.

After we sat there saying nothing for a long time, Codie took my hand. My fingers had gone colder than the Breezers, but hers felt warm and soft as rising bread dough around them. "Cabooskie, be happy, okay? It's nothing. It's a couple of years when I would have fucked off and dropped out of community college and worked a bunch of crap jobs. It's just a way to pay for a real college. If I ever decide to go. It's not like colleges are going to come after me the way they're already coming after you, Miz Four Point Three."

"Codie, you don't know that. You're so smart. Smarter than me."

"Smarts don't count if you can't put them on paper."

Even though Codie had a classic case of dyslexia, we moved around so much in her early years of school that by the time it was diagnosed when she was in fourth grade, she'd already absorbed the idea that she was a dummy.

"Cabooskie, I know that you want what you think is best for me, and it's hard for you to believe that the air force is it, but it is. You just gotta trust me on this. Besides, Mom's up for a transfer, and if I gotta move anyway . . . ?"

"But what if you get sent to . . . ?"

"The Sandbox? No worries. Pretty much all the troops except rent-a-soldiers are already being withdrawn. Besides, I'm a female! In the air force! It's not like they're gonna put me out in an up-armored Humvee sweeping for IEDs or something. Statistically, driving I-25 would be more dangerous."

I didn't feel or look convinced.

"Cabooskie, don't stress. Mom already said that she'd pull strings to get me a cush assignment." She looked straight into my eyes and promised, "A safe assignment."

"But, Codie, we hate the military. We hate Gung Hos." *Our mother is a Gung Ho. She's not like us. She's the anti-us. You can't trust her. You can't abandon me.*

Codie shrugged, muttered, "YOLO," drained her bottle.

"YOLO? Don't be all You Only Live Once. This isn't like bungee jumping or some other onetime dumb-ass thing."

Codie pressed her lips together and nodded without saying anything.

When I saw the finality of that nod, I started blubbering so hard I could barely get the words out. "Please, come on, you can't do this. Please."

"Luz, it's done." She went inside and slid the patio door shut behind her.

I made myself stop crying and tried to swallow the lump in my throat with a chug from my bottle. It tasted like perfume and chemicals. I've never drunk Breezers since.

"Jace, hey, Jace, are you watching this?" Like a kid overamped on sugar, Kirby tries to divert Jacey's attention away from Zavie Plutino's vaporizer and big muscles.

"What?" Jace asks, annoyed.

"Cooking an egg with my flashlight."

Kirby is, indeed, swishing an egg around in a tuna can set atop a flashlight the size of a baguette. Beams of blinding light escape around the rim of the can and throw a halo up into the black sky like Batman signaling. The smells of burning tuna oil and can label blend with cooking egg as Kirby stirs the clear yolk around with a stick until it turns white because, yes, the ultimate Gung Ho flashlight *will* cook an egg.

"Hey, look!" Kirby holds the can up to show Jacey, who barely notices because she's still mostly involved with her short GI and his crafty vaporizer.

"Jesus!" Kirby drops the hot can and flicks his burned fingers in the air to cool them off. Scrambled egg spills onto the sand. Out of everyone's sight, tears flood my eyes at the thought of Kirby Kernshaw with his spindly arms and freckle-smeared lips packing an empty tuna can and an egg, *an egg*, down a cliff just so he can impress his latest batch of new friends with the special trick he can do with his special toy. I know it is totally stupid to be bawling for Kirby Kernshaw, but that knowledge does nothing to slow the stream of tears. Instead they fall harder as I watch the guys windmilling karate kicks and Jacey oozing over her latest interchangeable drug source. We're nothing but little baby birds in a nest, all open mouths, begging to be fed, to be liked, to have someone sit with us at lunch, to send us a Christmas card when we're gone, to remember that we were ever here when our two—three, if we're lucky—years are up and we have to start all over again at a new school with new Quasi-friends. Who'll also forget us as soon as we're gone.

Then, in the way I've been doing ever since it happened, I shift straight from sadness to anger, and Kirby's naked show of need starts to work on me like a dentist's drill, and I despise him. How has he not had it drummed into him that brats don't whine? We don't plead. We don't need. We require nothing. Not even real roots. We're air ferns. Kirby Kernshaw annoys me so much that I want to club his head in with a rock. I scrub the black mascara slurry off my face with the back of my hand.

I edge away from the fire. No one notices when I leave. I didn't expect them to. There's a myth that, because we move so much, military kids are geniuses at making friends. That we're social chameleons who can blend in anywhere. And for a few freaks, it's true. There are a minute number of brats who can strut into any school, anywhere in the world, get the social scene wired by second period, assemble an entourage by third, work their way up to the cheerleaders' table by the end of lunch, be elected president of student council by the last bell, and reign over homecoming court that night. There are mutants like that in any group. Maybe we have a few more than average because all the moving gives us more practice and turns some of us into ingratiation whores. In the end, though, what all military kids are truly gifted at, the social skill we've mastered better than any other, is unmaking friends. We're geniuses at leaving people behind.

And I was better at it than most. Why shouldn't I be? Codie was the one who mattered. A few days after she received her diploma from Pueblo Heights High, then Frisbeed her mortarboard across Tingley Coliseum, Codie left for Basic at Lackland. For the first few weeks the air force held her and all the other new recruits incommunicado. Then we got a preprinted card telling us where we could send mail, and even a time when Codie would be allowed to call us and talk for exactly three minutes. The card warned us not to worry. "Your recruit is adjusting to a new way of life and will sound scared, unhappy, and uncertain about whether he or she has made the correct decision." But when we finally spoke, Codie was confident, happy, and utterly certain that she *had* made the correct decision.

"I was born to do this," she'd crowed. "There's always someone to tell you what to do, and it's always a succession of random, unrelated tasks that you're not expected to understand. And best of all, there are never any papers to write and you almost never have to read. Dyslexia with a touch of ADHD is like having a superpower in the military. I'm such a rock star here."

"You were always a rock star, Kimchi."

"You can't call me that anymore. The big deal now is that we're pivoting our forces into Asia."

"'Pivoting' our forces?"

"Yeah, don't you love that? Like we're just gonna do a sweet little pirouette and vanish from Afghanistan, then pop back up in Yongsan, South Korea. No, listen, the Middle East? Yeah, it'll always be hot, but not cool like the Far East is gonna be. China, Korea, Japan. It's gonna be all about the Pacific Rim now, baby. How perfect is that? I even look the part. Hey, I've got a whole career ladder and everything."

"A career?" I thought that I could just about hang on by my fingernails for two years until she got out; then I had it all planned: We'd go to college together. With her SF experience, Codie would be a shoo-in for law enforcement. "You mean you're not coming back when your hitch is up? You're staying in?"

"Don't say it like that. Luz, I think I can get commissioned."

"An officer?"

"Yeah, why not? Because we were raised noncom?"

"No. Of course not. Absolutely you could be an officer. I just never in a million years thought that—"

"What? I'd be a lifer? I can hardly believe it myself. But, Luz, listen, for real, for once in my whole existence, I am seriously good at something. I am seriously good at being a soldier. I guess I just needed the structure or something."

"Like we didn't get enough structure growing up? Like our lives weren't run by Mom's Duty Rosters?"

"At home, sure. Sporadically. When she wasn't falling in or out of love."

"In and out of bed, more like. Mom had to have the military for structure or she'd be so far off the rails it wouldn't be funny. But you? Codie, you don't need it."

"Luz, you don't know that. You don't know what it's like in my head."

"Tell me, Codie. Make me understand."

"I got people in line behind me waiting for this phone. They won't give us back our personal ones for another month. Can't you just accept that this is my choice? It's what I choose to do."

"Or maybe you're just doing what Mom programmed us to do."

"You got the same programming and I don't see you rushing out to enlist. Come on, Luz, be happy for me. For the first time in my life I don't feel like a retard loser."

"That's the thing; you never were. You said it yourself so many times. It was because we moved so much. By the time a teacher figured out that—surprise!—even if you spelled 'stop' 'pots,' you were really fucking smart, and even if, maybe, next year, they'd get you assigned to the right class with the right teacher, we'd be gone by then."

"Boo-fuckin'-hoo. It is what it is."

It is what it is? I can't believe she uttered the ultimate Gung Ho statement of idiocy in any way except making fun of our mother, who says that exact thing way too often.

"Is Mom around? I need to ask her if she knows my DI."

Though I knew what a DI is, I tried to shake her out of Gung Ho mode by asking, "Your what?"

"Drill instructor. Is Mom there?"

I put our mother on and she barked, "What's the sit rep?"

She meant "situation report." Mom was still wearing her camo BDUs, her hair pulled up tight into a French braid that didn't extend more than the three inches in bulk that the air force authorized. They talked to each other in the foreign language that I'd resisted my whole life and my sister had secretly become fluent in, and it was all MTIs and MEPs and BMC.

"Forget that HUT! Two, three, four, shit," my mom advised. "It's HUT! Twop! Threep! Fourp! Put that 'puh' in and you'll get the cadence right." Talking to Codie, my mom was happy and animated in a way I could barely remember her ever being with us. A strange mix of jealousy, sadness, and revulsion forced me to leave.

After Basic, Codie went into Security Forces training, where, besides learning to direct traffic and what to do about barking dogs in base neighborhoods, she studied capture and recovery of nuclear weapons, IEDs, and military operations in urban terrain. Codie was good at everything, but utterly excelled at BEAST, Basic Expeditionary Airmen Skills Training, the week when they all went *Lord of the Flies*, lived wild in the field, and made war on one another. Codie was elected leader of Reaper Zone, and, in spite of being half the size of most of the guys on her team and still wearing full body armor and humping a pack containing three MREs, all her MOPP gear—chemical warfare suit, gloves, boots, and gas mask—and carrying two canteens and an M-16 rifle, she was officially credited with the most kills. Because she was not only an honor graduate but got a ribbon for highest small arms marksmanship, *and* made Warrior Flight, Codie was rewarded with the assignment that everyone dreams of, Hickam Air Force Base, right next to Honolulu and across the bay from its sister base, Pearl Harbor.

Meanwhile, I was surviving my junior year at Pueblo Heights as best I could. Which, without Codie, was not too sparkly good. Codie had always been the filter between me and the world. Doing school without her was a root canal minus the Novocain. I killed two birds—social group and numbing the pain—with one group of Quasis, the stoners, when I discovered how easy it was to hang with the slouchy kids who liked to get high. How open and welcoming they were. How essential and mood-elevating their drugs were. My favorite of this crew were the kids who were bused in from the rez. The sweet-faced Navajo girls who carried their weight in their tummies and favored low-rise jeans on their skinny legs and baby-doll tops with ties in back over their barrel chests. I liked them because they had even less interest than I did in getting acquainted. As soon as a brief, initial giddiness was over, we'd all clump together, say nothing, and kill time in as painless a way as possible. None of us was under the delusion that these were the best years of our lives or pretended that we'd "stay in touch."

When Mom got her orders for Kadena, "Keystone of the Pacific," the largest U.S. air base in Asia, near the end of my junior year last April, my reaction to her was, "No! You can't do this to me. There is no fucking way that I'm transferring my senior year. Period. End of discussion. I'll live on the street before I move again."

"Why? So you can stay here with a bunch of loser dopeheads? That is not going to happen. Besides, this is going to be different. We have family there."

"What family?"

"Your grandma's family. I have some names."

"Why haven't I ever heard about this family before?"

"You have. Your grandma used to talk about them a lot."

"I was eight when she died."

"I remember lots from when I was eight."

"She barely spoke any English."

"So? You should have learned Japanese."

"So! *You* should have taught me."

"Why is everything always my fault? When are you going to step up and take responsibility for your own life? Where would I be if I'd had your attitude? I'd be sitting around in Bumfuck, East Jesus, waiting for the world to hand me something. You can think whatever you want about the air force and your sister's decision, but at least she's doing something with her life."

"What? She's doing exactly what you raised her to do. She grew up on air force bases; she joins the air force. You grew up on air force bases; *you* joined the air force. Maybe if either one of you had been given some other options—"

Mom jumped in at that point and went off on how my attitude was what was wrong with this country and how, at my age, she was working two jobs, and America was for winners, not whiners. When I tuned back in, she'd returned to promoting Okinawa. "The point is, I have names. Aunts, uncles, cousins. You said you were always jealous of people with big extended families. Now you'll have one. Okinawans are good about family. Tight. Your grandma always told me that. You'll probably have a huge gang of cousins waiting to party with you."

Someone to party with was sort of the goal of my mom's life. Eventually I agreed to go. Cousins and a big extended family sounded good, but that wasn't what changed my mind. What changed my mind was that, after almost a year at Hickam, after almost half of her hitch was over, Codie got deployed. I don't know whether Mom's strings didn't reach to Hawaii or she just stopped pulling them, but Codie's orders came in a month after ours, and they were for Afcrapistan.

The only string Mom actually was able to pull was to get a buddy of hers to work some magic with our orders, so that we had a five-day layover in Hawaii right before Codie was scheduled to leave. So going to Okinawa was the price I had to pay to see my sister before she deployed.

When Codie picked us up at the airport, I almost didn't recognize her. She was taut and tan. Every soft place on her had been hardened into muscle. She had her hair skinned back in the same French braid Mom was wearing. When I hugged her it was like my sister had been compressed into a dense antimatter version of herself. I felt shy around her and hung back while she and Mom went into their pod-person Gung Ho routine.

"What's your tempo band?" Mom asked.

"A," Codie answered.

"Suh-*weet!*" They high-fived. "And what's your max deployment time?"

"Hundred and twenty days."

"Piece of cake. You can do that standing on your head. Just don't leave base. For anything. Never go outside the wire."

"No worries, I'll be the best little fobbit ever."

They laughed while I figured out that a fobbit had something to do with being stationed on a forward operating base away from the action.

Listening to them bond over "ABUs" and "CST reporting instructions" made me want to stow away in the luggage compartment on the next flight straight back to Albuquerque. Then suddenly, miraculously, the Gung Ho talk was over. Ever the party girl, Mom had us drop her off at the NCO club, where she knew half the noncoms and planned on speed-dating the rest. Once I had her alone, Codie turned back into my sister. As we walked across the NCO club lawn, I took the first full breath I'd inhaled since she left. After New Mexico, the moist air was a plumeria-scented miracle.

"What did I tell you?" Codie asked, twirling around beneath a tree that showered us with brilliant red flowers when a breeze rippled through the high branches far over our heads.

"You were right," I admitted, grinning up into the rain of crimson petals. I wanted to remember everything about the moment when I got my sister back, so I pressed one of the blossoms into the copy of *The Hunger Games* I had bought to read on the plane. Later I looked up the name of the tree that had rained red happiness on us and found out that it was called a coral tree. And *Erythrina variegata* became my favorite botanical specimen.

That's when Codie unhooked the opal pendant necklace she was wearing, fastened it around my neck, and we fell back into sync so completely, it was as if the past year had never happened. As if she'd never told me she'd enlisted and we'd gone straight from counting lightning strikes to dancing beneath a shower of petals. We were so mind-melded that neither one of us had to say out loud that we weren't going to even mention her deployment. With the full force of our combined sister power, we would keep it outside of our charmed circle forever and it would never be able to touch us.

Codie drove us to a secret cove she'd found. Unlike the cove where my fellow waste cases and I gather every night now, which is mostly pebbles and crushed coral, this one had soft powder-white sand. The water was the aqua of a movie star's swimming pool, and it was encircled not by jagged black cliffs, but by royal palms with straight, ringed trunks and a starburst of fresh green foliage geysering from the top.

Codie stuck swim fins on my feet, a circle of glass in front of my face, a tube in my mouth, and told me to follow her. I put my head in the water and was stupefied by beauty. A stained-glass window came to life beneath my mask that fractured into clouds of fish like wriggling jewels and petrified forests of coral in Disney colors. She'd undone her hair, and bubbles glistened in a row along one strand as it swayed around her head like a Samoan warrior princess's. She took my hand and we flippered through a forest of translucent streamers of shamrock-green kelp while a mosaic of wobbling parallelograms undulated across the white sand bottom.

Codie tugged at my hand and I looked her way. She was so excited that the mask smushing the flesh down around her eyes made her look like an ecstatic Pomeranian as she pointed in underwater slow motion. I followed her finger and found a huge armored hulk, like something out of the Jurassic period, hovering in the water below. With one lazy stroke of its flipper, the green sea turtle rose and headed straight for us.

It stopped right in front of me, calm and still as a boulder, and I stared right into the turtle's mysterious face, into those heavy-lidded eyes. Above her permanent frown, tiny bubbles of air escaped from the two dots of nostril at the top of her hooked beak. As the turtle oared a flipper and surged past, a current of water brushed against my cheek. Codie and I held hands and shrieked high-pitched, closemouthed insect shrieks of joy deep in our throats.

Fortunately, right on schedule, Mom had fallen in love with a staff sergeant in an operations support squadron at Hickam who looked like Kanye West but with even less charm than that arrogant a-hole. With Mom occupied, Codie and I got to spend every day of her leave at the cove. And every day the turtle came back. We decided that she was a mother turtle who would lay eggs on a secret beach at the next full moon. On our last night, Codie swore to me that I had nothing to worry about; all her unit was going to be doing was helping the transition to let the Afghans take over.

"I promise, Cabooskie: I won't be anywhere near a hot zone. So stop worrying, okay?"

"Okay," I agreed, and something that had clenched tight within me finally relaxed.

The next day, my mom and I left at dawn on a space-available military flight to Okinawa, where we checked into the Shogun Inn to wait for base housing to open up. Two days later, Codie deployed to Afghanistan. One week after that I scratched through seven days on the calendar and calculated that my sister only had 113 days to go.

Codie had done twelve days in Afghanistan and we were finishing our second week on Okinawa when two chaplains knocked on the door of our room at the Shogun Inn. After that the words scrambled and all I can remember are "Afghan insurgents," "transitioning to joint control," "details uncertain at this time," and "the ultimate sacrifice for a grateful nation." No matter how many times I arrange and rearrange the words, they always end up saying the worst thing I could ever hear.

· EIGHT ·

The living one is coming, Anmā. I can feel the one the kami are sending approaching.

I feel it too. An urgency beats through me that reminds me of how women had described childbirth, when the wisdom of the body seizes control and what must be done is done whether they are prepared or not.

Who will it be?

I don't know.

Your sister, Hatsuko!

No, it won't be anyone from our clan.

A stranger.

Of course, it will have to be a stranger.

Do you know what to do?

We don't need to understand the plans of the kami. Only to be ready to act as the instruments of their will.

But the stranger is coming, right? The one we will use to free ourselves?

No more questions. All that remains is for us to be ready.

Ready for what? To kill the one they send?

Ready to do whatever the kami set before us.

Anmā, do you feel that?! The water is lifting us up! I'm frightened! Help me!

There is nothing to fear. Let it move you; it is what the kami want.

We are being swept away! Anmā, save me!

I am with you! I am with you! Be happy! The kami are delivering us!

· NINE ·

*P*uh-WHOOSH! Puh-WHOOSH! Puh-WHOOSH!
    The distant sound of a round of syncopated pops follows me down the beach as Kirby cracks into his magic treasure chest of malted delights. The offshore breeze grows stronger as I walk closer to the water's edge. Fuzzed-out moonlight shines along the trail of foam left by retreating waves, outlining a gentle curve where the shoreline bends toward the far end of the series of cliffs.

Behind me my people, the other military kids cast by our government onto this microdot of an island, are silhouettes outlined by flame. The shimmying blaze makes them jerk around like the puppets we are, which causes the question that military kids hate the most to pop into my head: *Where are you from? What's your hometown?* The way all my thoughts—without ever asking my permission—always loop back to Codie, this one causes me to recall those girls in Wichita Falls when they asked my sister that exact question.

It was halfway through my seventh-grade year. I remember because I'd just gotten my braces off right before we were transferred from Mountain Home to Sheppard Air Force Base outside Wichita Falls, Texas. Since base housing was full, Mom used our BAH, basic allowance for housing, and rented a dinky two-bedroom apartment off base in a complex where all the neighborhood cats used the empty pool for a litter box.

I don't know why, but having a new, braces-free smile without the big funky gap in the middle that my old one had made me believe that this assignment would be different. At the bus stop on our first day of school, I found out big gap, no gap, braces, no braces, none of it mattered to civilians. We were outsiders. We were different.

It was January, and Codie and I walked through a freezing wind thick with dust and gravel to the bus stop half a mile away. As we got to the stop, the three girls already waiting there watched us with sour expressions, like we were Christmas presents no one wanted. Socks or cotton underwear. Finally, a skinny girl with mean hillbilly eyes and thin lips asked Codie where we were from. We never knew how to answer that question. Whether to say the base we just left. Or the one we were born on. Or the town where our father's parents lived, even though we hadn't seen them since I was a baby. Or Missouri, since our mom's parents lived there. So Codie just pressed "play" on our standard answer and started counting off the assignments. "Okay, we just moved from Idaho. Our mom was born on Clark Air Base in the Philippines. But that base is closed now. I was born in Germany, but then we moved to California, where Luz was born, then San Antonio. After that was Nevada, then back to Germany, then . . ."

I watched the girls' eyes narrow as the litany of countries and states went on. The bright light of the group, a girl with the congested voice and under-eye shadows of someone with chronic sinus problems, stared hard at Codie's antique gold skin and her cloud of espresso-brown hair, then observed with canny, shitkicking arrogance, "You don't look German."

Her friend, wearing a "Support Our Troops" T-shirt, said, "They're base kids," in a way that meant, *They'll be gone soon, too soon to be friends with. But not too soon to bully.*

While they studied us, I saw my future in Wichita Falls like it was showing on a crystal ball: me getting picked on for the next two years by these inbreeds, and I mentally started erasing them. Codie saw the same vision, and, never one to erase or ignore, dropped her weight back and sank down into The Stance. My sister would have been a killer jock if we'd ever stayed anywhere long enough for her to get on a team. Instead, she channeled all her natural athletic gifts into martial arts. It was her major bond with our mom. Some mothers and daughters scrapbook or read *Little House on the Prairie* together. Codie and my mom sparred. In her prime, my mom was a female Bruce Lee, and she taught Codie her own mix of karate, kung fu, street brawling, and some system from Israel called krav maga. So, essentially, my sister could kick your ass in half a dozen languages. She could knock your hat off your head with the back of her foot, then crush your windpipe with her elbow when you reached for it. The girls circling us at the bus stop had enough animal cunning to be able to read serious danger coming off of Codie like stars and squiggles from a KO'd cartoon character.

They backed off and even let Codie and me get on the bus first. Those girls never spoke to us again the entire time we went to that crappy school. Hardly anyone else did either. But I didn't care. I had Codie. Codie was my hometown.

I follow the curve in the shoreline until the fire disappears from view and there's no sign at all of the kids on the beach. The shoreline straightens out. I stop and let the tide wash in over my ankles. Ahead of me moonlight paints an avenue of silver across the waves so broad that it seems I could simply stroll across it.

Where do you want to be buried?

That question is the mind-fuck version of the hometown/where-are-you-from one. Brats hate it even more, since it highlights the fact that not only are we not from anywhere, but some of us have nowhere to go back to.

We had Codie's funeral in Hawaii. The air force took care of most of it. An honor guard of soldiers wearing white gloves marched in formation, then handed Mom an American flag folded into a tight triangle with the white stars on the blue background facing up. Seven people from Codie's unit came, including her sergeant. They were all nice. They all said nice things about Codie. But they didn't know her. The chaplain who conducted the generic, interdenominational service didn't know her, so all he could talk about was how our nation owed a debt to Codie and she'd given her life defending what she believed in.

That was wrong. Codie wasn't defending what she believed in. She was just a girl who didn't have the grades to prove how smart she was, and not much else going on at the moment she enlisted. It was also wrong that there were no cousins or friends from grade school. No aunts or uncles just because our grandmother was from Okinawa and our father checked out early and my mom hates his family. Or they hate her. The story keeps changing. But it was still wrong. There should have been people there who remembered Codie from before her permanent teeth came in. Who knew that she loved the Black Keys and Flamin' Hot Fritos. That if the skin of a mango so much as touched her lips they would swell up like a starlet's after too many collagen shots. That her handwriting was comically unreadable. That she could run the four-forty in under a minute. That her favorite movie was *Princess Mononoke*. That when our mother was too busy to go to the commissary or her car needed a new transmission more than we needed groceries and the money ran out before the month did, Codie would make us mustard-and-sugar sandwiches and ketchup soup. But no one said any of these things at her ceremony.

All any of them wanted to talk to me and Mom about after the service was what a one-in-a-million fluke Codie's death was. How weird it was for not just a female, but a female air force, to get killed by mortar fire. How it had something to do with her just getting there and not being fully briefed on SOP. How someone must have really screwed up if they hadn't told her never to go outside the wire.

That was the first I'd heard about Codie dying outside of the base. When I asked what had happened, why no one had told us about this before, their gazes ping-ponged around from Mom then back to me, and they all went mute until someone asked Patterson, the guy who'd made the comment, whether he was so stupid because his mother is his sister or if it was from being dropped on his head. Then they started in on how no one really knew how Codie had died. How details were sketchy. How the jerkwad fobbits were too fucking illiterate to even write a decent report.

"So why did you say that?" I asked Patterson. "About Codie being outside the wire?"

He didn't answer, but a staff sergeant with a head too small for his beefed-up shoulders whispered to me, "Don't worry. We'll get them for you. We'll get the sons of bitches who did this to your sister."

I wasn't trying to get in the sergeant's face when I asked, "Is that supposed to make me feel better?"

"We understand," he said. "We've all been where you are now, and it sucks, and sometimes it just helps to stay angry."

"I'm not angry, I really want to know if you're planning to get the person who was actually responsible."

"Just give us a name."

"Her." I pointed at my mother. "The person who signed her enlistment papers."

Before my mother could say anything, I walked away from all of them and went back to the cemetery. I half liked and half hated that an enormous coral tree shaded it. I liked that a fluffy quilt of crimson blossoms had already settled over Codie's grave. I hated that I'd never be happy again when I thought of twirling with her in a shower of coral tree petals in Hawaii. My mother and I didn't exchange one word on the long flight back to Okinawa. That was her version of being under-standing and forgiving me. It was my version of being true to Codie.

I trudge through the sloppy waves and the ocean is cool against my overheated calves, thighs, belly. I slide forward and the water gently lofts me up. It looks like molten metal around me, a silver syrup streaming ripples in a wide V from where it parts at the tips of my out-stretched fingers as I breaststroke toward the moon.

I swim until I can't take another stroke, flop over onto my back, and let the sea rock me to a lullaby rhythm. During the day, looking down from high atop the black cliffs, this shallow part I'm bobbing above now is a collar of pastel blues and greens ringing the island. At the point where the coral reef wrapping around the island drops down as steeply as the cliffs at my back, the color abruptly changes from soft tropical shades to a midnight blue that's black at the deepest spots. That's my destination.

I flip back over and continue on. I know I've reached the outer reef of dark blue when the water grows chilly. Beneath me now are hun-dreds of feet of sea snakes, moray eels, sharks, and grouper big as bears. Ahead is the East China Sea, then China, South and North Korea. Behind me, out beyond Okinawa, is the Pacific Ocean all the way to Codie's cove where the mama green sea turtle swims.

I glance back. In the misty fog the island looks like a place out of a fairy tale. An imaginary land that would vanish entirely if I asked why I, why any of us Americans, were there. A fairy tale that my mother and grandmother invented so we'd all have the comforting illusion that we belonged someplace.

That lie was pretty much blasted to smithereens by three phone calls not too long after we arrived on the island but before the chap-lains came. When the first call came and I heard my mom resurrect her halting Japanese, which she'd barely spoken since my grandma died, I knew she was talking to the Okinawan relatives I'd heard so much about. I was excited and asked her when we were going to meet them. But, even though Mom and I were still talking then, she wouldn't give me any details. She said her Japanese was rusty and she couldn't under-stand what they were saying, and obviously they didn't understand what she was telling them, but that she'd try again.

The second call was short and tense. It left my mom bristling worse than a rottweiler about to attack, and I knew better than to ask her about it. The third call was loud. Apparently her Japanese had come unrusted, because she was screaming like a Green Bay Packers fan in the language I hadn't heard her use since my grandma died. I never even had a chance *not* to ask about that conversation, because she left right after it, went to the NCO club, and must have made a new friend, since she didn't drag herself back to the Shogun Inn until dawn. Later that morning, a Saturday, a letter arrived.

It wasn't the normal kind of letter that came through the air force's APO system that you had to pick up at the base post office. It was local, and a messenger—an Okinawan girl who rode up on a moped and had some sort of special badge clipped to the pocket of her blue blouse that allowed her to get on base—delivered it. She wouldn't give it to me and I had the extremely unpleasant duty of waking my mother so that the delivery girl could bow and hold the letter out to her on the palms of both upturned hands as if it were a sacred offering.

Pausing only to grab her pocket Japanese dictionary, Mom took the letter into the bathroom, slammed the door shut, and switched on the fan, which let me know that she was smoking the cigarettes she swore she was going to give up when we got here. An hour later, she came out smelling like a bar at two in the morning and refused to tell me what was in the letter. All I knew was that after it was delivered, the phone calls in Japanese and the talk about the Okinawan relatives who were going to open their hearts and homes to us stopped dead. A few days later, the chaplains knocked on our door, and I forgot all about the letter and most everything else.

I turn back around and keep swimming. The seawater is cool and leaches warmth from my body. My arms and legs feel noodly. I wear out easily these days, since I don't—can't—eat or sleep much. If I swim out any farther, I won't have enough energy to go back. Should I turn around or keep swimming? I stop and dare the ocean to make the choice for me.

My back is turned on Okinawa, on Kadena, on my latest group of Quasis. The vast dark of sea and night sky swallows me up. I am alone. The only person on earth who really knew me, who would really, truly care if I vanished, is gone. That awareness starts to pull me down. I tread water for a few seconds and panic shivers through me.

This is a bad idea. I have to turn around.

The panic adrenaline gives me a jolt of energy and I think I can make it back to shore. Then, suddenly, in the black night two orbs of shimmering light appear. They're the eerie bluish green of phosphorescent waves. They hover around me, one on each side, like guardian angels. They're so oddly companionable that the panic vanishes. An unexpected peace fills me with a warmth like five tequila shots, and the words "Stop struggling" form in my mind, like a command spoken by my sister, who always took care of me. I let my body go still as glass and sink down under the waves. The orbs follow, dimly lighting the water around me. As the dark sea closes in above my head, I have one last thought: *Codie, if this isn't what you want me to do, if this isn't what you yourself did when you enlisted, send a sign.*

But no sign comes. I go down so far that the moon shrinks away to a tiny pearl far overhead. My lungs scream for oxygen. The phosphorescent orbs wobbling beside me show me how easy it is to breathe water. All I have to do is exhale the dead air in my lungs and breathe in and it will all be over. In the same instant, a swoosh of water swirls up against me and the shadow of a large sea creature passes by. Drowning is one thing, but I do not want to be eaten by a shark. I flail at it, and my hand hits what feels like the rounded edge of a heavy table. It's solid as furniture and not sandpapery the way sharkskin is supposed to be. Then the shadowed thing tips its head up toward the last glimmers of moonlight penetrating the dark water and I see the hooked profile of a sea turtle. She hovers directly in front of my face so that the beat of her flippers lofts my hair up and down.

Codie has sent a sign.

I struggle to rise to the air. But I'm too far down. I fight toward the surface, but a wave like a giant fist slams into me, holding me down, pushing me farther and farther back under. It bashes my head against the reef at my back, and, with a crack that shoots a bolt of pure white pain through me, the film in my brain stops.

· TEN ·

Anmā, *where are we? The water is gone. The girl is gone. Why did the wave put us here?*

Because the kami *willed it.*

Where is the girl?

The girl is where the kami *will her to be.*

But we need her.

The kami *know that. They will bring her to us again.*

· ELEVEN ·

The next thing I am aware of is rolling over onto my side and vomiting up roughly ten gallons of seawater along with another couple salty gallons that pour out of my sinuses.

I sprawl on the gritty sand, too exhausted to even roll over, until a chill sinks into my bones. I hoist myself up on wobbly arms and see that I've been spit out on a steep patch of deserted beach. The sand is smooth except for the tracks left by a handful of busy crabs. I can't see any marks from where I came ashore. It's like a giant hand has dropped me here. Cliff walls jut up all around, caging me. The tide creeps closer, and I realize that very soon I'm going to be trapped. Codie didn't save me just so that I would be battered to death against a cliff. I study the stone walls locking me in and search for a way out.

The moon is operating-room bright over my shoulder. It casts a pattern of pocked shadows across the sheer stone faces and reveals that rather than rising, the rock walls tilt outward. I don't have the strength to climb a regular cliff; you'd have to be Spider-Man to scale a jagged cliff that leans out like that.

There seems no way out until I notice a crevice where the cliff walls join. With no other choice, I haul myself up, and, hoping the opening leads to an escape route, or at least to higher ground, I scramble into the slit. There's just enough moonlight for me to make out that the opening leads back into a tunnel. I follow it. The instant the rock walls close in around me, I am overwhelmed by a monstrous stench. With the tide rising behind me, though, I have no choice but to forge ahead. As the last few flickers of moonlight fade, darkness worse than a nightmare of being buried alive closes in around me.

As I go farther back into the cave, the sand turns to hard rock ground beneath my feet. I am on an incline that rises slightly as I follow it even farther back, praying that it leads to an escape route or at least to ground high enough for me to wait out the incoming tide. I feel my way along with a hand on the clammy stone wall. The ocean roars at my back, echoing off the rock walls and filling the narrow tunnel with a salty mist denser than the densest fog. I glance back. The moonlit mouth of the cave is lost in a whiteout of surging surf as the tide roars in. Soon the opening will be completely blocked, and even if there were a way out on the beach, I won't be able to get there. I briefly regret not taking the swan-dive option from the top of the cliff when I had the opportunity. Even worse for my mom than Codie's closed-casket funeral would be if my body gets trapped in this stone labyrinth and she has nothing to bury.

A second later, the rock walls echo with a thin chirping cry. All I understand from it is that the crier is female, Asian, young, and scared.

The water rises up around my ankles and I pray that whoever's back there calling for me knows how to get out. I run up the gentle slope toward the far end of the cave. The voice grows louder and a glow appears. At first I think the phosphorescent orbs have returned, but the closer I get, the brighter the glow grows. Its source is hidden behind a bend in the cave walls. I hurry toward the feeble glimmer. When I round the bend, I catch a whiff of kerosene.

The cries are so strong now that, even above the roar of the waves, they grow louder. I rush toward the voice and scraps of memories of my grandmother speaking to me come back. *"Konbanwa!"* I call out.

As I get closer, the light from the kerosene lamp quivers, reflecting wetly off the oozing cave walls. It draws me closer with its homey incandescence. I turn the corner and there she is, an Okinawan teen-ager, collapsed beside a kerosene lantern that is sending up a black snowfall of soot. Her wavy black hair hugs her round face in a bowl cut. A few dingy scraps of what was once a school uniform cling to her skeletal limbs. She is so emaciated by hunger and disease that she lies sprawled on the damp rock floor of the cave, her torso barely propped up against the slick walls. A bandage black with dried blood hangs from one stick arm.

As ravaged as she is, however, the girl's eyes light up when she sees me. She stretches hunger-hollowed cheeks in a grin and joins her hands in a prayer that seems to be thanking and begging me at the same time. I realize she thinks that I have come to rescue *her*.

"Who are you? How long have you been trapped here?"

Of course, she doesn't understand English. In fact, from her expression, it almost seems as if she's never heard it before. As if the sound of my voice terrifies her. I grab the lantern resting beside her on a flat rock, hoist it up, and shine it around the cave. No crevice, no chink in the rock, no way out is revealed. Worse, I see now that the rising tide is pushing the line of foam deep into the cave. The drowning waves will follow.

The cold salt water flows in and she speaks, a pleading stream, her hands pressed together in front of her heart, begging me to help her. Her eyes are bright and so filled with intelligence that they shine in spite of the gloom of the cave and her dire condition. What is she ask-ing? She's beckoning me forward, begging me to come to her. Does she expect me to carry her out? Is that what she's asking?

"I can't." I point to the dot of pearly foam blocking the exit. "The waves. The tide is coming in. We can't go out that way. How did you get here? Show me the way out."

Of course she doesn't understand. I curse my mother for never teach-ing me Japanese. The roar of the advancing waves echoing off the rock walls rises to a deafening level. The girl locks my gaze with hers and, without the slightest gesture or word, compels me to come forward.

I lean in closer, feeling as I do as if the ground is tilting under me, tip-ping me toward her. The closer I come to the girl, the softer the sound of the waves behind me becomes. By the time our foreheads are nearly touching, the roar is a silence more total than any I've ever known. Into that quiet comes a sound so soft that at first I can't identify it. I listen hard and hear a sick mewling coming from somewhere beneath her blouse, as if she has the runt of a litter of kittens hidden there. It's the whimpering of a newborn. An infant. A dying infant. That is who she is pleading for. That is who I was saved to save. The strange gravity pulls even more strongly at me, dragging me forward.

The girl raises her arms, begging me to save her baby. The bandage around her wrist slips off, and maggots like dancing rice boil out from the blackened gash of a wound on her forearm. They spill out over her body in unstoppable white waves. It is a vision from the nightmare I've had every night since Codie died. The image imprints itself on my mind and only gets worse when the kerosene light goes out and the cave falls into blackness. I feel like I'm being pulled down. And then I am falling. Wind rushes through my hair. There is no end to the descent.

Exhausted, I sag down onto the cave floor. It is far cozier than my own bed. I could rest in this dark place, silent except for the white-noise roar of the sea. Really, truly rest. It would be unimaginably peaceful to simply lie here as, one by one, all the torments of life dwindled away until I could finally sleep. And all I have to do is lie quietly until the tide comes in to fill this stone hole like a swimming pool.

"Luz? Luz, are you back there? Luz?"

I consider answering the distant voice, but even as I do, a weariness so complete overtakes me and my eyelids droop shut and I am asleep before I can open my mouth.

"Luz!" Jake's voice echoes as it recedes, moving farther and farther away from me. The first touch of a wave reaching back into the cave shocks me for a second. It is cold and alarming; I almost jerk awake, but the wave recedes and, easy as switching TV channels, I tune back in to the program where I am warm and carefree. I'm snuggling up against the luxuriant rock when I bump into what must be a sea urchin, because a spine like a steel pin pokes me, and I cry out from the pain.

Suddenly I'm awake and there's a girl and a baby who need help. I feel blindly for the wall. My hands scrape against rock on all sides as I make my way out into the main tunnel. A pulse of light gleams faintly against the wet walls. I follow it into the tunnel, where the beam from a flashlight is disappearing.

"Jake, wait!"

"Luz."

The beam bounces crazily off the damp walls as Jake runs, sloshing through the rising tide, back to me.

"Hurry, she's in here."

Jake, who's wet from the waist down and holding the flashlight over his head to keep it dry, follows without any questions. He gives off a vibe like my mom when she's in emergency mode and is just thinking about what needs to be done and how to do it. I rush ahead back into the dark. The kerosene lamp is still out, but the flashlight throws a smear of illumination onto the entrance to the chamber.

"She's back in there. She has a baby."

Jake nods, as if this is what he expected to hear.

I step aside and let him go in first. I can't make myself face my nightmare, of Codie wounded, suffering. Not with a full light. I wait at the entrance to the chamber. The tide rises higher against my ankles.

"Jake, hurry. We have to get them out of here."

I wait to hear Jake speaking to the girl in Japanese. But no sound emerges until he says, "Luz?"

I take a deep breath to steady myself and notice that the stench has disappeared. The cave now smells like stone washed by clean seawater. The only way I can make myself go back into the chamber is by keeping my eyes trained on Jake's face. He's calm in a way I'll never be able to fake in a million years. My skin prickles from feeling the girl, lost in the black shadows at our feet, watching me, waiting for me to save her and her baby. The tide pulls away, back out of the cave, as Jake directs the flashlight down to the girl at our feet.

"Luz?" There's a tenderness in his voice I've never heard before. "Is this what you mean?" I brace myself to see the girl revealed in its glare. Images flash through my mind of prisoners in dungeons, lepers in caves, shrinking from a harsh glare. But the light falls on nothing except bones. Bones so white and bleached they're pieces of art made of ivory. There's not even anything definably human about them.

Jake touches my shoulder. His hand, warm and steady, makes me aware that I'm shivering. "We have to leave." Seawater splashes in, rising this time to our shins. "Now. Before the tide completely floods us in."

Jake takes my hand and pulls me away. At the last second, something makes me turn back. I grab at the space where the sea urchin was, snatch up what I find there, stuff it into a pocket that I zipper shut, and Jake and I haul ass as fast as we can back down the tunnel.

The opening is lost in the foaming roil of water rushing in through the chink in the cliff that is our only way to escape. The waves surge in, pushing against our legs.

"The tide is in!" Jake yells. "We can't get out!"

"No!" I scream back over the roar of the waves. My death is one thing, but Jake is absolutely not going to die too just for being kind. This time I'm the one who channels my mom, and when we catch each other's gazes in the sputtering beam from the dying flashlight, we both know what we have to do. We brace ourselves against the battering power of the water, and Jake, using his surfer's wisdom, calculates. At the exact moment that the flow reverses, he orders, "Dive!" The flashlight dies. I plunge forward into the torrent and am sucked into the wet darkness.

· TWELVE ·

A nmā, *she's leaving; the stranger is leaving. You can't let her leave. She was the one the* kami *sent to us.*

Don't fret; she will be sent again.

You should have killed her. She was ready. Why didn't you kill her?

The kami *stopped me.*

But why? Why did they bring us up from the bottom of the sea here to this place to meet her if they didn't wish us to claim her?

The kami *knew we weren't ready.*

They made a mistake.

The kami *never make a mistake. It is only we who make mistakes when interpreting their will.*

No, Anmā, they made a mistake. They sent a demon who speaks demon language. And a girl besides. Why would they send a demon girl?

Because our fate is bound up with hers.

How do you know this? You've never even encountered a demon before.

I block the terrible memory that tries to twist into my mind.

Listen, my son: We knew long before the war came to our shores that the Americans were demons.

Because that is what you were taught in school?

No, Hatsuko and I didn't need our Japanese rulers to teach us that. My father, your grandfather Shojin Kokuba, had already proved to us that our enemies were soulless monsters when he took us to the foreigners' cemetery near the port of Tomari. Since we have to wait now, shall I tell you about it?

Yes.

All right, then. The visit was dangerous. To express any interest in the imperialistic enemies of the emperor was a treasonous crime, punishable by public flogging if the commander was merciful and beheading if he was not. But our father took the risk, because he believed it essential to impress upon his daughters that, in the unlikely event that the Americans did manage to overcome the invincible Imperial navy and invade our island, we, the young women of Okinawa, had to understand that Americans were not human, and that we would be used in beastly, unspeakable ways.

The round lenses of Father's spectacles flashed like the beacons of the great lighthouse at Zanpa Saki as he nervously checked in all directions before we entered the neglected plot. Who knew what spies might be lurking about? But the only soul who passed was a bowlegged old man with whiskers long and white as Confucius's, and a stack of dried pandanus leaves taller than himself lashed to his back. When Father was certain it was safe, he shooed us in like our mother driving her silky-eared goats before her.

At our approach, chartreuse-spotted monkey lizards skittered away from the weeds and vines choking the strangers' graves. I reached for my big sister Hatsuko's hand. Even in the still afternoon heat, her fingers were chilled by the presence of the unquiet spirits that occupied this shunned place. Weathered headstones lay flat on the ground, where any passing dog could lift its leg on them. Odd stick-letter words were etched horizontally into the foreigners' grave markers.

I caught Hatsuko's eye and jerked my head from side to side like a crazy girl, pretending to read the strange letters that made a person's eyes twitch back and forth in such an unnatural way. Hatsuko rewarded me with a tight smile that she immediately covered, and I made the crazy-girl face again.

Our father cracked his walking stick against my backside. "Tamiko," he hissed. "Do you think this is funny?"

"No, Father." Fortunately it was his stick made of bamboo, not the sturdy one of banyan wood, and the smack only stung for a moment. Overall, I preferred the bamboo cane to the times when Father disciplined me by making me kneel on rice with my hands tied behind my back for so long that when my punishment was over, Hatsuko had to help me stand, then dig out the grains embedded in my knees with the tips of her fingernails.

Father had been a schoolteacher before the day when he both married our mother and was adopted by her father, your great-grandfather, Masahide Kokuba. My mother's father was a well-off farmer cursed with six daughters and no sons to inherit the family's land or mortuary tablets or carry out the funeral rites that would ensure that Grandfather Kokuba would be with his kin group in the next world. That day in the barbarians' cemetery, Father was once again the stern schoolteacher as he tapped the stick letters engraved on the tombstones, and said, "These are the names of four of the sailors who came with Commodore Perry on his expedition to force open the closed door of the mighty Japanese Empire and lay it bare to America's imperialistic greed. When our king would not meet with him, Perry marched on Shuri Castle with two hundred of his men and they bullied their way through Shurei Gate like the barbarians they are.

"Though there had been no weapons on our island since the Japanese claimed Okinawa in 1609, and Commodore Perry and his men wore gleaming swords at the high waists of their white trousers and were guarded by soldiers carrying rifles with bayoneted tips that reached to the top of their impossibly tall hats, our brave king refused to meet with him. Instead, with smiles and gentle words, Perry was put off and forced to meet with a lowly regent in Hokuden Hall, where only the most minor of trading envoys were received. The people of Okinawa rejoiced at this brutal snub. They were certain that their king had shamed the mighty American commodore so thoroughly that he would slink away in disgrace."

Our cultured father made a sour face and spit in disgust at such foolishness. "How stupid those pitiful fools were not to understand that shame is a useless weapon against men with no honor. Remember this, daughters, should war come to our shores: Americans have no honor. You cannot imagine how they will defile you." Hatsuko lowered her head in embarrassment and I, as always, copied her.

"If you don't believe me," he said, though we didn't doubt him in the least, "look at this." He tapped the dates on the tombstones when Perry's sailors, dead of disease and accident, had been put into the earth of Okinawa. Hatsuko and I gasped as we read the year: 1853.

Faster than a Chinese merchant with an abacus, Hatsuko did the calculation. "Ninety years ago?"

"And they're still here?" I was stunned.

Our father nodded. "Yes. And in all that time the sailors' oldest male relatives have never come to wash their bones and take them home."

I shivered in the stifling heat, thinking of the spirits of these wretches, abandoned by their families and trapped for all eternity among strangers. I could not imagine such loneliness. Even though they were imperialistic invaders and enemies of Our Beloved Father the emperor, it made me sad to think that the spirits of the lost sailors would be trapped here forever. Alone. Alone and forgotten.

Once Father saw how stricken we were by this evidence of the Americans' cruelty in abandoning their own, he hurried us from that unholy place. Still the restless spirits imprisoned there haunted my dreams ever after. Hatsuko and I could not imagine a people so callous or a fate so cruel, and we swore that no power on earth would ever keep us apart in this or, more important, the next world.

Did Aunt Hatsuko pray to the kami to send the demon girl to us?

She must have. She promised we would be together in the other realm.

But, Mother, if we claim a stranger's body, won't we be condemned to spend eternity with her ancestors?

Once in the next world, we will find our clan.

But I don't know our clan and they don't know me. Anmā, what if we are separated?

That was the worst of all my fears. That we would be separated and my child wouldn't know who his people were. Wouldn't know where he belonged. Without intending, I recalled a song that had frightened me as a child.

> I let my innocent child
> Journey to the netherworld alone.
> Morning and night, looking for me,
> He must be crying.

I don't want to be alone.

Don't cry. Please don't cry. You won't. I promise you, you will never be alone. That is why the kami have given us more time. So that you will know the story of who I was and how you came to be. You must have all my memories so that you will know your clan and they will know you.

Even the painful ones you have pushed from your thoughts?

Especially those. You must know my story, for it is the story of the munchū we are part of and that you will be with for all of eternity.

Even if we are separated?

Even then.

Will there be time?

There must be time.

Then tell me quickly. Tell me what I must know.

I will begin on March twenty-third, 1945.

Don't tell me numbers, Anmā. Tell me what I understand. Tell me colors. Remember the colors again. The pink of the baby piglets. The gold of the trunks of your bamboo grove. The purple of your mother's sweet potatoes. The yellow of the flowers on the sea hibiscus hedge that lined the narrow oxcart path. The red of the flowers on the deigo tree, so bright that the entire side of the mountain seemed to be on fire.

Yes, and everything in between was green. Leaf, vine, grass. More greens than you can imagine.

I can imagine so many greens, Anmā.

Imagine all of them and then imagine above and below was blue. The sea was the blue of jewels. The sky was the blue of softness. I believed that my life would change forever on that day.

And did it?

Yes, but not in the way I had imagined.

Tell me. Tell me.

Will you be quiet now and listen?

Yes.

It is a very long story.

I will be quiet.

All right then, I will begin.

· THIRTEEN ·

Like every other fifteen-year-old in Okinawa I was nervous that morning, my son, the morning your story begins, and I woke long before dawn. I wished that my older sister, your aunt, Hatsuko, was awake, but she snored softly on the futon we had shared for my entire life. She had come from Shuri late the night before in order to stand by my side when, in a few hours, all across the island, we would learn which students had been accepted to one of the few prefectural high schools. Those whose names were not read out that morning would be condemned to be farmers or fishermen, maids or shop clerks. But if our names were on that short list, we could dream of careers as teachers, nurses. Perhaps even positions as administrators with the exalted Imperial Japanese prefectural government.

In the big city of Naha, families rushed out at dawn to purchase the first copies of the *Ryūkyū Shimpō* on the newsstand to read the list printed there. In small villages such as ours, we would all gather around the photo of the emperor to hear the headman read the list, whose contents only he knew. In our village of Madadayo that man was your grandfather. As our village's highest-ranking man, Father was responsible not only for announcing official proclamations, such as the high school lists, but also for collecting taxes and making sure that all orders given by our Japanese governor were carried out.

The thought of humiliating your grandfather and grandmother, your great-uncles and great-aunts, and all the ancestors who protect and guide us so long as we bring honor to their memory made my stomach tighten into a fist that punched against my heart.

To calm myself that morning, I stared at my sister's school uniform hanging from its own special peg. The night before, I'd helped Hatsuko brush the dust from the shoulders of the sailor blouse and scrub at the smudges on the collar with a cloth dipped in Fels-Naptha until it was again so crisp and white that it shone in the darkness as brightly as the lily pin that designated that she was the head girl, gleaming on the breast of the navy-blue blouse. I knew that I would never be elected head girl and wear such a special pin, but I wanted just an ordinary Princess Lily pin so badly that my chest ached with longing.

Hatsuko's name had been announced two years ago as one of the few girls from the entire island admitted to the Himeyuri Girls High School in Shuri. Known as the Princess Lily girls because of the pins they all were honored to wear, Himeyuri students represented the finest of Okinawan society. They were so elite that some graduates were even allowed into the restaurants and hotels in Naha that Okinawans were forbidden to enter, since only true Japanese were admitted. Just like true Japanese girls, the purity of the Princess Lilies was prized above all. A student could be expelled for so much as exchanging a note with a boy. Our Japanese rulers had taught us that only the lower classes allowed the sexes to have any contact after childhood and before a suitable marriage had been arranged.

I never had the slightest doubt that Hatsuko would be one of the few selected to go on to high school. Your aunt was so smart that she even learned to speak English from our uncle Chūzō Shimojo, who worked on a sugar plantation in Hawaii for most of his life before returning to Okinawa so his spirit could rest here with our ancestors when he died.

Not only was Hatsuko always the best student, but, like our father, she was very Japanese-looking. Quite tall—nearly 160 centimeters— she had the long, straight black hair, high brow, angular features, pale ivory skin, and refined ways of a Japanese noblewoman. She'd even adopted their genteel way of walking pigeon-toed. Yes, your aunt Hatsuko was as fine and delicate as an actual lily. The only other girl as lovely as Hatsuko was Uncle Chūzō's daughter, our cousin Mitsue. In truth, Cousin Mitsue, with her large, luminous eyes, thick lashes, and full lips, was far prettier than any girl ever born in Madadayo. Mitsue was Aunt Toyo's daughter and had been born fully two years after Toyo's husband, Uncle Chūzō, had left to work in Hawaii. Mitsue's real father was rumored to be a sugar importer from Tokyo who was as handsome as a movie star. It was said that the sugar importer insisted upon testing the sweetness of the local product before he made any purchase. The baby Mitsue was a year old when Uncle Chūzō, who knew nothing of the child, returned. Aunt Toyo was terrified that Chūzō would turn her out and she'd be forced to flee with her bastard child to Naha and work as a *juri* in the pleasure quarter to keep them alive. And though Chūzō was furious, and he did beat Toyo terribly, he was as charmed by Cousin Mitsue as every other male she ever encountered would be, and ultimately Uncle Chūzō claimed her as his own.

Mitsue and Hatsuko were born only a week apart, and though there was always an edge of competitiveness between them, they became good friends, and went off to Shuri together. I was always so proud of my cousin the great beauty, and my elegant and intelligent big sister, and tried to be like them in every way, though I knew that I would never truly measure up since I took after our mother.

I was very *Uchinānchu*, and my mongrel Okinawan blood showed up clearly in my short stature, in my round face that was all blunted nubs, and in my skin, dark as an ancient banyan tree, no matter how careful I was about wearing a sun hat. And because our mother foolishly allowed me to go barefoot when I was a child, my toes were splayed out like a hairy Ainu's, the most mongrelized of the impure races in the vast and invincible Japanese Empire that our Japanese teachers told us occupied one-fifth of the entire globe—all the way from Java in the South Seas to Manchukuo at the northernmost tip of China.

I shudder now to recall how Mother also allowed, encouraged me even, to squat down over the open privy flowing into the pigsty and do my business with no more shame than a goat releasing pellets onto the ground. She was such a typical Okinawan peasant that she actually believed that a bit of a person's spirit is discharged with the excrement and that the only way for a family to reclaim this lost spirit was by eating the flesh of pigs fed in this manner. Who could blame our refined Japanese rulers for despairing that Okinawans would ever become truly civilized? Ever be worthy of being called Japanese?

The only small hope any of us had of escaping the poverty and ignorance of Okinawa was high school. Four of my five older siblings had honored our family and our ancestors by being accepted. Your uncle Ichirō, Forest Orchid Boy, had already been drowned by that time, claimed by the *fiidama*, which left my remaining three older brothers, your uncles Takashi, Mori, and Hiroyuki. All of them honored our clan by being accepted to the elite boys' high school. Upon graduation, they had all, in turn, enlisted in the Imperial Army and been allowed the privilege—rare among Okinawans, who were usually too short and skinny to qualify—of fighting for our emperor. The second-born, Takashi, was serving with the emperor's forces in Manchukuo to liberate the native Manchurian people from the cruel Russians. My third brother, Mori, was helping to liberate the Filipino people from the colonial dictators. And my fourth brother, Hiroyuki, was battling the British aggressors in the jungles of Burma. Even Hatsuko had the honor of serving the emperor. She and her classmates at Hime-yuri High School were training as nurses in case of the remote possibility that the Imperial Army might need them. I alone had thus far failed to serve our emperor.

I dreamed of joining Hatsuko. Even before she went to Shuri, on the outskirts of Naha, Hatsuko and I always visited Naha several times a year. You can't believe how exciting those trips were. Before the Imperial Army took control of the railroad, we would rise before dawn and catch the train that ran from Itoman in the south all the way north to the village of Kadena. On every trip one of our fellow passengers, invariably a man, would point out that the tracks were made in Pennsylvania by the Carnegie Steel Company and that tickets for more than three million journeys were sold each year. Oh, we were proud of our railroad!

I loved watching scenes flash past my window: housewives squatting at the edge of a stream, washing potatoes and squeezing and pounding dirty laundry on the stepping-stones; old men sitting in the shade of a banyan tree transforming strips of bamboo into baskets; peddlers pushing carts down village lanes advertising their fresh tofu or sweet red-bean cakes; children bouncing balls of rubbery sago-palm pulp, spinning around and catching them as they sang in our native Oki-nawan language:

>Mai-mai, nuri-nuri, nuran yaraba, inu shimabuni ukite,
>   noshite yarachi!

>*Spin, spin, obey, obey, else you will be set afloat on the Devil's*
>   *Island boat!*

I especially liked peeking into farmers' backyards when they were making sugar. While their half-naked young children chased one another through the fields where the cane's golden tassels swayed in the breeze, their fathers and big brothers would feed the stalks into grinding machines driven by patient horses plodding around an endless circle. Then the mothers and older daughters, their hair tied up in white kerchiefs, would boil the juice in large iron pots until it thickened into a sugary black paste. Beyond the cane fields, luxuriant rice paddies either rippled along the sides of terraced mountains in undulating rows, or shimmered in flooded fields like mosaics of silver and green.

In Naha, we were always awed by the majestic port where ships from Japan, Taiwan, China, and the South Sea Islands came and went. Waves lapped against the concrete piers and seagulls cried overhead. There the dockworkers, all brown as bark and naked except for their loincloths, would load and unload huge crates. Rickshaw drivers dressed in starched black jackets scrambled to be the first to pick up disembarking passengers, usually government officials sent from the mainland. As I watched, another childhood song would run through my mind. This one captured the excitement from centuries gone by, when the great tribute ships came and went from China. It reminded us of the hundreds of years when Okinawa was a trading center with silks, dyes, spices, perfumes, wine, folding screens, feathers, exotic birds and animals, swords, gold, books, medicinal herbs, even eunuchs, passing to and from Java, Thailand, Korea, Japan, and, of course, the country we were aligned with for centuries, China.

After Hatsuko left for school, I would take the train to visit her by myself. She would meet me at the station and we'd rush off to catch one of the trolleys that crisscrossed Naha from its international port all the way to Shuri, home of the palace of the Ryukyuan kings and, of course, Himeyuri High School. I could have ridden those trolleys the entire day, marveling at the rickshaws and motorcycles and, very occasionally, an auto purring along the broad, palm-shaded avenues. We were thrilled when we spotted a fine Japanese lady in the backseat of her limousine driven by a chauffeur wearing a peaked cap, white gloves, and a double-breasted uniform.

Our first stop was always a little shop that Hatsuko had discovered that sold *mochii* balls as fine as the ones made in Tokyo. There would be no boring *beni imo* cakes made of purple sweet potatoes, or any other Okinawan food, for us on those special days. After our special Japanese treat, we would stroll along the avenue, peering into the elegant hotels and restaurants built exclusively for the mainlanders, and whisper about the day when we were both Himeyuri graduates and would be allowed to enter with the rest of our elite classmates.

The highlight of those trips, though, was a trip to Naha's best picture palace, the Golden Star. There we would watch one movie after another. Before they were banned, we also used to watch energetic, fast-moving films from America. Once, we saw a cowboy movie that caused Hatsuko and me to weep when the Indians—handsome braves, noble old women, babies in their mothers' arms—were slaughtered simply for defending their homeland. We thought the Americans a cruel people indeed. Not just for what they'd done in the past, but for forcing the defeated Indians to reenact their conquest for the camera. From our allies the Germans came our favorites, horror movies about vampires and monsters constructed by mad scientists in which the wicked always threw their heads back and cackled in a horrendous way that made Hatsuko and me shriek and grab each other in fear.

The movie that invariably packed the theater, though, no matter how many times it played, was *The Coming of Satsuma*, which told how the Japanese had captured our beloved King Shō Tai in 1879. In the movie version, when our king was about to be thrown alive into a cauldron of boiling oil, he grabbed two of his executioners and leaped with his screaming victims into the boiling oil. Though the Japanese had told us that the story was a lie, and that Shō Tai was a trader in league with the Koreans who were plotting to enslave us, everyone in the theater would clap and shriek their approval. Everyone, that is, except Hatsuko, who found the entire display treasonous. The officials must have agreed, because a few years ago, the film was banned entirely and never played again.

Late that night, exhausted by the excitement of the city, I would ride home, imagining the time when I, too, would be a Princess Lily girl and live with Hatsuko. She would help me with my writing exercises, since she was famed for her elegant calligraphy, and mine looked as if a chicken with muddy feet had walked across the paper. After I earned my certificate, we would teach in classrooms next to each other, and our adoring students would follow us around like ducklings trailing after their mother. Everything, my entire life, depended on my name being on the list of those accepted into high school.

· FOURTEEN ·

*A*nmā?
  Yes.

What if the demon girl forgets about us?

She won't forget us. That girl will never forget us.

But what if she does? What if we are trapped here forever? I will stop existing, won't I?

I told you that I will never allow that.

But you fear it, don't you? More than you fear our being separated. I am growing weaker. It will happen soon, won't it?

Yes.

That frightens me.

Your fear won't help us. Don't you want to know whether my name was on your grandfather's list?

Of course it was. You had a Princess Lily pin until the demon girl stole it.

Yes, but does that mean my name was on the list?

It wasn't?

Listen and you will find out.

Though I was more nervous than I'd ever been in my life, there was one good thing about the upcoming announcement: At least, for that one day, no one would talk about the war. It had gotten so bad over the past few months that some dared to suggest that the conflict might come here, to Okinawa. Even though we had air-raid drills, our Japanese teachers told us not to worry. Yes, there had been bombing, but the American navy could do no serious damage. We knew from our teachers that our divine emperor's brave aviators had destroyed the Americans' Pacific fleet at Pearl Harbor.

What could our island possibly have to fear? It was so tiny that it didn't even appear on most maps. No Westerner had found his way to our shores since Commodore Perry's brief visit nearly a hundred years before. Of what possible interest could Okinawa be to any of the greedy imperialist powers? We had no weapons, no minerals. All we had were pineapples, papayas, sugarcane, and pig shit.

Still, that did not stop our teachers from educating us about what would happen in the highly unlikely event that the Americans did invade. Posters hung on the walls of our classrooms that depicted those sweating monsters with their red faces and monstrously long pointed noses. One showed the demon leaders Churchill and Roosevelt, devil horns curling out of their heads, squatting on a pile of bones, their clawed toes wrapped around skulls, eating the flesh of innocent Japanese. In voices trembling with horror and disgust, our teachers told us of the Americans' unnatural and insatiable appetites. In the few small, weak countries they had managed to conquer, these beasts had roasted and eaten every child they could trap, and raped every female they could find, from infants in cradles to ancient crones. All that stood between us and that unspeakable fate was our emperor and the brave Imperial soldiers he had stationed in Okinawa to protect us.

On the day the names were announced, for a few moments we would all forget those well-documented atrocities as we discovered what our futures held. That morning, a moment before dawn, Kobo, our old rooster, started in. His crows grew in volume as the first rays of day slanted across our small farm and he announced to the world that he, Kobo the Mighty, had once again singlehandedly caused the sun to rise. I hoped that his crowing would wake Hatsuko, but, exhausted, she slept on. The new principal had transformed our beloved Himeyuri High into a training center for girl warriors. Last month, Hatsuko had told me, a girl had died of exhaustion during a twenty-seven-kilometer forced march. The death had only inspired him to institute harsher measures so that the Himeyuri girls who were honored to wear the Princess Lily pin would have the discipline necessary not to disgrace him.

Gradually other sounds joined in the symphony that I had woken to every morning of my life: the pigs grunting as they rooted through cooling mud for the bits of sweet potato my mother threw out; the chickens clucking and pecking about for tasty bugs; the goats bleating out their impatience to be fed. Missing was the mooing of our cows, since they had all been requisitioned by the Imperial Army.

A rustling in the thatched roof that was so high overhead it kept our house cool even on the hottest days was followed by a series of happy chirps. In the darkness, I imagined the gecko that brought luck to our family, the sac at his throat puffing up into a lovely pink bubble as he did his morning push-ups. A second later, he darted away to do his job and keep the high roof free of cockroaches.

The groaning of wood against leather signaled the arrival of our ox, Papaya, carrying a cartload of night soil. The leathery leaves of the tall sea hibiscus that lined the narrow path slapped against the cart as he made his way out to our fields. Soon the workers who tended our rice paddies and fields of soybeans, sweet potatoes, millet, and sugarcane would arrive to receive instructions from my mother. Bit by bit, as my father had grown more refined, more modern, more Japanese, my mother had taken over the daily operation of our farm. When Father refused to ever speak another word of *Uchināguchi*, our coarse local dialect, there was no longer any reason for him to meet with the men, since none of them spoke Japanese. That's when my mother officially became the boss.

Since nearly all of our men had left to serve the emperor's glorious struggle against the imperialist forces of the West, most farms and businesses were now run by women. My three older brothers were gone. Father had tried to enlist but, to his shame and sorrow, was turned away because, even with spectacles, his eyesight was too poor. And now it was my turn to learn whether I had been judged worthy to serve the emperor by going on to high school. I thought of the intolerable disgrace our father would be forced to bear if the name of his youngest daughter was not on the list that he, as headman, would read out today before the entire village. The shame of that possibility stabbed me with such force that tears sprang to my eyes.

Though I neither moved nor made the slightest sound, my sister, always eerily sensitive, woke and asked, "Tami-chan, what's wrong? Why is my Little Guppy crying?" She took my hand. Hers, usually soft and white as a true lily, was rough and calloused. Her tone, however, was still gentle and refined, and it caused me to blubber as wetly as the big-eyed, round-faced guppy I'd been nicknamed for. The first rays of the morning sun slanted in, and the blue mosquito netting around us turned the light into a pastel cloud.

"What if my name is not on the list?" I wailed. "What if I can't come to Shuri with you and study to be a teacher? What if I have to stay here and marry a farmer who makes our children poop into the pigsty? Whose teeth are rotten from sucking black sugar and who drinks too much millet brandy? What if I have to sleep on *gōyā* melon seeds for the rest of my life?"

Hatsuko's face was creased with concern until the mention of the *gōyā* melon seeds. She laughed then at my typically Okinawan habit of eating the roasted seeds of the deliciously bitter *gōyā* melon in bed at night and hiding the shells by tucking them into the straw of the tatami mat.

My big sister put her arm around me. Her sleeping kimono was soft against my skin. Our aunt Yasu, the second-oldest of Mother's sisters, wove on her backstrap loom the finest *bashōfu* cloth made from the purest banana fibers, so that our kimonos were light and cool in the summer heat. "Oh, Little Guppy, I'm laughing because I was just as fretful as you on the morning when they read the names for my class."

"Yes, but you're so smart. The smartest girl ever to come from Madadayo."

"Guppy, you're smart. You're certainly much smarter than Cousin Mitsue, and she was admitted."

"Because she ..." I stopped myself before I could utter the word "beautiful," and said something that amounted to the same thing: " ... looks like a real Japanese girl! I bet Fumiko Inoue is on the list." I named the smartest girl in my class.

"Fumi has hair like a *shiisā* lion dog."

I grinned at Hatsuko's wicked comment. It was true. Fumiko washed her hair with hand soap and it always puffed out around her head like a fierce guardian dog's. Hatsuko covered her own grin with her hand in the refined manner of a proper Japanese girl, reminding me to do the same. We giggled in the sophisticated way she'd learned at school, making a high-pitched, silvery sound as pleasing as the ringing of tiny silver bells.

Later, at breakfast, the three of us, me, Hatsuko, and my father, knelt at the foot-high table where the treats my mother had prepared in advance for this special day were laid out for us. Sea-snake soup, always eaten for courage; bright pink, spicy *tofuyu;* sweet potato with green-tea sauce; deep-fried whale tripe in peanut sauce; and my favorite, *gōyā chanpuru*, made with bitter melon, pork, and tofu.

It was quiet and a bit lonely with my brothers gone. I even missed my mother, who had gone to the fields early so that she could finish the day's work in time to be by my side when the names were read. As annoying and uncultured as her loud, braying laugh and insistence on speaking our native dialect were, the morning felt leaden, almost ominous, without them.

I studied my father's face. His spectacles caught the early morning light and turned them into two circles of silver hiding his eyes. He had known since yesterday whether or not my name was on the list. Hatsuko saw me peering intently at Father and shook her head at my foolishness; of course he would reveal nothing. Until the names were read, I would not know whether he was hiding pride at my acceptance or humiliation that I had been rejected. Unlike so many of our uncivilized relatives and neighbors, whose every feeling was allowed to play across their broad, brown faces, my father had mastered the fine Japanese art of masking all show of untoward emotion.

Father held up his chopsticks horizontally. We all bowed our heads and said the blessing with him, "Itadakimasu"—"I gratefully accept"—then began our meal.

I had given up on Father betraying the tiniest hint as to what fate had in store for me when I noticed something that turned my belly to ice: As he lifted his bowl of soup, his hand trembled. His hand had not ever trembled before on any of the other mornings when he knew in advance that the names of his children were on the list of those admitted to high school.

Hatsuko's own hand reaching for her chopsticks halted as we both stared at that telltale quiver. Her eyes, wide now with distress, found mine. My sister's reaction confirmed what I feared most: My name was not on the list. I would not be going on to high school.

Reflected in my own bowl of sea-snake soup, I saw my future self: skin like my mother's—tough and brown as ox hide—married to a farmer with brown teeth rotted away from sucking on black sugar and stinking from never cleaning himself properly after doing his business into a pigsty.

Heartbroken, our dream of teaching together vanished, neither Hatsuko nor I could force down a single bite of the delicacies my mother had prepared. My tears dropped without a sound into the bowl as I lowered my head, accepted that my name was not on the list, and whispered, "*Itadakimasu.*"

· FIFTEEN ·

When he finished his meal, our father carefully replaced his chopsticks, stood, and nodded once at Hatsuko to indicate that it was time. We both trailed him out to the veranda. I copied Hatsuko and walked in the delicate, pigeon-toed way of a true Japanese girl, rather than the splay-footed manner of an Okinawan peasant. On the veranda, we followed our assigned roles. As I always did before he appeared at any public function, I trimmed our father's steel gray hair with the pair of long-bladed silver scissors kept for this precise purpose. Hatsuko stood up tall and elegant, and, swallowing the ashen lump of disappointment that I'm certain was choking her as badly as the one blocking my throat, she began to recite the Imperial Rescript on Education.

The silver blades in my hand flashed against my father's silver hair as Hatsuko recited the words that every Japanese schoolchild knew by heart. I tried to draw strength from our former emperor's wisdom to face the disgrace that awaited me.

Know ye, Our subjects:

Our Imperial Ancestors have founded Our Empire on a basis broad and everlasting.

A fly buzzed about my father's head, but his attention was so focused on the words of the Emperor Meiji that he did not sweep it away. A tear slid silently down my sister's cheek, yet I felt her making her leaden heart as pure as possible as she poured it into her recitation.

Ye, Our subjects, be filial to your parents, affectionate to your brothers and sisters; as husbands and wives be harmonious, as friends true; bear yourselves in modesty and moderation . . . always respect the Constitution and observe the laws; should emergency arise, offer yourselves courageously to the State; and thus guard and maintain the prosperity of Our Imperial Throne coeval with heaven and earth.

Though it didn't seem possible, my father stiffened his spine even further than it already was, and I knew that he was steeling himself to accept the blow to his honor that was to come. The certain knowledge that our Emperor Hirohito, one hundred and twenty-fourth holder of the Chrysanthemum Throne, was a god, descended in an unbroken line from the Sun Goddess, Amaterasu, who brought light to the world, and that his every act and thought were blessed by heaven, made all hardships endurable. I focused on how trivial my sorrow was in comparison to the threat that our dear Father Emperor was now facing from the despotic Western powers. The emperor's divinity eased our worries: my father's about his three sons, Hatsuko's and mine about our brothers.

Really, it was silly to worry. In school we had learned that never in history had foreign soldiers invaded Japan. Kublai Khan had tried in 1281, but a *kamikaze,* a divine wind, had arisen to destroy the mighty Khan's fleet, a naval force five times as large as the Spanish Armada would be some three centuries later. As long as the Sun Goddess's descendant sat on the Chrysanthemum Throne, no enemy could harm our sons or brothers defending him. Though I would not serve our glorious cause as an educated subject, I would do my best to bring honor to my family and to our emperor no matter what my destiny might be.

"Oh, Father," Hatsuko called out, startling me. "What has Tamiko done?"

Blood dripped from the tip of Father's ear in a steady stream down the side of his face and onto the collar of his *yukata.* I had nipped the tender flesh of his ear. Our father had not uttered one sound, one word, not of pain or of reproach. Instead, he pressed his handkerchief against the wound, and, without a word or glance in my direction, took the scissors from my hand and gave them to Hatsuko. I sank into myself as Hatsuko finished the job I had botched.

A few hours later, all the inhabitants of our village had gathered in our courtyard. It was rare that they'd all stopped work this way. Everyone's workdays had grown longer, since Tokyo needed every sen we could provide to help in the fight against the Western imperialists. And, since we were such a backward place that required so much additional administration, we were taxed twice what other prefectures were. Many of the lazier farmers claimed that these necessary taxes were bankrupting them. I smelled them now, their sweat, the stink of night soil from their fields, as all the other villagers crowded in next to me in the courtyard of my family's house while we waited for my father to speak. I shuddered at the thought that I would be condemned to marry one of their sons. Father and Hatsuko stood on the long veranda that ran the length of our house. The ear I had cut was covered with white gauze. The noonday sun grew hot on our heads and the drone of the cicadas rose to an unbearable pitch.

On the shaded veranda, Hatsuko cradled a case made of *hinoki* wood, the whitest and holiest of all woods, for it contained the photo of our father, the emperor. Usually it was safeguarded inside the *hōanden* built in the yard of our school, where we could bow to it each day, but today was special, and, with great care, the photo had been transported here to watch over the proceedings. With great solemnity, Father put on a pair of white gloves, then carefully took the case of pale wood from Hatsuko. Since none of us was worthy of gazing upon the emperor's image, we all bowed our heads even before he could unlatch the case.

My twin cousins, Shinsei and Uei, stood beside me, heads lowered. The acrid scent of their nervousness wafted over to me. They were good students, but they had both been caught too many times speaking *Uchināguchi*, and been punished with whippings and by having to wear the humiliating "dialect tag" on strings around their necks that they couldn't remove until they caught someone else using our backward language. Those infractions would eliminate them from consideration; they would not be going on to high school either. Like mine, their lives would end in our small village. I wanted to reach out and take my old friends by their hands, to stand next to them as we endured our shame together. But it had been many years since we'd fought with screw pine swords or slid down hills of silvery *susuki* grass. Not since Hatsuko had explained to me how coarse and Okinawan it was for boys and girls to play together. She had shared what she'd learned in her Moral Education class about how making love was a painful duty that a wife endured for the sake of her husband. And until a suitable marriage was arranged, a girl had to remain a model of Japanese purity. That meant no contact with boys whatsoever. No talking, no exchanging notes, and, if I really wanted to be above reproach, I wouldn't even look at a boy. I didn't know whether this applied to cousins, but I didn't want to take any chances.

A ripple ran through the silent crowd as everyone shifted to make way for a newcomer elbowing in from the rear. In loud *Uchināguchi*, she brayed out, "Excuse me, excuse me, I'm sorry I'm late." Only one person would have the effrontery to speak out so coarsely in the presence of our emperor: my mother.

Of course, Mother's favorite sister, Aunt Junko, was with her, along with Aunt Junko's grown daughter, Chiiko, and the youngest of Chiiko's three children, Kazumi, a baby girl as sweet-tempered as her mother. Kazumi was so pink and tiny that we all called her Little Mouse. Little Mouse, strapped to Chiiko's back, popped her head up above her mother's shoulder.

Hatsuko lowered her head in shame as our famously bigmouthed mother stopped to address one of our neighbors. "Tokashiki-san, old friend, it's all your fault that I'm late, you know. Your bull escaped and tried to mount our old water buffalo, Papaya. We had our hands full getting that randy devil off of her. Does he take after you? I'll have to ask your wife."

I started to laugh, but the sight of that courtyard filled with farmers and their wives hooting, exposing mouths full of blackened or missing teeth, stopped me. I did not want to be one of them. I creased my lips into a hard line of censure and glanced up at Hatsuko. She gave me the tiniest nod of approval.

"Make way for my fat behind; I want to stand with my second daughter, Tamiko, when her name is read out."

She didn't know my name wouldn't be read. Apparently Father didn't consider her worthy of sharing even this disgrace. It was probably all her fault that I hadn't been admitted. Who wanted a girl with a mother who joked publicly about animals mating? It was all so typically Okinawan. I burned with humiliation as my mother shoved her way in next to me. Beneath her work trousers, tied at the ankles, her broad, leathery feet were bare and spattered with stinking night soil. Just as mine now would be for all the rest of my life.

My head still bowed, I heard Father snap the *hinoki* wood case closed; our emperor could not be subjected to such crass insolence. If Mother had been anyone else it would have been Father's duty to either beat her bloody for such a show of disrespect or to turn her in to the Japanese authorities. People had been executed for lesser crimes. For a second, the air around me crackled with Father's rage, and I glanced up, fearing that this time, Anmā had gone too far. But only the muscles bunching and unbunching at Father's jaw betrayed his fury. That and the blossom of blood as red as a *deigo* flower that bloomed anew on the white gauze covering his cut ear.

Father gathered himself and read the first name on the list, Ritsuko Amuro. Just as Father started to read the second name, a loud noise boomed out and the ground beneath our feet shuddered.

"Earthquake!" my mother shouted, and the crowd commenced to shriek and mill about like crazed geese. Women pulled their children flat onto the ground to wait for the next concussion. Our house shook in the thundering. In the goat shed, the horned male ran in panic around the post he was tied to, until the rope coiled tightly around his neck. His eyes wide with fear, he bleated out his terror in cries that sounded eerily human.

"Gunboats!" my father yelled, bounding off the veranda with a strangely exuberant step. Ignoring the danger, he set off, nearly running, toward the high black cliffs that towered above the ocean beyond our village.

We followed my father, our manor lord. As we ran, clouds of frightened black crows swirled overhead, cawing and flapping their wings. Father led us to the great field high above the ocean where, long ago, all the thousand lords of Okinawa were said to have once gathered. We crowded right up to the edge of the cliff, looked to the West, and a silence far more complete than the one that honored the emperor's photo fell upon us.

Where the vast blue of the East China Sea should have been, now there was only the dull gray of painted metal. In every direction, as far as we could see, the water was filled with warships of every size and description, all of them bristling with immense cannons pointed directly at our small island. Farthest away, off in the mist, were the largest, the battleships. They squatted on the horizon like sumo wrestlers waiting to destroy an opponent.

Gazing down at the terrifying armada, my father's eyes took on a fevered glaze. Excitement that he could barely suppress caused an unfamiliar quaver to oscillate through his words as he announced in an oddly exultant voice, "It has begun. Operation Shō has begun. Okinawa, this pathetic, useless little island, is about to become the scene of our emperor's greatest glory." My father's eyes glittered as he explained, "Soon the Imperial Navy, led by that floating leviathan, the *Yamato*, the greatest battleship ever constructed, will arrive and obliterate what is left of the United States' fleet."

The village elders nodded joyfully at Father's forceful words. A couple of the oldest among them had wispy white beards so long that their whiskers brushed the black rock at their feet when their heads dipped in eager agreement.

"The trap was set with care and now it is about to be sprung!" my father exulted.

All the men cheered my father's patriotic words except for Masa Akamine. Akamine-san, our village's calligraphy master, stood and asked, "Why do you all cheer? Will none of you speak the fears and doubts that you whisper secretly?"

Silence greeted Mr. Akamine's traitorous words. Our neighbors glanced about nervously. Who knew who might be listening? Who knew who might be receiving secret payments to report treasonous comments to the Imperial Army? Higa-san, a bachelor fisherman who once supplied us with the finest bonito on the island, had disappeared after making a drunken jest about the emperor, never to be seen again. Word reached us that he had been tried as a spy in front of the high command in Naha and beheaded with one swift chop of a sword.

All the men glanced down as the calligraphy master continued. "Why don't any of you ask the question I know you're all thinking? Weren't all the Americans' ships supposed to have been destroyed at Pearl Harbor?"

There was a moment of silence when those guilty of having had exactly that traitorous thought studied their feet.

"Akamine-san," my father spoke. "It was only the Pacific Fleet that was destroyed. There is still the Atlantic. And besides, it is clear to anyone who has eyes that most of those ships are decoys, fakes. Why, I can see from here that they're made of wood and painted to look like real battleships. Their only real purpose is to scare us. Which, I see, they've succeeded in doing."

Hearty laughter broke out then, and even I smiled with relief.

But Masa Akamine was not finished and went on growing increasingly frantic. "Does it not worry any of you that all the mainland Japanese who run our island sent their families home long ago? And now even the few remaining Japanese who are not in the army are leaving. We should be talking about evacuation."

"Evacuation?" Father mocked him. "Don't any of you farmers understand? It has been the great Admiral Yamamoto's plan all along to lure the American navy into this trap. A noose is drawing around them. At this very moment the greatest battleship ever to sail the waters of any ocean under any flag, the *Yamato*, is cruising at full speed, leading the entire Imperial Navy to encircle what remains of the demon's navy and crush it in one swift blow even more devastating than the one we dealt them at Pearl Harbor!"

"We have caught the lazy oafs napping again!" yelled Masaoka-sensei, a true Japanese who'd come from the mainland to be the principal of our local elementary school. A drunk and a wife-beater who liked to summon the older girls to massage his temples while he lay with his head in their laps, he had plastered the walls of our classrooms with posters showing us the sweating, apelike enemy, the "GI Joe" who lived to slaughter "Japs" and "Nips." Masaoka-sensei had instituted a Victory or Death program at the school. Even the kindergartners were required to practice marching at five in the morning. Marching was followed by an hour of drills with our bamboo spears, their tips sharpened and hardened in fire until they were as deadly as steel blades, while Masaoka-sensei exhorted us, "Concentrate your hatred in the tip of your spear." We ended each day's drill by swearing allegiance to our emperor and promising to die a thousand glorious deaths in his honor.

"Let us speak no more words of cowardice!" my father said, his voice rising with a thrilling patriotic fervor. "They are unworthy of the brave soldiers who have come here to our poor island to fight and die for us. For Japan! For our father, the emperor!"

"*Tennō heika banzai!*" the principal bellowed.

They all, even the ancient old men whose trembling legs bowed out like a chicken's wishbone, joined the cry: "Ten thousand years! Long live the emperor!"

"Right half turn!" my father ordered. "Bow full ninety degrees!"

They bowed toward the east, toward mainland Japan and the Imperial Palace.

Assured of the humiliating defeat soon to be dealt to the Americans whose very own Commodore Perry had once shamed us, the villagers grew celebratory. We turned our backs on the battleships and returned to the courtyard of our house, where bottles of millet brandy were produced and passed around. Even Father, who usually disdained the harsh local brew, took several swigs.

All talk of evacuation was abandoned. Besides, hadn't some already tried sending their loved ones to safety? I glanced at the faces of Mr. and Mrs. Taira. Their slender bodies tilted toward each other as if they would fall down if one weren't there to prop up the other. A year ago they had evacuated their three young children on the passenger-cargo vessel the *Tsushima Maru,* and sent them to the safety of the tall mountains and deep valleys of Japan. The 826 children who boarded that ship were excited that they would see maple leaves turn red in the autumn and even, wonder of wonders, witness snow in the winter. On August 22, 1944, at two in the morning, our merciless enemies torpedoed the ship. No one ever spoke of the incident, not even to offer consolation to the heartbroken parents. Instead we all pretended that the children, all 826 of them, were too busy making snowmen to write their parents.

Hatsuko beckoned for me to follow and we went into the number one room of our house, which contained our family altar, where we prayed for good marks in school or asked forgiveness for some childish misdeed. It was dark with all the wooden doors shut. Hatsuko stopped to light a stick of black Okinawan incense and pray that the spirits of our ancestors, all those ghostly names inscribed on the framed wooden tablets, would protect and guide us.

We rushed on to our sleeping area, where Hatsuko knelt on the tatami mat and handed me her comb. Without a word, I began combing her lustrous black hair. Carefully, I pulled a part down the center, divided each half into three equal sections, and braided them into a shiny rope. I wished for the millionth time that I had inherited my father's straight black, good Japanese hair, instead of the wavy Okinawan hair of our mother's family.

"Father is right," she said, as I finished tying the second braid.

"We must all do our duty now," I finished.

She reached over, grabbed her black leather school satchel, and stuffed in some books, her ink stick, the comb, a bar of soap, and her extra pair of socks.

"Hatsuko, you're not leaving, are you? Surely your studies will stop now for a few days."

My sister ceased her flurry of activity and held her hands out to me. "Tami-chan, do these look like the hands of a student?"

I touched her palms. They were rough as a pineapple.

"There have been no studies, no classes, for many months now. All the Princess Lily girls are training to be battlefield nurses. We'll assist the regular nurses who work in Red Cross hospitals. But, in addition to that, my unit has been assigned to help Lieutenant Nakamura's unit with . . ." My sister paused, glanced around, leaned in, and whispered, " . . . a top-secret project." Then, in one motion as fluid as a palace dancer, Hatsuko stood. "I have to leave now, but tell me that you will follow."

"Follow you? To Himeyuri? But we both know that my name isn't on the list. I wasn't accepted. I can never be a Princess Lily girl."

"Can't you see, Tami-chan? None of that matters anymore; we are at war. Lieutenant Nakamura says that we're all soldiers now. We must all fight with our tough Japanese spirit. Even he, who was trained as an English translator, is joining the struggle. You are needed in Shuri, Tamiko. You will be welcomed. I promise you that."

"That may be, but *Anmā* will never allow me to leave."

"Do not let our mother stop you. Persevere, Guppy. Use the strength of your Japanese spirit to overcome any obstacle. Come." She led me to the kitchen. There she spread her *furoshiki* wrapping cloth on the table and heaped sweet potatoes onto it.

"What are you doing?"

"Oh, Little Guppy, the soldiers get so hungry and food is so scarce. I thought I would take my share to them."

I helped her to pile even more potatoes onto the large piece of fabric. "Take my share as well of these unworthy potatoes to the emperor's soldiers in Shuri." She tied the bundle, and set it atop her head.

I walked beside Hatsuko down the dusty path that led to the main road to Shuri. Even balancing a great bundle of sweet potatoes, my big sister was noble and elegant. The lily pin on her breast shone, announcing to all who passed that she was illuminating the world with her purity and her patriotism.

I walked with her down the shaded path that led away from our village. "Why can't I just come with you right now?" I begged. "Your Lieutenant Nakamura has never seen a worker like me." Neither one of us took my plea seriously; it would be unthinkable for me to leave without our parents' blessing.

Hatsuko grinned. "When you do come, the lieutenant will like you; I'm certain of it. Even though he is purebred Japanese, he finds our backward country ways amusing. Wait until you see his sword. Only officers are entitled to wear swords. He always walks with his right arm crossed over his waist so his hand is on the hilt at all times. And he speaks English!"

"You speak English," I reminded her.

"No, Lieutenant Nakamura speaks the beautiful English of poets. He even writes poetry himself, Tami-chan. Listen to this." Hatsuko stopped as she recited: "'The bright yellow blossoms of the chrysanthemum bushes behind her looked like bursts of golden light. The moon, it changeth not. This night and yesteryear. But that which ever changeth is man's fickle heart.'"

She sighed a sigh as vast as the Pacific Ocean, and I understood then that Hatsuko loved this lieutenant. I worried that his poem was about man's fickle, ever-changing heart, but said nothing. "I must go. It is still a long walk back to Shuri." With that, she turned off our shadowed path and stepped out onto the road.

Before the Imperial Army took over the railroad, then requisitioned all the petrol on the island, there were buses on this road that would always stop to pick up anyone who needed a ride. Now all one saw anymore were military vehicles, trucks filled with soldiers, and they never stopped. Farmers driving carts, rickshaw drivers, herders with flocks of goats, they all had to step lively to get off the road in time, because the trucks wouldn't even slow down for them. But that day, the prospect of the long walk to Shuri didn't bother Hatsuko, and as she set off, her step was lively, lightened by the exhilaration of the important work she was doing and by thoughts of her gallant lieutenant. Her dark braids streamed out behind like the reins to a beautiful horse that had slipped away from me. I watched until she disappeared from view, then trudged home.

Back in the village, the men drank millet brandy and argued over whose family had the purest samurai lineage and who had sacrificed the most to help turn back the greedy American and British colonizers. Just as the sun was setting, my mother returned from the fields and entered the house, shaking her head and muttering about "the idiocy of men."

That evening when marchers from all the nearby villages in the area gathered in the Madadayo village square, my mother went to bed, saying that only people who didn't work all day had enough energy for such foolishness. My father and I, however, hurried off holding paper lanterns decorated with our emperor's fiery red rising sun. We sang songs about how we all yearned for the privilege of dying for the emperor, how we could not imagine any greater glory than to give our lives in his service.

A huge bonfire was built in the center of our village. In the light of its dancing flames, the men, now thoroughly drunk, set out to prove which one of them had sacrificed the most for our emperor. Everyone began gathering piles of food, bits of metal, scraps of cloth, anything we had left that we could contribute to the brave Japanese soldiers who were fighting on our behalf.

Sometime during this debate, Father disappeared. When he returned, he was leading Papaya yoked to her cart. He hurried her along as best he could by snapping a short leather whip against her thick hide. Piled high on the cart were the crocks that contained our barley, rice, the fish Mother had dried, as well as the miso pork she'd preserved. Beside them were stacked coops containing most of our flock of chickens. Two goats were tethered to the rails of the cart.

"I will drive this cart myself to Shuri this very night and present our humble offerings to the emperor's soldiers!" my father announced. But when he tried to climb up onto the cart, his legs turned to rubber, and he slid back down, landing on his bottom on the damp ground. I was shocked; I had never seen my austere, elegant father in such a state.

My mother appeared out of the darkness and yanked him back to his feet as if he were a sleepy child. "What do you think you're doing with our fish and miso pork and chickens and goats?"

"They are no longer ours, woman," he boomed out. "I have requisitioned them in the name of Emperor Hirohito!"

"Oh, shut up with these idiocies about your precious emperor. There is a great and terrible war coming, and your family will starve if you give away our chickens, our food."

The crowd fell utterly silent at such a treasonous pronouncement.

"Have you forgotten," my father roared, loud as a Kabuki actor, "that my family is descended from a long line of samurai who died defending their king?"

"And have *you* forgotten that the kings they died for were Okinawan kings? Not the ruler of our invaders?" I gasped, unable to believe what my mother had said. She reached out to grab the yoke. "Now, stand aside so that I can take our food and animals back home, where—"

My father raised the leather lash and cracked it against my mother's cheek. My hand leaped up to cover my mouth, but I did not dare move. If I intervened, it would be yet another blow to Father's honor, and my mother would have to answer for that as well. As blood trickled down Anmā's cheek, her eyes darkened to a shade beyond black, and a silence descended. It was as ominous as when the deceptive calm of the eye of a typhoon passes through, and I feared the terrible storm that was to come, for not only had Mother disgraced my father, she had insulted the emperor.

The awful silence was broken by my aunt Junko yelling out, *"Fii-dama!"* We followed her trembling finger to a glowing apparition hovering in the sky above the Sacred Grove beyond the edge of the village.

When I glanced back down from the small phosphorescent blur of a fireball wobbling in the sky, all five of my aunts had taken positions beside my mother, their sister. Next to them were their daughters. At the front of the line of my girl cousins was Chiiko with baby Kazumi, Little Mouse, on her back. Like Mother, all five Kokuba sisters were weathered, their skin tough and dark as ox hide from working the hereditary plots of land in their care.

"An uneasy spirit hunts for a body to claim," an old-timer called out in a voice quavering with terror. The others like him who were close to dying moved away from one another so as not to make such an inviting target for the phantom predator.

My aunt Junko, who had a wide space between her front teeth through which she liked to spit melon seeds and a headful of uncensored thoughts, announced in a somber voice, "This *fiidama* hasn't come to steal anyone's *mabui*. It is a sign that the *kami* are unhappy."

As a *noro* priestess, Aunt Junko was the village's spiritual leader, and, though Father and the other modern ones like him disdained our native religion in favor of Japan's more advanced Shinto, she still commanded respect. The bowlegged old men muttered assent and nodded in fright, their long white beards bobbing up and down in the darkness.

"Enough of your superstitious Okinawan twaddle about fireballs!" Father proclaimed. "The scientist from the mainland who came to investigate has already explained that this phenomenon is nothing more than a pocket of phosphorus gas released from one of the many tombs in this area."

At that, the old men cooed like doves in agreement.

None of my aunts joined in. Instead, they closed in even more tightly around my mother. "Perhaps," Aunt Junko said, wrapping a sheltering arm around her little sister, "but why then did the *kami* choose to release this *pocket of gas* at exactly this moment if not to voice displeasure?"

This time, the murmurs of assent were louder and they were against my father. "I will not listen to you ignorant traitors betraying our emperor," he thundered. "Tamiko, you shall be the one to deliver our offerings to the brave men who fight for us and our emperor. Go home now to prepare. In one hour you leave for Shuri!"

· SIXTEEN ·

You lost my flashlight?" Kirby asks Jake. "You dickweed. Do you know how much that flashlight cost? I had to pay for shipping from England. It was—"

Jake punches Kirby in the mouth with one quick snap of his fist.

Though I'd warmed up a little on the hike back to the cove after Jake helped me through the narrow crevice he'd found earlier that led to the trail, I'm still shaking from being batted around by the outrushing waves that funneled us back out through the cave opening. I'm even more chilled, though, by what I saw in the cave. I can't force the image of the starved girl or the sound of her mewling infant out of my mind.

"What the fuck?" Kirby taps a finger to his lip; it comes away glistening with blood. Kirby's tongue flicks out. He tastes the blood, and, still not believing, says, "You busted my lip, man. The fuck you do—"

"I told you about that bath-salt shit," Jake says in a level, information-dispersing tone. "I told you it can cause psychotic episodes. Did I not tell you that, Kernshaw?"

"And I told you I haven't got the shipment yet."

Jake ignores Kirby and asks, "What? You decide you'd do a little test? Put a dose in the Cuervo? That it? You spiked the Cuervo. Listen, jerk-wad, this ain't the homecoming dance, and that shit is not vodka you swiped out of your dad's liquor cabinet." Jake does a pretty good mean redneck when he puts his mind to it.

"Why do you even think I did that?"

Jake pauses, glances my way. "Luz, she . . ."

. . . *saw shit that wasn't there.*

" . . . she's having a rough time."

"Luz? Dude, you don't look right."

"Jesus, Kirby," Jacey snaps, then hisses, "her sister." She steps up next to me, takes my free hand in hers, makes a sandwich of it, warming my fingers. None of them ever said anything directly to me about Codie, but after the *Stars and Stripes* did an article last month about heroes that mentioned Codie, Jacey sent me a card. Just something from the BX. A photo of some purple tulips on the front and a verse from Scripture inside. "Peace I leave with you; my peace I give you. I do not give to you as the world gives. Do not let your hearts be troubled and do not be afraid." She tilts her head and her expression is a blobby mush of concern. I want to reach over, ram the heel of my hand into her face, and smush it around like Silly Putty.

"You do realize who her mother is, don't you?" Jake asks Kirby, assuming that, as usual, Kirby is lying about the bath salts.

"Yeah, but—"

"Do you have a fucking death wish?"

"If you would shut up and let me—"

"No, I'm not going to let you open your mouth and tell me again how they sell bath salts in head shops and it's such a safe, great high. Did you not hear me the first time, when I told you that it causes strokes and hallucinations and psychosis? Did I only imagine telling you all that?"

"A. It *is* legal—"

"Kirby, you *are* tripping. I mean, you have got to be seriously, *seriously* high to say something that stupid."

"It's not stupid, dicklick. I read up on it. They keep changing the formula so that the DEA can't actually write a law making it illegal. So, eee-yaah, it *is* legal, dude. And B. You sucker punched me like the little bitch you are."

"Sorry. It's the only way to get you to shut up sometimes."

Kirby gives him a fair-enough shrug.

"As for all your DEA technicalities? You really think OSI gives a shit about that?"

Everyone takes a collective inhale at the mention of the Office of Special Investigations. OSI is the air force's FBI. They're the agents in black T-shirts who investigate felony crimes. And they're actually a lot more like the Mafia than the FBI. They get your name and you and your family just disappear. Overnight. No questions asked. Due process is a civilian concept.

Since there is no arguing with OSI, Kirby stomps away, dragging the empty cooler behind. He hurls back, "Even if I actually had any shit, I wouldn't waste it on you losers."

The moon is setting behind the cliffs above, making a pointy crown from the zigzag of peaks at the top; the fire has burned down to embers, and the night has grown darker. A general agreement passes through the group that it's time to leave. They gather their things and follow Kirby up the winding path.

"Luz," Jake asks, "you ready?"

I pick up my shoulder bag from the sand and we trail behind the others.

Kirby spiked the Cuervo. Kirby spiked the Cuervo. I repeat the words like a chant to ward off evil spirits. Except that the spirits aren't evil. They can't be. I asked Codie for a sign and she sent a mama sea turtle that saved me from drowning. I don't want that to be a figment. But the Okinawan girl with an infant crying for help? They had to have been products of whatever evil chemical Kirby snuck into the Cuervo. I wish Codie were here to help me figure out what the hell is going on.

In the dark, I start to wander off the path, and Jake grabs me. "Luz, look out. That's Devil's Claw." He points to the tangle of tough, scrubby vegetation bordering the path. "It's got thorns like needles that'll rip your skin to shreds."

With him still close, almost holding me, I ask, "Jake, did you drink any of the tequila?"

"Yeah. Some."

"Did you . . . ? See things?"

"Luz, that shit affects everyone differently. Body weight. Mental state. You know, you've been through a lot lately."

Body weight. Mental state. Body weight. Mental state. Jake is so reasonable. I hope Christy appreciates him. I carefully work the syllables through the snarls in my brain, then, with exaggerated casualness, ask, "So, you really think Kirby spiked the Cuervo?"

"All that shit he was talking about bath salts? He probably did actually get some and was running his perverted idea of a test."

"But no one else who drank out of the bottle seemed, you know, affected."

"Like I said, it hits everyone different. Shit, look at you." He does just that. "Your body mass index is what?"

I shrug.

"Have you even eaten today?"

"I had some yogurt this morning." *Or was that yesterday morning?*

"We should go find you some soba or something when we get back."

"That would be good."

Being taken care of, someone looking out for me, is like my Kryptonite; it makes me weak, and I have a sudden, overwhelming desire to tell him about Codie. It seems really important that he know that she has an unnatural passion for Cheetos, sucks limes like they're Jolly Ranchers, and celebrates her birthday every year by doing her age times three in push-ups. And not girl push-ups either. Real ones. But I don't say anything, since it would involve using the past tense, and I can't do that to Codie, because she's not "was." She's "is." Mostly, though, I want to tell him about seeing that girl in the cave, but I can't figure out how to arrange the words so they don't sound either drug-induced or insane. I hate being so pathetic and weak. I ask him logical questions, like how he managed to find me.

"There aren't that many places you could have disappeared to. I just planned to try them all."

"Why?"

"Process of elimination."

"No, why did you come and look for me?"

"Be kind of crappy if I hadn't."

Jake moves on ahead. I study him for a moment then follow him to the base of the long, steep trail. The slushy roar of the East China Sea dims as we zigzag higher and higher up the cliff face. The farther we go from the ocean, the less and less sure I become of what I saw. What I think I saw or experienced makes no sense on dry land. By the time we reach the top of the trail, everyone is already pulling out, cutting crazy beams through the dust with their headlights as they rock off the tilting shoulder and turn back onto the road.

Jake looks back at me. "Where's your car?"

"I walked."

"You walked? From the base?"

"Just from the bus stop."

He glances at the narrow, twisting road. "That's not safe."

"I can't argue."

"Come on, Surfmobile's right up ahead."

I get into his ancient station wagon. I've never seen it without a couple of boards sticking out the back. Jake pulls off the shoulder and a breeze blows in through the open windows. The night air is all soft and heavy with smells that remind you you're eleven time zones away from the States. As we lurch down the hill trying to keep up with Kirby, who is pinballing around turns like the lunatic he is, I stare out into the dark, unable to stop the image of the girl in the cave, which I apparently hallucinated, from strobing through my mind.

"Hey, come here." Jake reaches across the bench seat, puts his arm over my shoulders, and pulls me to his side.

I lean against him, and the instant I make contact with his body, the visions disappear. His warmth makes me realize that I'm sodden. "I reek."

He leans over, puts his nose against the top of my head. "No, you smell like my favorite thing, the ocean."

He starts rubbing my arm, and I know I have the choice of a quick hookup or something else. Because I don't want some random sleazy encounter to be his last memory of Luz James, I pick "something else" and kill the moment by asking, "Where's Christy?"

The rubbing stops dead. "She's off somewhere."

"Where?"

"You really care?"

"Should I?"

He withdraws his arm, puts it on the steering wheel. "She's up in the *yambaru*. Up north in the backcountry. Doing Obon stuff with her family like a good *Uchinānchu*."

Uchinānchu. The funny, singsongy word rings like a nursery rhyme in my memory and causes smell tags to pop up in my brain: Pond's cold cream, cigarettes, a vinegary body odor mixed with the wet-hay fragrance of green tea. They're all the smells I associate with my grandma Overholt, who'd been born Setsuko Uehara, but whom Codie and I called *Anmā*, the Okinawan word for "mother," since that's what we grew up hearing our mom call her. I see *Anmā* in my mind pointing at me and saying that word, *Uchinānchu*, then pointing at me and saying, "You, you *Uchinānchu*." Then she'd point at Codie and say the same thing. She always made us repeat the funny word, then, when we said it correctly, she'd smile and kiss our cheeks and give us pieces of hard candy that smelled like violets. Gradually, we figured out that the word *Uchinānchu* meant Okinawan.

I do the translation and ask, "What Obon stuff are the other Okinawans doing?" Codie always said that being a brat is good training for being a spy. Since you're always coming in cold and having to pick up cues fast, so that you can fake knowing more than you do, you learn to make a little information go a long way.

"Just the usual three-day blowout when the whole extended clan, the *munchū*, gathers."

I can feel Jake trying to decide what slot to put me in: crazy druggie girl, quick hookup, or, maybe, someone who's a little bit like him. I go for door number three and say, "Yeah, Obon, I remember my grandmother talking about that."

"Your grandmother is . . . ?"

"Pure *Uchinānchu*."

"So your mom is *hāfu*?"

Half-oo, the word that explains itself. "Yeah, Oki and Cawk."

Stripes of light from the oncoming cars flash across Jake's face as he studies me, sees something that doesn't add up, and I explain, "My father was pretty dark."

"You never know. Genetics is such a crapshoot. I have this one *hāfu* friend, his dad was long gone before he arrived. His mom. Bar girl. Too poor to raise him. Farmed him out to her family up north, so he was brought up very old school, right? Pure *Uchi*. Barely speaks a word of English. And this guy, he looks exactly like Will Smith. I mean big grin, jug ears, completely round eyes."

"Wow."

"Yeah, plays the *sanshin* and everything. Very traditional. Was your grandmother?"

"Was she what?"

"Traditional?"

"Definitely." Codie used to call us chameleons. Said blending in was the best protective mechanism until you figured out what was going on. "Obon was always a really big deal in my family."

Jake laughs in a way that's not either flirty-sexy or worried I'm going to have a mental meltdown. He laughs like we're friends. "God, my mom and all my aunts go into total overdrive. They even left a day early to consult with their favorite Utah back in Henza."

"Yeah, Utah," I repeat, having no idea on earth why he's talking about consulting with a Mormon state, but not wanting to show him what an outsider I really am by asking.

"They've all been cooking like maniacs. Huge batches of *sātā andāgii*, since all the grands and the great-greats back for forever loved their Oki doughnuts. Spam for some long-gone uncle who developed a taste for that in the camps after the war. *Gōyā chanpuru*, because it was my great-aunt Hide's favorite. But really? What *Uchinānchu* doesn't love their *chanpuru*?"

"Really," I agree, having no idea what "*chanpuru*" is, but liking how amazingly normal I feel when I talk to him. Like I actually do belong here and I just imagined everything: the girl in the cave, the rogue wave that saved me, a sea turtle sent by my dead sister. I start to believe that it was all drug-induced and has nothing to do with me. As if to literally prick this new bubble of coziness, whatever it was that I swiped from the cave and stuck in my pocket pokes me. Tilting away from Jake so he can't see my stolen goods, I unzip the pocket and dig the item out. When I uncurl my fingers, a brooch rests on my palm. It is in the shape of a flower and is made of iridescent mother-of-pearl. The trumpet-shaped flower hangs from a long stem that is bent over in a humble way. I think it's a lily.

I'm still surreptitiously staring at it when Jake asks, "You plan on doing anything for Unkeh later today?"

I stuff the pin back in my pocket. "Yeah, Unkeh, I remember my grandmother talking about that," I lie, "but I can't exactly recall what it is."

"Unkeh? First day of Obon. Welcoming day."

"Welcoming who?"

Jake looks over to see if I'm joking. "The dead. Today is the day the dead return."

· SEVENTEEN ·

Anmā, *she knows that today is Unkeh. How do I know what the demon is thinking?*

Because we're with her now.

Oh. Because you made her take your pin?

Of course.

Are we kami-sama *now?*

No, far from it.

But you are happy.

Yes.

Because the kami are helping us?

Yes.

Will there be time for you to finish telling the story?

There has to be. Where did I stop?

Your father had just told you that you were going to Shuri to give your chickens and pork miso to the emperor.

Just so.

So your name was on the list.

Oh, you're a greedy one. Listen, the story must be told as it happened. Now, I will begin again.

I was going to Shuri! I would join Hatsuko and our cousin Mitsue.

The words sang in my mind, accompanied by the creaks of the cart's wheels and groans of the leather strapping as Papaya strained against the great wooden yoke. Blue shadows cast by the full moon slid over her broad back as we swayed along. The long branches of the sea hibiscus hedge lining the path scraped the sides of the cart and rat-a-tat-tatted against the bars of the chicken coops piled in the back.

What a day! Just when I thought that my dream of going to Shuri as a student had died, it was brought back to life in an even more magnificent form: I would arrive at the headquarters of the Japanese army as a hero, with wonderful gifts of food and livestock. I imagined the handsome face of Hatsuko's Lieutenant Nakamura bright with gratitude at our family's largesse. Perhaps this display of devotion to the emperor would prove how Japanese my sister truly was and inspire him to propose marriage to her. I knew that Hatsuko had always dreamed of marrying a pure Japanese and fleeing our backward island.

While I imagined my sister's joy and gratitude, Papaya snorted, yanked the reins from my hands, and came to a dead halt. At first I thought that she must have spotted a *habu* viper, and I grabbed the machete from where it swung by a hook on the side of the wagon to chop off its poisonous head. Instead, six ghosts blocked the path.

I screamed and the machete clattered to the bed of the cart.

"Stop screaming," Aunt Junko ordered. "It's only us." My mother and her sisters, all of them, oldest to youngest—Junko, my mother, Yasu, Toyo, Sueko, Yoshi—stepped out of the shadows.

In front of them all stood my impetuous cousin, Junko's daughter, Chiiko, who told her aunts, "Yes, be quiet. We certainly wouldn't want to wake up *your brother.*"

All the women laughed at Chiiko's sarcastic comment. The women had long ago agreed that the decision to adopt my father into their family had been a terrible mistake that only laughter could allow them to bear.

"Wake our brother?" Aunt Junko asked. "After all the millet brandy he drank? Nothing will wake him."

When my mother joined in the laughter, the deep cut from my father's lash that sliced beneath her high cheek like a dark shadow seemed to lighten a bit. Even Little Mouse, tied to her mother's back, peeked over Chiiko's shoulder and grinned. Little Mouse's baby teeth had come in, and, just like her mother and grandmother, Chiiko and Junko, she had a gap between the front two. Our father always said that it was that space that allowed all the foolish words in the women's foolish heads to tumble out. Father warned Hatsuko and me that blurting out whatever thought crossed your mind was a very Okinawan trait and we must strive to keep our thoughts and especially our feelings to ourselves in the refined Japanese manner.

"Let's get this cart unloaded," Aunt Yoshi ordered. Though she was the youngest of the sisters, she was the tallest and the strongest, since she'd been the baby adored by her siblings, who regularly went hungry so that she would have extra treats to help her grow strong and healthy. They also never allowed her to carry heavy loads on her head, as they did, which caused her to grow taller than the others. Aunt Yoshi was the mother of my twin cousins, Shinsei and Uei. Since everyone knows that multiple births are a sure sign of a shamefully animal nature, it was generally agreed that all the spoiling was the reason.

"What are you doing?" I asked, as my aunts and cousin carried off the chicken coops and crocks of pork miso.

"We are undoing what should never have been done in the first place," Mother answered firmly, untying the goats and leading them away from the cart.

"Those are for the emperor," I protested. My mother caught Aunt Junko's eye and all the sisters laughed, their merriment an enchanted piping in the still night.

My *anmā* and her sisters carried the cart's contents to the narrow footpath that led into the dense growth of the jungle.

"Where are you taking the emperor's gifts?" I called after them, but they'd already been swallowed up by the night. I jumped down off the cart. Papaya was slewing her head to the side as she yanked off a wad of weeds, then calmly chewed. Confident that she wouldn't wander away until every blade had been consumed, I left the empty cart and ran down the footpath.

The narrow, twisting path cut through the sacred grove thick with tall red pines that smelled of resin. The path led to the tomb of my mother's clan, where we gathered several times a year. Especially at Shiimii and Obon, my mother and her sisters would spend days weeding the family plot and cleaning the tomb. Then they would produce a multitude of square lacquered boxes filled with rice cakes, wafers, seaweed rolls, boiled octopus, and potato pudding for us to share with our ancestors. There were no lacquered boxes that night.

At the end of the path, I found them gathered in front of our family tomb. The tomb was the pride of the Kokuba family. It had a granite roof high as a man's shoulder. Some said that such tombs resembled a turtle's back. But Anmā laughed at that, saying only one thing had such a voluptuous curve: a woman's womb. It was where all life started and, in the form of this tomb, where it would return.

Because there'd been a bone-washing ceremony just a few days ago, the large squared-off stone that usually blocked the entrance had already been pushed aside. Working as they always did, like a jolly colony of ants that liked to sing and make bawdy comments, my mother and her five sisters carried the crocks of food they'd taken from the oxcart into the tomb.

The millet-seed oil lamp was lit, and the tomb glowed with its soft illumination. Our tomb was one of the largest on the island, with rows of shelves for holding ceramic urns arranged in chronological order, containing the bones of generations of family members. It did not smell of rotting flesh as so many did, since all my female relatives were careful about cleaning the bones before they were stored in here. They understood that all the rituals had to be observed perfectly or the dead would never complete their transformation into ancestral spirits.

When the last crock had been stored away, and the goats and chickens distributed among her sisters to hide on their farms out of Father's sight, Mother took a handful of rice from one of the bags, clapped her hands together to catch the attention of the kami, and prayed. "Dear ancestors, today the Americans have begun destroying our island. Please guard your many descendants that we may live to honor you. And protect this food that we leave in your safekeeping, so that when my proud husband and foolish daughters are starving after Japan has been defeated, they will have food."

"Mother! You can't speak that way. Remember what happened to Ashitomi-sensei?"

"Of course I remember one of our few Okinawan teachers and how those Japanese soldiers took him out and beat him like a common criminal for stating the truth: that Okinawa is nothing to Japan. A shield, at best."

Even in this dark and deserted spot, I glanced around. If anyone overheard her, my mother, and probably me as well, would be shot on the spot as a traitor. "Mother! What treason you speak. What insults to all the brave soldiers who have come here ready to sacrifice their lives in our defense."

Aunt Junko and Cousin Chiiko hooted the raucous laughs they were famous for. "Ready to eat every *kin* of our rice," Chiiko said, "steal every chicken, drink every drop of millet brandy, and put babies in every pretty girl they come across."

Though all my aunts laughed, my mother was deadly serious when she stared hard at me and said, "Listen now to your *anmā*, Tamiko, for only I will tell you the truth. Ashitomi-sensei was right: The Japanese don't care about us. They will sacrifice every person on all the Ryukyu Islands down to the last child to protect their sacred motherland. And when they are defeated, it will be even worse."

My heart stopped; if a spy overheard such a treasonous remark, we would all be beheaded. "Defeated? *Anmā*, what a silly joke you are making. Why, everyone knows that in all its glorious history, Japan has never been conquered. And she never will be as long as her subjects remain loyal to our father, the emperor."

"Tamiko, there is no more time to pretend. Though we never wanted it, have nothing to gain by it, and did nothing to provoke it, Japan has brought a great and terrible war to our people, and we shall be crushed by the *Amerikās*."

"Our sister is right," Aunt Junko said, cousin Chiiko and the others nodding their heads in sad acknowledgment. Even sweet Little Mouse, the happy baby grown into a happy toddler, looked on wide-eyed and somber.

"No!" I protested. "For more than a thousand years Japan has—"

"Daughter, listen. We will be conquered. I know this from your aunt Toyo's husband, Uncle Chūzō, who worked all those years in the sugar plantations on Hawaii. He has told me that the generals did a very stupid thing when they attacked Pearl Harbor. They awoke a sleeping dragon."

"But size does not matter," I argued. "It is spirit. The pure Japanese spirit will always prevail. Japan has already destroyed the enemy's navy at Pearl Harbor and defeated them in the Philippines and Corregidor and Singapore and . . ." I tried to remember the names of the other sites of Japanese victory.

"You speak like a rabbit. Perhaps the rabbit, cornered by an ox, can hop about for a bit, dash between the giant beast's hooves. But eventually? The foolish rabbit will be crushed."

Doubt squeezed my heart then, and did not release its hold until I glanced down at my mother's feet. As usual, they were bare, and her toes, spreading out as wide as a stretched hand, were leathery and brown as an ape's. It was just as the school inspector visiting from Tokyo had told our principal, when he saw how many of us were barefooted. The inspector in his brown suit, hair neatly parted and gleaming with pomade, had asked then, "We do the best we can, but really? What can you expect from these little brown monkeys?"

Little brown monkey. That was exactly what my mother was.

And still she chattered on, seeming more like a little brown monkey with every word. "My great-great-grandmother Uto, who was called Old Jug, and drowned in the Great Typhoon of 1872 and has always taken an interest in our family, spoke to me soon after Third Brother left. She told me that he would never return. That none of my sons would return. That they would die from the sun spinning too close to earth—"

"See?" I interrupted, unable to contain myself at such ignorance. "This is why I must ignore you. This is why I must go to Shuri and become educated and worthy to serve our emperor. You don't even know that the *planets* rotate around the *sun.* You can't even read. You can't appreciate all that Japan has done for us because you're too ignorant."

My mother slapped me hard across the face. "You will never speak to me like that again. I am your mother. You will respect me in this life and honor me in the next as you honor all of your ancestors, or we will punish you with sorrow and misfortune in this life *and* in the next."

My aunts and cousin Chiiko sucked in stunned breaths; never before had they heard such a terrible threat spoken aloud.

"And now, *baka*"—Anmā spit out the word "fool," and went on— "you will listen like a good daughter with your eyes lowered and your mouth closed. Here. Take this." She shoved a tube made of fabric at me. It was stuffed with more money than I had ever seen in my life.

"Tie that around your waist beneath your kimono."

I did as I was told.

"Do not ever allow yourself to be parted from that money. My mother gave it to me in secret so that I would never have to stay with any man who was unkind to me. I should have used it long ago and left your father, but now that you need it, I am happy I didn't." Next Anmā placed a bonnet on my head and tied it tightly beneath my chin. It was quilted with thick wads of cotton padding and extended down until it covered my shoulders. "This will protect you when the bombs fall." She shoved another into my hand and told me it was for Hatsuko, and that I must always tie my older sister's bonnet on before my own.

"Most important of all," Mother said, leaning in close and holding up a thick document. "Remember that this is here."

"Why have you brought our family's *koseki shōhon* here?" I asked when she held up the certificate that she'd gone to great trouble to register in Tokyo. It documented our lineage and proved that this land belonged to our family. We all thought she was stupid to have gone to the bother and expense of proving something that everyone already knew to be a fact. "Why isn't this in the house?" I asked. "Safe in our *butsudan?*"

Anmā shook her head, as if my question about our family altar were a pesky fly. "Safe in a house of wood with a roof of palm thatch? Only stones will be safe when the bombs fall. Here." She shoved my leather rucksack, which the Japanese principal had insisted all students must have, into my hands. "I have packed dried kelp, roasted soy beans, and dried bonito for your journey."

"*Anmā*, where are you sending me?" I asked. My lip trembled and tears gathered in my eyes. "To Aguni Island to work for Great-Uncle Eikichi?" I thought of the island that no one spoke of because the inhabitants of Aguni made their living slaughtering animals. Already my aunts had sent three of my rowdiest boy cousins to that desolate place. They'd returned chastened, with moons of dried blood beneath their nails, their arms flecked with white scars from the knives, and tales of being driven like beasts of burden by our cruel uncle. "Mother, please, don't send me to Uncle Eikichi."

"I'm not sending you to Aguni Island, *baka*. You will go to Shuri."

I was too surprised to speak.

"Your sister is a goose. A lovely, refined goose, but with no more sense than a goose. She is like your father. Ready to die for beautiful words that have no truth. Though you aren't happy about it, you are like me. Your feet are wide and rooted to the earth. Your sister's head is filled with airy thoughts that will make her float away. You will go to Shuri and keep her alive. Do you understand me?"

My smart, worldly big sister, I was to be her caretaker? Me? Little Guppy?

My mother grabbed my arms and shook me. "Do you understand me?"

I nodded, feeling as I did when I rolled down the long, steep hill above the Oigama River. The world was topsy-turvy.

"Pay attention and mind this well: From now on your life doesn't belong to you. It belongs to me and to your father and our mothers and fathers. Because even though we may all be killed, we will go on living through you. You and your sister have our blood. It is your duty to take care of it and to live as long as you can. *Nuchi du takara*. Life is the treasure. Do you understand?"

I nodded.

"Say it," she ordered me. "*Nuchi du takara*."

My tongue fumbled over the words. "*Nuchi du takara*. Life is the treasure."

"*Nuchi du takara*." All the women folded their hands and repeated my mother's words like a chant. Cousin Chiiko clapped her hands several times to call the *kami-sama*'s attention to their prayer, then excused herself; she'd left her two older children asleep with no one watching over them, since her husband had been drafted and sent to Manchukuo to fight the imperialist oppressors there. Plus, hers was the only home with a stable free for Papaya, so she'd have to deal with the balky ox. With Little Mouse fast asleep, lolling on her back, she hurried away.

Anmā went on. "When you need help, when you need guidance, pray to our ancestors. Especially Old Jug. Ask for her guidance. She will help you. Do you understand?"

I nodded. *Anmā* stared for a long time into my face, then clapped my upper arms with her open hands, and commanded in a thick voice, "Good. Go."

The moon had set and the forest was lost in darkness by the time my mother pushed me off, down the path. I stumbled away from the tomb, then paused and looked back. Mother yelled angrily for me to stop dawdling. As I walked away, she shrank, becoming a pale moth in her summer kimono until the black night swallowed her up entirely. When I reached our village road, Chiiko was there leading Papaya away.

"Travel safely, First Daughter," she called back to me. First Daughter was her name for me, since she'd carried me on her back when I was a baby, long before her own children were born.

"Good-bye, Second Mother."

The sun was beginning to rise as I reached the first bend in the road and glanced back to catch a final glimpse of my cousin and her baby. Little Mouse had awoken and managed to squirm around in the sling binding her to Chiiko's back, so that she was staring at me. I wondered whether Little Mouse would call me Second Mother one day, since I used to carry her on my back. The first rays of the new day slanted into her face and I waved. Though the toddler's arms were free and I had been the one to teach her how to flap her hand downward in fare-well, Mouse did not return my wave. This made me sad, for it seemed my first daughter was withholding her blessing from me and my mis-sion. I kept waving in vain until Little Mouse and Chiiko disappeared in the distance. A bubble of love for my cousin and her child rose up and filled my chest so full that it hurt, and I almost turned away from Shuri and ran back to them. Back to Madadayo.

But I forced myself to draw on my true Japanese spirit of sacrifice and persevere. Back on the path, I sensed the presence of uneasy spir-its hovering around who had not received a proper burial, and wished that I were traveling to Shuri in a cart loaded with a hero's bounty of gifts for the emperor. Mouse's sad face haunted me. I began to think that the *kami* were sending me a warning, as they often do through tod-dlers not yet able to speak, and once again I was tempted to turn back. But the prospect of serving the emperor by Hatsuko's side was so excit-ing that I pushed on.

By the time I reached the main road, the sun was shining full in my face, and my heart was light again as I set off for Shuri.

· EIGHTEEN ·

At Kadena's front gate, the guard, a young Okinawan woman in the short-sleeved khaki uniform of a host nation civilian employee, asks for our IDs. From my shoulder bag, I dig out the card that all dependents are issued at the age of ten. Codie and I used to talk about how we dreaded the day when we turned twenty-one and would have to surrender them.

By the time Codie was twelve, she hated the goofy photo on her card so much that she "lost" it so she could get a new one. Always Luz the Caboose, following my sister and copying everything she did, I "lost" the brand-new card I'd gotten when I turned ten. Before we went in for new ones, Codie spent a lot of time making us up. Eyeliner, mascara, blush, lip gloss. Her breath on my face as she told me to look up so she could put mascara on my bottom lashes smelled like Sucrets from the lozenges she was sucking that day for a sore throat. We thought we looked stupendous. The photos, however, taken by a bored GI under flickering fluorescent lights, were worse than the first ones.

"Oh. My. God," Codie said when we got our cards, still warm from the laminator. "We look like Jodie Foster in that old movie where she's a ho. We're baby hos."

The IDs became another secret in-joke between us. Mom, however, was not amused. She ordered us to redo them. Codie promised we would. ASAP. But we never did. We loved being baby hos together. Plus, we both considered our mother a giant hypocrite, because she was such a ho herself, and only transformed herself into the perfect, by-the-book soldier girl for work.

Eventually Mom confiscated the baby-ho IDs, torched them into a dripping mass of molten plastic with her lighter, and took us herself to get replacements. This time the only makeup we were allowed was ChapStick, and the photos were taken by an airman terrified of screwing up in front of a superior. I'm actuallly rolling my eyes in my ID photo.

At the gate, the Okinawan guard studies Jake's ID, then mine, shines a flashlight in our faces to make sure they match, hands our cards back, and waves us on. Going through the gate into the base is like watching one of those tiny sponges packed tight into a capsule miraculously expand into a dinosaur when you put it in a glass of water. In the instant that it takes to drive through the opening in the miles of chain-link fence encircling Kadena Air Base, the world opens up. The claustrophobia of Okinawa, with its narrow, twisting roads, and buildings crammed together right up to the street, expands into a sprawling world of wide, tree-lined avenues and rolling green lawns, endless acres of parade grounds and runways, a commissary and BX lavished with jumbo parking lots.

"Hey, there's my house," Jake says, slowing down to point out a big one-family unit at the edge of the most extravagant spread of open land of all, a golf course. The just-watered fairway perfumes the air with the scent of newly mowed grass. The house he points out, secluded from the rest of the neighborhood, is so large, I ask, "How many are in your family?"

"My parents, two brothers, two sisters. My aunt and her family were living with us, but they moved back to Naha. Two cousins are semi-permanent. They're all gone now, though, back at the ancestral home."

"Oh, yeah, right, Obon."

"Couple of uncles even flew in from Hawaii. This guy I surf with, his grandparents came in from Peru. Lots of relatives from the mainland."

"So why did you stay behind?"

"It's a long story. Is that Kirby?"

We easily catch up to Kirby, who's creeping along way under the forty-kilometer-an-hour speed limit. He has trouble with converting kilometers to miles, so he just cuts the KPH figure in half and never drives over twenty miles an hour on base. His stepdad has promised that he'll ship Kirby off to military school in Arkansas if he screws up one more time. And Sergeant Kernshaw, a Desert Storm vet with arms like tree trunks, does not play around. Kirby's brake lights flash.

"Why is he pulling over?"

Kirby slides to a stop beside the parade ground, where, on review days, row after row of airmen in their freshly pressed service blues, their shoes like black mirrors, march in perfect unison. He jumps out of the car, grinning, the cut on his lip forgotten, holding up his phone like he's caught the game-winning ball. One thing you have to say about Kirby: He doesn't hold a grudge. Codie was the same way. Always said her ADHD made it impossible for her to concentrate on one person long enough to get a good hate on.

Kirby pops his head in Jake's open window. "Hey, I just got a text from Jacey. She's dumping the Italian Shetland at the barracks before curfew—"

"Curfew?" Jake interrupts. "Curfew's not for another hour."

"They changed it to ten because of those navy guys."

"Oh, right." Curfew had been pushed back all across the island because some sailors had raped an Okinawan woman.

"Anyway, Jacey's up for hanging out some more. You guys in?"

"Luz?" Jake asks.

"No, I'd better . . ." I point off in the general direction of our housing area. "Curfew." None of us are supposed to be out after curfew, not that we care that much. I only observe the rule when it's convenient. And it's convenient now. My nerves are fried; I have to get something to take the edge off.

"What about you, jackwad?" Kirby asks Jake.

"Hang out? With you?"

"Yeah, me, rim job. What's your problem. Not like I busted *your* mouth open or anything. I'm the aggrieved party here. Come on, we'll—"

"Yeah, okay. Cool. Text me."

Kirby leans in, gives us his blue-gummed smile, "You two. You're good together. I can see it."

Count on Kirby to zero in on and say the most awkward thing imaginable.

"Good to know you approve," Jake says dryly. "Means the world to us."

"Dude, you're the one always talking about how you want to break up with Christy, but you're afraid the whole Smokinawan world'll turn against you if you do."

"Thanks for sharing, Kirbs." Without another word, Jake starts to roll up the window.

"Gahhh!" Kirby, his head still in the window, sticks his tongue out, pretends he's being decapitated.

"Pull your head out of the window, Kernshaw, and put it where it usually is. Up your ass."

Kirby backs away. "See you later, masturbator!"

"After a while, pedophile."

I direct Jake through a series of crisp right-angle turns. We pass a neighborhood of midgrade officers' housing with neat yards trimmed to the specified three-inch-height maximum. Farther on is enlisted housing, where I live. As the rank goes down, the number of cars and trucks clustered around the multifamily units increases.

"That's us." I point to the one empty carport on the block.

"You don't have a car?"

"Yeah, but my mom parked it at the flight line."

I don't add that Mom not letting me use her car while she was gone was why we had a shrieking fight right before she left that had ended with her telling me, "You have an anger issue that you need to see someone about. Did you get in touch with the TAPS program like I told you to?"

I tried and failed not to wince at the acronym. Tragedy Assistance Program for Survivors. Motto: "Caring for the families of our fallen heroes." It physically hurt me that our mother didn't understand how much Codie would have hated that. The "fallen heroes" part. All of it. What made me sick, literally, physically sick, was how she acted like Codie's death was a problem, a problem that was impeding the efficient accomplishment of The Mission. And, like every other facet of life that related to accomplishing The Mission, the air force had a solution, and setting up the TAPS program and Web site was it.

"Oh, yeah," I told her. "I have an online mentor and everything. We're always texting and Facebooking and tweeting and twatting and everything."

Mom gave me her badass law-enforcement face, the one that told all the airmen stealing paper clips, and skeevy noncom window peepers, and brat taggers defacing government property that she knew who they really were. That they could lie to her all they wanted, but she knew. Just like she doubted that I had an online mentor walking me through the stages of grief. So she took the car. Her last words to me were, "You need to get your shit wrapped up a whole hell of a lot tighter than it is now or there is going to be trouble. Serious trouble."

"'Going to be'?" I'd asked her, flabbergasted. "There is *going to be* trouble? As if there hasn't been trouble already? As if we're walking through a fairy-tale dreamland of happiness and cotton-candy clouds and have no idea what 'trouble' is?"

The words I hadn't spoken when the chaplains came vibrated then between us like a hologram of Codie. Like my fury had summoned her to bear witness to the truth I was not allowed to speak, the truth I was being punished for even thinking: *Your daughter, my sister, the one person on earth who loved me and whom I loved, is dead. And it's your fault.*

My mom twitched with the effort of not slugging me. At that moment, I wanted her to crack out a little krav maga. I didn't care if she beat me to a pulp, as long as I could get a few serious shots in on her. But she didn't go martial arts; instead, she muttered, "Consequences, Luz, consequences," and left before I could scream at her about what bullshit *that* was.

Jake pulls into our carless carport, leaves the engine running. "You want me to walk you to the door or something?"

"No, no. That's cool. Daughter of the head base cop, who'd mess with me?" I pivot toward the door handle. I really don't want to go into the empty apartment; there's too much night left. But I've used up all the fake extroversion I can muster.

"You want me to come in with you?" he asks, quickly adding, "You were saying some pretty extreme things tonight."

"Ex-STREAM THINGS!" I sing in a fake heavy-metal way. Literally and figuratively, I hit exactly the wrong note.

"Whatever. I just thought, after what happened, you might not want to be alone."

"Are you suggesting yourself to solve the alone problem?"

"Fuck you. Jesus, Luz, get over yourself."

"Sorry. I'm an asshole."

"You don't exactly make it easy to be your friend."

"'Friend'?"

He squeezes his eyes shut and scratches the back of his neck where irritation is making it prickle.

"You're sweet, Jake." Though I don't intend to, I sound like a condescending bitch. I jump out before I can embarrass myself any worse than I already have.

Outside, the still air smells like Okinawa when it exhales its night breath, a sick fragrance of too much green. The base is sleeping. I watch the station wagon's red taillights crest the rise at the end of the block, then disappear on the other side. I stay out on the porch until the mosquitoes drive me inside.

The edifice we currently inhabit is a nice enough two-bedroom unit, assigned on the basis of Mom's pay grade and number of dependents. The white paint and tan carpets are new. To stay under our weight allowance, we didn't move any of our furniture from Albuquerque. Everything in the apartment is borrowed from the base, and it's fine in an anonymous Motel 6 way. All the upholstery has been drenched in Febreze to kill the smell of past owners. Which just creates its own new superodor of Febreze plus sweat and cigarette smoke overlaid with the corn and cumin smell of Doritos.

Mom hasn't hung up any of our usual stuff on the walls. Not the giant wooden fork and spoon from the Philippines, or the cuckoo clock like a little brown chalet from Germany, or the red-and-gray Navajo rug we got in Albuquerque, or the blue eye pendant from Turkey for warding off evil that she brought home from her last TDY. Mom had to hit the ground running when we arrived. Command was losing their shit because of a dependent crime wave. Brats staying out past curfew, stealing traffic signs, scrawling "gang signs" on the side of the commissary, getting GIs to buy alcohol for them at the Class Six, doing drugs. Pretty much all the activities that I enjoy with Kirby and his crew.

Plus, since the walls are made of typhoon-proof concrete, you need a drill to put anything up. So the fork and spoon, the clock and the pendants are leaning against the wall in the spot where, eventually, they'll be hung. Everything else except our clothes and cooking things is still in boxes. Which is different. Before, no matter how short the assignment was going to be, Mom always made a big effort to make a new place homey. But home is just the people who live there, and we both know that we'll always be one person short of ever having a real home again.

The only thing that looks normal is the battered old box with "Anmā's Stuff" written on the outside in my mom's handwriting. Of course, that box has never been opened again after the day we got it eight years ago. We were in the middle of PCSing to Germany when we found out that our grandmother had died. Since Mom had no one to leave us with, she couldn't even go to the funeral. *Anmā's* box had bounced around the APO system for weeks before it caught up to us at the Ramstein Prime Knight Inn, where the billeting office had us staying until base housing opened up.

Inside the box were all the things *Anmā* had left my mom. A broken string of pearls, a cloisonné bracelet missing two panels, some dangly rhinestone earrings, a wedding ring, stock certificates for a company that had been out of business for twenty years, and the Smith & Wesson .38 service pistol that my grandfather Eugene Overholt had carried in Vietnam. On the bottom were a dozen albums from the sixties. Mostly Motown, Smokey Robinson, the Four Tops, all the music that Codie and me and Grandma Setsuko used to dance to when we visited her in Missouri. But only when Grandpa Gene wasn't around. It would crack Codie and me up to watch our grandmother do her little dances: an old-timey twist and some all-purpose swaying and bouncing that she called "Fuggoo." Grandma Setsuko, for never really learning English, had still managed to pick up a lot of classic moves. Even though my stolid grandfather Eugene was stationed at Kadena sometime in the late sixties, early seventies, I couldn't see him teaching her those dances. Especially since, whenever he did catch us dancing, he'd yell at *Anmā* to stop "jumping around like a jungle bunny."

I search through *Anmā's* box for her favorite album, the one she took out of its secret hiding spot and played only when Grandpa Gene was gone for an entire evening to one of his Agent Orange meetings. I find it at the very bottom of the box and pull out the album. It's clear and red, as if it were made out of candy-apple coating. Like all the albums she had that were produced locally, this one's cover is made of low-grade, speckledy cardboard. It has a photo of a soul group on the front. Only the hair suggests that everyone in the group is Okinawan except for the singer, an American guy, either black, Latino, or, maybe, Smurf. The picture has faded so much that he's now a pale blue. He wears white pants and a white vest with nothing under it. A corona of curly hair puffs out around his head. Back when we first heard the album, Codie and I figured that the group must have been like the Beatles on Okinawa, because Grandma Setsuko would play it over and over again, dancing or just swaying to the Motownesque beat with a dreamy, far-away look on her gentle, round face.

In the apartment above ours, the weight-lifting beef kebab starts grunting and clanging dumbbells down on the ceiling. I put the album back, flop down on the couch, listen to the barnyard noises, and am suffocated by the usual combo cloud of Febreze, loneliness, and the kind of sadness that's beyond the reach of tears. All I feel is a jittery exhaustion, too wound up to sleep but with barely enough energy to get out of bed. I click the TV on, but after only a few seconds the firewall of snarky late-night talk-show hosts and psychic crime fighters is breached by the image of the girl in the cave lifting her wounded, maggot-ridden arm out to me. Drug-induced or not, the vision makes my heart pound so fiercely that I jump to my feet and pace until I can breathe again.

In the kitchen, I use the broom to sweep out a bottle of Chivas from between the refrigerator and counter where Mom hid it. She's selfish with the good stuff and doesn't want me helping myself. Still in its velvet bag tied at the neck with a gold cord, the scotch was a present from Eli, some marine stationed at Futenma that Mom met in July at a joint training exercise on the north end of the island. My mom believes that everyone understands that deployments are like marriage recess. I doubt that Eli's wife back in South Carolina with three kids understood any better than my dad understood when she cheated on him. Even if she did maintain that she was only doing it so he'd know what it felt like.

"Some people just aren't meant to be married." That was her entire defense.

Almost none of the soldiers who killed themselves had an "intact family."

I most definitely do not want to think about that evil factoid. Or the one about how most of the soldiers didn't seem suicidal. Instead, I take the scotch to my bed and work on switching off my brain before it forces me to ask questions I don't want to know the answers to. My phone is there where I left it on the night table. I make a point of not keeping it with me, since the only person who ever calls is my mom. Sure enough, as soon as I turn the thing on, it starts making the horrible *Psycho* shower-murder scene *eek-eek* tones that I put on to warn me I was getting a text. I have nine new messages. All from her. I delete them. That—just thinking about her—makes my heart jackhammer so bad I'm like a drop of water skittering around a hot grill. I take a slug of the Chivas just so I can get calm enough to sleep off whatever Kirby put in the Cuervo. The scotch has zero calming effect, so I kneel down beside my bed and stretch an arm under the mattress, feeling for the slick plastic of the Ziploc bag with its gravelly wad of pills inside. My chest relaxes just imagining the lovely, serene blue of the Ambien. The soothing lilac of the thirty-milligram Oxy. The very grounding sage green of the Percocet. When I can't immediately find them, I sweep my arm from one end of the mattress to the other. Fighting a panicked, nauseated sensation, like being on an elevator that drops too fast, I do one more sweep before I tip the mattress up and shove it off the bed. The Ziploc is gone.

"That bitch."

Consequences. I can hear my mother saying that as clearly as if she were in the room with me.

Consequences? I want to ask her. *What did Codie do that she had to suffer you and your fucking consequences? Trust you? Love you? Who would be that stupid?*

I was. I actually did believe my mom when she told me that everything would be better on Okinawa. That because of some half-understood words her mom had told her about us having family here, about how Okinawans are so warm and honor family above all else, that we'd be welcomed into a cozy island paradise.

Fuck that. The only family I ever really had was Codie, and you took that away.

I hate going in my mom's bedroom, but I have to find that Ziploc. Her room smells like her: pressed ABUs, vanilla-musk body lotion, and gun oil. I understand an arsonist's glee as I root through her drawers, leaving devastation in my wake. I rip apart the socks that she still rolls into tight balls and arranges in perfect rows like she learned in Basic. Like she taught Codie so that her daughter would have "an advantage." I yank the camouflage uniforms off hangers spaced exactly three fingers apart. They momentarily stay upright, held there by starch and discipline, before melting onto the floor of the closet, where I stomp on them, wipe dirt from the cliff trail on them. I knock the head-shaped metal hat shaper she uses to keep her blue service cap rigidly upright off the lamp it sits atop.

I flip *her* mattress over, delighting in violating her hospital corners. I tear *her* room apart and find nothing until I push the chest of drawers over and discover, not my baggie of delights, but something almost as interesting: the letter that was hand-delivered to her by the Okinawan messenger girl on a moped the day after my mom had her third and final phone call with what I assumed were our relatives. Though she never did tell me what was in the letter, it was obviously not good, since, after coming out of the bathroom smelling like a tobacco factory, she went directly to the NCO Rocker Club, came home very late and very drunk, wearing an XXL Lakers fan jersey with Kobe Bryant's number on it, and refused to say another word about our alleged Oki relatives.

I'm disappointed that the letter is all in Japanese characters—until a photo falls out. The date stamped in red across the bottom shows that it was taken at the beginning of the summer, the day before the letter was delivered. The color photo appears to have been shot with a very long telephoto lens on a gray and cloudy day somewhere in a dingy urban landscape. Possibly Chicago, I'm guessing from the small segment of an elevated rail line visible between the two buildings that dominate the image. The subject of the photo obviously didn't know he was being surveilled. He looks like he's in his sixties, Latino, or maybe a really light-skinned black.

For a second, I think I recognize the guy. Then I realize that I don't know him at all. He's just some anonymous, old street-corner guy, slouching against the side of a building, looking warily off to the side, studying the street with a tense, alert expression on his face. Above his head is part of a sign that reads, "apLand." The one thing that's not dreary and monotone in the photo is a patch of sidewalk at the guy's feet, which is covered by some sort of red fluff, as if a parade had just passed by and one of the floats had exploded.

Though he's only a guy standing on some random, big-city street corner, and there's no way I could possibly know him, I still can't entirely shake the feeling that there's something familiar about him. My mom trailed a lot of men through our lives, mine and Codie's, but this one is too old to be one of her hookups. She doesn't demand much, but she does require buff. And nearly always young.

I try but can't see any connection between the letter written in Japanese from what were supposed to be my Okinawan relatives and an old street-corner dude in Chicago. I finally have to conclude that the photo must be from an investigation my mom was involved in and she just randomly stuffed it in the envelope the letter came in. Who knows how many stakeouts she's been on? She certainly never would have told me about them. Probably she's secretly in OSI and has trunks full of surveillance shots, including ones of me stealing prescription meds.

I'm about to wad up the tissuey letter when I notice one word written in English on the envelope in my mom's handwriting: "*yuta.*" I say it out loud and realize that that is what Jake was talking about, not the Mormon state. A phone number is carefully written next to "*yuta,*" and underlined several times. A time, 1500, and a date the day after she received the letter follow. Why would my mother make an appointment with this "*yuta*"? Is there a connection between that and the photo? A strange sense of urgency overcomes me, as if I were intended to find the photo and the envelope. As if, like the sea turtle, they might be signs from Codie. Signs that I have no idea how to interpret. I'm so clueless that I feel like I'm trapped in a video game called "Okinawa," where I don't know the rules, but the person I love most will be hurt if I can't figure them out and act according to their logic.

Or I'm buzzed on bath salts.

Or I'm deranged.

The possibilities are limited.

The wreckage of the sergeant's room, all the tidy sock balls lying unspooled, the starched uniforms crumpled in a heap, the decapitated hat-shaper, rocking on the floor, certainly votes for deranged. Suicidally, death-wish deranged. My heart thumps and my guts twist from needing the confiscated baggie of calming pharmaceuticals. The psycho-killer *eek*s ring out, startling me so bad that I let out a little shriek. I shove the photo and envelope with the number written on it into my pocket, and the stolen pin jabs me. I grab the phone, ready to hit "decline." I cannot hang up on my mom fast enough. But it's not her. I answer.

"LOOZER! Get your ass over here, Lulu. ASAP. We're going in."

"Kirby, what—"

"Quit being a little bitch and come out and party with us." He lowers his voice. "Luz, seriously, come; Jacey won't go with us if you don't come."

"Go where?" I ask.

"Murder House."

"That place you keep talking about? And every time you bring it up, Jake freaks out and won't let you take us?"

"'Let' me? Luz, that guy is not my CO. And he's straight-up cray about all this Oki stuff. Besides, he left. Not that it was ever his call anyway."

"He left?"

He raises his voice to its typical bray. "Yeah, got his kimono all up in a bunch when I told him where we were going and that it wasn't up for debate. You coming?"

"I don't know."

Kirby whispers again, "Luz, please come, okay? For me? If you don't come, Jacey won't go."

In the background, Jacey asks, "Kirbs, is she coming? 'Cuz I'm not gonna go without my best friend."

Best friend? Jacey Bosfeld just called me her best friend? This throws me for a loop, since she's never even been to my house and I've never been to hers. *Best friend.* I can't think of what to say. Codie was always the only best friend I ever had. The only one I needed.

"You talk to her," Kirby says, his voice fading out as he hands the phone off.

"Are you in?" Jacey asks. Her voice sounds different—louder, clearer—like she'd been talking to me through a window before and has stepped inside to where I am. Before I can answer, she whispers, "You should have seen it, Luz. Jake totally went off on Kirby. For once, though, Kirby didn't back off." She lowers her voice even more. "Wanna know why?"

"Why?"

"Me. Because I said I wanted to go. I think he's into me."

"'Think'? Jace, he's been crushed out on you all summer." Having a normal girl conversation feels like speaking in a language that I haven't used in a long time, but one that comes back with no effort.

"Really?"

"Uh, yeah."

"Hey, what's the deal with you and Jake?"

"No deal. Flirting while his girlfriend is away, I guess. Why, did he say something?"

"Like he needs to? With the way he looks at you?"

"What 'way'? There's no 'way.' So he's not there now?"

"God, no. He was really pissed about Kirby taking us to Murder House."

"Why?"

"You know. His usual Oki stuff. He says it's this big desecration to go in there."

"The house?"

"Yeah. It was supposedly built on some ancient Oki family's tomb."

"And that's why it's haunted?"

"I guess. I tune him out when he goes off like that."

"So you don't remember any of what he said?"

"I don't know. Something about Murder House being all sacred and everything."

"Why?"

"I don't know. Oh, wait. Now I remember. It's where the dead wait to make contact with the living and steal their souls."

Grabbing my shoulder bag, I stand, and as I walk to the door, say, "I'll be right there."

· NINETEEN ·

Anmā! Anmā! *Who is that? The warrior on the horse.*

He is a palace guard who died defending our last great king, Shō Tai. And the beautiful woman washing her long hair is his third wife. I don't know who the pale Amerikā *crying in the corner is.*

Can they see us?

No, they aren't kami *either. They are the displaced, not* kami, *not living, waiting here like us.*

For the girl who came to the cave?

Perhaps.

But she is ours. Didn't the kami *send her to us?*

No more questions. If I answer all of them, there won't be time to tell you
the story. You do want to be with our clan when you enter into the other realm,
don't you?

Yes.

All right then. Where was I?

You were sad because Little Mouse didn't wave good-bye to you, but then the
sun came up and—

Yes, yes, the sun came up and I was on the road to Shuri to be with my sister.

Because the Imperial Army had seized control of the railroad, I had
to walk all day to reach Naha. Though we had heard that the city had
been bombed a year ago, all the reports had downplayed the damage,
and I was not prepared for the devastation. Where once there had been
trolley lines and fine restaurants, exclusive hotels and tree-lined boulevards, only piles of jagged cement and burned timbers remained. I
made my way out of the ravaged city to the ancient capital of Shuri,
home of the Okinawan kings that my father's family had once served
as hereditary samurai. Fortunately, Shuri and its castle were far enough
from Naha that they remained untouched. The royal palace sat atop a
hill like a potentate elevated above the subjects who knelt at his feet.
I comforted myself with the knowledge that the Imperial Japanese
Army had located their headquarters in our capital and had dispatched
two of their finest generals, Ushijima and Chō, to command it.

I went straight to Himeyuri High School to find Hatsuko and discovered that the Imperial Army had claimed most of the school. I told the
Japanese guard at the gate that I'd come to see my sister. He said only
soldiers and Princess Lily girls could be admitted, and that all students
were off taking nursing classes at headquarters. I asked where headquarters was. The guard gave me a fierce look and demanded, "Are
you a spy?" He raised his rifle until the bayonet pointed straight at my
heart. "You speak Japanese like a spy."

I thought of all the Okinawans who had been whipped, imprisoned,
or beheaded by suspicious soldiers for speaking our dialect, and, my
heart hammering in my chest, I turned and fled into the crowd. I ran
for several blocks, expecting at any moment to be shot in the back.

When I was safely out of range, I took refuge in an alley and caught my breath. Huge army trucks rumbled past. The asphalt streets were already cracked and rutted from their weight. Japanese soldiers in khaki were everywhere. A rickshaw passed carrying a stern army officer with the high black collar of his olive green tunic buttoned tight beneath his chin. His black leather boots came all the way up to the knees of his jodhpurs. The officer had removed his sword from its scabbard and thrust it between his feet. The barefoot driver wore a long vest that slapped at his pumping legs, and a conical straw hat that bounced on his head as he ran.

Other high-ranking officers with fierce scowls rode past enthroned in the sidecars of motorcycles. In spite of my fright, I marveled at all the evidence that my little island had been transformed into the mightiest fortress in all the Pacific. Still, with no official papers, or letter of acceptance into Himeyuri, I was worried about being taken again for a spy. So, as night descended, I climbed the wide stone stairway that led out of Shuri to the one place where I felt secure: the great castle at the top. Even when the Japanese forbade teaching the history of the Ryukyu Islands, Mother had made sure that her children knew that Shuri Castle was the heart of our country. Besides being the capital, where our kings had once ruled, the castle held the long history of the Ryukyu Islands, the chronology of all the kings, chronicles of battles fought, and, most important, *Anmā* always emphasized, all the property records throughout the islands. She was proud that, while Shuri Castle was not quite as old as the Roman Coliseum, our ancestors had created this structure centuries before the Cathedral at Notre Dame was even started.

Though I was upset at not finding Hatsuko, and by having a bayonet pointed at me, a sense of ease suffused me when I reached the forty-foot-high wall that encircled the royal palace and its grounds. The wall had stood for five centuries. Even the imperialist aggressor Commodore Perry, whom our king had insulted so grievously, had not attempted a serious invasion. I knew then that what we Okinawans always said was true: "As long as Shuri holds, our kingdom will hold." I passed beneath the grand gate inscribed with the Chinese characters meaning "Land of Peace" and entered the safety of the enchanted world within.

The castle painted in gold and vermilion could have been plucked from a fairy tale. It was just as I remembered it from my childhood visits with Mother. The tips of the castle's vast tiled roof swept up at the edges like the horns of a water buffalo. Carved stone dragon heads spouted cool water from underground springs. Gardens and shaded forest walks sprawled out beyond the vast courtyard, suffusing the air with the tender scent of lilies.

Out of sight of the castle keepers who were shutting the gates for the night, I slipped unnoticed into the woods, where I imagined generations of kings and queens strolling down the same cobbled path I followed. It crossed over the high arch of a bridge above a pond where fat red and gold koi fish from Japan undulated through the water. The path ended at the base of an ancient banyan tree so large a thousand men could have cooled in its shade. I spread my *furoshiki* wrapping cloth on the ground beneath its latticework of aerial roots and sat down to rest. Overcome by exhaustion, I dropped immediately into a deep sleep filled with dreams of feudal princes and princesses.

Early the next morning, I awoke to the sounds of a squad of Japanese soldiers executing bayonet drills on the main square in front of the castle. I crept through the garden that hid me until the soldiers were in sight. They wore sleeveless T-shirts, bands of white were tied around their foreheads, and olive green leg wrappings held the bottoms of their pants tight. They lunged in formation, bellowing out one loud grunt as they thrust into the guts of invisible enemies.

My empty stomach churned in response. At the far end of the courtyard, a tea vendor was pushing his two-wheeled cart among the patriotic spectators who had gathered to watch and cheer the valiant warriors. Still hidden by the dense foliage, I dug a bill from the mouth of the snake of money Mother had tied around my waist, replaced the rest, and then stepped out to make my way through the crowd. I purchased a millet cake and a cup of tea, knowing that Mother wouldn't object to the expenditure; I would never be able to find and safeguard Hatsuko if I starved to death before reaching her.

I stuffed the delicious cake sweetened with sugarcane juice into my mouth. At my feet, pigeons gathered to peck at a shower of crumbs thrown by one of the spectators. Cooing, they approached the crumbs with their jerky, deliberate gait, and then nibbled away at the windfall until it was gone. After a moment, another shower of crumbs fell.

When I saw the source of this generosity one word flashed across my mind: *juri*. I knew that the woman tossing crumbs to the birds was a prostitute by the sheerness of her *tonpyan* kimono, by the careful shaping of her black eyebrows, by the way her thick black hair was held in a bun atop her head by a long silver pin that flashed in the morning sun. Decent women wore their buns offset to the side so that the tops of their heads were free to carry a basket of potatoes or a piglet tied at the ankles. Her rouged cheeks were pink as a doll baby's, and her face was pale and velvety with powder. She'd even stained the tips of her nails a delicate coral by binding *tinsagu* petals to them overnight, something decent girls were forbidden from doing. But mostly I knew she was a *juri* by the shameless way she wore the sash of her boldly patterned kimono high on her waist to make herself look taller, more slender, and more youthful than the virtuous women like my mother and my aunts, who tied their sashes low on their hips.

"They're hungry today, aren't they?" the *juri* asked me.

I glanced away, embarrassed that she'd caught me gaping at her.

"Oh, look at The General bullying all the others into letting him take more than his share." She pointed to a big pigeon with his chest puffed out and laughed a laugh of such silken refinement that I had to stare at her. She had lovely teeth: white, without the slightest hint of decay from sucking sugar. Watching the fat pigeon she called The General strutting about, chasing the other pigeons away, I had to laugh as well.

"What are you doing in Shuri?" the *juri* asked.

"I'm going to meet my sister at Himeyuri High School."

"Oh a Princess Lily girl," she said. "She must be very smart. Are you a student there as well?"

I nodded, wanting her to think that I, too, was very smart.

"So you must be on your way then to join the others at the Japanese high command headquarters."

"Yes." Though I still didn't know where this high command headquarters was, I was pleased that I had learned where Hatsuko was without revealing that I wasn't actually a Princess Lily girl.

With no warning, the *juri* reached out, took my chin in her fragrantly powdered hand, and tilted it from side to side, studying my face as if I were a horse she was considering buying. She had a forward manner that I assumed must be due to her profession.

All trace of her former gay demeanor now vanished, she asked intently, "You are a true *Uchinānchu*, aren't you?"

It was pointless to deny; besides the obvious fact that we were speaking in *Uchināguchi*, no one had a more Okinawan face than I.

"You come to Shuri because you love our history, don't you?"

I didn't correct her. I thought that our history was charming in a backward way, but the modern, exciting future we'd have once Okinawa had proved her loyalty to the empire, that was really what I loved.

"You know that we have not always been impoverished farmers. You know that in the fifteenth and sixteenth centuries we were traders welcomed in China, Korea, Java, and the South Sea Islands. That Japan, though she invaded our islands and extorted heavy taxes and tributes, was but one of our many trading partners. And not even a favored one."

I said nothing; my mother and her sisters were always making treasonous statements just like these. Besides, I needed the *juri* to show me the way to headquarters.

"Yet you are also educated." She stared into my face for so long that I brushed at my nose, fearing that something unpleasant might be protruding.

"Yes, I think you just might be smart enough and Okinawan enough to survive what is coming. I won't. Most of us won't."

It annoyed me to hear her speaking the same backward, traitorous thoughts as my mother, and I wanted to leave. But she still gripped my chin as she went on. "You with your true Okinawan eyes and heart and soul, remember all that you will see. Remember and then tell the tale. Tell the truth of what happens." With that, she released my chin and set off at a furious pace. When I didn't follow, she glanced back and snapped, "Come along."

I was torn between prudence and curiosity. As it always did with me, though, curiosity won out and I scurried after her. A cluster of silk cherry blossoms dangled like a cute pink tail from the long silver pin stabbed into her high bun. I followed that bobbing pink tail down the steep stairway back to Shuri below. Even at this early hour, the town was bustling. Vendors yelled out that their *gōyā* melons were fresh or their *suzuki* fish had been caught that very morning. Delivery girls balanced pots of tea and baskets of *andāgii* still warm from the fryer atop their heads. At the base of the stairs, we passed beneath a high *torii* just like the ones in Japan and onto a broad avenue that was lined on both sides by stone lanterns as tall as a man. At a Buddhist temple next to the avenue, a priest sprinkled water on the steps to keep down the dust.

A mother and her daughter emerged from the temple. The girl, probably only a year or two younger than me, ran ahead of her mother. When the mother saw her nearing the *juri* she called out sharply, "Watch where you are going! Remember what I told you!"

The girl stopped, stared up at the *juri*, and froze in horrified recognition. The mother rushed up and yanked her stunned daughter away.

Though the *juri* acted as if she hadn't noticed the insult, a red welt appeared on the pale skin of her neck, as crimson as the mark of a lash. With her head held high, we continued on. When she spoke, her voice was calm and deliberate, and since she didn't so much as glance my way, it almost seemed as if she were speaking more to herself than to me. "No one knows what fate has in store for her. This very day, for example, a *habu* viper hiding and waiting for just such an opportunity might strike at that mother's ankle as she walks to the gate of her fine home. And in spite of the desperate prayers her daughter offers for her beloved mother, the heart of her hearts, her protector and comfort, the mother will die that night. Then, in what he says is his grief, but all know to be his selfish cupidity, the father will marry his young and stupid mistress and bring her and her stupid family and all their debts into their house. The father will drink even more as the debt collectors' demands grow ever more impossible. When everything has been sold, except for all the mistress's fine goods and expensive presents, which she has hidden away, the father, who must save his honor at all costs, will sell his daughter, and all his shame will be transferred to her.

"Mind where you're going," the *juri* snapped at me, and I jumped out of the way of a motorcycle. A Japanese naval officer, splendid in his sparkling white uniform and peaked hat with its black patent-leather visor, sat in the sidecar, serenely observing the passing scene. A class from the Shuri Boys Prefectural High School approached. They were dressed in long-sleeved white shirts, crisply ironed white pants, and white shoes. They wore black ties and their hair was neatly combed and shone in the sunlight. When the boys passed, the fragrance of sandalwood and mandarin oranges hung in the air behind them.

"Careful, you'll catch a fly." The *juri* laughed at me for gaping, open-mouthed, at the handsome boys. The *juri* stopped and studied me. "Well, aren't you going now to high command headquarters to join your fellow Princess Lilies?"

I glanced at the chaos around me with no idea what direction to set out in.

The *juri*, seeing my confusion, said, "Come along; follow me. Even a very, *very* smart girl can get turned around in Shuri."

As I followed her farther into the heart of Shuri, the town on the outskirts of Naha that I had visited so often became more and more unrecognizable. Gone was the peace I'd always found strolling the sleepy streets canopied by banyan trees. The sound of horse hooves slowly clopping against the cobblestones and the jolly cries of vendors were replaced by the harsh voices of commanders barking orders at soldiers marching past in crisp lines, by the sputter of motorcycles and the rumble of truck engines. Where once the air had been perfumed with the fragrance of vendors' papayas, pineapples, mangos, and bananas, now a pall of diesel fumes enshrouded the town.

We approached what had once been a shady park with stone benches for resting beneath a thicket of ancient Ryukyuan pine, some of them said to have been planted during the reign of King Shō Tai, and I found that all the trees had been cut down. The barren field, trampled now into mud, was surrounded by a tall barbed-wire fence with loops of razor wire at the top. Inside were rows of crude, hastily constructed huts, each one with a door that opened at the top like a stable. All the doors had a number on them; most were shut. At the few open ones, women stood looking out, like horses waiting to be fed. Their faces seemed made of stone, statues with no expression at all.

Outside the fence, a line of soldiers—low-ranking ones in baggy uniforms, crumpled, sweat-stained caps, and dirty leg wrappings—waited beneath a sign that read, "Welcome Soldiers of a Holy War." When each man's turn came, a sergeant gave him a number and pointed to one of the doors. Clasping his number, the soldier would hustle over to the appointed stall, step in, and both sections of the door would be closed behind him. Two briefly unoccupied women exchanged a few words in a language that wasn't Okinawan or Japanese.

"Korean comfort women," the *juri* informed me. "Don't stare; they've been brought here to keep you Princess Lilies pure."

I didn't understand why her tone was so harsh, and she gave me no time to ask as we hurried on to an area where there were no civilians at all. Everyone was in uniform. Suddenly I recognized what had once been the home of Okuda Seitoku, who'd become the richest man on the island by selling lumber to the Japanese. I wondered what had happened to him, since his vast, Western-style mansion now had a magnificent flagpole out front with the rising sun whipping in the wind at its top and a sign that identified it as the headquarters of the 32nd Imperial Army.

"You, Okinawan whores, you aren't allowed here!" A skinny guard with snaggled teeth braced his rifle across the *juri*'s chest, barring our way.

In perfect, high-class Japanese without the slightest trace of an Okinawan accent, the *juri* responded, "And you, you ignorant, cat-toothed bumpkin who smells of his own shit, you had better step aside immediately if you know what is good for you."

The guard's face purpled with fury, and he spoke in a hissing whisper that boiled with rage: "You have insulted a soldier of the emperor. You have insulted the emperor. You will be executed."

As soldiers, bayonets pointing at us, closed in, I cursed myself for being so stupid as to fall in with a crazy woman; there was no hope of running away this time.

· TWENTY ·

The *juri* whirled on the soldiers and demanded, "What are you idiots doing? Do you dare impede my passage? Move aside immediately or I shall be forced to report your insubordination to"—she pulled a pass from the sash of her kimono, and with a theatrical elegance handed it to the cat-toothed guard as she pronounced the name— "General Chō."

The look of horror that dawned on the guard's face froze into wide-eyed terror as he read the signature at the bottom of the *juri*'s pass.

Holding the pass with the sacred signature above his head, the guard prostrated himself at our feet. The other soldiers followed suit. The *juri* plucked her pass from the guard's trembling fingers, stepped around the cowering figures, and led me away, tossing over her shoulder, "I detest bullies, don't you?"

A road, so new the asphalt was still black and sticky, led us to a massive construction area. Through the clouds of dust raised by dump trucks, I saw an army of Okinawan workers streaming in and out of a building guarded by soldiers in khaki uniforms, rifles slung over their shoulders, who glared fiercely at all who approached.

The workers were a mix of men in loincloths and women in baggy trousers, all with cloths tied over their mouths and noses to keep out the dust. They left the building tottering beneath the weight of baskets filled with large rocks balanced on their heads with only a coil of thin cloth as a cushion. One after another, the laborers dumped their loads onto a huge pile, then turned around and went back to the building, holding their now-empty baskets.

"Well, here we are," the *juri* said, stopping behind a pile of discarded stone. "Just show the guard your Himeyuri ID card and you'll be admitted." She watched my nervous expression for a moment, then added, "Or you could simply slip in with the work crew." She smiled; I hadn't fooled her.

"How did you know?"

"No real Princess Lily girl would ever speak to a woman like me. It was one of the first things our Japanese teachers taught us."

"You . . ."

"Were a Himeyuri girl?"

Instead of answering, she folded back the inner collar of her kimono and revealed the distinctive lily brooch pinned there. Turning to leave, she said to me, "Don't ever let them make you forget that you are *Uchinānchu*. The blood of kings runs in your veins." With the slightest of bows, she disappeared in the dusty haze. The last I ever saw of her was the pink cherry blossoms at the end of the long silver pin in her beehive bun bouncing gaily behind her.

Before I could be noticed, I pulled the *furoshiki* from my satchel and tied it around my face so that only my eyes were visible, then hurried to the stone pile, snatched up a discarded basket, stuck it atop my head, and fell in with a crew entering the work site. The Japanese guards, seeing only the bracket on my head and my round face and brown Okinawan skin, barely glanced my way as they waved me in.

Once inside, we all funneled into a single narrow line and descended down a steep staircase carved into the limestone and lit with naked bulbs strung up above our heads. The stairs plunged farther and farther into the earth until we were deep beneath the ancient capital. When we had descended twenty meters beneath the surface, we arrived at a main tunnel. I glanced around and my mouth dropped open in astonishment, for stretched out in front of me as far as I could see was a vast underground kingdom.

Side tunnels with plastered walls and polished concrete floors fanned off in every direction from the main one. Soldiers on vital missions marched briskly past stooped laborers. I followed the crew I'd entered with. We passed large rooms filled with officers bent over maps. Okinawan boys my age and younger, members of the Blood and Iron Student Corps, stood at attention nearby, waiting to serve as couriers. An officer called for a boy, snapped a message into his hand, and he bolted away to deliver it. In a kitchen area with a chimney dug up through the ground, a red-faced cook bent over a large kettle that wafted the delicious odor of boiling rice. Room after room was stacked with sleeping planks, a vast barracks large enough for hundreds of men.

Farther on was a dispensary, a roomful of typists, and, most astonishing of all, a telephone switchboard with operators wearing headsets pulling out and plugging in cords. And all of it was buried deep in the earth, safe from American bombs. As this marvelous warren hummed around me, I knew then that my mother and the *juri* were wrong and that Hatsuko and my father were right: The Japanese Empire *was* unconquerable.

I shivered as a thrill of pride ran through me at the thought that I, too, might be allowed to be part of this magnificent enterprise. Even if I had to do it as a rock carrier, I was determined that I would serve our emperor. For a moment, it appeared that this was exactly what would happen. The crew came to a halt at the end of a tunnel that rang with the clanging of picks striking rock as men burrowed farther into the earth. The workers scrambled to refill their baskets with the loosened stones.

I gently slid my basket to the ground and was backing away when a squat sergeant wearing a cap too small for his melon-shaped head stopped me and, wagging his finger at the student's satchel strapped across my chest, demanded, "What are you doing here?"

I didn't know whether to answer in my best Japanese or to prove that I was nothing but a local laborer by speaking in *Uchināguchi*. Even though I decided on Japanese and was answering in his language, the impatient sergeant made a face, stopped me, and said, "Never mind. I can't understand your Okinawan gibberish anyway. You must be one of the new Himeyuri girls straight off the farm. You are in the wrong wing entirely." Speaking slowly, as if to a not-very-bright child, he gave me directions, adding, "And don't get in the way. There are a thousand soldiers down here serving the emperor. Don't disturb them!" I nodded my head and hurried away before he could demand my school papers or notice that I wasn't wearing a lily pin.

Though I tried to follow the sergeant's directions, I quickly became lost in the labyrinth. To hide how bewildered I was, I would straighten up every time an officer, his heels clicking smartly on the concrete floor, right hand resting on the hilt of his sword, strode past. If he was especially handsome, I wondered whether he might be Hatsuko's lieutenant.

I was at a loss as to how I would ever find Hatsuko without revealing that I was an intruder, when a group of girls passed by, all neatly dressed in sailor blouses with the brooches of the Princess Lily students gleaming on their chests. I followed them to a large ward where a class of more than a hundred students watched a nurse with a name band tied around her right arm that identified her as Head Nurse Tanaka. A heavyset Japanese woman with a deep voice and a sallow complexion, Head Nurse Tanaka was demonstrating how to inject salt water into a tangerine. I searched frantically for Hatsuko's face, but there were so many girls crowding around the nurse I couldn't find my sister.

Head Nurse Tanaka clapped her hands sharply and all the girls immediately fell silent. "We have no time to waste today. We must finish our lesson quickly, because the photographer is here to take portraits for your records. So let us begin without—"

Head Nurse Tanaka saw something in the doorway that caused her to stop and come to rigid attention. All the girls followed suit when an

Imperial officer strode into the classroom. He was tall and slender with the bearing of a prince and, when he conferred with Tanaka, he never once removed his white-gloved hand from the hilt of his sword. This had to be the famous Lieutenant Nakamura. I searched the crowd even harder for Hatsuko.

Head Nurse Tanaka clapped her hands sharply and called out, "Girls, attention! Our liaison officer, Lieutenant Nakamura, has been kind enough to leave his far more important duties for a moment and deliver a message to us. Because your backward country never developed a system of dams and reservoirs such as we have in Japan, water supplies are running low."

I joined the other girls and bowed my head, ashamed of Okinawa.

"The lieutenant reminds us that water is not to be wasted on bathing or for any purpose other than drinking. Do you all understand?"

As one the Princess Lily girls shouted out a rousing, *"Hai!"*

The lieutenant bowed in response, his long, curved sword sweeping out behind him. In the split second before he stood back up, his gaze locked on someone in the crowd. I followed it and found Hatsuko in the moment that her eyes met his. Hatsuko jerked her glance away from the lieutenant's, but not before a blush had crimsoned her face. Nakamura gave a barely perceptible nod in her direction and left.

"Group leaders!" Head Nurse Tanaka called out brusquely. Four students stepped forward. Of course Hatsuko was one of them. "Gather up your supplies." She nodded toward three sopping tangerines already heavily perforated from earlier practice groups, and one rusty old syringe.

I joined the girls who clustered around Hatsuko. My beautiful cousin Mitsue was the first to notice me. She smiled such a wide smile that two dimples dented her cheeks, and she rushed over to hug me. I hadn't seen her since she'd gotten engaged to a soldier, Masaru, whose name meant Victory, and she seemed even lovelier than she had before. When my sister spotted me she squealed, clapping her hands over her mouth to silence the shriek.

"Little Guppy, you came! I can't believe that Mother and Father actually allowed you to leave. Aaah, you're so dusty, and your hair!" My sister plucked a dead leaf from my hair, smoothed the crazy waves down with her fingers, turned me to face her friends, put her arms around me, rested her chin on the top of my head, and, squeezing hard, whispered to her friends, "Look, everyone, it's my little sister, Tamiko. My darling Tami-chan. We call her Little Guppy. Doesn't she look just like a little guppy? A cute little guppy?"

"She does!" a girl with straight, shiny bangs whispered back. "She reminds me of my little sister. Oh, I miss my Kiko-chan so much. Will you be my little sister too?"

The six other girls in Hatsuko's unit all agreed on the spot that I had to be their little sister as well. Just as Hatsuko had promised, I was not only welcomed but adopted as a mascot. The Japanese were another story. In order to ward off any suspicion that I might be a spy, Hatsuko took off her Princess Lily pin.

"Here," Hatsuko said, "put this on."

"Big sister, I can't. That's your school pin."

She brushed aside my protest, pinning the lily on my blouse herself. "You need it more than I do. Everyone knows me. I'm head girl. That's the head-girl pin. Though the soldiers don't know us by name or face, they all recognize a head-girl pin. They won't question you if you're wearing one." I glanced down and tried to see what the difference was between her pin and the other girls', but they all looked identical to me.

Before I could ask what distinguished a head-girl's pin, Hatsuko interrupted with a question of her own: "So did you see the secret we've been working on?"

"The tunnels? They're astonishing."

"And there are dozens, hundreds more like them all over the island."

"Even hospitals," Sachiko added. "Where we will serve as nurse's aides, helping patients write letters and cheering them on as they prepare to return to battle. All safe beneath the flag of the Red Cross."

The other girls nodded, excited by the grand adventure they were all on.

"Girls! Girls!" Head Nurse shouted. "Stop gabbling like a bunch of silly geese! Your turn to have your photographs made will be next. You may take ten minutes, no longer, to return to your room and prepare."

We rushed to the girls' room, where Mitsue gave me a uniform she'd outgrown. As the girls smoothed their hair into sleek braids, I bemoaned the sorry state of the short, wavy mop atop my own head.

"I'll fix it," Mitsue volunteered. In an instant, she had produced two rubber bands and swept my hair into pigtails that everyone agreed were *chura*. Without a mirror, I trusted that my new hairstyle was truly as cute as they had proclaimed it to be. More than my hair, though, I yearned to view myself in the uniform of a Princess Lily girl. But there wasn't time to find a mirror large enough before we rushed off to the empty classroom that had been set aside for the photographer's use. There we stood in line and waited while he opened the heavy metal case containing his equipment. He tacked up a large piece of canvas over one wall for a backdrop, set up a wooden tripod, then mounted a camera with a bellows on it.

The photographer wore a soiled white shirt with a battered tie knotted at his scrawny neck. His most notable feature was large ears with points at the top like a bat's wings. In spite of his scary ears, he was a jolly soul who made silly jokes as he asked each girl her name and the name of her village. He carefully recorded the information in a notebook, positioned the girl in front of the canvas, stared down into the viewfinder of his camera, held a bulb out, then said, "Oh, you, I know your type. You have too many boyfriends to count, don't you?" When the girl laughed, he squeezed the bulb and the shutter clicked. No matter how many times they'd heard his silly joke, each girl in turn smiled when the photographer accused her of being a heartbreaker.

The only girl he didn't tease was Mitsue. In fact, when he looked into the viewfinder and beheld her he was struck dumb. As if not believing what his camera was recording, he glanced back up at his subject. Instead of flapping his hand one way or the other and saying to her what he'd told the rest of us—"A bit more to the right. Now back to the left. Chin down. Hold it. I bet you have too many boyfriends to count, don't you?"—he stepped over to my cousin and touched her, gently positioning her first one way, then another. He arranged her hands, her arms, pivoted her shoulders. He smoothed imaginary wrinkles from her uniform as if she were a work of art and he the curator. We all stopped laughing and something uneasy passed through us as we witnessed the power of female beauty to enslave the male beholder, a power that the rest of us knew instinctively we would never possess.

After he took so many pictures of Mitsue that the bat-eared photographer had to change the film, it was Hatsuko's turn, then mine. He snapped off our individual photos in a glum, automatic manner without any boyfriend teasing, as if Mitsue had made him feel like a heartbroken suitor. When he was finished with our photos, my sister begged him to take one of the two of us together. "Please," she explained, "she's my little sister."

"There are lots of sisters here," the photographer grumbled, speaking in our native dialect. "I'm supposed to take individual photos for your official records just the way they do them in Japan."

I put on my best backcountry accent and said, "But this one will be for our sweet little *anmā*. Please, sir, please." I made my silliest Little Guppy face, popping my eyes out and puffing up my cheeks before I took a chance and added, "I thought big ears were supposed to be the sign of a generous nature."

The photographer laughed then, seeming relieved that I'd turned his job back into a silly game, and said, "Oh, what the hell, get in there with your sister." He waved me back into the frame. "In times like these a little silliness is worth a lot."

I stood in front of my sister and she rested her hand on my shoulder. I knew I looked even more like a guppy than I usually did as I grinned into the photographer's camera, but I couldn't help myself from smiling so wide that my cheeks ached, because I had done it: I was with Hatsuko and the Princess Lily girls in Shuri.

· TWENTY-ONE ·

O h, we are in-country now, motherfuckers," Kirby says.

Me, Jacey, Wynn, and DaQuane are following Kernshaw through a wooded ravine on the edge of base housing. The Apes are out in force, patrolling the streets, looking for curfew breakers to bust, so we're sticking to the overgrown ravine that runs behind the neighborhoods. The jungly undergrowth is slick and has a squishy, tropical smell. It is alive with trip wires of vine and sticky nets of spiderweb. I'm hanging back with Jacey, who's wearing strappy sandals and having trouble picking her way over the roots that run through the ravine like veins on the back of a man's hand. Up ahead the guys are talking about Jake.

"Why's he gotta be that way?" DaQuane asks. "It's not like anything would ever happen to him even if we did get caught."

"Shit, no," Kirby agrees. "As long as generals like to play golf and his family keeps the course looking like fucking Pimlico, he is untouchable."

"Pimlico is a horse racing track, turd munch," Wynn points out.

"Okay, but that other one? Where they wear the green jackets and shit. That's why the Furusatos are royalty on Kadena. Jeez, they live in base housing, right? Go to base schools? Get to shop at the commissary? You cannot tell me that they are not majorly connected."

"They have to be," Wynn agrees. "They're probably the reason that angry mobs aren't protesting about so much prime real estate being used so American generals can knock white balls around with a stick."

"Don't get me wrong; I love the guy—"

"Except when he goes off on his Oki shit."

"Except when he goes off on the Oki shit. Precisely."

Jacey and I hang back, letting the guys drift out of earshot. "Look," she whispers, and I follow her finger to a dense grove of low-lying vegetation. It sparkles with fireflies. "Wow, I can't remember the last time I saw fireflies."

"Me neither. When Codie and I used to go stay with our grandma in Missouri, they were everywhere. Codie loved fireflies. We'd catch them in jars outside Grandma's house and light up entire rooms with them bright enough to read by."

As we watch the enchanted circuitry blinking on and off, it takes me a minute to realize that I've just spoken Codie's name out loud. And talked about her in the past tense.

"Luz?"

"Yeah?"

"I'm really sorry about your sister."

I nod, tamping down the little flare of anger that blazes up anytime anyone says something terminally lame like that, something about being sorry.

Jacey heads up the path, but I remain rooted to the spot. She pauses. "You okay?"

"Yeah, sure."

She holds a branch out of the way and waits for me. I stoop under; she's nice. She's just a nice person who said the wrong thing because there is no right thing to say. There never will be. We rush to catch up to the guys.

The ravine trail ends at the USO parking lot on the edge of junior officer housing. Kirby points to the house nearest to us. The number 2283 is stenciled in black letters on the front. "That's it."

The boxy white cinder-block house is indistinguishable from all the other boxy white cinder-block houses around it. Except that the other houses each have a nameplate with the last name and rank of the soldier assigned to the house, and there is no name attached to number 2283.

"Really?" Jacey asks. "That's it? That's Murder House? It just looks like your average dumpy base house."

"What were you expecting?" Kirby snaps. "All kind of haunted-house shit? Bats flying out the windows and a hunchback with a limp answering the door? It's a freakin' base house, dude. Jeez."

"Sorry," Jacey apologizes.

In the thin drizzle of violet illumination cast by the streetlight half a block away, number 2283 does feel haunted in its own way. It appears smaller, more compact than the other houses. As if those other houses have expanded to hold the lives within them, but this one, isolated at the edge, though exactly the same size, seems smaller, shrunken. Like it was standing off by itself, holding a grudge.

"Is anyone living here?" Jacey asks.

"Not for years," Kirby answers with a new authority in his voice. "The air force stopped assigning families to it a long time ago."

DQ bobs his head from side to side, only glancing at the house out of the corner of his eye, the way you don't look directly at a growling dog. "So it's all locked up? What? We gonna break a window? Destruction of government property. That is a federal offense. Leavenworth, man."

Kirby grins and dangles a key on a string hanging from a metal-ringed tag with the number 2283 written on it in black Sharpie.

"How the *hell* you got a key?"

"When you clear base, just take a second and check out the name on your inspection sheet."

"Your dad runs Inspection?" Wynn asks with appropriate deference.

Like his superpower has been revealed, Kirby nods in modest acknowledgment. We have all felt the lash of Inspection, the corps of anal-retentives who swarm over your quarters when you move out, making certain that your family isn't trying to pull a fast one on them with old tricks like not cleaning the dusty air vents or spackling over your nail holes with toothpaste. Everything has to meet the housing inspector's standards or your transfer will get held up.

"Why is it called Murder House?" I ask.

"You don't know?"

"Usually the reason someone asks 'why,' isn't it?"

"I don't know, Luz. Maybe you're working undercover for your mom. Undercovers ask a lot of random questions."

"That's it, Kirby. You got me. I'm wired up the yin-yang. Here." I stretch out the neck of my T-shirt toward him. "Speak into this."

"Way I heard it," DQ starts in, "some captain choked out his wife when he caught his best friend nailing her. Who was also, like, the navigator in the crew he was on."

"That sucks a bag of dicks," Wynn sympathizes.

"Not the story I heard," Kirby argues. "I heard that the wife wasted the captain because she caught *him*. With the navigator!"

"Dude!"

"You're both wrong," Jacey says, her voice a low rumble that slices through the monkey chatter. "It was a fourteen-year-old girl. Back in the early sixties. Her stepfather was . . ." We all wait for her to continue. Something in her tone, her intensity, makes me stop breathing. " . . . interfering with her."

DQ's brow crinkles, the old-fashioned word has confused him.

"She threatened to tell, and he choked her to death."

Wynn and DQ start asking all kinds of stupid CSI questions about whether they had the "forensic capabilities" back then to conduct a proper investigation. Through the whole boneheaded discussion Kirby, for a change, doesn't say a single word; he just watches Jacey. When Wynn and DQ start going off about JonBenét Ramsey, Kirby steps over next to Jacey and says, "Jerkwads, shut the fuck up. Jesus."

They are silent for a moment; then Wynn asks, "So why is this place supposed to be haunted?"

Kirby answers, "Whole bunch of weird shit. Water faucets and

lights turning off and on by themselves. Bloodstains on the curtains
and floors that wouldn't wash out. Candles blowing themselves out in
closed-up rooms. Children crying in rooms no one was in. Just weird,
freaky shit. The next family they moved in told base housing they
couldn't live there. Obviously, BH don't give a shit. Refused to move
them. Whole family bugged so bad that they made their dad take the
first transfer available. They ended up PCSing to Armpit."

"Harsh."

Armpit is slang for Offutt Air Force Base in Nebraska. Not a dream
assignment.

"After them, it got *really* interesting. The next family saw an Okinawan woman dressed like an old-timey princess washing her hair in
the laundry room sink. And a samurai warrior dude with the winged
helmet and everything, riding a horse through the living room."

"What does *that* have to do with the girl?" DQ asks.

"Everything. Her getting murdered was such a major release of negative spirit energy that it opened up a sort of wormhole there for all the
forces of evil to enter and—"

"God, Kernshaw," Wynn interrupts, "would you please stop talking
out of your ass. Jake already told us the whole story. The house was
built on an Okinawan family tomb. After the war, they came in and
bulldozed this site where ten generations were resting."

"Oh, wow, like in *Polter Guys,* where the house was built on an ancient
Indian burial ground."

"That was a hella scary movie."

"Yeah, that part when Jack Nickels hacks through the door with an
ax and goes, 'Here's Jack!'"

"No, dumb ass, that was that other one. The one that had the lady
from *Popeye* in it."

The chatter rises to such howler-monkey levels that I have to say,
"Okay, you morons are going to have to shut up now. Your stupidity is
physically hurting me. Kirby, you going in?"

"Me? Why me?"

"Uh, because you're the one with the key."

"Second wave. I'll go in with the second wave."

"What if the first wave never comes out?" DQ asks.

"Wynn?" Kirby holds the key up, jiggles it at Wynn. "YOLO, bro."

Wynn shakes his head. "Hey, I'm with Jake on the whole desecration deal."

DQ swats Wynn. "You're a pussy. Big tough cowboy. You're a scared little pussy boy."

Wynn swats back, which starts a whole slapping, fake punching war. While they're occupied determining who the bigger pussy is, I pull Jacey aside and whisper, "Can I ask you something?"

"Sure. Of course."

"Did Kirby put anything in the Cuervo?"

She doesn't hesitate before shaking her head. "No, if he'd actually had anything he would have pulled it out when I said I was leaving. I mean, he's seriously into me."

She's right. Kirby wouldn't have been cooking an egg with a flashlight if he'd had exotic designer drugs to impress Jacey with. "So there wasn't anything in the Cuervo?"

"No. But don't stress. About the way you were? You know, after the cave and all?"

I look away, praying that Jace gets the message that I don't want to talk about this anymore. She doesn't.

"Don't feel bad, okay? This one time? Back at my friend's when we were stationed at Lackland? We were like eleven or something. Her brother gave her a joint and we both got so high, we were laughing our asses off. Had the monster munchies. Everything. Then her brother tells us it was oregano and grass clippings. But, I swear, I was super, super high. So, you know, it happens. You think you're doing some shit and your mind plays tricks on you. It's no biggie."

Even though Jacey can't see me, I nod, not knowing what to say as I consider the possibility that it all really happened. The instant that I allow the image of the girl in the cave into my thoughts, the fireflies either reappear or I just notice them again. Either way, it's like someone has turned the intensity all the way up. The dots of light brighten to diamond pinpoints.

I grab the key out of Kirby's hand. "I'll go."

"Luz," Jacey says, "are you sure?"

I shrug. "YOLO, right?"

Jacey turns so that only I can hear her. "I don't think you should be the one to go. Not after—"

"That's why I have to go." I take the flashlight from Kirby.

"Wow, you see that?" DQ asks, holding his palms up. "It started raining right when she said she was going in."

"Rain?" Wynn asks, holding his palms up to the drizzle. "This is like extra high humidity. Mist at the most."

"Whatever."

I take the key and walk alone across the parking lot to the place where the dead communicate with the living, and the question I've tried so hard to tamp down, the one only Codie can answer, bullies its way into my head. I shove it down and glance back. The group is now mostly hidden in the woods around the lot, right on the edge of the area illuminated by the security light. The mist makes them look fuzzy and washed-out, like a fading photo of people I used to know a long time ago from another assignment, another base.

I turn back to the house and am nearly to the door when Jacey scampers up beside me. "I'm going in with you."

"Jace, really, you don't have to."

"I know, but you'd do it for me."

As I try to open the back door, first Kirby, who squeezes in next to Jace, then DQ and Wynn arguing about who's the pussy now, join us. A patrol car passes. Its spotlight rakes the yard, and everyone presses into the shadows as the car passes.

"Hurry up, Luz," DQ hisses as I fumble in the dark. "He's turning around. He's turning around! He'll see us when he comes back this way."

"Oh, fuck," Wynn whispers. "My dad is gonna have my ass."

"*Your* dad," Kirby says. "Mine'll lose his job."

We all shove in the door the instant I get it open. A second later, stripes of high-intensity illumination from the patrol car's headlights slash across the empty back porch and slice in under the blinds.

Everyone freezes. The closed-up house is pitch dark and hot as an oven. It smells like an empty base house, like dust and Pine-Sol, but it feels different from any other empty base house I've ever set foot in. It feels inhabited.

"Kirby," DQ hisses, "turn the fucking flashlight on."

"No! We have to be sure they're gone."

Codie?

I wish I was alone. In the darkness, while the others make nervous jokes, I try to conjure my big sister by bringing to mind the way she looked on the day of her graduation from Basic. She was a recruitment poster in her pale blue blouse with brand-new chevrons on either shoulder. Her hair was braided tight against her head and tucked under her dark blue cap. A LEGO block of colored medals and awards was pinned ruler-straight across her chest, right above her heart. She was so proud. I wish I had been proud too, instead of angry and bewildered and jealous of my mom and the air force for taking her away from me. I wish I'd known that my anger was a luxury that I squandered too much of the time we had left on.

Kirby switches his flashlight on and, of course, the beam falls on nothing. There are no bloodstained curtains or floors. No faucets and lights turning themselves on and off. No children crying. No samurai warriors or Okinawan princesses doing shampoo commercials. The house is as dead and done as the cheerless words the Hickam base chaplain spoke at Codie's service.

I'm turning to leave when Kirby yelps, "Holy shit!"

"Is that what I think it is?" DQ asks the question on one long, shrieky exhalation.

Kirby has the beam focused into the pitch dark of the next room, where it reflects off of a pool of dark liquid so wet in a house that has been closed up for years that it gleams. "That's blood, isn't it? I'm getting out of here."

It is blood. My heart stops.

"That must have been her bedroom," Jacey says.

"So that has to be her blood," DQ, completely freaked out, says. "Almost fifty years old and still fresh."

"Or it could be . . ." I go into the room, pick up a white plastic cup with the Teen Center logo, "Being a teen has never been this much fun!" written on it, " . . . spilled soda from some other kids as dopey as us who also managed to break in."

"Oh, snap!" Wynn cackles. "Diss on you, DQ." He snatches away the plastic cup, grabs DQ in a neck lock, and shoves the cup into his face. "Drink the blood, infidel! Drink!"

DQ slaps the cup away. "Get that outta my face, snowflake."

That's it. There is no sign that a girl died here. No spirits reach out to me from beyond the grave to explain what's happening and what

I'm supposed to do. No displaced samurai or dirty-haired princesses. No spirit of a starved girl trapped in a cave trying to make contact. No Codie.

So now that I've eliminated the possibility that either my sister was trying to reach me or I was tripping my ass off, that leaves only one explanation: I am even more seriously screwed up than I already knew I was. All I want now is to be alone. I can't keep up a front for one more second.

"We're out of here," DQ says, making his voice deep and manly. "This place is about as haunted as a petting zoo."

"Yeah, plus, it's hot as balls in here."

They stampede out, taking the noise and light and struggle with them. For a moment, the empty house is blissfully peaceful and oddly cool and I could stay here forever. In the next instant, the question I've been running from, the one that only Codie can answer, forms in my mind. The instant it does, every ounce of energy in my body washes out, leaving me too weak to move. An unimaginable thirst overtakes me, and my stomach cramps violently from hunger. I open my mouth to cry out from the pain, but no sound emerges. Needle pricks of pain stab my scalp, like I'm being eaten alive by biting insects. I try to claw at them but can't raise my arms. My heart drums with fear and I try to run, but I am frozen. Literally. I shiver with cold.

With every bit of strength I can summon, I force my right foot a fraction of an inch forward. As soon as I lift it the tiniest bit, a shaft opens up and I am falling. I hurtle down so fast that my hair and arms are blown straight up over my head. Air punches up into my nose, my mouth, with a nauseating force.

I see where I will land: spiked rocks poking up above churning waves. I scream, and the sound is sucked away before it leaves my throat. But I don't land. Instead, the rocks, the sea, the darkness disappear, and I'm in a place where the sky is a shade of indigo more exquisite than I could ever describe. The air smells like lilies and pineapples. I watch a child that I know is my child as he tumbles down a grassy hill.

"Luz?"

It's Codie. I stop breathing. She's here. We're together again and I understand that we can be together forever. I know what I have to do. The debate is over. I have all the answers. Except one. Of course, she knows the question I won't allow myself to ask, and though she scolds me for even letting it form in my mind, she answers it. "Cabooskie, what does it matter how I died? Even if I did kill myself, that's no reason you should."

"It matters, Code. It's all that *does* matter. Just tell me you didn't. That you were happy. You were, weren't you? Happy? Being a soldier?"

"Yeah, sure."

"So why are they saying you were outside the wire?"

"I don't want to talk about that."

"But I have to know. You had an intact family. You had me. You always had me, Codie. Right? You were going to come home to me. Codie. Codie?"

"Codie?" The sound of my own voice startles me and I awake to excruciating pain. My back is broken on the rocks, a wave is rising up to claim me, my sister is gone, and I have made a mistake. A terrible, terrible mistake. This isn't what I want. This isn't what Codie wants for me. As clearly as if she were standing next to me, she says one word, "*Yuta,*" and then I am alone again.

"Luz? You coming?"

The beam of Kirby's flashlight hits me in the face, bringing with it the smell of dust and Pine-Sol.

"Kirby, point it down," Jacey orders.

"Oh, sorry." The light disappears.

Jacey takes my hand and leads me outside.

· TWENTY-TWO ·

Anmā, *where is she going? Why did you allow the demon to escape again? My son, stop worrying. Can't you see that the* kami *are helping us? They inhabit her now. What they want shall be done. Our time is short. Let me finish.*

That night in Shuri a space was found for me next to Hatsuko on her futon in the room she shared with the twenty other girls in her group.

We were crowded in tightly, since most of the dorm had been requisitioned by the Imperial Army.

I stayed up late listening to Hatsuko and her best friends—Sachiko, Miyoko, and, of course, our cousin Mitsue—talk. I learned that Sachiko, the tallest of the group, was the fastest runner of all the Himeyuri girls, and that her father was a schoolteacher in a small village at the northern end of the island. That Miyoko, who had a merry, laughing face, was spoiled because she was an only child, and her father owned a large distillery that supplied the Imperial Army with the rice brandy, *awamori*, that they preferred. As for Mitsue, the hard labor and limited rations that had left the others bony and drawn seemed only to have refined the essence of her attractiveness further, making her full lips seem even fuller and her large, luminous eyes even larger.

Mitsue showed me a photo of her fiancé, Masaru, and told me that he was fighting for our freedom from Western tyranny in the Dutch East Indies. Though Masaru was from Hotaru, a village very near our own, they had met when he was training here in Shuri. I told my lovesick cousin that the true Japanese spirit that shone from her fiancé's face was certain to guarantee us the victory that he had been named for.

Amid the other students crammed into the room, I noticed a thin little girl with a long face off by herself in the far corner. "What is that child doing here?" I whispered to Mitsue.

"Oh, that's Katsuko," Mitsue answered in her soft voice.

"She's the youngest Himeyuri girl," Miyoko added. "Very smart. She's only twelve but still scored the highest marks on the entrance exam of any girl on the island. Her sister, Natsuko, is somewhere over there. Natsuko, Katsuko, and Hatsuko, funny, no?"

I was still staring at the pale little girl, wondering how a twelve-year-old could be of any service to the emperor, when Mitsue held up a meter-long white sash and handed me a needle threaded with red. "I am making a *senninbari-haramaki* belt for Masaru. Won't you take some stitches? I've already drawn the pattern for you to follow."

Ideally, Mitsue should have had a thousand virgins stitch one red knot apiece into the sash, so that the soldier on the front line who received the belt would know that one thousand pure women carried him in their hearts. Instead, the five of us stayed up as long as we could keep our eyes open, passing the sash and red thread back and forth until we'd each added two hundred and fifty knots.

I don't know when I fell asleep, but I was jolted awake in the middle of the night when I was heaved up off my sleeping mat.

"Earthquake!" I yelled to alert the others.

"Bombs, Little Guppy," Hatsuko corrected me. "They're bombing what's left of Naha. Don't look so scared. You'll get used to it."

The other girls said nothing as the concussions from bombs dropping just a few kilometers away fell into an ominous rhythm. Each detonation would momentarily drown out all other noise. A second later we would hear the rattle of our soldiers' antiaircraft guns. Soon even more frightening noises reached us: the tinkling of shattered glass falling, and the crackling of fire as the bombs landed closer to Shuri.

When the entire dorm started to shake as though a typhoon were roaring outside, Hatsuko and the other girls exchanged worried looks. "They've never reached this close before," she whispered to me.

Head Nurse Tanaka's harsh voice rose above the bombardment: "Quickly, girls! Quickly! We leave at once for Haebaru Hospital. Don't dawdle. Those left behind will have to deal with the *ketō* on their own!" She used the word that meant not just "hairy savage," but also implied a beast with uncontrollable lusts. An animal that lived to rape.

"We're leaving?" I asked Hatsuko, blinking, my eyes and brain not adjusting rapidly enough. She had jumped up immediately, stuffed her few extra clothes into her rucksack, and was ready.

"Yes," Hatsuko answered, gathering up my belongings and cramming them into my satchel. "But it will only be for a short while. The invaders will be repelled in a matter of days. A week or so at the most until they are destroyed by our majestic Imperial fleet."

"But why can't we stay here? We would be safe in the tunnels."

"Those tunnels are for the emperor's soldiers, silly. Come on. Hurry. We'll finally get to see what a glorious hospital has been built for the brave soldiers wounded defending our emperor."

In the corner, I noticed twelve-year-old Katsuko carefully sliding her schoolbooks into her rucksack, so she'd be able to keep up with her studies.

All 220 Princess Lily girls assembled silently in the night. From the distance came sounds I would have taken for drums had I not known better. As we set off at a brisk pace, the rhythmic booming had a lulling quality, like the beating of a massive heart.

"Look, Naha is burning," Sachiko whispered. "I wouldn't have thought there was anything left to catch fire." Off to the west, the sky above our mighty port of Naha glowed orange against the black of the night.

"The flames haven't reached Shuri, though," Hatsuko said. "As long as Shuri stands we will be fine."

"When is Operation Shō going to begin?" Miyoko asked. "Shouldn't the Imperial Navy destroy the American ships now that they've all been lured into the trap? What are they waiting for?"

Cousin Mitsue shot Miyoko a warning look and pressed her finger against her lips to remind her how dangerous it was to give voice to such traitorous thoughts; spies were everywhere. "Don't be silly," she said in a too-loud voice. "We will all be back in Shuri in no time. In fact, I think I hear the sound of the engines of our White Chrysanthemums right now."

The other girls agreed with too much enthusiasm, though none of us would have been able to hear the sound of a kamikaze plane flying off on a suicide mission to destroy the American fleet above the boom of exploding bombs.

Outside, though the night was cool, the air was heavy with the smell of burning wood. The other girls hurried away, but my sister, her face orange in the light of the flames creeping upward toward Shuri Castle, stood transfixed. When I reached out and took Hatsuko's hand it was damp with sweat. "Don't worry," she said, her voice a wobbly chirp. "We'll be back in no time."

"We've got to hurry," I said, tugging on her moist hand. "The others are getting ahead of us." Though we set off, marching as fast as I could make my sister go, she continued to glance back toward Shuri. I guessed that she was watching for Lieutenant Nakamura, and we fell farther and farther behind the others.

The main road churned with panicked refugees fleeing the city. A squad of soldiers on their way south to Haebaru marched past in lockstep, their boots pounding against the dusty road like pistons. For a while, we matched the warriors' ferocious pace. I felt like I was one of them, all of us bound by the love of our emperor, and a soaring exhilaration overtook me.

Eventually we reached the country, yet the bombs followed us. Even worse, though, were the flares that lit up the night, leaving us all exposed. In their terrible bluish light, I saw my fellow refugees. Old men pushing carts loaded with pots and baskets and futons. Women tottering beneath the weight of baskets balanced on their heads. Children as young as five struggling along with babies tied to their backs.

Coming in the opposite direction, toward Hatsuko and me, we met a woman with an infant lashed to her back, leading two small children by the hands. She yelled to us, "We heard there are hundreds of kilometers of air-raid shelters in Shuri. Why are you leaving?"

"We are Princess Lily girls," Hatsuko answered. "We've been assigned to the hospital at Haebaru."

"Will my children be safe in Shuri?"

"Yes, of course you all will be safe. The emperor's Imperial Army is there."

"*Nifee deebiru!* Thank you, sister." Relieved, the woman grinned and rushed off toward Shuri.

We marched on in silence; finally I asked, "Will she be safe in Shuri? Will the soldiers allow her or any civilian who isn't a worker into the tunnels?"

"No, of course not. Don't be ridiculous."

"But then why did you—"

"Tamiko," my sister snapped, "what would you have me say? As a Princess Lily girl it is my duty to spread the pure Japanese spirit and maintain morale. The emperor is our father and, like a good father, he will watch over us. But only if we honor him by not betraying him with doubt."

Her own speech bolstered Hatsuko, and she marched on with new vigor in her stride, while I became the dawdler, troubled by the sight of all those trusting country folk flowing north toward Shuri, where the bombs were falling. Mostly, though, I worried about everyone back at home, and rushed forward to ask Hatsuko, "Do you think Mother and Father will be safe?"

Hatsuko whirled on me and hissed, "You must never again mention our family. Haven't you noticed that no one speaks of their families? We all carry that burden in silence. To do otherwise would only cause sad thoughts and show lack of respect for the emperor."

I shut my mouth and clung silently to the faith I had in our mother's hardheaded resourcefulness. She knew where every cave near our village was. She would make sure that she and Father and my aunts and uncles and cousins were safe.

At our quickened pace, we soon rejoined the rest of the girls from Himeyuri. The moon had risen and reached its zenith by the time we arrived at Haebaru. We craned our necks, searching for the emperor's magnificent hospital, where we would read to wounded soldiers and bring them glasses of water, safe beneath the shield of the Red Cross.

But no red crosses greeted us. Instead, Head Nurse Tanaka led our group to a series of grassy hills with cave openings hastily concealed behind some withered foliage that looked like animals' dens and told us that this was our destination. "What are you waiting for?" Head Nurse demanded. "You lazy Okinawan girls will have to wake up if you're to be of any use to our emperor. Now get in there."

We entered the nearest opening. It was immediately apparent that this cave was nothing like the plastered tunnels beneath Shuri, with their polished concrete floors. It was little more than a hole in the ground fit only for bats. A kerosene lamp cast a dismal drizzle of light that revealed walls and ceilings dripping condensation, and stalactites hanging down like grotesque icicles. The smeared letters of patriotic slogans written on the walls—"Don't die until you annihilate your foes!" "Stick to your guns until you die!"—ran in wet black streaks over the oozing limestone.

"Move back! Move back!" a burly soldier gripping a rifle ordered, pushing us roughly down a long entry passage. "If you're caught here in the entrance when a bomb explodes nearby, the air pressure will kill you. You'll die like a deep-sea fish yanked up from the bottom, with your guts hanging out."

The entryway dead-ended in a chamber that was already packed so tightly with fifty Himeyuri girls who had arrived before us that we all had to sit; there was not enough room to lie down. By the light of a single kerosene lamp, Hatsuko managed to find our friends, Sachiko, Miyoko, and Mitsue, and we groped our way toward them, stumbling over bodies and bundles.

The ventilation system had never been completed, and the odor of unwashed bodies was choking. Flakes of soot floated up from the bottle of kerosene with a wick of twisted rag that served as our lamp. The soot drifted back down on us like a black snowfall.

It was too dark to see who was speaking, and the girls chattered over one another, each comment louder than the last. "Did you hear about the nurse the Americans captured? After the whole platoon raped her many times, they impaled her on a flagpole and left her for the maggots to devour." "The demons get their laughs by castrating any prisoners they take. Then, before they've bled to death, they run them over with their tanks and bulldozers!" "The marines, though, they are the worst. In order to qualify, they must kill both their parents." "And drink their blood!"

In spite of the horror stories, the long night of marching caught up with me and, wedged in between Hatsuko and Mitsue, I fell into a sleep darker than the cave became after the kerosene lamp was extinguished. I don't know how many hours later I was dragged from my dreams by the stench of all those bodies crammed into such a small space and the urgent need to relieve myself.

Outside, the sunlight dazzled me. The early afternoon air was cool and fragrant with the scents of spring, new grass, and fresh leaves. The cloudless sky was bluer than I had ever seen it, and I recalled that the name of the nearby village, Haebaru, meant "meadows of southerly winds." The previous night felt as if it had been nothing but a bad dream that was over now, and life would again be as it was meant to be. High overhead, flashing across the sun, I caught a glint of silver. I shielded my eyes to see the insect or bird better.

"Oh, no, a *tombo*." Hatsuko appeared at my side.

"A dragonfly?" I asked. "It's too big."

"No, that's what we call the *Amerikās*' reconnaissance planes. Remember how we used to chase real *tombos*?"

I thought of the long summer days when we would run through the millet fields, the shimmering wings and big, all-seeing eyes of the dragonflies dancing ahead of us.

"Well, now the *tombos* are chasing us. We are the prey they search out." An instant passed before Hatsuko laughed, almost as if she had to remind herself to make the sound of silver bells. "Where the *tombos* fly, the bombs will follow." For a long time we watched the planes that were watching us.

Hatsuko's words proved correct, and the next day a steady bombardment of the green meadows, fields, and woods around the cave hospitals began. All day we were trapped inside by the fall of bombs that paused only briefly at dusk, when our enemy stopped to eat dinner.

Over the next few days, before any patients arrived, we had nothing to do but huddle inside the cave and wait and listen as the explosions grew closer and louder. With no water for bathing or washing our clothes, it wasn't long before we were all afflicted by the tormenting bites of the lice that hid in our hair and the seams of our dirty clothes.

When word reached us in our gloomy cave that the ketō had come ashore on our beaches, and that they were equipped with monstrous war machines that moved like huge blocks of iron, crushing everything in their paths, we had to hide how downhearted and frightened we were. Though I knew enough not to ask aloud, I wondered about Operation Shō, the crafty trap that my father and Miyoko had spoken of in which the Imperial Navy, led by the mightiest warship ever created, the invincible Yamato, would trap the American fleet and wipe them out like sitting ducks. Why hadn't the trap been sprung before our enemy came ashore?

Though we were afraid to voice our doubts for fear of not showing our true Japanese spirit, I knew that Hatsuko shared them. After a detonation so near that the shock waves rumbled through the cave, she called out in a voice too bright with false excitement, "Think of our brave soldiers lying in wait in the tunnels beneath Shuri like a thousand habu snakes, hiding until the right moment to emerge and strike. Tennō heika banzai!"

Our answering Banzai!s were drowned out by a furious series of staccato blasts. By the guttering flame of the stinking kerosene lantern, I saw the faces, pale from hiding in caves for so many days, go even paler as we imagined the Amerikās with their red faces and long noses trampling across our island, hoisting infants on their bayonets, ripping toddlers in half with their massive hands, torturing our parents, making their way to us so that they could use us in the unspeakable ways Father had warned Hatsuko and me of in the foreigners' cemetery.

That evening when the bombing stopped at our enemy's dinner hour, we rushed outside and beheld, in the place of Haebaru's green meadows, a barren wasteland of smoldering tree stumps and bomb craters. Nonetheless, we hurried out to feel the sun on our faces, to fetch water, relieve ourselves, gather our meager rations from the quartermaster, and visit with the hundreds of others who poured out of the honeycomb of caves.

Mitsue and I were filling our buckets with water when a woman from her fiancé Masaru's village rushed up, her face a pudding of sorrow, and said, "Oh, dear Mitsue-san, I was so sorry when I heard the news about Masaru."

"News of my fiancé? What news?" Mitsue demanded. Her lips, plump and full as a cartoon goldfish's, trembled with fear as she waited for the answer her heart had already spoken.

The woman pressed her fingers against her mouth as if she could bottle up the words that had already been released. "You don't know? I was certain that you would have known."

"What? Tell me. Masaru, is he . . . ?"

She couldn't say the word, but none of us needed to hear it.

The neighbor nodded. "His parents received the white box over a month ago."

The Imperial Army sent the ashes of the dead home in a white box. Mitsue wept all night for her fiancé named Victory, and there was nothing any of us could do to comfort her.

· TWENTY-THREE ·

At the end of the second week in that gloomy cave, before casualties reached our part of the hospital system, we had little to do other than pluck and crush lice, and scratch at the maddening bites the chalky white insects crawling in and out of our clothes left. Our spirits were quite low when we received news that made us all leap to our feet and cheer as wildly as we had when we learned that Japan had devastated the U.S. fleet at Pearl Harbor: President Roosevelt had died! This proved to those few doubters that the emperor truly *was* divine. Just as the gods had sent divine winds to destroy Kublai Khan's Mongol fleet when he tried, not once but twice—in 1274, then again in 1281—to invade Japan, the deities had intervened again to protect our beloved homeland.

It was obvious that the bullying Americans were being punished for provoking Japan into attacking them. Surely now the war would be over. The Americans could not possibly go on without their leader. But the onslaught not only continued, it increased in ferocity. We couldn't understand such callousness. If our emperor were to die, we would be incapacitated by grief. Our reason for fighting to the death would be gone; the *ketō* had to be even more monstrous than we thought.

Time for these desolate reflections vanished when patients began to arrive from the front. We were summoned to the main hospital cave to receive our assignments. The rainy season had commenced and rivers of mud now ran between the bomb craters. At the entrance, we were told to wait while our leaders, the Himeyuri teachers, consulted with the authorities inside. All around us wounded soldiers lay on stretchers, moaning with pain. They had obviously been waiting for hours, since their uniforms were soaking wet. We stood outside with them, the rain running in rivulets down our faces.

After several hours we were ushered in by Nurse Tanaka. The air of the main corridor was thick with fluffy black soot from the kerosene lamps mounted on the walls. "No talking," Tanaka hissed at us. "We're coming close to the officers' quarters. They've just arrived from the front."

All the rooms were open to the main corridor, so we fell silent and bowed our heads as we passed the officers' quarters. To look directly at an officer in such circumstances would have been a sign of disrespect that the more capricious among their ranks would punish with a severe beating. But that didn't stop Hatsuko from glancing around until she found Lieutenant Nakamura in a room stacked with sleeping planks. My sister stopped dead. Nakamura had his back to us. He wore only trousers and a sleeveless T-shirt that revealed broad shoulders and a fine, slender physique. In his hand was a tin of Jintan breath mints with the navy commander on the front wearing his trademark old-fashioned commodore's hat. Carefully, almost reverently, Nakamura plucked a mint from the tin.

As he was bringing the Jintan mint to his mouth, he felt my sister's eyes burning a hole into his back and turned to face us. In spite of being caught in a state of undress, he was the essence of dignity as he bent at the waist in a courtly bow and held his last mint out, offering it to Hatsuko. My dazed sister barely had time to offer a stunned wave of thanks and refusal before I hurried her down the hall.

Hatsuko's hand in mine trembled from the force of her emotion. Sachiko and Miyoko were reacting like silly schoolgirls to the sight of the handsome lieutenant, their heads pressed together, stifling giggles. Mitsue, on the other hand, hadn't even noticed the half-dressed lieutenant. Her grief had lent her a detached serenity, and she seemed to float among us like a spirit summoned back from the dead.

Beyond the officers' quarters was an operating room. It was lit by a naked electric bulb that blinded us after our confinement in the dim cave. Two masked doctors bent over an operating table while a nurse stood by, holding a tray piled with gleaming instruments. Their patient groaned in agony. The harsh illumination threw jagged, dancing shadows across the cave wall, and I felt as if I were watching one of the German horror movies that Hatsuko and I had seen in Naha.

"Stop gawking!" Nurse Tanaka ordered, swatting the back of my head with a hard slap.

The patients' ward was at the end of the corridor. Here stacks of bunk beds six high filled with wounded men lined the bare cave walls. In addition to the usual odors of cave life, there was the stench of rotting flesh, pus, urine, and acrid medicines. Nurse Tanaka gave us our assignments, and we broke into three groups. Hatsuko and Miyoko were sent off to surgery ward one. Mitsue went to surgery ward two, and Sachiko left for the internal medicine ward.

Nurse Tanaka stared sharply at the pin on my chest that designated me a head girl, and, without looking at my face, asked, "Name?"

I told her. And, just as Hatsuko had promised, she wrote it down without question.

A nearby patient began calling out to us, "Nurse, please, a bedpan. Please, I've been asking for hours. Please." The man was so emaciated and dehydrated that his head was little more than a skull with eyes sunk deep into their sockets and dark hollows shadowing his cheeks.

"Help this man!" Head Nurse shouted at me, as if I had been the one ignoring him for so long. Before I could tell her that I'd received no training and didn't even know what a bedpan looked like, she stomped away.

I stood, rooted to the bumpy floor, overwhelmed by the men around me, who all began crying out for help the instant Nurse Tanaka left, as though they knew better than to make any requests in front of her.

"Please, Nurse, a bedpan," the first man begged again.

I wanted to tell him that I wasn't a nurse. I wasn't even a Himeyuri student. But the years of having it drilled into me that no respectable young woman would ever speak to a man silenced my tongue.

"Please, you have two hands." The soldier's voice was so piteous that I couldn't refuse. I searched the ward for a receptacle and found a foul-smelling basin, which I intended to hand to him, then turn my back while he relieved himself. At his bed, however, he wouldn't take the pan.

"Nurse, please, I need a bit of help. If you could pull back the sheet . . ."

I did and found that both the man's arms had been amputated.

"And now," he continued. "I'm very sorry, but . . ." He nodded his head toward his crotch.

I, who had not so much as spoken to a boy since I was a young girl, and certainly never seen an unclothed man, had to remove his loincloth and hold his member as he urinated. I breathed through my mouth so as not to faint and repeated to myself, *I am doing this for my emperor and my country. I am doing this for my emperor and my country.* When he was finished, other patients begged for the same service. Some had the use of their hands. Some did not.

As the shock of what I would be required to do wore off, I reminded myself that these men had been wounded defending me and my island from the predatory Americans, and I forced myself to speak to them. The effect of a few kind words was remarkable. Men who'd seemed little more than pathetic, groveling animals a moment before retook their human form and told me where they were from and how they had been wounded. More than one had tears in his eyes as he whispered that I reminded him of the little sister he'd left back home in Japan.

Then they began talking about the enemy. "The *ketō* are even worse than we'd been told," a man with a soiled, bloody bandage wrapped around his torso said. "They're grotesquely large and covered in hair, furry as an animal's pelt. We even saw some of the black ones. True ogres. Terrifying."

"And many of their bodies are tattooed," a patient whose foot had been blown off put in. "Like pirates."

The first man added, "The worst, though, is that their weapons are as massive as they are. They have tanks that come at you with the force of a mountain moving. They crush everything in their path. They ran over a wounded man and I heard his bones crunching like matchsticks."

"But we're still winning the war, aren't we," I said, more statement than question.

"Of course, of course," they all rushed to reassure me.

The man who'd lost his foot declared, "Japan's never fought a war she couldn't win. The Americans and their weapons' bloated size just make them easier targets for us!"

The injured men answered that plucky declaration with a *banzai* cheer for our emperor. Because of their debilitated condition, however, it sounded feeble and uninspiring, and we all fell into silence.

Certain that I knew what would cheer them up, I announced heartily, "It will all be over soon anyway once the emperor unleashes Operation Shō and crushes the American fleet just floating out there like sitting ducks. Wait until the mighty guns of the *Yamato* are turned on them!" I finished with a flourish, proud to know the name of Japan's indomitable warship. I waited for the patients to join me in a cheer.

It never came. Instead an uncomfortable silence greeted my pronouncement. The men's gazes flickered away, refusing to meet mine. After several long moments, a patient crammed into the back of the cave, beyond the glow of the kerosene lamp, let out a dry, bitter laugh.

"Shut up, Nishihara!" another patient barked at him. "Don't say anything in front of Miss Mighty Guns."

"You shut up, Aoki!" Nishihara growled from the darkness. "Why should our little Okinawan princess here be the only one who doesn't know that Japan has no fleet. And that her precious *Yamato* was sent to the bottom of the East China Sea five days ago."

I searched the faces of the other men for proof that he was lying or delusional. That he had been driven mad from the pain of his wounds. And though a couple of the men did mutter, "He's crazy," and, "Pay no attention to Nishihara," the truth was plain on their downcast faces: The *Yamato* had been sunk. No invincible warship was coming to save us. There was no Operation Shō. No help was on its way. Okinawa was all alone.

PART II

NAKANUHI THE MIDDLE DAY

Celebrating with the Dead

· TWENTY-FOUR ·

*Y*uta. The word jangles in my head as I step out of the stifling house.
I gulp down deep breaths of cool, sweet night air, trying to calm
myself enough that I can make it home. Kirby and the others are sauntering across the parking lot. The instant a pair of headlights tilts down
the hill toward them, however, they run for the Dumpster next to the
USO and scurry behind it.

Jacey hangs back with me and, tipping her head to look into my
face, asks gently, "Luz?" She takes my hand. "Girl, what's wrong? You're
freezing. Luz? Say something."

I'm so rattled that I can't stop the words from slipping out, "I . . . I
think . . . I'm probably losing my mind."

She takes my other hand and squeezes them both between hers.
"Did you see something in there?"

I nod.

"Her? The girl who was killed?"

"No, nothing like that."

"Your sister?"

"Not exactly. I have to go."

"I'm coming with you."

"I actually really need to be alone."

"No, you don't. Whether you know it or not, you actually really
need to have someone watching out for you. You're not as tough as you
think you are."

"I don't think I'm tough. I'm a mess."

"You aren't. It's stress. Stress and drugs and not sleeping. That will screw with your head."

"Yeah, my head is pretty screwed with."

"I'm coming home with you. Period. End of story."

I'm desperate to be alone and start edging away. "Thanks, Jace, seriously, but I think you're right. I need to sleep. So I'm just going to go home and sleep."

"Luz, you don't look good. Are you sure?"

"Yes, I just really need to be alone."

"Okay, but call me. If you need anything. Anything at all. You want my address? You could come over, in case you change your mind and want some company."

"No, I'll be fine. Really."

I follow the ravine back to my neighborhood and crawl out right behind our apartment. I'm halfway across the backyard when I get hit in the face with the high beam from a passing patrol car. Knowing that most of the base cops are fat fucks who get winded tying their boots, I decide to make a break for it; no base cop would venture into the *habu*-infested ravine.

I'm just starting to crawl back down into the ravine when the patrolman yells out, "Luz? Luz James, that you?"

I shield my eyes from the glare of his high beam and catch a glimpse of the patrolman from under my hand. "Oh, hey, Boone, hi."

It's Airman Dwyce Boone, a short, squirrely guy barely older than me who works for my mom. He kills the spotlight and I walk over to the car. Boone jumps out, holds the back door open like he's my prom date. I get in and he hops in the front.

"Well, good evening, Miss Luz." Boone is a little too gleeful about busting the boss's daughter and makes a big show of picking up the clipboard with his incident reports attached. He takes out the pen and circles it in big loops above the clipboard, like he's warming up to write.

"Boone, come on, don't log it."

"Rules is rules, Miss Luz. Are you asking me to bend them?"

"I'm asking you just not to be a jerk."

"It's almost midnight. You're out way after curfew. That's an automatic citation with a copy to the SOFA member's CO."

He's especially pleased that my mom's boss, the Duke of Douchebaggery, Colonel Manness, whom Mom nicknamed Manliness because he's so not, would have to be notified. Manness is a by-the-book, old-school stickler who is threatened by everyone, but especially by women like my mom who could kick his ass three ways into next Sunday. The citation would give him the chance to ask her, "If you can't command your own family, how can you command a unit?" And that would land hard on her, then a whole lot harder on me.

"Let it slide, okay? Look, our apartment is right there. I could say I was just playing in my backyard."

"And everyone else could say that if I don't cite you, I was just sucking up to the boss."

"Boone. Dude."

He laughs, puts the clipboard down. "I was just messing with you."

"Very funny."

He twists around in his seat, gets comfortable. "So what do you hear from your mom? Can't believe they pulled her off when we're already so shorthanded."

I act like I'd read even one of her texts. "Sounds like it's going fine."

"No shit, I'd give my left nut to be out in the Sandbox doing what I actually trained for."

The Sandbox? Afghanistan?

"I heard they're transporting some high-values."

High-value enemy combatants. I scrub the scared quaver from my voice and say, all casual, "Yeah, she mentioned that."

"Really? Damn it. *That's* what I trained for. Not babysitting brats and keeping guys from beating on their wives. I mean 'Security Forces'? Come on. What strings did your mom pull to get to go?"

Get to go?

I see my mom again, packing, filling her duffel with ABUs in the new blue-gray camo pattern. When she'd thrown in her tan boots, I'd asked, "Aren't those only authorized in theater operations?"

In answer, she popped her eyes at me, said, "Listen to you, all 'theater operations,'" zipped up her bag, hauled it out to sit by the front door, ready for her 0500 departure time, and left to meet her buddies at the Rocker Club.

Now I want a real answer and say the one thing I'm certain will open Boone up like a can of tomatoes. "Probably because she's a woman."

"I didn't say it, but it sure ain't like she could have volunteered any quicker than me."

She volunteered to go? I open my mouth and take shallow breaths, so that Boone won't see or hear that my heart has accelerated so much I'm panting at the thought that my mother volunteered to go to a war zone. Where her daughter was killed. I thought I'd made myself invulnerable to my mom's behavior, but this evidence that I mean so little to her that she'd risk leaving me entirely alone in the world, that I really, truly, in fact, don't have anyone, panics me.

"But," Boone adds, "on the real, you got a high-value female, it's a whole cultural deal. No males allowed. You need a female on the transport. I get that. The pool of females with the right training just ain't that big. So they pretend like it's open to all us humps stuck here on the Rock, but basically? They already tapped who they wanted. So your mom, I get her. But Wheeler? Vinger? Maldonado?" He names the guys chosen to go with her. "Why'd those guys get to go? I smoked Maldonado in Counterinsurgency. And Urban Terrain. I was like, 'Dude, did you never play "Counter Strike"?'"

"Yeah, sucks for you."

She chose to leave.

Boone's radio crackles. He takes the call—barking dog—starts the engine. "Duty calls. Luz, who you staying with?"

"Here. This is our place."

I start to open the door; Boone catches my eye in the rearview, holds it, asks again with lots of added emphasis, "No, Luz, for real, who are you staying with, because I *know* that your mom knows the base housing reg that states that 'In the event of leave or an extended TDY in which the service member is absent from her quarters for five days or more, dependents under the age of eighteen will not be left unsupervised.'"

Of course my mom knows the reg. And of course she knows I know and expected me to be smart enough not to get caught breaking it.

"I *maybe* can let the curfew thing slide, but not this. So let me ask again, Luz: Who are you staying with? Because I cannot allow you to remain in base housing without supervision."

I run through the list of my latest Quasis. I really wish that one of them was an actual friend. Someone who'd cover for me if I showed up at their door with an MP, acting like I was staying with their family. But

I don't even know where any of them lives. Except for one. "Uh, yeah, not a problem. I'm staying with the Furusatos."

"They on base?"

"Of course. That's regs, right?"

"What's the address?"

"Over by the golf course."

"I need an address, Luz."

"Yeah, it's something-something.... Shit, I can't remember the name of the street."

Boone shakes his head, starts the engine. "Give me directions."

· TWENTY-FIVE ·

Fortunately, when we get to the Furusatos' house, Jake is cool, saying in a casual, unsurprised way, "Hey, Luz."

I start talking then. Fast. "Yeah, Jake, hey, hi, here I am. Again. As usual. Because I'm staying with you while my mom is TDY, since she'd never leave an underage dependent unsupervised in base housing."

Jake doesn't miss a beat. "Which is why you've been staying with me. Us. My whole family, including my parents."

Boone takes a minute to size up the situation. He glances around at Jake's house. It's nice. Not just officer nice. Civilian nice. Walls a non-reg color, shelves filled with the ultimate weight-allowance buster—books—stuff hanging everywhere: paintings, photos. So many nail holes drilled into the concrete walls.

Boone puts on his official voice, asks, "Might I have a word with your father?"

"Yes, sir, no problem, sir. If you're really sure that's what you want. I'm just saying that because my dad, Colonel Furusato, has a predawn briefing and he might not be too happy about being woken up, sir."

I'm surprised by what a convincing liar Jake is and almost believe myself that his father is an officer giving predawn briefings instead of a glorified lawn boy in the civil service. It's lucky that it's too dark outside to see that there's no plate with a name and a rank on Jake's house. "But it's your choice, Airman . . ." Jake carefully reads off the name tape. "Boone."

Boone nervously crimps the insignia on his black beret between his palm and fingers so that the screaming eagle is all erect, as he weighs the joys of fucking with me against the dangers of annoying an officer. Before the opportunity for Boone to call Jake's bluff even arises, I step through the door and stand next to Jake like we're a fifties couple and Boone is the dinner guest who has overstayed his welcome and we're trying to ease him on his way.

"Okay, then, Boone, I guess we're cool here. We should wrap this up. Don't want to wake the colonel."

"Yeah," Jake agrees, "he's kind of hard-core, know what I'm sayin'?"

Boone blinks, furrows his brow.

I wave nightie-night, call out, "Thanks for the ride," as I gently close the door.

Jake and I huddle by the door until we hear the car pull away. I crack the door. When the white cruiser has finally disappeared, I start to step outside. "I should leave. I can get back to my place without anyone seeing me."

"I don't think so." Jake pulls me in and shuts the door. "Not now that you're officially listed as staying here. If anything happens, my father will get reported, and that would be so not good. You would not believe how far under the radar we have to stay to be able to keep living here."

"Jake, I'm sorry. I didn't know who else—"

"No worries."

In the living room, behind Jake, a large cabinet dominates a wall. A pair of doors is open, and sticks of burning incense poking from a holder lacquered scarlet and gold send twines of smoke up, scenting the air with a fragrance both floral and ancient.

"So you went with them," Jake says with obvious annoyance. "To see the 'haunted house.'"

"I did, but—"

"But what?"

His hostility catches me off balance, and I can't figure out how or whether to tell him about what I experienced.

Jake takes my silence for shame, and his tone is beyond dismissive when he says, "Yeah, right. You're really *Uchinānchu*. Did they even bother telling you about that place?"

"That it was built over a tomb?"

"You knew and you *still* went in?" He shakes his head in something between amazement and disgust. "Wow, you are so not who I thought you were. You're not even who you were pretending to be, are you?"

"Jake, it's not like that. I had a reason to go in."

"What? To check out the freak show? See the superscary Okinawan ghosts?"

"No, nothing like that."

"So what then? You writing a paper on primitive superstitions of Ryukyuans? An anthropological study of strange funeral rituals?"

"Jake, listen. The reason I went in was . . ." I stop, tripped up by the sight of the gallery of family photos haloing the cabinet. Lots of cute little girls in kimonos with high obis snugged up under their armpits. Bowlegged grandparents on wooden *getas* leaning on canes. Couples on their wedding days, husbands standing stiffly beside brides made up like geishas with powder-white skin and cherry-red rosebud mouths. Some of the black-and-whites are so old that the subjects have the rigid, unblinking look of people photographed with flash powder who had been ordered not to move. How do I explode the mess of my family, my life, my possibly deranged imaginings, in front of them?

When I don't speak, Jake shrugs, says, "Yeah? Pretty much what I thought." He points down the hall. "I think there's clean sheets on the bed in the guest room. See you in the morning." Walking away, he tosses over his shoulder, "Or not."

Just before he closes the door of his bedroom behind himself, I call out, my voice louder and tighter than I expected, "I went in because they told me you can communicate with the dead there. I went in to try to make contact with my sister. I may be going crazy, but I've been getting signs that I'm supposed to do something. Except I don't know what. I don't know what a *yuta* is, but I think I'm supposed to go to one. And I . . ." I stop because I feel a warm gush of tears rising in my chest. I stomp them down so hard that I sound almost hostile when I say, "I need your help."

Jake doesn't turn around, and for a moment I'm convinced he won't. That he'll shut the door on me and my psychotic rambling. He doesn't even face me when he says, "Maybe I'll help you, but there are some things you have to understand first."

"I know, Jake. There's so much I have to understand."

He comes to me then, gets right in my face. "First off, this isn't any folkloric bullshit or cultural awareness field trip. This is Okinawa. This is how it is: We live with the dead and the dead live with us. It's not spooky or creepy or woo-woo; it's just how it is. Got that?"

"Yes."

He studies me. "How do I know you won't be standing back, taking notes, judging?"

"Because if I don't figure out what Codie wants me to do, if I have to live the rest of my life completely alone, I'll kill myself."

Jake nods, and though he doesn't say anything, I know he understands more than I have any right to expect him to. I want to tell him the whole truth—that I saw a dead girl in the cave and she needs me to save her and her baby—but I can't get the words out. That part is so crazy that it will make him miss the real point: Codie. Codie is always the point.

Jake leads me to the back door, slides it open, and we stand for a moment with the air-conditioned inside air rushing past us. In the living room a clock bongs out. Jake says, "Midnight. Happy Nakanuhi."

"Come again?"

"Second day of Obon. Starts right"—the clock chimes a final time—"now." He steps out the door, stops. "Okay, I'm going to show you something that no other base kid has ever seen. But if you ever tell anyone about it, you'll wreck a lot of lives."

He doesn't wait for me to promise that I won't ever say a word, just stalks off across the course, which the streetlights shining on the freshly watered grass has turned into a lake of silver.

I follow him into it.

· TWENTY-SIX ·

Eight small villages once existed where Kadena is now," Jake says as he spins numbers into the lock on the gate of the Deigo Tree Golf

Course. A sign on the gate informs members, "Course closed in obser-
vance of Obon." An illuminated display next to the fence shows photos
of various holes taken in the early summer, when the trees were in full
bloom. They're coral trees like the ones shading Codie's grave. A small
plaque says that on Okinawa they're called *deigo* trees, and that the red
blossoms were named the prefectural flower in honor of the blood that
was shed during the Battle of Okinawa.

Jake opens the gate, we step in, and he locks it behind us. As we walk
through the dark, empty course with its perfect swells and paths, it's
like being in Disneyland after hours. It's the perfect place for a quick
hookup, and for a split second I wonder whether that's where we're
headed after all. But the determined way Jake strides forward elimi-
nates that possibility.

As we go farther in, away from the lights, it grows dark and all I can
hear are the sounds of distant air conditioners cycling on and off, frogs
croaking, birds singing lonely songs, and the rustle of a breeze swirling around in the high branches of tall trees. It takes no effort for me
to imagine that this was once the site of a peaceful, rural village. I try
to imagine what secret could possibly be hidden here. Jake leads me off
the fairway into a heavily wooded area. Signs warn golfers, DANGER:
SNAKES. REMAIN ON FAIRWAY.

I stop. "Jake?"

"Don't worry. I've got antivenin at the house. Most likely you won't
die before I can run back and get it."

"'Most likely'?"

"I'm messing with you. There aren't any snakes. Come on. We're
almost there."

Once we turn off the fairway, it is so dark that I have to hold on to
the back of Jake's shirt to follow him. The trail ends at a large concrete
platform surrounded by a high fence with razor wire at the top. A
sign on the gate has "Danger" and "High Voltage" written in Japanese
characters, English, and Spanish, and the icon of a lightning bolt stabbing a guy in the chest as he falls backward. Inexplicably, the fragrance
of jasmine and sandalwood incense perfumes the air. Jake pulls the
unlocked gate open and gestures for me to go in.

I point to the signs. "Uh, *electricidad? Peligro de muerte?*"

Jake bangs his hand against the nearest of several tall metal sheds. It
clangs hollowly. "They're fake. The only things that are real are these,"

Jake says as he lights several of the candles sitting on the concrete. Hidden behind the sheds is a small stone shrine in the shape of a house with a thatched roof. It is encircled by coins, incense, fruit, small cakes, glasses of sake. Each group of offerings is carefully placed within one of eight outlines.

Jake points to them and says, "Every one of those is the outline of one of the eight villages that were eradicated when the U.S. military claimed all this land."

I look more closely and see, etched into the concrete, drawings of streams with tiny fish swimming in them, plots of land with images of potatoes, stick figures dancing, the distinctive turtle-shell shape of tombs. They're hieroglyphics describing a vanished world drawn by people still mourning the hometowns that they can see on the other side of a barbed-wire fence, but that are lost to them forever. It's like the brat hometown curse taken to an unbearable level.

Jake taps the drawing of a tomb. "After the war, after the military seized their homes, their farms, that's what the displaced villagers wanted most. They wanted their ancestors. They would never be at peace if they weren't allowed to return to the spot where their tombs had once stood in order to fulfill their obligations so that their ancestors could enter the next realm and then be able to guide and protect them.

"And that was the deal the villagers, led by my great-great-grandfather, managed to get from the base commander. In exchange for the villagers not protesting the golf course, their representative, my great-great-grandfather, was made manager of the course. A section of the course was set aside, and each year during the three days of Obon, the course is closed and the oldest male of each village family is allowed to bring offerings and pay his respects. But the deal was never official, so—"

"So that's why you and your family pretty much have to live and work at the course and put up with ignorant comments from people like Kirby."

"Oh, did Kernshaw tell you what a big sellout I am?"

I shrug. "Sort of. Not exactly."

"Don't worry. It's nothing he hasn't said to me in person."

A sudden stillness comes over the course. Even the trees stop rustling. I glance around, feeling like we're being watched. And not just by one or two people—it seems as though a great crowd is studying us. But there's no one there, and I'm overwhelmed again by the same sensation I had in Murder House: that I am hurtling downward toward my death. Again, the strength drains from my body and I sink to my knees. The instant I do, the earth is solid beneath me once more. My heart still pounds with fear. I look up at Jake and beg him, "I need to know what to do."

Jake kneels next to me. "It's okay, Luz. You're doing what you're supposed to do. What the *kami* want you to do. You're showing respect."

"*Kami?*"

"Spirits. Deities. Ancestors. All of the above. There's no exact English translation. Should we ask them for their help?" Before I can answer, Jake claps his hands sharply, then begins speaking in a casual, conversational tone. "Hello, this is Jake Furusato, great-great-grandson of Eitarō Furusato, who had this shrine built for you. And this is my friend Luz James. We've come to ask for your help."

Jake takes out all the change he has in his pockets and neatly arranges the coins at the edge of the shrine. I take off the opal necklace that Codie gave me and put it next to the coins. Jake nods approval. The loneliness that has haunted me since Codie died disappears. It's like the good moment in Murder House and, for once, I feel as if I am exactly where I am supposed to be.

Jake tips his chin toward the candles. "Tell them what you need."

"Don't they already know?"

"No, this isn't like the Christian god who's everywhere and knows everything. You have to tell them."

I think about what an idiot I'll feel like, speaking to the spirits of the Deigo Tree Golf Course. But one glance at Jake, kneeling beside me, his hands folded, who has shared a secret that could destroy his family, and that fear leaves. "I need help—"

"Get their attention first," Jake interrupts. He mimes clapping.

I clap several times, then begin again. "I would like your help to find out what my sister—"

"Tell them her name, your mom's name, and your Okinawan grandmother's name."

"My sister is Codie James." I like the *kami*. I like that Codie is in the present tense with them. "My mother was born Gena Overholt. Now James. Oh, I forgot to introduce myself. I'm Luz James. My grandmother was Setsuko Overholt. She's Okinawan. Her Okinawan name was Setsuko Uehara. I need to know what I'm supposed to do."

I stop then because what I really want to ask the *kami* about is the girl in the cave. But even here, I can't reveal the full extent of that disturbing vision. Instead, I take the crumpled envelope from my bag, put it down on the cement, and say, "This is the phone number for a *yuta*. Since they're supposed to be able to communicate with the . . . those who are gone, maybe you know whether my mother consulted this person. Maybe you know why. Maybe this *yuta* knows what I'm supposed to do." I look over to Jake.

"State the problem," he advises.

"Should I see the *yuta*? Will this person be able to help me? What if this *yuta* only speaks Japanese?" I glance over at Jake. "Now what?"

"Now we pray."

"Out loud?"

"However you want."

"And then?"

"We wait until they put the answer in our hearts."

I don't know how long we kneel in front of the shrine. Long enough for the sky to lighten to a pearly gray and for streaks of apricot to appear along the eastern horizon.

When he finally stands, Jake picks up the envelope, puts it in his pocket, says, "We'd better get a few hours' sleep. We'll need to be rested tomorrow. I'll make the appointment."

Before I can ask any more questions, Jake's phone buzzes. He checks it and says one word, "Pilgrims."

· TWENTY-SEVEN ·

Back in our sleeping cave that evening, I said nothing about the *Yamato* being sunk and the fleet destroyed. The others probably already know of this tragedy and have been showing true Japanese spirit by not giving voice to such gloomy information. Hatsuko and our friends were unusually quiet and somber; their first day as student nurses must have been as shocking and unsettling as mine had. My sister, however, was the most demoralized. Like the rest of us, Hatsuko had lost weight, but even beyond that, she seemed to be shriveling into a smaller, more frightened person. I tried to coax a smile out of her by saying that it was lucky we'd grown up on a farm with goats and pigs, so that men and their odors weren't such a surprise to us.

Miyoko and Sachiko perked up at this touch of levity. Sachiko, her nose wrinkled in disgust, finally felt free to ask, "Did you have to touch their . . . you know? Down there."

This triggered nervous giggles as we realized that we'd all had to endure the same humiliation. The only one who denied herself the release of our shared humor was the one I'd intended it for, my sister. "Don't laugh at the emperor's soldiers," she snapped at me. "How would you like it if some nurse in the Philippines or Manchukuo mocked our brothers in this way?"

Too late I remembered that Hatsuko had always been excused from cleaning the goat pen and feeding the pigs because the smell alone would make her vomit. I could only imagine how badly what my sensitive sister had experienced that day had affected her.

A bit later, a skinny corporal poked his head into our cave and barked out the order that a new mess had been established to handle the influx of patients and soldiers, and that two of us were to come with him immediately to draw our rations for the day. I jumped up. "Hatsuko, come with me. The air will do us both good."

Hatsuko refused with a weary shake of her head and continued scratching listlessly at the lice tormenting her.

"Mitsue?" I asked. I knew that this day must have been particularly hard on her as well, what with being around so many soldiers who surely reminded her of her dead fiancé. Always struggling to be pleasant, in spite of her sorrow, Mitsue agreed to come with me.

The new kitchen was a fifteen-minute walk away. It had been erected next to a cave that contained a natural spring. There was already a long line when we arrived. As we waited, wooden tubs so huge that they required three men to carry them were hauled out from the cave kitchen to the distribution shack. In the shack a portly mess sergeant with a voice harsh as a crow's squawk yelled orders. His underlings, their faces flushed from the steaming tubs, used shovels to dump rice into the ration pails of those ahead of us.

Mitsue and I each held a pail. Our job was to collect enough rice for the fifty of us in our cave. I was glad that Mitsue had agreed to accompany me; we always received generous portions when she was by my side.

Though it was lovely to be outside on a perfect day in late spring and to feel the sun on my face, I couldn't stop worrying about my sister; she didn't have my ability to put unpleasant thoughts out of her head.

There was always one of two side dishes to accompany the rice, either seaweed or bean paste. I hoped that today we would have bean paste, since Hatsuko preferred it. Somehow I'd try to wangle an extra serving for her. I wanted my strong, noble big sister back, and whispered a prayer for help to Old Jug, the ancestor who Anmā maintained had always taken an interest in our family.

Just as I finished, a group of the newly arrived officers ambled in, talking and joking among themselves. Officers never appeared in the mess line, and we all stiffened at the sight of their swords glinting in the sun. Since their rations were delivered to them, they were obviously simply out for a stroll. In the middle of the group I glimpsed Lieutenant Nakamura and was seized by the certainty that Old Jug had brought him to me in answer to my prayer.

"Lieutenant Nakamura!" I called out.

"What are you doing?" Mitsue hissed, horrified that I was addressing an officer. Everyone's attention snapped my way at this breach of protocol. Nakamura looked over at us. I shoved my pail into Mitsue's free hand, hissed, "Please, cousin, play along. This is for our Hatsuko," and hurried over to the lieutenant.

Fortunately, either Nakamura wasn't as rigid as most of the officers, who gave me fierce scowls, or my guppy face amused him, because he regarded me with a kindly expression as I approached. Bowing deeply, I blurted out the mission I had fabricated. "Please, sir, forgive this impertinent intrusion, but yours is the only name I happen to know, and I am in desperate need of assistance."

"'Desperate'?" he repeated with the hint of a smile.

"Yes, yes, if you could, please come this way." With a shrug toward his friends, Nakamura followed me back to Mitsue, whose expression had gone from puzzlement to annoyance. "My friend needs help carrying our rations back to the others in our chamber," I explained. "A dire necessity is forcing me to leave. Immediately."

He understood at once; dysentery was sweeping the caves. I took my bucket from Mitsue and shoved it into Nakamura's hands.

Mitsue grabbed it back and snapped, "I don't need any help."

I couldn't believe that my cousin was so wrapped up in grief for her dead fiancé that she wouldn't help me out. Fortunately, the gallant lieutenant held out his hand and said, "Please, I insist. It would be my honor to aid you in this small matter, Miss Shimojo."

I was encouraged that, somehow, he already knew Mitsue's name. Still, my cousin hesitated for a long moment and heaved an impatient sigh before she finally handed the bucket over to the lieutenant. At that, I darted off with an urgency that lent credibility to my story. I ran all the way back to our cave, entered breathless, and yelled to Hatsuko, "Quickly! Get ready. Lieutenant Nakamura is coming."

For several seconds, my sister sat frozen, staring at me. When she saw from my expression that Nakamura truly was about to appear, it was as though a current that had been switched off was turned back on. She asked me whether there were any specks of soot on her face from the oily kerosene smoke, and I used the edge of my blouse to clean them all away. Then Hatsuko scrambled about, begging the other girls for a few leaves of tea and some lumps of sugar. Somehow, she managed to have a cup of tea brewing when Nakamura, carrying both pails, arrived. Being the gentleman he was, he stopped and stood aside so that Mitsue might enter first.

The lieutenant's gaze followed my beautiful, bereaved cousin until he caught sight of my sister and saw what I saw: a magically pretty girl whose eyes sparkled and whose cheeks flushed pink as a rose. His bow was especially deep and respectful. My sister returned it, then tilted her head down and to the side, swept her hand with all the fingers pressed together so that it resembled the ivory petal of a lotus blossom, and bade the lieutenant to enter in a voice soft and high as a geisha's. My heart burst with pride; no Japanese noblewoman could have been more elegant than my sister.

Nakamura seated himself. We all knelt in a circle around him and watched the lieutenant drink his cup of tea. He slurped loudly to express his appreciation and compliment my sister, finishing with a sigh of satisfaction, as if he'd just consumed a banquet. Using only the tips of his joined fingers, he carefully passed the empty can his tea had been served in back to Hatsuko and asked, "If it pleases you, I should like to sing a song to express my gratitude."

We all clapped and begged him to sing, but he waited for Hatsuko's permission. Eyes downcast, she nodded and the lieutenant sang.

> Whether I float as a corpse under the waters
> Or sink beneath the grasses of the mountainside,
> I will willingly die for the emperor!

Nakamura's voice, though slightly nasal, was pleasant enough. When he finished, all of us except Mitsue clapped and begged for another. I was pleased to see that Nakamura's eyes instantly leaped to Hatsuko's face to seek her approval. "Hatsuko, what do you think? Would you like another *gunka* to bolster our spirits?"

"Of course," she implored, her voice, filled with new, high trills and a soft breathiness, sounding strange to me. "Your patriotic songs are a gift to us. They are strengthening our love for our emperor."

"As you wish," Nakamura answered in the old-fashioned, formal way that many officers adopted. His voice, however, was strong and direct as he sang.

> Fields burn up, and the time to exterminate has come!
> Wipe out all vicious Americans and Britons!
> These mountains must be our foe's tombs and monuments!

After singing all the *gunka* he knew, the lieutenant asked, "Would you girls like to see proof that we Japanese are destined to rule the world?"

We all competed to show who could agree with the most eagerness.

Nakamura waited for us to quiet down; then he carefully plucked an empty cigarette package from his pocket and held it up triumphantly. In the center of the small white package was the perfect red circle of a rising sun.

"*Lucky. Strike.*" Nakamura touched each foreign word as he pronounced it. "Don't you see? Even the enemy begs for our good fortune and power."

We bounced on our knees, clapped and shouted, "*Banzai!*" considerably buoyed up by the lieutenant's proof of our invincibility. Before he left, his gaze swept the dark corners of the cave until he found Mitsue; when their eyes met, he bowed and my cousin dipped her head. I guessed that Mitsue must have told him about her dead fiancé and he was showing his respect for a fellow soldier in arms.

When Nakamura was gone, all the girls except my sister and Mitsue whispered and giggled like silly children. Hatsuko merely sat with a faraway look on her face, so transported that she even stopped scratching. Mitsue simply sat apart, looking sad. I chastised myself for forcing her into my scheme; obviously Nakamura had brought up painful memories of her dead sweetheart. Still, I went to sleep that night happy that my plan had worked so well. A Lucky Strike, indeed!

· TWENTY-EIGHT ·

Over the next few weeks, Lieutenant Nakamura became a regular visitor to our cave. We needed the bit of cheer he offered, because our work in the wards grew ever more difficult and distasteful. The rooms carved into rock became crowded with patients, both those who had been wounded in battle and the far greater numbers disabled by typhus, dysentery, malaria, and dengue fever. When all the bed planks had been filled, patients were laid directly on the rocky ground. There was no medicine for any of them. No sulfa for infections. No morphine for pain.

They all suffered, but the worst were the tetanus and gangrene patients. Those afflicted with tetanus would bite anything they could lay their hands on, whether it was a rag or another soldier. In the end, their jaws locked together so tightly that it was a struggle to pour a thin stream of water into their mouths, and they groaned deep in their throats as thirst drove them mad. The gangrene patients screamed in unbearable agony as their limbs turned dark and swelled grotesquely, before they finally went rigid and silent.

Even as conditions deteriorated, and their patients needed them more than ever, the regular army nurses from Japan, like Tanaka, took to disappearing with greater and greater frequency. While their patients suffered unendurable agonies, those nurses simply left the wards and gathered secretly in a distant supply closet to smoke cigarettes that they rolled out of newspaper and pine needles. If one of us had the temerity to disturb them to ask whether they would administer an injection or change a dressing, these hard women, many of whom had been prostitutes before enlisting, would subject us to the harshest of tongue-lashings. None harsher than the ones delivered by Head Nurse Tanaka.

No one dared bother Tanaka because of the rumors that she poisoned patients she found too disruptive. I tried not to believe this, but couldn't help thinking of how the young private with dysentery who couldn't control his bowels and constantly soiled himself had died so suddenly in his sleep. As had the gruff old sergeant who bellowed all day long for bedpans, water, food. As had the haughty captain who called Head Nurse a fat slob because, while all her patients were wasting away, she kept getting suspiciously plumper and plumper. He accused her of stealing her patients' food and threatened to have her investigated. That night he, too, died in his sleep.

I could dismiss the rumors that Head Nurse Tanaka was the cause of these deaths, until the roof of our cave collapsed. All of us escaped the cave-in except for a senior girl, Hanashiro, who was one of our best student nurses, renowned for her unfailing cheerfulness. We all worked furiously, bloodying our hands dragging rocks off of her, and, though we did succeed in saving our friend's life, her brain had been damaged. From then on, Hanashiro would wander around with a vacant smile on her face, unable to work or even speak, squatting in front of us with no shame and relieving herself whenever she felt the need.

In honor of the person Hanashiro had once been, we were all, even the officers, kind to her. The only one she seemed to bother was Head Nurse Tanaka, who would rail on about what a disgrace she was and how taxing it was that we all had to watch over Hanashiro so she wouldn't hurt herself, and that, generally, she was a menace to the group. No one paid Head Nurse any attention, since she was always complaining about something. But one night, when Tanaka was on duty, Hanashiro, who was perfectly healthy except for her brain, died in her sleep. From then on I stayed as far from Head Nurse as I could.

· TWENTY-NINE ·

When we return to the front gate of the golf course, we find a group of a dozen Okinawans waiting. Jake exchanges a few words with them, then holds the gate open for the pilgrims who'd texted to let him know they were waiting to enter. "Go on ahead back to the house and get some sleep," he tells me. "I've got to take them to the shrine, then lock up after they leave. It'll be a while."

In the guest room, I clear a bunch of Jake's little sister's dolls off the futon. They look like a tribe of Barbies crossed with space aliens fully accessorized with tiny shoes and purses. I lie down, certain that I won't be able to sleep.

A second later, I'm wandering through a vast open meadow where bison, giraffes, and white cats wearing red capes nibble at the grass. I glance down, and at my feet is the gray-speckled linoleum that covered the floors of one of the three schools I attended when we moved so much during fourth grade. When I look back up, I'm standing in front of the class being introduced as the new girl. An iguana in a tall cage stares at me, one eye goggling forward, the other pivoting around to take in the back view.

Codie appears and begins brushing her hair with a tiny silver fork. With each stroke, her curls and frizz straighten until her hair flows like satin around her head. In the next instant, our grandmother takes the fork and is combing the curls back into Codie's hair. It is not the grandmother I knew, though. Instead, it's Grandma Setsuko as she was in my favorite old photo of her. She'd told us that the black-and-white had been taken at an Okinawan club in the late sixties, early seventies, sometime around when she met my grandfather Eugene. Her eyes are thickly lined; her hair is ratted into a bubble that rises behind the shiny band of ribbon holding it back from the pouf of bangs that fall over her broad forehead. She is planted front and center, gazing adoringly up at the group playing onstage. They're the band from the cover of her favorite album.

Always embarrassed by the gap between her front teeth, my grandmother hides most of her smile with a hand in front of her mouth. Still, the corners of her lips show on either side of her hand. They're painted with a lipstick so pale they seem white. She could have been Elvis Presley's girlfriend instead of Eugene Overholt's. That's the grandmother I see in my dream, who lifts up a curly, unstraightened section of Codie's hair, lowers her head into the unruly curls, and kisses my sister's wavy hair as if each strand were a beautiful flower with a heavenly scent.

"When are you coming back?" I ask my sister, eager to work out the details so that she can return.

Before Codie can answer, brown water splashes against my ankles and the taste of caramelized sugar fills my mouth. In that instant information way that dreams have, I know that the droplets come from bullets being shot into the puddle of mud at my feet. I know that my sister and I are being hunted and we have to find safety before the planes come again. I grab her hand and pull her along. But no matter how fast we run, the bullets stitching a deadly seam in the earth follow right behind us. The seam fills with blood, but I know that if I can only hang on to my sister until the bullets make ten thousand red stitches, we will be saved. We run harder, but the dirt turns to mud that sucks away our frantic strides until we're not moving at all.

I drag my sister forward and then I shelter her body under mine when a thousand dragonflies attack us like angry wasps. When I rise up, however, all I find beneath myself is an amputated leg. I remember that my sister is dead, until she calls to me from another room in an empty house stacked with boxes. I can't tell whether we're moving in or out. I search for Codie, but one room leads to another in an endless warren. Finally, I look up and see her. She is outside on the vast lawn, exposed; the planes will come and she will be killed, and it will be my fault. I was supposed to take care of her; I promised our mother. Frozen in place, I call to her, but no sound comes from my screaming mouth. My sister twirls slowly beneath a rain of crimson blossoms, trampling the flowers at her feet into a red stain, her hair a rippling curtain swirling around her.

Maybe I stopped sleeping because I hated to wake up crying. I thought that the worst mornings were the ones when I was certain that I'd been able to convince Codie not to go and she never enlisted and we were together again. On those mornings, for three seconds after I opened my eyes, Codie would be there, absolutely there. The fourth or fifth second, though, was worse than when the chaplains came, because I'd be crashing straight down from the dream happiness. This, though—waking up in Jake's sun-blasted guest room being stared at by dolls with bugged-out alien eyes, certain that my sister is about to be killed and I have to save her and I don't know how—this is worse.

· THIRTY ·

I'm in the kitchen when Jake comes in from guiding another group of pilgrims to the shrine. An older gentleman in a white guayabera shirt is with him.

"Luz, meet Shingo-san."

We exchange bows as Jake explains, "He's agreed to stay here to help any other villagers who come so that I can take you to the appointment with the *yuta*."

"You already made an appointment for me?"

My surprise surprises Jake. "I said I would."

"But won't your family be upset? Didn't they leave you in charge?"

"They did, and this is what I'm deciding to do. We gotta book, or we'll be late."

Outside, as we walk to the car, I see that what I'd thought was your average tribal tattoo encircling his right biceps turns out to be a linked series of what look like Chinese throwing stars. The black ink looks so good against his tan skin that I touch one of the circular symbols. Trying to hide how much I just wanted to touch his skin, I ask what the symbol means.

We stop next to the car, the metal warm against my back as Jake studies the tattoo, his finger rubbing against mine where we're both touching it. "It's the *hidari-gomon*. It used to be the royal crest of the Ryukyu Kingdom." He's so close, I can feel his breath against my cheek. My heart thuds. His other hand rises. I think he's going to kiss me. Instead he holds the keys between us and asks, "Can you drive? I'm trashed from no sleep."

"Jake, you can just tell me where the appointment is. You don't have to come with me. I'll figure something out. You don't have to go to all this trouble, leaving the course and everything."

"Actually, yeah, I do. The *kami* put it in my heart that I have to help you."

"They did?"

"Yeah, when we were at the shrine. Also, I have to go because the *yuta* doesn't speak English." As he heads for the passenger door, Jake adds, "Mostly, though, I'll be punished if I don't do what the *kami* want." He says it in such a matter-of-fact way, like he's just told me that gravity will make a person fall down and bump his ass, that it ends the conversation, and we get in the Surfmobile.

Even without the surfboards that he usually keeps hidden under the blue tarp in the back, the car smells like seawater and board wax. I start up the engine. "Which way?"

"The A&W south on 58."

"Like the root-beer stand? This *yuta* person is meeting me at an A&W?"

"That's what she said."

Jake is asleep before I can ask whether that's weird.

I drive at fifteen miles per hour through the wide streets lined with sprawling green lawns. The housing area slips past in slow motion, like I'm on a train gradually leaving a station that I will never return to. Sprinklers click through their orderly arcs, throwing water onto the ruler-straight yards. A pack of boys riding BMX bikes stand on the pedals and lean forward into their adventures. An elderly Okinawan lady, most of her face covered by the scarf tying a broad-brimmed hat to her head, pushes an ancient lawn mower up a steep hill. In a playground, little boys in baggy shorts, their noses peeling from sunburns, ignore the swings and jungle gym to jump out of the cockpit of the husk of an old fighter jet that is the centerpiece of the area.

The hot, humid wind blowing in the station wagon's open windows lifts the hair off my neck. I zone out, and images from last night's dreams fill my head. I don't understand why Codie and I were running from planes strafing the earth behind us. Or what the amputated leg was about. Or why those dreams felt so real, as if they'd happened to us, when the only memory I'm certain is an actual memory is the one where my grandmother buries her nose in Codie's curls, because she really did used to do that. With both of us. She'd smell our clouds of curly hair as if each strand were a beautiful flower. As if we, her granddaughters, were the loveliest beings ever born. That feeling, of being adored, was what Codie and I got from *Anmā* and no one else.

We leave through Gate Two. When we pass through that opening in the miles of chain-link fence encircling Kadena Air Base, we go from a world where the rules are black-and-white into claustrophobic chaos, and all I have time to think about is driving. I've had so little opportunity to get behind the wheel on Okinawa that when I pull out into Okinawan traffic and an armada of tiny clown cars hurtles directly at me, the stomach-dropping wrongness of driving on the left side hits me with full force.

On the off-base side of the fence, a line of Okinawan protesters wearing white headbands and carrying signs marches back and forth. Most of the signs are in red characters. A few are in English. "NO U.S. BASE!!" "WW2 OVER IN 1945!!" "WHAT IF OKINAWA OCCUPY ONE-FIFTH OF US?!?!" A bullhorn crackles and one of the protesters yells at us in Japanese.

I hear a crinkling coming from the back of the car. In the rearview mirror I catch a glimpse of Kirby emerging from beneath the blue tarp. Hair spiked up on one side where he slept on it, Kirby gapes at the protesters and comments, "Dudes, you lost the war. Deal with it."

Jake sits up, going directly from sleep to fully awake. Apparently used to Kirby appearing without warning in the back of his car, he says, "You did not seriously just say that."

"What? That you all lost the war? Truth hurts, brah."

"Kirby, we've been over this before, remember? Okinawa was essentially a colony of Japan."

"So you keep saying, but colonists can kill them some motherfuckers too. Ask Benjamin Franklin. He fried some redcoat ass with electricity."

Jake catches my eye and we exchange indulgent smiles, like we're taking our developmentally delayed cousin out for the day.

"Look at that, boy-san." Kirby points to the businesses lining the streets outside the base: tattoo parlors, bars, strip clubs, restaurants with giant cheeseburgers and tacos painted on them, clothing stores selling oversize gangsta clothes, and clubs blasting aggressive hip-hop with bitches-hoes-suck-coochie-cock lyrics. "Bet them dudes is happy we're here. All those places'd be belly-up tomorrow if the bases closed. Okinawa's economy would totally tank."

"Yeah, Kernshaw, what a blow it would be to lose all those high-paying stripper and tattoo artist jobs. To say nothing of the great BX cashier, gate guard, and lawn boy positions."

"Hey, Furusato, glass houses, dude. You and your family haven't done too bad sucking off the teat of the USAF."

Jake just shakes his head, but I say, "Lucky Charms, you don't know what you're talking about. You really don't."

Kirby, distractible as a lemur, rolls his head from side to side, wings his right arm out, stretches his shoulder. "When are you going to get some foam back up in here?"

"Sorry if the accommodations aren't up to your standards, m'lord."

"Inflatable mattress, that's what you need."

"Not getting too shit-faced to make it home to your own bed's what you need."

"Naw, I like it back here. Like camping, but you don't got to wipe your ass with leaves."

"Kirbs." Jake laughs, his irritation gone. "You are so worth the price of admission."

"So, where are we going this fine day at hungry thirty?"

"'We'?"

"Why? What? This a date? That it? You two on a date?"

"No," Jake and I answer together.

"Did you officially break up with Christy?"

"Kernshaw. Shut up."

"What? You've only been talking about it since, like, sophomore year or something."

"Seriously. Shut. Up."

"Well, if it's not a date, then I can come, right?"

"No, you can't come," Jake answers.

I spot the orange-and-brown oval A&W sign and flip on the turn signal.

"A and Dubs! Oh, hells, yes! I'm so hungry I could eat a gas station hot dog. I'ma get me one of them Melty Riches. Drive this piece of shit like you stole it, girl."

"You're not sitting with us," Jake warns.

"Wouldn't if you begged me, bro-bro."

I pull into the parking lot of one of the many A&Ws on the island. Almost vanished from its American homeland, the classic fifties franchise is inexplicably popular on Okinawa. In the drive-in section, an Okinawan carhop in an orange polo and orange-and-brown-striped skirt, the ponytail of her black hair squirting from the back of an orange ball cap, hurries out with a silver tray. I park in the lot near a mechanical, potbellied bear wearing an orange tam, licking his chops with an orange tongue, and waving a happy welcome.

"You got a shirt back here, brah?" Kirby asks, plucking his tank top away from his spindly chest. "I'm all gym locker up in here."

"You left one back there somewhere after your last sleepover."

"Coo. Meet you inside."

The restaurant is loud with Japanese pop music, the clatter and beep of food prep machines, the happy chatter of customers. Covies of schoolgirls in sailor blouses and tiny white ankle socks lean over tables, gossiping and slurping frothy drinks. Mothers sit on benches outside and watch their children crawl through the giant hamster tubes of the orange play structure. A cluster of old men in guayaberas occupies a booth in the back, sipping coffee, passing judgment on the scene, nodding and laughing at one another's comments.

"How are we supposed to find her?"

"She said she'd find us."

Just as we slide into a booth by the big windows facing onto the parking lot, Jake's phone rings. He checks the number, jumps to his feet. I assume it's Christy. "I'd better . . ." He points outside as he answers while walking out the door. Kirby, buttoning his shirt, passes Jake on his way in. Guessing who Jake's talking to, Kirby pokes him with an accusing finger until Jake karate-chops him with his free hand. Kirby comes in, his shirt buttoned wrong, one side hanging down half a foot more than the other, and slides in across from me. "So, are you and Jake together?"

"'Together'? What's that even mean?"

"It means his girlfriend is ripping him a new one right now because someone probably saw you two together and called her."

"No reason for that."

"Really? So Jake wouldn't kick my ass if I hit on you?"

"*I'd* kick your ass if you hit on me."

"Harsh, Caboose, very, very harsh."

"What did you just call me?"

"Caboose? Cabooskie? That was your nickname, right?"

"Yeah, but no one ever called me that except—"

"Your sister. I know." He stares at me, realizes something, and explodes, "Fuck, no! You really don't remember. All this time I thought you were just being cool."

"Cool? What was I being cool about?"

"If you don't remember, forget it."

"No, tell me. You knew Codie?"

"God, you really don't remember." He shrugs. "You *were* pretty young."

"Tell me."

"Jeez, this is embarrassing."

"Isn't embarrassing your specialty?"

"Okay, remember the Sheppard NCO pool?"

"Yeah, but I was like nine or ten when we lived on Sheppard. Oh, no. Now I remember. That was you? You were such a shrimp. How did you get so tall?" And then all the details of the incident he doesn't want me to recall come back and I explode. "Yes! That was you! That was totally you!"

"God, Luz, I was a kid. I didn't know what I was doing."

"What didn't you know you were doing?" Jake asks as he slides into the booth next to me.

"He showed my sister his wiener at the pool on Sheppard."

"Get. Out."

"I didn't make her touch it or anything."

"Yeah," Jake says. "Probably because she couldn't find it. Thought you dropped a Hot Tamale in your swimsuit."

Maybe it's because Kirby is such a complete goober that talking to him is like talking to a big, slobbering, but ultimately lovable dog. Or maybe it's just such a thrill to meet someone who knew Codie that, like with Jacey, talking about her, thinking about her doesn't hurt. "Codie sort of actually liked you."

"She did? *Now* you tell me." Kirby shakes his head. "Codie James. Jesus, she was like my sexual awakening. She was like this perfect anime warrior princess. Badass but so cute."

I grin; it's the perfect description.

"I used to come out of the pool all pruned up and shivering, and I'd lie on my stomach on the hot cement and put a towel over my head and watch her just being so cute that I kind of wanted to squeeze her to death. Just *aaarrrr*. She kicked my ass after I . . . You know."

"Say it, perv," Jake interjects. "Exposed yourself to her."

Kirby slugs Jake on the biceps. Hard.

"Yeah, she told me." I smile at the memory of Codie going krav maga on the skinny white boy. "Also told me that the carpet matched the drapes."

"There wasn't any carpet! I was a kid."

"I was messing with you. She never said that."

"She scared the shit out of me. Said what I did was a federal offense, since it happened on federal property, and I'd go to Leavenworth if she told your mom."

"No! She never told me that. That's good."

"She was such a badass. She was killer with all those Oriental martial arts. I could totally see her enlisting."

The happy-memory vibe screeches to a halt. He hadn't known Codie at all. "Really? Because I couldn't. I never could." My tone is so weird and intense that no one says anything after that. We pull menus out of the holder and study them until a waitress approaches and asks, "You look *yuta?*"

"*Yuta*, yes. *Hai!*" I answer eagerly.

She holds a tray with a mug of root beer and burger off-greasing onto wrapping printed in Japanese with the words "Melty," "Chubby," and "Lite" sprinkled around, points me to the private meeting room down a short hall, and says something in Japanese to Jake.

"She's waiting for you back there," Jake translates, giving the girl some bills and taking the tray. "We're supposed to bring this to her."

"I'll pay you back."

"Don't worry," Jake says as we leave Kirby at the booth ordering half the menu. "It's good karma."

"Okinawans have karma, too?"

"Everyone has karma."

The back room is deserted except for a grandmotherly lady, sitting with her hands folded in front of her, at a booth covered in orange Formica. The *yuta* has short, frizzy hair and is wearing glasses so enormous they cover half her face and magnify her round cheeks and the pouches beneath her hooded eyes. When she spots us, she waves for us to come over, then turns her entire attention to the order that Jake slides in front of her, peeling the top bun aside to check the toppings on her burger. The pineapple, onions, cheese, and bacon meet with her approval. She takes a bite as she motions for us to sit. As we do, she leans forward, grabs the straw poking from her root beer, presses her lips together in a prim seam, and pipelines half the mug down while staring intently at me. Not that I necessarily would have liked a séance atmosphere with incense burning, but the overhead fluorescent lights, poppy music, and the *yuta*'s obvious fondness for all-you-can-drink root beer in a frosted mug don't build my confidence that she will be any help at all.

I expect her to pull out a deck of tarot cards or take my hand and read my palm. Maybe a crystal ball, something with tea leaves. Instead, she unlooses a clattering barrage of Japanese.

"She needs your list," Jake translates.

"List of what?"

"Ancestors," Jake says, as if it were the most obvious thing in the world. "All *yutas* start with the list. Sorry, I should have told you that."

Jake tells her that I don't have a list. The *yuta* looks perplexed but reaches into a shiny vinyl tote bag printed with the face of a smiling Corgi dog and extracts a notepad and ballpoint pen that she shoves toward me.

"She wants you to write down as many of your family members that you are related to by blood as you can remember. She can't help you without the list. Just write all the names you can think of."

"Does she read English?"

"She doesn't need to. She senses from the list who is unhappy."

The *yuta* adds a few other specifications.

Jake nods and tells me, "She needs you to go as far back as you can. Preferably at least six generations. Married and maiden names of blood relatives."

"You're kidding."

I make the list starting with Codie and go back through my mother and father, and the few other relatives whose names I've even ever heard. As I write, the *yuta* listens to the music and studies the ceiling tiles while she chews her pineapple burger, as serene as a cow in a pasture working her cud. The list is pathetically short; I think of Jake's house, of the constellations of ancestors dancing around his family altar and feel like an orphan compared to him. When I finish, I twirl the sheet around and slide it back across the table.

As she studies the first few names, her cud-chewing expression tightens dramatically. She pushes the burger aside, carefully wipes her hands, screwing each finger into a napkin to clean all the grease away. When she's finished, she squares her shoulders, closes her eyes, chants softly to herself under her breath, and lets her hands hover above the list like someone waiting for the spirits to make the planche of a Ouija board move.

Her eyes still closed, her finger comes to rest, time and again, on Codie's name. Each time her fingers contact the letters, her eyes screw shut even tighter and her entire face contracts in an expression of pain. She opens her eyes and strokes Codie's name, her fingers resting on the letters and smoothing them as gently as a mother soothing a fretful child.

I clutch Jake's arm. "What? Ask her what she sees."

Jake starts to speak, but she holds up a silencing finger, bends forward, clamps her lips around the straw, sucks down the rest of her root beer, shoves the empty mug toward Jake, and dispatches him for a refill. Waiting until the door closes behind him, she pushes her trash to the side, and holds her hands out until I place my palms atop hers. She cradles my hands and studies the ceiling tiles some more, her eyes occasionally flickering. She nods as if the transmission had ended, lets go of my hand, taps Codie's name, and says, "Cry. Make sick. Sad."

"My sister? Codie? Codie is crying? Why? Why is she sad? 'Make sick'? What does that mean? Is she making me sick?" The old lady has no idea what I'm asking. "My mother? My *anmā*." I throw out one of the few Okinawan words I know. "Did my *anmā* tell you to say that? Did you speak to my mother?" I pull out the crumpled envelope and point to what I hope is my mother's name written in characters on the first line of the address. "You know? Did she call you?" I pantomime making a phone call as I point emphatically toward the *yuta*.

She studies the characters and shakes her head no.

In all my pantomiming, the surveillance photo falls out of the bag. The *yuta* notices and reaches across the table for it. As she studies the photo the furrows deepen on her forehead.

I tap the street corner dude. "Do you know this man?"

Instead of dismissing him, she tilts her head back in order to study the photo through the bottom part of her glasses. When she gets the image in focus, her expression curdles even more. Her lip curling up, she looks from me back down to the photo; there's something about the photo that has upset, disgusted her.

"What? Did my mother show you this photo? Do you know this man?" Even as I ask the question, an answer begins forming in my mind. I shove it away as less than a distant possibility, the far-off sound of thunder in the summer that does not signal rain.

When Jake returns, the *yuta* hurriedly shoves the photo back and, with rapid, emphatic waving gestures, orders me to hide it away. Without knowing why, I feel ashamed as I stuff the photo back into my bag. Jake slides the refill in front of the *yuta*, who reattaches to the straw and suckles like a baby pig with a bottle. She finishes with a gasp then proceeds to unleash a nonstop stream of Japanese on Jake.

Jake listens, interjecting crisp head nods and several explosive *Hai!*s to indicate that he's following her. When she's done, Jake turns to me. "She can't help you because your list is incomplete. You have to get more names of ancestors, blood relatives, otherwise she can't give you a full reading."

The *yuta* nods vigorously as Jake translates, pausing only to reach over, grab a stack of sugar packets and a handful of creamers from a box on the table, stuff them into her tote, and extract a tissue-thin envelope that she pushes across the table to me.

I open it and a bill for sixteen thousand yen flutters out. I have all the commissary money my mother gave me in my bag, and I hand her nearly two hundred dollars. Jake sees the money, explodes in annoyed

Japanese, takes most of the bills back, and hands them to me. "That's an insane amount. She didn't even give you a decent reading."

The *yuta* gathers up the remaining bills, scoots to the end of the bench, and stands. She is even shorter than she appeared while sitting, barely reaching my shoulder. She pushes past me and rushes out. Leaving Jake to collect Kirby, I intercept the *yuta* outside in the parking lot, next to the mechanical bear. "Wait, you can't leave." She hurries away from me, tacking toward a bus stop with a red clay-tile roof next to the highway. I run after her and block her escape. "You have to help me."

She looks up, goggling, the big lenses an aquarium in front of her eyes, and says, "Need list. List too short. Find all ancestor."

"I don't know any more ancestors. Did you talk to Codie? My sister. Did my sister have a message for me? I can get more money. *Takusan yen.* You picked my sister's name out, and then you got an expression on your face like you saw something horrible. What does my sister want me to do? Why did I see that dead girl in the cave?" I scrape my brain for phrases my grandmother used to say, press my hands together, and plead, "*Onegai,* please, tell me what I need to do?"

She scribbles something on a scrap of paper, thrusts it at me, and rushes away to catch the bus hissing to a stop on the edge of the highway.

Jake appears at my elbow, takes the slip of paper from my hand, and studies it. "It's the name and address of her teacher in Naha who's a master *yuta.* I've actually heard my aunts talking about her."

"But won't she need the same list of ancestors?"

"Maybe not. She's much more on the spiritual side. Supposedly just being in her presence, it, you know"—he pauses, his voice becoming gentle—"helps."

"Even if you're a total psycho—" I'm surprised and embarrassed when a sob almost hijacks my attempt at humor. I choke it back as fast as I can.

Jake puts his hand on my back in a comforting way and whispers, "*Shi, shi, shi.*" The hushing syllable—*she,* not *shhh*—strikes a chord of deeply buried memory, and I recall another voice whispering it into my ear long ago, when I was very young and had hurt myself. I struggle to remember who it was who had once dried my tears.

Just as it almost comes back to me, Kirby struts across the lot holding his phone above his head like a trophy. Jake pulls his hand away as Kirby announces, "*Gomen nasai*, young lovers, but this is where I'm going to have to leave you. Shortie's on her way right now to pick me up."

When neither Jake nor I take the bait and ask who the "shortie" is, Kirby whines, "Don't you want to know who she is?"

"Just the luckiest girl in the world, right?" Jake answers.

"You got that right," Kirby agrees gleefully. His thumbs popping across his phone's keyboard, he mutters, "Yeah, baby, daddy's gonna beat them cakes like Betty Crocker."

"Ew," I say. "Just ew."

Jake puts his hand out, I give him the keys, and we walk back to the car. "Kirbs, you coming?" Jake yells.

"Seriously, I got a hot date coming to pick me up."

"Don't talk about your mother like that," Jake riffs.

"Watch and learn, son," Kirby yells back. "Watch and learn."

Before he starts the engine, Jake advises me, "Keep your phone handy. Kirby will be calling any minute for us to come back and get him 'cause his 'shortie's' car broke down or got hit by an asteroid or something."

As we pull out of the A&W, I glance back just in time to see Jacey turn into the parking lot.

Jake checks the rearview mirror. "I did not see that coming."

"No kidding," I agree, stunned.

"What do you think? Is Kirby her act of charity for the month?"

"Or her total psychotic break with reality."

"More like."

As we head south to Naha, I zone out for a moment, stare at the clouds stacking up in an indigo sky, and let myself sink into the luxurious feeling of someone being on my side, someone looking out for me. As soon as I identify the source of my contentment, I realize how undeserved and inexplicable it is. "Jake, seriously, you can just tell me how to get to that address and put me on a bus to Naha."

He looks over, gives me a slow smile, and asks, "Now, why would I want to do that?"

I don't know whether Jake truly believes that his ancestors have ordered him to help me, or if he does want to sleep with me. The only thing that comes across for certain is that he actually wants to be with me. The instant I accept that, a remembered scent of Pond's cold cream, green tea, and a not unpleasant, vinegary body odor overwhelms me, and I recall that, of course, the person who used to comfort me as I sat in her lap and she whispered, "*Shi, shi, shi*. No cry," was Grandma Setsuko.

· THIRTY-ONE ·

Most of the month of May blurred into a never-ending round of too much work and too little sleep and food. And far, far too little water. An instant after the rain stopped, the moisture all disappeared, sucked away by the coral and limestone of our rocky island. And although every surface in the cave was damp, all the moisture, contaminated by salt or human waste, was undrinkable. Though it seemed futile in the face of the round-the-clock bombing, we continued to set out whatever container we could lay our hands on to collect rainwater. Invariably, we found them either filled with dirt or completely overturned by the constant explosions. Or, worst of all, smashed to bits. So we lived with constant thirst and hunger.

One thing did happen near the end of the month, however, to brighten the drudgery: Hatsuko and I received a letter. All mail from overseas had ceased long ago, when the enemy cut off our shipping lanes. Even within the island, it was impossible to communicate with our families left behind. This letter, however, was delivered directly to us by Kenta Higa, our oldest living brother's best friend. Kenta, a handsome boy with fine, long limbs and hair that shone as if it were lacquered, had been sent home from the Philippines when the leprosy he'd contracted there had worn his fingers and toes to nubs. After he delivered the letter to our cave, he left us and continued on, making his way to the Airakuen leper colony where he would live out what remained of his days. We waved good-bye from the safety of the cave opening as Kenta walked away in broad daylight, his stride still strong and straight, with no apparent concern for the planes buzzing through the sky above his head.

Her hands trembling, Hatsuko carefully unfolded the tissue-thin paper that doubled as an envelope. "It's from Takashi." We both had always idolized our second brother. Where Ichirō had been the most handsome of the boys, Takashi was always the smartest. I pressed my fingers against my lips to silence the little yips of joy breaking forth, and Hatsuko read.

"'Dear Sisters, Since I am certain that nothing could have stopped my hardheaded little Tamiko from joining First Sister, I know that wherever this letter finds you that you will be together. So I send you both greetings from a spot on the Pacific Ocean that I am not allowed to divulge. I am in the top level of the "silkworm shelves," what we call our bunks because we are stacked in here so tightly. We are suffocating with the heat and sick as dogs from the waves batting us about. Yet I couldn't be happier, for guess who occupies the two shelves beneath mine? Your brothers Mori and Hiroyuki.'"

We gasped with delight. Not only were our brothers alive, they were together. We both covered our mouths then, and tears spilled down over our fingers.

"Go on! Go on!" I finally urged Hatsuko.

"'Mori has stopped vomiting long enough to send his greetings.'"

Hatsuko and I laughed. Mori was even more squeamish than Hatsuko. As a boy he threw up at the smell of a rotten papaya.

"'Hiroyuki has stopped singing now long enough to do the same.'"

We shook our heads. That was our Hiroyuki, always ready with a song or a joke. He had the carefree temperament of our mother's family. Hatsuko's and Mori's nervous stomachs came from our father's.

"'Our Okinawan good luck has continued to hold, and all three of us have been transferred back to the headquarters of the 2nd Army at a city on the mainland, the name of which I am not permitted to divulge. There we will be part of the defense of all of southern Japan.'"

Hatsuko gently pressed the letter to her chest. "They've done it, Tami-chan," she exulted. "They've been accepted as real Japanese, sent to defend the mainland. Father must be so proud. It is all he's ever wanted."

"And Mother must be happy, because they are together and will be safe on the mainland."

"Yes, no enemy has ever invaded the homeland."

"Read the rest! Read the rest!"

"There isn't much more. He asks, 'How are Mother and Father? We have sent several letters but have received no reply. I know that conditions don't allow you and Tamiko to write, but we three brothers are so hungry for news from home.'" Hatsuko looked up at me, stricken. "But we have written. All those letters before the mail stopped. Did they not receive any of them?"

I shook my head and she continued. "'In closing I will leave you both with a selection from the Imperial Rescript for Soldiers and Sailors that always heartens me: "Obligation is heavier than the mountains but death is lighter than a feather. Do not disgrace yourself by being captured alive, but kill yourself first." Mori, Horuyuki, and I send you our best wishes and ask for a letter in return as soon as your duties allow. From Second Brother, Takashi.'"

"They're safe," Hatsuko exulted.

"They're safe and Mother and Father are safe," I added. "I just know it."

Hatsuko didn't break her vow never to speak of our parents, but she did blink away tears and nod her head.

We read and reread Takashi's letter so many times that the thin paper became limp from the dampness of the cave and spotted with black where flakes of soot landed on it.

· THIRTY-TWO ·

The next morning when I reported for duty, Head Nurse Tanaka informed me that the surgery ward was swamped and she had assigned me to assist with operations.

"But I've had no surgical training," I objected. "Really, I've had no training of any kind."

"Do your best. Show true Japanese spirit, and don't disappoint the emperor." With those words, she retreated to join the other nurses in the supply cave.

I had avoided the surgery ward because it frightened me with its glaring horror-movie lighting. Weeks had passed since the hospital had had any supplies of aspirin, much less morphine or ether. As I made my way through the maze of tunnels that led to the surgery ward, shrieks of agony echoed out. They grew even more piercing when I entered and saw that where there had been just three operating tables before, now six were crammed into the same space. All of them were being used. The shadows of the doctors and nurses bent over patients danced across the cave walls as if they were demons capering before a fire.

"You!" A nurse with a face like a dried gourd and a smock splattered with blood yelled at me. "Come help us here! Hold his leg down!"

A soldier, naked except for his loincloth, thrashed on the table. It had grown unusual to see a patient move. Their rations had been reduced to two servings a day of gruel so thin it was little more than cloudy water, and most of them had only enough energy to lie on their bunks, hollow-eyed and filled with despair. The patient thrashing on the table was as handsome as Ichirō, my first brother, who had been drowned by a vengeful spirit on the third day of Obon. A strap around the patient's waist held the young man's torso in place, but he still flailed his limbs. Feeling as if my hands belonged to someone else, I clutched the soldier's ankle. He screamed as the doctor poked his gloved fingers into a gaping wound so deep that the femur showed through the blood.

"We can't save it," the doctor barked. "Prepare to amputate."

"No! No! No!" the young soldier screamed. "No. Please let me die! Let me die!"

"Stop disgracing yourself, your family, and our emperor," the doctor ordered.

"Yes, yes, yes," the soldier muttered, weeping uncontrollably.

For a moment, as the doctor began, I could hear the bone being cut into; then that sound was drowned out as the soldier's whimpers rose to the howling shrieks of a beast that faded away until a sharp pain in my upper arm brought them back. I returned to my senses to find the nurse with the gourd face pinching me as hard as she could.

"Don't you dare faint," she commanded me.

I gripped the soldier's leg and he writhed beneath my hands like a python. Time seemed to derail like a film that had unlocked from its sprocket. The soldier's mouth still gaped open, but his screams no longer reached my ears. In fact, all sounds fell away and a blessed silence blanketed me, until an insistent voice ordered, "Take the leg away."

The nurse jabbed a sharp elbow into my side and repeated her command. "Stop your daydreaming! Take the leg away."

She laughed when I looked from her to the leg and found that the soldier was no longer attached to it. "What's wrong with you? Didn't you notice that he'd stopped struggling? Come on! Come on! Get it out of here. That leg's of no use to anyone anymore."

I staggered out of the cave, not able to understand how a limb could feel as if it weighed more than an entire body.

"Dump it there," a soldier with a shovel barked at me from the safety of a shallow cave, where he was digging graves for the bodies piled next to the opening. I laid the leg down carefully, but when I straightened back up nothing around me made sense. I wondered why *Anmā* had allowed the pigs' pens to become so filthy that their rank odor made me gag. And why hadn't this muddy field that surrounded me been planted? At this time of year, it should be lined with neat rows of sugarcane and sweet potatoes poking chartreuse buds out of the dark earth.

"Idiot!" A harsh voice exploded the word in my ear as strong arms closed around me and dragged me into the cave. A bomb detonated only a few meters from where I had been standing. The grave digger threw his body over mine to shield me from the spray of rocks and gravel that pelted us.

"What's wrong with you?" he asked when the debris stopped falling. "Are you deaf? Didn't you hear me yelling at you?"

I almost asked him where my mother was. But abruptly, the film that had come unspooled began running at its proper speed again, and I was in a cave filled with graves, and *Anmā* and our green fields of sweet potatoes were far, far away.

· THIRTY-THREE ·

Damn, I forgot about all this mess," Jake says when a man with a hard hat atop his scarf-wrapped head appears, waving a red flag on a stick, detouring traffic around the massive road construction project up ahead. The diverted traffic funnels into a clogged bypass.

"Back route," Jake mutters before whipping a screeching U-turn that leaves drivers honking and swerving out of his way.

Jake switches on the radio. An Okinawan singer warbles out a tune, accompanied by several ukuleles. The song ends and two deejays, a man and a woman, come on. The man barks out aggressive sentences in Japanese. The woman giggles a lot as she chatters away in high-pitched baby talk. Whatever they're bantering about makes Jake snort and shake his head. He stops laughing, though, when we come to a halt at a light next to a vending machine, with its perky sound track and *Close Encounters* lights selling drinks right next to a massive cement structure in the shape of a turtle shell.

"That is so wrong," he mutters, speeding away. "I can't believe the fucking Japanese put one of their fucking machines next to a family's tomb."

The fucking Japanese. I try to figure out Jake's animosity. Isn't Okinawa a prefecture of Japan? Isn't he Japanese? I don't ask, but it's like hearing a Californian, or an Iowan, talk about fucking Americans like they belonged to a whole other country. He snaps off the radio.

We make a bewildering number of turns until we're in an Okinawa I've never seen before. The roads narrow and traffic dwindles to nothing. English disappears entirely from the signs. We pass through a succession of small towns and villages. Houses and businesses crowd in to the very edge of the road. Tanks for collecting water sit atop the flat roofs. Water rationing is in effect across the entire southern half of the island, with supplies being shut off entirely every other day. High concrete walls and bars across the windows protect buildings from the flying debris and wind damage of a possible typhoon. The rare traditional Okinawan house with a red-tiled roof and a pair of ceramic *shiisā* dogs guarding the gate stands out.

Big, round mirrors at intersections keep Jake from colliding with oncoming cars. Brightly lit vending machines pop up everywhere on an empty stretch of road beside a field planted with pineapple bushes. Next to a bus stop on a deserted stretch of road between two towns, we stop at a red light and the machine on the corner there chirps out a greeting to us in Japanese.

Jake's back route leads to a road that hugs the eastern coastline off to our right. Waves break against a seawall protected by thousands of loosely stacked, pyramid-shaped chunks of concrete. In the distance, immense freighters—black and rust monsters—inch across the far horizon. We climb a long hill that falls away steeply down to the ocean in a series of steep black cliffs. Beyond them the East China Sea glitters in the sun. The shifting aquas and jades darken to a hard Prussian blue where the Pacific stretches out toward China.

Naha appears. From a distance it looks like a city made of white building blocks. An armada of miniature vehicles and skinny men on scooters riding with their knees cocked out buzz past us. Traffic picks up on the multilane highway and we are swept into the surge flowing toward the capital of the Ryukyu Islands.

On the outskirts of the city, strip malls pop up. Mama-san stores selling dried squid jerky and *bentō* boxed lunches mix with Starbucks and McDonald's. Two-headed speaker horns for typhoon alerts are nailed high on utility poles. A round, five-story emporium towers over the small businesses. It is crowned with tall letters that announce SLOT & PACHINKO.

As we move from the gray outskirts, the city rises up around us, bustling in a sunshiny, tropical way as the streets turn into wide boulevards lined with stately palms and broad sidewalks. Workers balancing on a scaffold seven floors above wear white hard hats and what look like long harem pants. A mailman with an official red lockbox above the rear wheel of his scooter weaves through traffic.

A big sign announces that we are on Okinawa's Miracle Mile, Kokusai-dōri, International Street, heart of the shopping district. The city that was white from a distance is pastel at street level. Shops with clear plastic awnings cast candy-colored squares of pink, yellow, baby blue light onto the passersby strolling past. A two-story-tall, splay-footed green gecko wriggles up the side of a store. Jake parks in the first lot we come to.

I pay the attendant while Jake studies the address, consults his phone, gets oriented; then we head off. The stores nearby cater to Japanese tourists, offering a king's ransom of Hello Kitty merchandise next to fierce rows of red clay *shiisā* dogs, all wearing sunglasses. Perched on the second floor of the souvenir store nearest us is a sculpture the size of a Dumpster of the Japanese lucky totem, a white cat with empty black eyes and big red ears. The cat with the dead eyes waves one motorized paw, beckoning customers to enter. On my past trips to the Kokusai-dōri, the sidewalks have been packed. The Obon festival has emptied the town, and we stroll easily past stores, many of them closed, with signs in Japanese and English saying they're off for the holiday.

We pass slender businessmen in white shirts tucked into black slacks, swarms of giggling, gossiping schoolgirls in pigtails pointing to clothes in store windows, and Japanese tourists in floppy hats and flowing cotton vacation clothes. They're all dwarfed by the occasional American serviceman, hair too short, nose burned red.

I follow Jake onto a covered street that has a green sign accented with white doves arcing over the entrance. In the sign's center, a translation of the characters—"Heiwa-dōri, Peace Street"—is printed in English. Inside, a high, vaulted skeleton of silvery steel, covered by a curved glass roof, encloses the maze of tiny shops and booths crammed together beneath it. Locals shuffling through the labyrinth in plastic shower shoes outnumber tourist shoppers. Shops sell more work clothes than aloha shirts and swim trunks. Dresses and trousers in easy-care poly-esters cascade down in rows so high that shopkeepers have to use a long pole with a hook on the end to snag the garments their customers are interested in.

One business, however, a souvenir store, is a clear tourist destina-tion. Shoppers examine lacquered sea turtles, branches of coral, and taxidermied *habu* snakes, fangs exposed, coiled up, ready to strike. The store is so well lit that the shoppers inside seem like part of a museum diorama. In this setting, it is easy to see how different the Japanese tour-ists pointing at bottles of *awamori* liquor with a *habu* snake curled up on the bottom are from the cheery Okinawan shopgirls bustling about them. The mainlanders are better dressed, taller, more angular, with narrower eyes. Mostly, though, they radiate a sense of entitled ease.

A kid about my age—obviously a base kid, from his slouchy, over-size jeans and Dallas Cowboys T-shirt—clutches one of the stuffed *habu* snakes as he sneaks up on his buddy, who is examining the fine assortment of shell figurines in shell hot rods, and pretends to sink the viper's exposed fangs into his friend's neck.

"Motherfucker!" his victim explodes, slapping his neck and whirling around to find the snake being poked into his face. He bats the snake out of his friend's hands. "You asshole!"

The friend's cackles echo up and down the alley. The Japanese tourists exchange looks of disapproval as the guys commence swatting at each other. Without a word, the nearest shopgirl carefully returns the discarded snake and shell figures to their proper places.

Farther on, Jake and I enter a bustling market filled with housewives buying food for the evening meal. Piles of silver fish with their scarlet flesh exposed sit next to packages of wrapped pig parts. Ears and entire pig faces are particularly popular.

"It's just a little farther," Jake assures me, as we step out of the enclosed arcade.

Outside the market, we find that the sun has disappeared and a light drizzle is falling. Vendors beyond the cover of the glass roof hurry to cover piles of purple sweet potatoes and a vegetable that looks like a shriveled, bumpy cucumber, with sheets of clear plastic. The rain beads up on the sheets and trickles in rivulets onto the pavement.

"What are we looking for?" I ask. Jake gives me the address and I search for a number. We are in the city's backyard, surrounded by utility poles and high concrete walls covered with graffiti. The air is dense with the odor of fried food venting from the restaurants. The bright, tropical pastels have gone gray in the dismal light, and we could be in the anonymous urban heart of any city in the world.

Jake looks up and down the long alley, then back down at the address. "This can't be right," he concludes.

"What? You think I scared the *yuta* so much she sent us on a wild-goose chase?"

Jake shrugs; in other words, that's exactly what he thinks. A kitchen worker, Okinawan, his spiky black hair held back with a headband, a dirty white apron wrapped around his waist, wheels a large trash can out. Jake shows him the address; they exchange a few words of Japanese. The worker, a kid really, maybe fifteen, considers. His perplexed expression and the way he points one way, then the other, do not give me hope. I glance around, frantic to find some sign that I haven't hit a dead end. There has to be someone in this stinking alley who can help. An odd sense of urgency overtakes me, and I hurry off down the alley. The wind picks up, shifts direction, and a fresh breeze blows in from the ocean, sweeping the stale odors away.

"Luz, there's nothing down there!" Jake calls after me.

I ignore him, and rush away, only to stop dead at the unexpected sight of a wooden fence covered with velvety purple morning glories. Atop the gateposts a pair of *shiisā* dogs glare down. A string of metal bells hangs from the latch. Inside the fence is a small courtyard and a bungalow tucked in the shadows behind a department store and a sushi restaurant. Above the door is a symbol carved in wood that exactly matches the whirling circle image, the crest of the ancient Ryukyu Kingdom, that Jake has tattooed around his biceps.

Jake catches up just as I'm about to open the gate. "Hang on. People around here keep crazy vicious guard dogs."

"It's okay," I tell him. For reasons I don't understand, I know that it is. I open the gate and step into the small courtyard. As soon as I do, the bustling city seems to fall silent and all I am aware of is the spicy, sweet scent of orchids from the potted plants on the porch. My heart races as I mount the porch steps ahead of Jake, almost as if Codie herself were waiting for me inside the little house. I'm convinced that the next-best thing is, though: a way to communicate with her. I'm so eager that my hand trembles as I rap on the door. I hold my breath and listen for sounds of footsteps, a door about to be answered. I hear nothing and rap again.

"Hang on," Jake says, coming up behind me; he removes a note written in Japanese characters taped to the front door.

"What does it say?"

"She's not here. She's off celebrating Obon with her family."

"Are you sure?"

Jake shakes his head. The same feeling I get every time I wake from a Codie dream to discover yet again that she's gone overwhelms me, and my eyes fill. I almost trip hurrying back down the steps.

Jake follows. I try to run away; I can't stop the tears and I can't let him see them. His hand on my shoulder stops me. I duck my head as fast as I can.

"Luz."

The tenderness, the pity in his voice undoes me. I feel my face start squirming around—chin trembling, lips twitching, eyes puddling—and squash it against his shoulder before he can see me losing control.

"I'm sorry," he whispers, his lips brushing against the top of my head. "I shouldn't have built your hopes up. Without a more complete list of your relatives, she probably couldn't have told you anything even if she'd been there. No decent *yuta* could have. It might take a while, but I'm sure that with your mom's help you can eventually put a better list together."

My mom. There is no way to make Jake, with his constellations of family photos, understand what a dead end my mom is. How she's spent her whole life fleeing real connection by escaping into fake ones. How, even now, she's running from her last real connection, me. Having mastered the stealth cry, I don't think that Jake will notice that thinking about my mom makes the silent tears flow even harder. But he does, and wraps his arms more tightly around me, and I think that I'll never be critical of my mother again for seeking this out, this momentary comfort, this break, no matter how brief, from aloneness.

Above the steady beat of Jake's heart, I hear a distant, mechanical whirring and look up at the exact instant that the two gray cars of a monorail with a red stripe through the middle whiz along near the tops of buildings several blocks away. As they pass from view, a clump of buildings higher than the rail hide part of the front car. In that moment, it appears as if the back car might be the last one in a long train. Might, in fact, be part of a big-city system. Like the El in Chicago. Like the one running behind the street-corner dude in the photo I found in my mom's room.

In my mind, I see the photo in exact detail and am certain of what I suspected but wouldn't allow myself to acknowledge from the moment I found the picture. I see the street corner dude's hair, which is my hair and Codie's hair and, almost certainly, the hair of the singer from the photo where my dazzled grandmother looks like Elvis's girlfriend. I see the man's coiled wariness as he glances down the street, and think of my mother's implacable restlessness. Far overhead, I see the gray monorail car in the photo and how it is identical to the one that just passed, right down to the red stripe through its middle. A stripe that matches the color of what I thought were tissue-paper blossoms from a parade that made a crimson carpet at the feet of the curly-haired man. Like the ones Codie stood on in my dream. Like the ones that cover her grave with scarlet flowers from the *deigo* tree.

"I can get a better list," I say.

"From who?"

"My grandfather."

· THIRTY-FOUR ·

I will never forget the date—May 29, 1945—when I heard the words, "Shuri has fallen."

The news spread among us like the deadliest of plagues, killing every hope we still had of victory. Worse even than that, we learned that our generals, Ushijima and Chō, had fled and no one seemed to know where they'd gone. The thought of being leaderless filled us with fear worse than any we had yet experienced.

"I don't believe it." Hatsuko dismissed the information as rumors planted by spies.

None of us wanted to believe it. Shuri was the soul of Okinawa. We were safe as long as Shuri stood. I could not imagine the vermilion-and-gold palace, the enchanted gardens where I'd met the *juri*, much less the Imperial Army's vast underground stronghold, falling into enemy hands.

"That's impossible," Hatsuko maintained stoutly. "Those tunnels beneath Shuri are impregnable. I won't believe that Shuri has fallen unless I hear it from an officer of the Imperial Army."

I knew immediately the officer she intended to seek confirmation from, and followed her as she strode purposefully down the long corridor to the officers' quarters.

"Hatsuko, Tamiko, how happy I am to see you," Lieutenant Nakamura, who was playing cards with his fellow officers, called out when he caught sight of us. "Won't you come in? I'm afraid we no longer have any real tea, but the boiled pine needles we drink don't make a bad brew."

"No, thank you," Hatsuko answered, lowering her lashes. "If we could just speak to you for a moment." She added, "About a military matter."

One of the other men pointed at his crotch and said that we were welcome to speak to his "little general" about any military matter we liked. That the "little general" would even stand up and salute for us. Hatsuko left then and didn't see how Nakamura smiled in a knowing way at their lewd laughter when he put his cards down and went into the corridor to speak with us.

"Is it true?" Hatsuko demanded. "Has Shuri fallen? Have the generals fled?"

"Does the huntsman flee when he runs ahead of the stag to set a trap to capture the great beast?"

"But no one knows where our leaders generals Ushijima and Chō are."

"They are here," Nakamura answered, and placed the palm of his hand over Hatsuko's heart. She looked up at him like a fish with a hook in its mouth. "They are but the mere embodiment of the noble Japanese spirit that will give us all the courage to make the ultimate sacrifice for our emperor when the time comes." At that moment, with Hatsuko's lips trembling and Nakamura's jaw set firmly, they looked like two film stars staring into each other's eyes. "The spirit that will join us forever when we have the honor of shattering like jewels defending our homeland from invasion."

Hatsuko gazed up as dreamily as if he'd just proposed marriage.

"What are you saying?" I demanded. Hatsuko shot me a sour look that warned me not to go on. I ignored her. "'Our' homeland has already been invaded. Okinawa *is* our homeland."

Nakamura spoke to me as if I were a slow child who required a simple explanation for something that was obvious to everyone else. "Oh, Little Guppy." I bristled at his using Hatsuko's nickname for me. "Okinawa is a finger, the littlest of the fingers, which will have the honor of being broken as we deliver all the blows needed to stop the American bullies from ever reaching the shores of our homeland and harming any real Japanese."

"A finger to be broken? Is that all Okinawa ever was to you? To any of you 'real' Japanese?"

Nakamura's expression hardened.

"Tamiko, you've said enough," my sister scolded. "You don't understand."

"I understand. You 'real Japanese' said you were defending *us*, but from the beginning we were nothing more to you than a shield for your own defense. Our deaths, our island, mean nothing to you and your precious emperor—"

A slap stung my cheek. "That will be enough!" Nakamura thundered, his handsome face twisting into that of a petulant child. "I could have you killed as a spy for voicing such unspeakable treason against the emperor."

"You, you with your long, shiny sword, you are the bully, just as much as the Americans." Barely believing myself what I'd said, I ran away. When I reached the safety of a bend in the corridor to hide behind, I stopped and looked back. Hatsuko had thrown herself at Nakamura's feet and was begging forgiveness for my transgression. He reached down, pulled her to her feet, tilted her tear-splashed face up, and gently stroked her cheek. I ran on, heavy with the knowledge that after such a display, Nakamura would surely propose marriage to my sister.

Hatsuko was still not speaking to me when, a few days later, the order came for us to evacuate the patients; the ketō ground troops were closing in. Head Nurse Tanaka had to go into the wards to determine which of the patients were mobile enough to make the journey south.

"You," she said, pointing to me. "You'll come with me and do something useful for a change and write down the names of the patients who can walk."

"What of the others?" I asked. "The ones who cannot walk?"

"What do you think? Quit being an Okinawan simpleton and come along."

A medic carrying a large brown box accompanied us, and we entered the first ward. None of the emaciated men with their maggot-infested wounds and missing limbs seemed capable of making the trip to the latrine, much less a hard march on hilly terrain. But when Head Nurse announced our mission, all the men struggled to stand. A few managed to hold themselves upright. Head Nurse told me to take their names.

Those not selected trembled with fear as they pleaded for her not to leave them behind. "The ketō will crush us beneath the treads of their monstrous tanks," they wailed. "I heard that they kill prisoners by skinning them alive. Please, Nurse, please."

"All of you, stop disgracing yourselves!" Head Nurse bellowed. She nodded at the medic, who passed among the men, handing out packets of white powder. "Mix this with water and it will speed you on your way to a glorious death in the service of our emperor."

I recalled the stories about Head Nurse's familiarity with poison, and a shiver ran through me.

"You men over there." She indicated a cluster of a dozen patients packed together on a couple of mats on the cave floor. "Since there is not enough powder for everyone, you will have a special honor." The medic handed the man in the middle a grenade.

"All you patients will remain silent when the enemy comes," Head Nurse instructed them, her eyes alight with a strange gleam. "When they have wandered far into the cave, then, and only then, will you pull the pin on your grenade. And, if luck is with us, the cave will collapse and those of the enemy not killed outright will be crushed. In this way your deaths will be of some small service to the emperor."

We helped the abandoned, bedridden patients arrange themselves in the proper posture of death, with their heads facing north. Their piteous cries, begging us not to leave them to starve to death or to die at a cruel enemy's hand, echoed out as we strode off to the next ward.

By that evening the ambulatory patients had gathered in front of the main cave. Men tottered on crutches; arms were in slings, heads bandaged. There wasn't a complete uniform among the lot of them, just a battered hat here, the scraps of a jacket there. Few even had boots. We stood in an eerie, ominous silence so unusual that it took a moment for us to identify its cause. A one-legged man who had his arm looped around the neck of a companion finally said, in a flat tone devoid of all emotion, "The bombing has stopped. Now they will come to kill us one by one."

As the sun set, I watched the army of broken bodies leave Haebaru. The stragglers at the end cast long, dark shadows that teetered behind them as they hobbled up the sloping hill.

In our cave, I felt Hatsuko's silence more keenly now that the incessant bombing had stopped. Sachiko, Miyoko, Mitsue, Hatsuko, and I were the only Princess Lily girls remaining. The others had left with the mobile patients. We had been assigned to stay behind until the next morning, in case the officers arriving then needed our help. We tried to chat, but our voices sounded stilted and too loud in the echoing silence. Soon the others were snoring softly, but I had become so accustomed to the sounds of war that I could no longer fall asleep without that constant rumble. I got up and went outside again.

It was drizzling, and a miraculous sound reached me: the croaking of frogs. The call of night birds joined their serenade. And then, most magical of all, I heard the chirping of a happy gecko, just like the one that had always brought luck to our family. I imagined the pink bubble of his air sac blowing up and down at his neck and was transported back to my room beneath our thick thatch roof. In that dark and serene moment, it was as if there had never been a war and there was nothing more natural in the world than for me to take a stroll. I followed the peaceful sounds out beyond the edge of our cave world. I would have gone farther, gone wherever those sounds led me, had a squad of twenty Japanese soldiers not marched past.

Each soldier wore full combat dress and carried a small square box under his arm. Their movements were crisp and forceful. It was exhilarating to see such a by-now-rare display of pride and spirit. These were the human bombs I had heard so much about. They would go out into the night and hide. When the enemy approached in their monstrous tanks, they would hurl themselves beneath the awful treads and detonate their bombs, destroying the machines, their occupants, and themselves in one final burst of glory.

As they came closer, I saw that the troops were not all Japanese. In fact, only those on the outer edges were. All the men, boys, really, inside the square of real soldiers were Okinawans of the Blood and Iron corps. One of the Okinawans glanced my way, and for just one instant, his mask of noble sacrifice fell away and he was only a boy again, young and scared, and I was the last girl he would ever see on this earth. He risked his sergeant's wrath by hissing at me, "They're here. The *Amerikās.* They're only fifty meters from this spot. Don't stay any longer. Go back to your cave. Hurry. Run. Save yourself!" His words were a dying wish. A wish not to be dying.

As I ran back toward my cave, I passed another group of soldiers carrying rifles. They took positions behind a windbreak, ready to fire at any enemy who should appear. Just as I reached the cave entrance, several cracking shots splattered the mud where my feet had landed only an instant before. The soldiers at the windbreak fired back and no more shots were aimed my way.

In the cave, Hatsuko, Miyoko, and Sachiko were stuffing what few things they had left into bundles. The moment she saw me, my sister rushed up and enfolded me in a hug. My heart soared with happiness that she had forgiven me. "Where have you been?" she demanded. "I couldn't find you. I was so worried. They're here! The order has already been given for us to evacuate for Makabe immediately. We're all ready to leave, but we can't find our cousin Mitsue."

"She must have left with another group," Sachiko said.

In the corridor orders were yelled for the evacuation to begin at once.

Hatsuko nudged me toward Miyoko and Sachiko, who were rushing to join the group assembling.

"Go with them," she ordered. "I have to do one last thing before I leave. I'll find you when we reach Makabe." I knew immediately what that last thing was. "No, we have to go now. Lieutenant Nakamura is probably already on the road ahead of us."

"He's not. His unit was ordered to stay behind," she answered, setting off without another word.

"I'm going with you," I insisted.

We shouldered our packs and rushed toward the officers' quarters.

"He must have just left," Hatsuko said, stricken, as we stared into the cave, empty save for a few playing cards and a can holding the butts of their pine-needle cigarettes. Some of them were still smoldering.

"Wait," I whispered. "Do you hear that?"

From around a corner, down the dark corridor came the sound of whimpering, as though someone might be trapped. Certain that someone was in terrible danger, I hurried off toward the distressing sound. I turned a corner and saw Nakamura far down the corridor. His back was to me. His pants were down and his slender buttocks shone in the guttering yellow light of the kerosene lantern at his feet. They clenched rhythmically as he thrust into a woman pressed between himself and the cave wall. Her legs were wrapped around Nakamura's waist. I tried to stop Hatsuko from seeing who he was with, but failed. The woman saw Hatsuko as clearly as Hatsuko saw her. The luminous whiteness of her arching neck. The profile perfect enough to be carved onto a cameo brooch. The unmistakable outline of her lips, as full as a cartoon goldfish's.

· THIRTY-FIVE ·

I lead Jake back through the Heiwa-dōri's maze of shops. Outside, beyond the high, arched roof of glass, the light drizzle has turned to a hard rain, and a field of colored umbrellas bright as Easter eggs has burst into bloom. Jake and I are both soaked by the time we jump back into his car, and the spot on the shoulder of his shirt where I wept has been washed away. The rain slithering down the windows makes it feel cozy inside the car, turning everything outside into a wobbly, Impressionistic painting. I dig through my bag, grab the photo, hand it to Jake, and point to the gray-and-red car that I had thought was part of Chicago's elevated train.

"Isn't that the monorail?"

Jake nods.

"And those blossoms at his feet?"

Jake studies the date. "This was taken when the *deigo* trees were in bloom."

"There must be one nearby, outside of the frame."

"And this guy? You think he's your . . . ?"

Jake waits for me to fill in "grandfather," but the certainty I had standing in the *yuta*'s courtyard dissolves beneath his hard-eyed scrutiny. I can't tell Jake about Codie's hair. How the silent, aggrieved man with his pale, patchy skin who was our grandmother's husband could not have been our mother's father. All I can say with even the smallest sliver of confidence is, "I'm pretty sure he knows something about my family history." I change the subject. "The photo had to have been taken here, though, didn't it? A *deigo* tree *and* a two-car monorail? How many other cities could possibly have that combination?"

"It has to be Naha."

"Of course, now the problem is to figure out where this was taken. Naha has, like, what? Half a million people?"

"Close to that."

I touch the corner of the sign above the guy's head. "'apLand.' My best guess is that it's a misspelling of App Land. Some tech store." I grab Jake's phone, regretting that I haven't brought mine along, even if it would have meant being subjected to Mom's texts. "I'll Google it."

"Don't bother." Jake's tone is weird. He flips the photo back onto my lap and pulls into traffic. "I know exactly where and what that is. It's pretty much the first place a certain kind of guy wants to see." Jake doesn't give any more explanation as we drive in silence, but his reaction, verging on disgust, reminds me of the *yuta*'s.

The rain has stopped by the time we leave the broad boulevards lined with royal palms and shops spilling out their glittering merchandise and turn onto narrower and narrower streets until we're creeping along a nearly deserted back road lined with dingy two- and three-story concrete buildings. We pass through a few blocks that look like a ghost town. Abandoned businesses with boarded-up windows and weeds growing through the concrete steps in front sport signs with letters so faded by the sun that I can barely make out the names: Club Kentucky. High Time Bar. The Manhattan. Girls Girls Girls. Beneath several of the names is the invitation "GI Welcome." High overhead, the gleaming silver track of the monorail skims above the rooftops.

Suddenly, amid all the gray buildings, we encounter one painted a vivid crimson. The shocking color frames a painting two stories high that depicts a beautiful woman in a red-and-lilac kimono sniffing a flower. A few blocks later there is another clump of equally gaudy bright buildings. The first is painted a shocking pink. On its far end, a two-story poster depicts a pair of anime girls in French-maid costumes, breasts overflowing laced bodices, while some invisible fishing line hoists up the backs of ruffled skirts to reveal the clefts of their butts. With a sarcastic tone, Jake translates the caption beneath the girls: "'Welcome home, Mr. Married Man. Your wife is out shopping for the day. Is there anything we can do for you before she gets back?'"

"Check that one out." He points to a place with a sign that translates as "The Girls' Nursing Academy." The two-story building is covered in bathroom tile and features giant posters of young Japanese girls in sexy nurse uniforms and pink scrubs. There is another caption, and though Jake does this translation in a high, girly voice, it's obvious that he doesn't think any of this is funny. "'Please come in! We need to check your pulse. Now please remove all of your clothes. We'd like to check your blood pressure, too.'"

On the street, a couple of businessmen in black suits crane their necks to study the photos of the nurse girls. A thuggy-looking guy with slicked-back hair steps out and beckons the men to enter, holding the door open, and pointing to other photos posted on the signboard next to him.

"What are these, strip clubs? Whorehouses?"

Jakes gives a dry imitation of a laugh. "Whorehouses? Technically, no, since prostitution has been illegal in Japan since the midfifties. No, these are 'bathhouses,' *sōpus*. Which is why what you pay for in a *sōpu* is just a bath. A very, very expensive bath where the girl washes you with her naked, soapy body. But if, during all the rub-a-dub-dub, the couple should just happen to realize that they are soul mates and fall deeply in love and can't keep themselves from having mad, passionate sex . . . well, it happens. That's just two strangers who've fallen in love. The money is for the bath. Period. That's the Japanese way."

"You sure know a lot about all this," I say.

Jake shakes his head. "No one who grows up here doesn't know about Soaplands. In a lot of ways, they're an essential part of Oki history. This, the *Tsuji* pleasure quarter, is the point where Japan, Okinawa, and, now that the dollar is so weak, to a much lesser degree America all literally rub up against one another."

I'm relieved that Jake's judgment and disgust are for murky political relationships. He drives on, pointing out the tiled, painted businesses as we pass them. "Okay, there you've got the Princess Heart, the Emerald, and Wave. And look." Jake tilts his head toward a couple of soldiers. "The first customers of the day."

Though they're in civvies, I figure them to be marines, since everything about them—from their bald-on-the-sides, high-and-tight haircuts, to their weight-lifter muscles, to their rolling gaits, like their balls are so enormous they have to straddle them with each step—is military on steroids. They're too big for the narrow street, too red-faced for the glaring sun. The marines pause in front of the Princess Heart and stare at the poster of a girl with a face like Betty Boop and breasts like a Jersey cow.

The soldiers shove each other as they study a price list that starts at twenty-four thousand yen for an hour, more than they make in a week. A tough-looking Okinawan bouncer wearing sunglasses, his hair gelled into a spiky 'do, slouching against a wall, straightens up, flicks his cigarette into the street, and closes in on the marines. He waves the soldiers away with broad gestures. The marines fail to take the hint and start to go in anyway. The bouncer, arms folded in front of his chest, blocks their entrance, and, with one nod of his head, two guys appear to flank him. The marines start to force their way past, and the three men drop down into the Stance. The marines recognize the serious ass-kicking potential on display, flip the guys off, and leave.

Jake takes a left, turns down a street drabber and drearier than the others, and stops in front of the drabbest and dreariest building in the neighborhood. It is, however, distinguished by three features: 1. down the alley that runs along the side of the building is a clear view of the monorail; 2. shooting straight up from a massive planter embedded in the sidewalk a *deigo* tree reaches for the sunlight above the roofline; and 3. the sign above the door is spelled out, not in Japanese characters but in straightforward English: SoapLand. "This the place you were looking for?"

"I didn't think it would be . . . You know." I'm embarrassed. Just as I feared, the instant I let anything about my family out, humiliation follows.

"SoapLand, that's the name of this establishment and the translation of *sopū*," Jake explains, as he backs the car into a side street and parks in a spot that allows us to see without being seen. "SoapLand is the only place around here that's so low-class they take foreigners, even the most despised of the *gaijin*, soldiers. U.S. GIs were what originally built the businesses, but all that's changed. Most *sōpus* now won't even let a GI stand outside and ogle the photos of the girls, because they'll scare away the customers with real money, Japanese businessmen."

The rain has stopped, and in the bright sunlight SoapLand looks even dingier. The aqua tile framing the frosted glass next to the front door has a filigree of mildew along the grout lines. The large photos of girls sporting ratted-up hairstyles, pale lipstick, and heavy eyeliner from the sixties and seventies, posted in glass cases outside, are so old they have faded to a lifeless blue. They remind me of the photo of my grandmother. Too much.

"Actually," I say, "I've changed my mind. I don't even know why I thought that I'm related to"—I wave at the scene on the other side of the windshield—"any of this. My grandfather was a farmboy from Missouri. My grandmother met him when he was stationed at Kadena."

As I speak, the marines rejected from the higher-class *sōpu* down the street appear. As soon as they move into view, there is motion on the other side of the frosted glass of SoapLand. The shadow of a man wobbles across the glass as he nears the open door. My heart gives a violent stroke.

"So, you want to leave?" Jake asks.

The shadow is inches away from being exposed at the open door. "Yes, we should leave. Now."

Jake starts the engine and pulls forward. He is about to turn onto the street and put the grimy realities of SoapLand behind us when the shadow man appears in the open door.

Jake stops. "Isn't that the guy in the picture you showed me?"

He is even more gaunt than he'd looked in the photo taken three months ago. The high knobs of his shoulders tent up his baggy suit on either side of his head. A rim of white hair outlines his face where the roots of his frizzy dyed curls are growing out. Though he could pass for Latino, even white, in person, his loose-jointed ease with a hint of swagger is all African American.

I want to say no so much it hurts. I don't want to be related to some skeevy guy working at a sudsy whorehouse. Or a skanky mom so messed up she needs the military to keep her on the rails. And I really don't want any of that to touch the only two good people who were ever in my life: Codie and my grandmother. I am cutting this loser out, excising him like a malignant growth. I'm saying the word, I'm denying that he has any relation to me when the old guy throws his shoulders back, stands up straight, and greets the marines with a smile that is Codie's dazzling smile. The years fall off of him and Codie is there in how he radiates the same quick but scattered intelligence.

The marines try to wave him away, but he gets out in front, cutting them off. They step around him, but he stays on their heels, a whippet herding buffalo. When they continue rebuffing him, moving farther down the block away from SoapLand, he grabs the sleeve of one of the marines. Instantly, two massive clubs of arms shoot skyward, throwing off the unwelcome touch. Both soldiers whirl on the pest and go ghetto on him, with aggressive head bobs and eye pops.

The skinny man with Codie's smile backs away, both hands up, declaring total surrender. The marines leave, fist-bumping each other, bonded again in *semper fi* brotherhood.

"What do you want to do?" Jake asks.

What I want to do is to tell Jake that I was mistaken, that my life has nothing to do with a broken-down old pimp dogging customers. I really want that. The only thing I want more is the tiniest scrap of my sister back. A flash of her smile. The name of the man who might be our grandfather. The list of ancestors that there's the remotest chance might let me contact her. I still could have denied it all, though, except for one indisputable fact: I am looking at the man, forty years older now, from the album cover. The one in the white vest that my grandmother used to moon over.

I pull the handle back; the car door cracks open. "I have to talk to him."

"Okay, I'm coming with you."

"No, I need to do this alone."

"Sorry, there is no way I'm letting you go by yourself."

He gets out, and we both head toward SoapLand.

· THIRTY-SIX ·

S ay what?" The man puts a hand behind his ear and wings it out. A tendril of wire connected to a hearing aid loops into the ear.

I glance over at Jake, standing down the street, grateful that he agreed to remain out of hearing. I give him a quick smile before repeating my introduction a bit more loudly: "I'm Luz James!"

"Don't have to yell. Just have to stop mumbling like you were before."

"Okay. Sorry. And my mother is Gena James. She was Gena Overholt. My grandmother was—"

"Setsuko?"

I hate hearing her name come from his mouth.

He points a bony finger at me, the joints swollen like the nodes on a stalk of bamboo. "You her kid? What? Change-of-life baby?"

"Grandkid."

He exhales a sharp bark of triumphant laughter, as if I've come to pay tribute to him with the fact of my existence. A fit of wheezing stops him mid-jubilation. When his ruined lungs stop laboring, he peers at me, asks, "They sent you, didn't they? Her crazy so-called relatives? Okay, okay, I get it now. You're the reason those lunatics came out here three months ago taking pictures of me, aren't you?"

"I don't know what you're talking about."

He folds his arms across his spindly chest as if to barricade himself against the fast one he's convinced I'm pulling. "Okay, let the shake-down begin. What's Sukie want?"

Sukie? He called my grandmother Sukie.

"College money? Back payments on child support? What's it gonna be?"

"I'm not here to—"

"All them crazy-ass relatives care so much about her, where were they when she needed them, huh? Think I didn't recognize them out there taking pictures of me? What'd she send them to take pictures of me for? Whatever it is, she knows it's some lame bullshit. She had a legitimate claim, she'd come herself."

"My grandmother . . ." I speak as loudly as I can, and Jake moves forward. I hold up my hand to signal that I'm fine.

He winces, adjusts his hearing aid. "Jesus, kid, quit saying that. Grandmother. You freakin' me out."

"She's dead."

"Sukie? Setsuko? She . . . ? When?"

"It's been a while. I was young. We were stationed in Germany when we got the news, so at least ten years ago."

"How'd she go?"

"Heart attack," I lie. I don't owe this stranger the truth. I don't have to say the word out loud: "suicide." Don't have to think about my grandmother all alone in a country where she barely spoke the language, her one child doing everything in her power to always be as far from her as possible.

He studies me, nods. "Oh, yeah, I can see it now. Can definitely see it. You got the good Vaughn hair."

Vaughn. His last name is Vaughn. My grandfather's last name is Vaughn.

"What about Gene?"

"Her husband? You knew him?"

"Stationed here together."

"He died before her."

"Gene? Gene's dead too? How? Throat cancer?"

"How did you know?"

He shrugs, drops his arms. "Informed guess." The high-tension force field of kinetic energy whirling around him sags and I can almost feel a vacuum being broken with a *whoosh*, like a rogue gust of wind blowing down the alley as time rushes in and catches up with him. He leans against the wall, looks up and down the street, searching for who or what just mugged him, stole his youth, his health. "So you're not here for money. Who sent you?"

"No one."

"Then how'd you find me?"

"A photo. I saw a photo."

"One of the ones they took? I don't get it; all they ever wanted was to get Sukie and me *out* of their lives. Why they bother takin' pictures of me?"

"They sent one to my mother. To keep her away, I think."

"So why are you here? You need an organ donated or something?"

Suddenly there is nothing I want from this man. All I want is my grandmother with her silly dance moves back. "Actually, forget it."

"I got it. You're doing a *Roots* thing. Tracing the ancestors, right?" I almost start to walk away, but in that instant, he tilts his head, and the light catches in his eyes. They are the same olive green as Codie's, and for the briefest instant, my sister stares back at me, and I would do anything to keep looking into her eyes. In them I see the truth of what the Okinawans believe: For better or worse, our ancestors are with us forever, and they won't be denied.

"So, you're my granddaughter." He studies me, nods like he guesses I'll do. "Well, come on up. We'll have some tea and go over the whole family tree."

I call Jake over, tell him the plan. He insists on coming with me. I can't expose him to any more sordid secrets. I just can't. "It's kind of personal," I insist. "I'll be fine."

"She'll be fine," Vaughn echoes. "Just gonna go over the family tree. I'll make sure nothing happens. She's my blood, you know."

Jake bristles. "You do know who her mother is, don't you?"

"I'm just getting caught up on all that."

"She's the head of Kadena base police."

Vaughn glances at me, impressed. "That so?"

"Yeah, and she's very protective."

"Good, that's good. Glad to hear it. Listen, chief," he tells Jake, "you can stand down. Nothing's gonna happen she can't tell her mama about. I promise you, man, you are looking at the last person on earth who'd want anything at all to do with the U.S. military. You feel me?"

"Jake, really, I'll be fine."

"You don't have your phone, do you?"

I shake my head no.

Vaughn hands me his. "Here, call him all you want." Jake gets Vaughn's number, calls it. The phone rings. Jake hangs up. "Okay, you've got my number now. Hit it the instant you need me, and I'll be there."

"'Whenever you call me, I'll be there.'" Vaughn walks away singing a song I recognize from one of my grandma's old soul albums. His voice erases any doubts I might have had about him being the one my grandmother loved; his voice is astonishing.

At the front door, Vaughn turns, sings out with special emphasis, "'I'll be lyin' in a coffin, baby! You know I'll be there!'" before disappearing inside.

Jake squeezes my shoulder and, after a moment's hesitation, I follow Vaughn into SoapLand.

Vaughn stands at the front desk where a broad-shouldered Okinawan woman with a bad perm, wearing a turquoise polo shirt and poppy-red lipstick is seated, drilling him with rapid-fire questions in loud, bossy Japanese. Surrounded by stacks of cheap white towels and busy folding more, the woman looks like a combination madam/team manager. Whatever Vaughn tells her—in a Japanese so American-sounding I can almost understand it—makes her mad, and she hectors him in a high-velocity, staccato tone, waving toward the front door, ordering him to get back to work.

"Catch you later, Mama-san," he says in English, flapping his hand at her dismissively. I follow him upstairs.

"Sorry," he tells me, unlocking the hollow-core door of his room on the second floor and standing aside to let me enter first. I don't know if he's apologizing for the studio apartment's small size, its threadbare furnishings, the trash can stuffed with Styrofoam take-out containers, or the interaction downstairs. The issue turns out to be a construction crew jackhammering down the block. He slams his one window shut. "Kinda noisy. I usually just turn my hearing aids off. I should move out, find a better place to live. But this dump comes free with the job."

I wait for the feeble air-conditioning to cool off the hot, airless room. Vaughn doesn't seem to notice the heat, though, as he studies a ceiling-high stack of boxes until he finds the one he's looking for, and unearths it. He gestures for me to have a seat, then extracts a photo album from the box.

"First ancestor you need to know about is me." He carefully places the book of photos on my lap and opens it to a color glossy. It's the original photo that was on the cover of the album my grandmother used to secretly dance to. Vaughn, minus forty years of hard living, stands in front of the four Okinawan guys in the band, dressed in a skintight white suit with nothing under the jacket except a deep V of glistening brown muscle. The guy staring calmly into the camera is not the fidgety old gent in the room with me but a star, charismatic and handsome, someone worth mooning over. Above his head are the words "The Soul Tronics. Appearing Every Friday at Club Girls A Go Go. Saturdays at the Peek-A-Boo, B.C. Street, Koza, Okinawa. Starring Motown Sensation Delmar Vaughn."

My grandfather's name is Delmar Vaughn.

"You were with Motown?"

"Woulda been. Had a contract and everything. Got drafted right out of the studio. They had me all positioned to be the next Smokey Robinson."

The easy smile, light skin, and olive-green eyes, startling in their pale brightness, as if an extra light were being shone only on him and none of the other band members, they all call the famous singer to mind.

The rest of Delmar Vaughn's photo album is filled with pages of good-times shots: Vaughn at the microphone, his flashed-out Afro a halo around his head; Vaughn hoisting drinks to the camera; Vaughn grinning, *Super Fly* pimp hat atop his head, a bar girl coiled under each arm.

"Green or turmeric?" he asks from the kitchen area, holding up two boxes of tea. "The turmeric tastes like shit, but it's supposed to make you live forever."

"You know, if you could just give me the names of everyone in my grandmother's family that you knew, plus your family tree, then I'll get out of your hair, stop bothering you."

"No bother. Not every day your past comes to life in front of you. Seems like you'd want to know about me."

"Maybe I could come back another time."

"Naw, I don't think it's gonna work like that."

The tiniest edge of a threat in Vaughn's tone makes me realize that he's a man who's been waiting for decades to tell his story to someone who cared. And he's decided that I'm that someone. Before he gives me what I want, he's going to make sure that I hear his story. He hands me his phone. "Call your boyfriend. Tell him you're fine and that you decided to stay awhile."

Jake tells me to take all the time I need, he'll sleep. "But call me the instant anything gets weird. Actually, call me the instant *before* anything gets weird."

I promise I will, hang up, tell Vaughn, "I'll try the shit tea."

He cackles a pleased laugh. As he busies himself heating water in a dorm-size microwave, I notice a large black-and-white security monitor split into nine different screens that takes up most of a shelf on a wall facing the bed. The upper left of the patchwork of screens is focused on Mama-san downstairs at the reception desk, folding towels. Other screens show the street outside. Most stare into small, empty rooms covered in tile. The only furnishings are a handheld shower snaking from the wall, its chrome head resting next to a large plastic stool with a split down the middle; a white plastic bucket; an inflated air mattress; and a stack of towels. Another camera is zeroed in on an overly bright room where three no-longer-young women in string bikinis slump on white vinyl chairs. Two look Filipina. The third, a tall, sturdy girl with narrow, single-fold eyelids and high cheekbones, sits away from the others and concentrates on picking at a scab on her right elbow.

All three are bored. The Filipinas flip through limp magazines, exchange listless comments, check their makeup in hand mirrors, and rearrange individual strands of their bangs. The third girl just sits and picks. A flurry of motion in the upper screen resolves into the backs of the shaved heads of the two marines I saw earlier. They step in front of Mama-san and cash is exchanged for towels. Mama-san takes the money but keeps her hand out. The marines wave her off. She starts to give the money back. The soldiers look at each other, shake their heads, pull out their wallets again, and both of them surrender their ID cards. Only then does Mama-san step out from behind the counter and lead them off camera.

In the same instant, both the Filipina girls come to life and assume rehearsed poses. One arches her back, sucks her middle finger; the second tips her head down and gazes up through a tangle of lashes at the marines. The third girl's smile is a wince, as if she's staring into the sun. The two petite Filipinas are chosen. They look like tiny Hindu elephant trainers as they lead the soldiers away.

Vaughn comes over with two mugs of hot liquid that looks like chicken broth. He notices me glancing quickly away from the monitor. "Sorry, wish I could turn that off, but Mama-san's got it rigged so it's on twenty-four-seven. Ignore it. It's just business. You've probably seen a lot worse on the Internet anyways."

Vaughn takes a seat on the edge of his bed across from me. "Want to see what killed your grand ... what killed Gene?" He leans over, flips the pages of the album back almost to the beginning, stops at a faded color snapshot of two slender young airmen riding a motorcycle across the open swath of a runway. Vaughn is the passenger, sitting in back, arms held out wide. In front, leaning over the handlebars into the wind, is a thin, fit Gene, my grandmother's husband. The reddish-blond hair he'd lost by the time I met him is a fringe flattened against his high forehead. His eyes are nearly lost behind the swell of his cheeks as he grins. He is so young.

Vaughn taps the photo, calling my attention to a row of fifty-five-gallon drums baking in the sun at the edge of the runway. Bands of different colors encircle each drum. "See those? Those are what killed Gene. What are killing me."

I glance up. Listen to the ragged wheeze of his breath.

"Called 'em the rainbow herbicides. Agents Purple, Pink, and Orange. According to the Pentagon, none of them was ever on Okinawa. But there they are. Only time and place military had 'em all together like that. Either testing for Vietnam or dumping the dented drums straight into the Pacific Ocean. I researched this shit. You better believe I did. It's all on the Internet now. Just look it up, you'll see.

"Back then, though? They told us that shit was safe as water, and we were so ignorant we believed 'em. No gloves, no hazmat suit. We humped those damn drums using our bare hands like the idiot kids we were."

Vaughn shakes his head, mutters to himself, "Young, dumb, and full of cum. Excuse me. Don't report me to your mother. Lucky for me, I was the biggest goldbrick you ever saw. Laid back much as I could. Gene, though, Gene liked running a front-end loader, liked watching those barrels with the colored stripes on them bumping down a long hill and splashing into the ocean. He was there every day handling that shit, breathing it."

I recall Gene, old before his time, rooted to his recliner, oxygen tube running into his nose, the end table next to him covered with pill bottles, always more of a glowering presence than a person. Vaughn glances at the security monitor. Two of the screens now show the marines in separate rooms, naked, sitting on the divided stools, being washed by their chosen woman. The women slosh soapy water across the men with as little emotion as workers at a carwash sudsing up a big SUV. When one of the men is thoroughly soaped up, his attendant positions herself behind him. I look away, thoroughly creeped out. But the image of the girl using both hands to reach under him and rhythmically wash his genital area with long swipes from his ass to his erect dick is already burned into my brain. Only my intense desire to hear my grandmother's story overcomes my nearly equally intense desire to leave.

Vaughn doesn't seem to notice the screen or my embarrassed reaction as he mutters, "Thank God, I had the Bush."

I wince.

"Naw, naw, not like that. The Bush is what we, me and the other brothers, called the five, six blocks of Koza that we owned. *Owned . . .*" He goes off into a reverie. When he speaks again, it's more for himself than me. "I'm telling you, this should be in the history books. The Bush was my kingdom. My domain. Me and the Soul Tronics. We were like the house band for the whole scene back then. It was ours, we owned it. Me and every other brother on the Rock. The Man did not dare set foot into the Bush. We set up the official Far East branch of the Black Panthers. Only we were more radical and better armed. You think getting pulled out the projects, then sent to Vietnam to get your ass shot up for some bullshit cracker war ain't gonna radicalize a brother?"

There it is, the anger always ready to flare, exactly like my mom's. With her gentle mother and silent father, I always wondered where it came from. Vaughn relaxes. When he speaks, he's once again one of the brothers who owned the Bush.

"Brothers going to or just coming out of 'Nam on R and R with their KA-BARS, their sidearms. Lot of green beanies too. Them Green Beret sonsabitches could kill a man with a ballpoint pen. Yeah, we had some desperate motherfuckers holed up in there. You hear lot of talk about, 'I was the only white dude ever go into the Bush.' Bullshit! MPs wouldn't go up in there. White man's military mighta ruled our lives on base, but not in the Bush. That was ours. And the Okis backed us up. Least the ones with any balls did. You want tough? Those were the motherfuckers invented karate. Japs took away their weapons, they turned their hands into weapons. Never needed a gun, a knife. They want you dead, didn't need no ballpoint pen, kill you with their bare hands. You think I didn't see them do it? Hell I didn't!"

Vaughn looks off, nodding to himself as if he'd just gotten the last word in. Then he remembers that I'm there and says, "Your grandmother, fine woman. Just wanted what she couldn't have."

"What was that?"

"Delmar Roquel Vaughn. You really want to hear all this old-timey shit?" he asks, now that he has my attention riveted.

Codie could nail down attention the same way. When she was around, you couldn't put your eyes anywhere but on her. Charisma. It astonishes me to witness its source. I nod.

"Okay, here's how it was back in the day. The girls who worked the Bush were there because they liked a brother, you know what I'm sayin'? I was fronting *the* hot band in the Bush. I could have had any female I wanted. Never a question of me paying. Hell, girls bought *me* presents. Beautiful Akai reel-to-reel, Seiko watch, Pentax camera, Denon hi-fi. Made me loans they never expected to see come back. Oriental women know how to treat a man. At least, they did back then. Not like the trash you got now." He waves vaguely toward the security monitor. "Damn Flips and Bucketheads. Sukie, though, Setsuko, now, she was a whole 'nother level. She was obsessed. I mean cuckoo stalker insane for me."

I almost stop him. Almost say, "That's my grandmother you're talking about," but I have made a decision: It's not. He's just telling me an old-time story from his life, and it can't touch or change who my grandmother was to me. I won't let it. I knew who she really was. I'm only listening to the story for the information I have to get.

"That's not just me talkin'," he continues. "Anybody'd tell you the same. End of a show, she was always right there with a nice, cool, moist towel outta the fridge, bowl of *sōki* soba with all that good pork in it, bottle of cold Orion." He grunts at the memory. "Even though she knew I was with a different lady every night, she'd lose control, try to scratch the new one's eyes out. Got to where I knew I had to cut her loose. I couldn't have that kind of discourse going on."

I like it that he uses the wrong word for "discord." Listening to him brag about what a stud he was makes me even more certain that he is my mother's father. I feel it in my blood, the cheater and the cheated. The left and the always leaving. The one who thinks connection equals entanglement. Whose idea of free is alone.

"I was just about ready to tell her not to come 'round no more when I got my orders. For 'Nam. All of us bloods making the scene down the Bush, we all got them the same day. Military knew the Bush was more powerful than they were, so they ganged up, air force, army, marines, navy. If you were black and not eatin' a yard of the Man's shit, you got orders that day. And there weren't any assignments sortin' mail at Hickam either. Naw, it was all front line. You got papers that day, you *were* gonna end up in the Central Highlands or the Mekong Delta. And you *were* gonna end up dead. Those orders were death sentences."

Vaughn looks out the window. The sun has come out and slants a harsh stripe of light across his face. His eyes glitter the way old people's do. He sounds even older when he says, "I wasn't gonna let the air force kill me. Took me a while to figure out they already had."

· THIRTY-SEVEN ·

Vaughn stares out the window. It's a long time before he finally picks up his story again. "The Bush was wild that night. Never been wilder. Girls were crying, making a fuss. Brothers all frontin' about how they ain't goin'. No way. No how. Then guess what happens?"

I shake my head, intent on what he is saying; I know the story is coming to the part where my existence begins.

"Typhoon! You believe that shit? Elsie, Typhoon Elsie, supposed to hit Guam; it veers off, heads right for the Rock. It was an official TC-1 alert. Base closed up, locked down. No one even supposed to be outside the fence. But after we got orders? We figured, *shee*-it, what they gonna do to us? Send us to Vee *Et* Nam? So we take it to the street. Ready to riot. *Hoping* they'd send some MPs after us, because we didn't care anymore. Whatever stockade they threw us in be better than dying in the Central Highlands next to some Montagnard fighting for a country he actually gave a shit about.

"So it's straight-up chaos in Koza, know what I'm sayin'? It's pouring rain, the wind is howlin' like standing in the prop wash of a B-52. All the club owners are freaking out, boarding up windows, pulling down the metal shutters, shoving sandbags under the doors. The mama-sans are filling up bathtubs, buckets, douche bags, anything they got for drinking water. Coupla shops still open are packed with people buying batteries, cans of Spam, jugs of water.

"What a trip. Our girls crying, hanging on to us. Wind whipping that rain sideways straight into our faces. Like a movie. And all us young, good-looking, renegade bloods were the stars. And our courage and pride and righteousness were going to beat back the damn United States air force, army, navy, *and* marines. Then someone with a radio starts yelling about how Elsie been declared a supertyphoon. Winds predicted to hit a hundred and seventy-five miles an hour. That is some serious shit. Blow a fuckin' anchor down the street's what I'm talkin' about."

I feel it, the winds howling through me, the winds that have always howled through me. Finally, I know where they come from.

"About then, lights flicker off. Shops close. Streets get dark and empty. We're standing in the middle a fuckin' ghost town. Then that siren goes off. You ever hear an Okinawan typhoon siren?"

I can barely force a word out, and whisper, "No."

"Make the hair on a dead man's neck stand up. Scary movie shit. Like they opened up the graveyards and ten thousand ghosts come pouring out, all wailing and flying through the streets. Man, eyes *popped* open when those sirens went off. No one be talkin' about blockading the streets, garroting the MPs one by one when they come for us. Everyone looking around for some shelter and all we see is doors closed, locked, and sandbagged. Brothers be thinkin' about those nice safe reinforced concrete barracks back on base. Next time that siren goes off, they gone. All the girls gone. *Poof.* Vanished. All except one."

"My grandmother." My *anmā*. I can see my grandmother so vividly, the way she always was. Always moving ahead, pushing forward no matter what, even if she was walking into a gale.

"Yeah, little Sukie. Not a dog out there loyal as that one. The wind about strong enough to blow her to China, and she just stand there, put her hand in mine, and led me away. Had a nice little studio. Had her a hot plate, four-blade ceiling fan, cassette player, nice double bed. Actual mattress on a frame. And the building was sound. Lot of buildings, shit whole department stores!, blew away when Elsie hit. Eight people killed. But we rode it out, me and Sukie, drinking *awamori*, smoking those funky Violet cigarettes, laughing. Made me happy to make someone as happy as she was just from being with me. I was like Elvis, Jesus, and Smokey all rolled into one for Sukie."

She pined for you for the rest of her life. I wonder whether I should hate him for breaking my *anmā*'s heart or if it really was better to have loved and lost than never to have loved at all. I wonder whether I'm like my grandmother or my mother.

"Even after Elsie moved on, Sukie stayed home from her bar hostess job. Bought me whatever I wanted. Beer, cigarettes, *sōki* soba. What can I say? Woman flat-out worshiped my ass. Loved to just pat me like I was some big, giant Christmas doll. My eyes, though. Man, she'd stare into them and whisper in her crazy Oki language. Not Japanese. Whole other language. And my hair? She'd bend over and kiss it like every curl was a baby that needed her to coo over it."

I think of her, transported, as she kissed my curls, Codie's. Of the adoration that oozed from her.

"At first, being a deserter was like staying home sick from school. I stopped shaving, grew me a fine Eldridge Cleaver, *Soul on Ice*, Black Power beard. But it wasn't the same. The Bush never recovered from Elsie. Typhoon blew the heart out the place. None of the cats who made the scene so cool ever came back after that night. Every last one of them was shipped out on the first plane that took off after Elsie passed. No more brothers strutting around in leather jackets, black berets, and purple granny glasses giving the Black Power salute.

"I got jumpy. Was sure they were coming after me. That they'd find me holed up in Suki's little apartment. Every time someone knock on the door, I'd slip out the window, hide in the alley until they left. But the MPs never came. No one came. Local police didn't even care. Once I realized no one was coming, I started wandering around outside. Sukie'd freak every time I opened the door. But I had to get out. I'd go up and down Gate Street. B.C. Street. If Sukie'd made enough the night before, I'd get me a hot dog, a few beers. Those five or six blocks were my prison yard. Went on like that for months.

"Eventually, I started going all the way up Gate Street, right to the edge of the base. Circled around all the way to the runway where Gene was unloading them rainbow barrels. Thought I was a ghost when he first saw me, then he had to know all about how I beat the air force almighty. Played it off for him. Acted like I was livin' the life, boy. Gene." He shakes his head at the memory. "Eugene Overholt."

"I was so lonely, I gave that hillbilly peckerwood my address and he started coming around. Got to be the highlight of my week when Gene'd show up with a loaf of Wonder Bread and a jar of Skippy peanut butter from the commissary. By then, he had this crusty rash all over his hands, arms. Told him it was from those damn drums. He just said, 'Not possible. PACAF has certified that it's safe.' Fool.

"Wasn't like I wasn't an even bigger fool, though. Bit by bit, it come to me why the air force wasn't coming after me: They already had me locked up. I was in a sixty-mile-long, three-mile-wide prison. I mean, where the fuck I gonna go? All they got to do is wait until I go stir-crazy like every other grunt ever gone AWOL on this Alcatraz of an island and they knew I'd turn myself in. Or they could just pick me up if I try to leave. Instant I flash my passport at the airport, I be in handcuffs and on my way to Leavenworth. And not just for desertion either. Hell, no. Okis had started protesting by then about all the rapes, murders, robberies committed by GIs and how U.S. military courts never done jack shit to a one of them. How Tokyo never stood up for them either, just hung 'em out to dry as usual. So military was looking for a scape-goat. They ever got me, they wouldn't just ship me out to 'Nam; they'd pin every murder, every rape, every cab fare ever got walked, and every pack of gum ever got stole on me and I'd be doin' some hard, *hard* time.

"Minute I realize I was never getting out, that's when I started losing it. The walls closed in on me. Koza, I had to get out of that shithole. I figure if I was going to be serving a life sentence on the Rock, at least I could do it in a decent city like Naha, where there's something beside strip clubs, tattoo parlors, and T-shirt shops.

"I didn't say nothing. Sukie, though, she was about half psychic, always getting messages from her ancestors. She knew we were played out. That I was leaving and wouldn't be taking her with me. She went crazy in her own quiet, moody way. Is it possible to rape a man? I woulda said no until then. That woman would not leave me alone. She was always pawin' at me, grabbing at my dick."

I stand. "Yeah, okay, that's enough. My grandmother was the best grown-up I ever knew and you were lucky that she gave you the time of day." As I start to leave, he stops me."

"I'm sorry. I haven't been around decent people in forty years. I can't even talk right anymore. You're right; I didn't deserve your grandmother. Stay."

I keep walking to the door.

"Hey!"

I stop.

"I'm not gonna be around a whole lot longer, and I need someone to know this story before I'm gone."

I don't move.

"I won't talk smack about your grandma anymore, but I am gonna tell the story true. You want that, don't you?"

I nod, sit back down.

"No surprise she turned up pregnant. I ask her what she want *me* to do about it. Sukie's a professional. She knew how to get it taken care of. I'm not saying that's the way I *shoulda* been, just that that's the way I was. But from then on, *she* was the one wouldn't let *me* anywhere near her. Sulled up like a possum. Prayed and lit incense. Only time she smiled was when Gene came by. She found some funky ointment for his rash. Rubbed it on him with her pretty little hands. Asked in this whispery baby voice if that made him feel better. Gene'd just nod his head like he was hypnotized. Being pregnant changed Sukie. What she wanted didn't matter anymore to her. Only my baby mattered. She needed someone to protect her, protect the baby, and I guess Gene seemed like the answer to all those prayers she was saying and all that incense she was burning.

"Pretty soon, Gene stopped even pretending he was coming to see me. Then he stopped coming to the apartment at all. Sukie'd leave, go meet him somewhere, come back smelling like that funky Jade East shit he wore. Few times I did see him, Gene looked at me like a dog got caught eating the Thanksgiving turkey. All ashamed, feeling bad for cheating with my woman. Only thing I felt was relieved. Didn't even tell her good-bye when I left. I'm sorry I did your grandma that way after she saved me, but once I had me a job lined up in Naha, place to stay, I was gone. Solid gone."

I guess a billion dominoes have to fall in exactly the right order for any one person to appear on earth, but the epic randomness of my being here because a typhoon veered off course and gave an Okinawan bar girl the opening to make her move on a guy she was crushed out on momentarily overwhelms me.

Vaughn's gaze flickers over to the monitor. What he sees there causes him to sit up straight, bristling with attention. The girl he's watching slithers over her customer like an eel with good rhythm, twining and rubbing until the marine arches his back, his glistening chest rising off the air mattress. He reaches out for the girl on top of him, and Vaughn zooms in. He watches with a steely gaze as the soldier grasps the girl's hips, tries to force her onto himself. Vaughn is on the verge of jumping up when the girl shakes off the marine's grasp and wriggles about on his crotch until the soldier shudders, his eyes fluttering and mouth gaping open as he sinks back down.

Vaughn, too, sags back down, the scene on the monitor forgotten. "So I assume she got Gene to marry her, take her with him when he left?"

I nod that this is the case. As Vaughn goes to a shelf and searches through it, I think about how I'd always been told that my grandfather's family had rejected us because they were racist and hated my "Oriental" grandmother. But I recall a family photo when my grandmother was pregnant, standing in front of Gene's husky Missouri farming family. They were all smiling. A big woman in a housedress stood between Gene and my grandmother, her freckled arms draped protectively over both of them. No such happy family pictures exist after my dark-skinned mother was born.

Vaughn pulls out an old leather-bound Bible, opens the tissuey pages to one showing a family tree. "There it is. Goes all the way back to slave times. Got a German in there. Seminole. Cuban. Irish. Little bit of everything. All ended up getting called black."

I ask him for some paper and a pen and begin copying. Vaughn goes from monitoring the girls with the marines to watching me and nodding with approval. "It's good to know who your people are. Important."

I copy the names. The oldest ones, from the early eighteen hundreds, sound either English or Old Testament. Nancy. Abraham. Bessie. Isaac. I write them down, but those aren't the names I'm really interested in. I doubt they'll help the *yuta*; I need Okinawan names. When I've gotten down enough of this stranger's family tree to be polite I ask, "What about my grandmother's family?"

"Sukie's people?" He blows out from between clenched teeth. "Okinawans and family, that's a whole other deal. Hard for an American to understand. We go around saying, 'Family's the most important thing.' Not even close. Minute family gets between an American and what's really important to him—money, power, pussy, being left alone—he'll cut 'em loose so fast. Not Okinawans. Ain't no cuttin' loose for an Oki. Family's yours in this life and all the ones to come. Worse than the damn Mormons.

"Sukie thought she was lucky that way. Bragged all the time about what an important family she come from."

"The Ueharas."

"Right. She even took me once to see the tomb. Bigger than her apartment, swear to God."

"Do you remember her father's name?"

"What was that sonabitch's first name? Haru? Hideo? Hiroshi, that's it. Hiroshi Uehara."

I write the name down, the first on my list for the *yuta*. "And her mother?" I ask, but Delmar Vaughn isn't finished yet with my grandmother's father.

"Old Hiroshi. Owned most of the land where the big marine air station is now. Of course, all the property titles were burned and bombed to dust during the war. U.S. military only too happy not to have any property titles to deal with when Japan gave them pretty much anything they wanted long as it was way off here on Okinawa and not on the mainland. Without the land, though, Uehara had nothing. That's why he adopted Sukie."

I stop writing. "Adopted?"

"Yeah, thought you knew that. Sukie was an orphan. Ueharas adopted her."

I put the pen down. I need the names of blood relations. "No, I didn't know that."

"Happened a lot back then. There were so many orphans after the war, they were handing them out at those detention camps like puppies at the pound. Sukie was too young to remember her real family, her mother. All she knew was that she was what they called a 'surplus person.' Thought she was lucky that the Ueharas took her in, even if it meant she worked like a dog all day and slept on a mat in the kitchen at night. The whole deal was tied to them allowing her to be buried in their tomb. That was supposed to be the big payoff for her, that she wouldn't spend eternity all alone. Always knew that her place was to serve that family however she could, 'cause if she ever let them down, all the Uehara ancestors would make her life hell not only in this world but in the next one too.

"The reason girls were adopted was to be maids or field hands. Then, if they were pretty enough and the family needed money because Dad gambled or whored around, they'd be sold to a house. All the shame would be loaded onto the girls, so the family would be cleansed when she was sold off as a prostitute.

"Very common, very accepted back then. Hell, happens now. The big Korean?" He points to the screen where the Korean girl sits, waiting. "That's why she's here. And her?" He nods toward a screen where one of the Filipinas is, alone, hosing down the tiled room. "Dad gambles. Got so far in the hole to the Yakuza, he had to sell her or they'da killed him. But these girls"—he waves dismissively toward the screens—"none of them are as smart or as determined as Sukie was. By the time I met her, she'd worked her way out of the suckee-fuckee business, and had a job as a hostess, getting dumb GIs to buy watered-down drinks."

A speaker emits a scratchy blast of staticky Japanese. Vaughn zooms in on the panel showing Mama-san having an angry conversation with the two marines, who are now standing in front of her reception desk; she's holding their ID cards hostage.

"Oops, gotta go to work."

I follow Vaughn downstairs, where he steps up and tells the marine,

"We got you on tape, buddy. You had your hands on the girl. That is illegal and you know it is illegal. So you can either pay the penalty or we call in the local popo, show them the tape, and see what they want to do."

As I slip out, unnoticed, I think of the Ueharas, the family my grandmother thought had truly accepted her, the one she told her daughter would be waiting for her with open arms. I think of my mother locked in the bathroom smoking her secret cigarettes and of the letter she'd read in there. How it had probably told her that she and her mother weren't related to them at all. That, no matter what Setsuko had told her, or even believed herself, she had no real, no blood connection to them and they owed her nothing. That the stranger in the photo, the street corner dude, was her only true, blood relation. It is dark outside when I leave. In the side room, the Korean girl is still sitting alone, waiting.

· THIRTY-EIGHT ·

Hatsuko's hand was ice-cold when I took it and led her away. In the main corridor one of the Himeyuri teachers, an Okinawan man, was addressing the student nurses. Nearly all 220 of us were there, listening anxiously as he said, "Each of you will receive one *go* of rice. We will follow the army south to Makabe. Only patients who can make the journey unaided will be allowed to come with us. Move only at night. Seek shelter before the sun rises. There are caves everywhere. Hide in them during the day. Stay away from our tombs. They have been used as gun emplacements by our brave soldiers; hence the enemy will blow them up on sight."

My heart constricted. I prayed that Mother and Father had fled to a cave near our home and not to our family tomb.

"And most important, know this: Anyone who attempts to surrender will be shot. Death before dishonor!"

A few girls answered by wishing the emperor a thousand years, but most of us scurried away, anxious to draw our skimpy rations before all the rice was gone.

There was no moon that night and our group set forth into a dark, expectant stillness. I hoped that Mitsue would remain out of sight; I didn't want Hatsuko to have to see her. Though we felt the presence of the enemy as if horrible beasts hiding in the darkness were watching our every step, it was heartening to be surrounded again by so many Princess Lily girls. I took strength from their courage. We barely whispered to one another, and then only to call out warnings. Hatsuko, though, said nothing and moved in a slow, mechanical way, still in shock from what we had seen in that dark corridor.

As we climbed a steep hill, the only sound was our own labored breathing. We had almost been lulled into believing that the enemy was sleeping when a shell burst lit the forbidding hill with a stark bluish blaze of illumination. The sky filled then with enough tracer fire and gun flashes for a dangerous twilight to leave us exposed. A shell landed on a pile of rocks nearby and sent hundreds of lethal fragments flying toward us. Bigger rocks, shaken loose by the concussion, avalanched down the hill. Shrieks of pain identified those hit by fragments or crushed by the boulders.

My body flooded with adrenaline strength at the sound of those death cries. I reached behind me, grabbed Hatsuko's hand, and dragged her off that hill and as far from the group as I could before collapsing. There was no safety anymore in our group. There was only the danger of being a larger target. I huddled with Hatsuko for a long time, letting the others drift far ahead of us, before we set out again.

After we had marched for several hours, it began to pour. The American flares glittered like long silver arrows through the sheets of rain. Water streamed down the ghostly faces of the refugees we passed. Villages had been reduced to piles of stone and ash, with an occasional bit of broken red roof tile. The stench of rotting carcasses filled the air. Worse were the occasional blazes of red and blue flames that burned even in the wet darkness, for we knew the flames were feeding on the burning fat of a body recently hit by shells. We hoped that it was animal fat but knew that many times it wasn't.

The rain stopped shortly before dawn. I managed to find shelter in a rare, intact farmhouse so recently abandoned that a fire was still warm in the white ashes. Hatsuko and I huddled together through the long day. That night we were unable to sleep for the constant bombardment all around.

By nightfall, we were back on the road to Makabe, and had no choice but to occasionally join the stream of refugees fleeing the bombing that, like a forest fire, was driving all creatures ahead of its destructive wake. The battle behind us rumbled as loudly as an approaching thunderstorm. Tanks roared; rockets shrieked; mortars landed with powerful whumps that we felt in our guts. The smell of cordite drifted in, mixed with the stink of decaying corpses.

Soon a heavy, drenching rain began to fall again. The night air turned cool, and, soaked and starved as we were, we started to shiver. In the downpour we splashed past mothers begging their exhausted children to hurry; old men pulling carts piled high with clanking pots, bent over so far that their wispy white beards dragged in the mud; young boys balancing huge bundles tied to either end of long shoulder poles, staggering beneath their loads; old women plodding forward mechanically while rain and tears washed down their wrinkled faces; mothers struggling forward with babies strapped onto their backs and heavy baskets wobbling atop their heads. The mothers carrying babies made me think of Chiiko and Little Mouse and I prayed that they were safe.

I could no longer hold back my concerns, and asked everyone I could where they were from, hoping to find someone from near our village who might be able to give us news of Mother and Father and the others. But I found no one. The rain stopped, but, exhausted by heartbreak, Hatsuko faltered and pleaded for rest. In a few hours, the sun would rise and we would be exposed to the *tombos*, the droning dragonflies searching for the slightest jiggle of motion. Because we were all streaming down this road together, soldiers and civilians, carts and army trucks mixed together, the planes swooping out of the sun would see only targets to be bombed or strafed. I had to keep Hatsuko moving. We had to find a cave, somewhere to hide, before the sun rose.

So when Hatsuko let her pack fall to the ground and started to slump down beside it, I lied, saying, "Ahead there! On the road. That platoon of soldiers that just passed us. Isn't that Nakamura with them?"

Even after what we had seen back in the cave, the lieutenant's name acted on my sister like a jolt of electricity. She retrieved her pack, shouldered the bundle, and told me to hurry; the platoon was getting away from us.

"I won't speak to him," she assured me, adding, "I will never speak to him again. I just want to make sure that he got out safely."

Because I knew that Nakamura wasn't with the soldiers, I became the one who dawdled; I wanted to keep Hatsuko moving, but not quickly enough to discover my ruse. Still, she summoned her last bit of energy and hurried us along. When we drew abreast of the soldiers, Hatsuko ran to the head of the platoon and stood watching as they straggled past. After the last dispirited soldier had marched by, she waited for me to catch up. Her body and spirit slumped dangerously as she said mournfully, "He wasn't with them."

"He must already be in Makabe then," I offered. And, though I hated the lie, I added, "He's probably waiting for you there, sick with worry. I'm certain that once we find him in Makabe, Nakamura will explain everything." Then I added the worst part of the lie: "Hatsuko, Nakamura is an officer in the Japanese Imperial Army, a soldier of the emperor. Which means that, by definition, he is incapable of doing anything dishonorable."

Hatsuko considered my pretty words, weighed them against the sight of Mitsue and Nakamura together, and found that they came up short. "I can't go any farther, Tami-chan. Leave me here. I will rest and find you in Makabe. Or in the next life, if that is my fate. I have to rest. I have no energy left." She collapsed on the wet ground and begged me, "Leave me here. I can't go on."

It was just as *Anmā* had warned me: My sister's head was filled with airy thoughts. And now that they had been punctured, she deflated like a balloon. For a moment I wondered why I had to be the one whose broad feet were planted on the earth; I was the little sister. She was my *onēsama*, my honorable older sister. Shouldn't she be the one looking after me?

A deafening explosion blew all such thoughts away as a bomb went off so close that fragments of smashed stone were driven into the side of my head. A sharp pain stabbed deep inside my right ear and I felt warm blood flowing down my neck, but could hear nothing except a loud ringing deep inside my skull. I knew that the next bomb would finish us off. I yanked Hatsuko to her feet and dragged her forward. Blocking out our own suffering and that of everyone we passed in the night, we tramped on in a state of oblivion.

"Look out where you're going!" an angry voice snarled, snapping me out of my stupor. At my feet was a man I'd nearly stepped on. He'd lost one leg and injured the other, and was dragging himself through the mud and bomb-crater puddles with his hands. No one stopped to help him. No one *could* stop to help him. To do so would be to choose a life that was beyond your power to save over your own, over your family's.

"Damn it, Hatsuko," I cursed, even my voice sounding strange now, hearing it with only one ear. "Move!"

We stumbled forward, leaving the one-legged man behind. Ahead was a steep hill. Halfway to the top, my knees gave way and I sank to the earth, almost too spent even to breathe. Hatsuko collapsed next to me. Though the rain had stopped, water still oozed from the porous ground and streamed down the hill. I lay against the limestone and let the water trickle into my mouth. Even after drinking my fill, though, I had no energy left. I could not lift my own body, let alone my sister's. I accepted that Hatsuko and I would die on this rocky patch of soaking ground. Then a cloud of flies with glaring red eyes—flies in the middle of the night!—swarmed about my head, buzzing into my eyes, nose, mouth, nipping at me with an uncommon ferocity. I smiled. This was Old Jug displaying her anger at my surrender.

"*Nuchi du takara,*" I whispered my mother's words to myself. "Life is the treasure."

The stinging pain of the fly bites jolted enough energy back into my body that, somehow, I managed to drag Hatsuko and myself to the top of the hill. Too tired to move another centimeter, we joined a group already resting there. Far behind us, back toward Haebaru, we saw long tongues of fire leaping out of the darkness. "Flamethrowers," someone in the darkness said. "They are burning alive the brave ones who refused to surrender."

"Death before dishonor!" someone called out.

One person answered with wishes for the emperor's long life: "*Tennō heika banzai!*" But the cry was not picked up.

Instead, someone said, "Do you smell that?" A rancid odor of diesel fumes and singed hair reached us. "That's the smell of human flesh being burned."

I did not want Hatsuko to concentrate on such ghoulish thoughts, and so turned from the sight of our island being incinerated and said,

"Look, a full moon." My sister followed my finger to the good-luck coin of a golden moon sailing through a filigree of navy-blue clouds.

"Remember all our moon-viewing parties?" I asked, simply to change the subject.

"That isn't until the middle of August. I won't live long enough to—"

I cut her off before she could speak the unthinkable. "Remember Anmā's muchi? How she mixed rice with black sugar and her purple sweet potatoes, then steamed the dough in fragrant ginger leaves?" My mouth watered thinking of the special treat.

Even Hatsuko couldn't resist the delicious memory. "Then we would tie a few of the bundles onto a long string and hang them from the eaves of the roof to ward off evil spirits?"

For a moment, we were not wet and hungry and scared, and flies, mosquitoes, fleas, and lice weren't chewing away at us, and we didn't smell worse than our goats ever had. We were beloved daughters, clean and fresh in the yukatas that Aunt Yasu had woven for us from the softest, finest banana fiber. Our stomachs were full of Anmā's muchi. And we were gazing at a moon that promised us the best harvest we'd ever had, while one of my uncles played his sanshin and sang a song about the beauty of Okinawa.

At the foot of the hill was the road to Makabe. The fat moon transformed it into a ribbon of silver that we would follow to safety after a bit more rest. Far up ahead, we caught sight of the platoon of soldiers I had lied about, telling Hatsuko that Nakamura was among their ranks. We watched them for a moment. The moonlight gleamed dully on the few bayonets they had left. Just as they were about to disappear from sight, a bomb exploded directly on them. For a split second the blast of the bomb was so bright that it outshone the moon and we saw silhouetted soldiers flying to their deaths. Not one of the soldiers rose from the spot where he'd been thrown; they were all killed, the entire platoon.

Though we no longer fooled ourselves that we would find safety, we had no choice but to keep moving south, toward Makabe, toward the end of the island. At least we would have the protection of our army there. With a weary sigh, I stood, prepared to move my sister forward by force if I had to.

Instead, to my surprise, Hatsuko jumped to her feet and whispered to me, "Those soldiers blowing up, that was a sign. It was a sign that Nakamura isn't meant to die yet. He wasn't in that platoon as you thought, because the gods are protecting him. Our destinies are intertwined; I can feel it. You were right; he *is* waiting for me. There *will* be an explanation."

Hatsuko's eyes glittered as she told me to hurry. I didn't say anything about how grotesque it was to think that all those young men had been slaughtered simply to send her a message. Instead, I pulled out the padded bonnets that our mother had made for us and tied one on her head and one on mine. It no longer mattered how I kept my sister alive, only that I kept my promise to *Anmā* and did it.

· THIRTY-NINE ·

Just before dawn, I managed to find the crumbled remains of a bombed-out bridge. We wriggled into the hollow formed between two large chunks of cement and, though water trickled beneath our hiding spot, soaking us through, we felt safe. After resting for a few hours in the damp spot, neither of us could ignore the rumbling of our empty bellies. We hadn't eaten since leaving Haebaru, and it was far too wet to make a fire to cook part of our ration of rice.

By scurrying out of hiding for brief periods, I managed to find some locusts, a lizard, and a handful of sweet potato leaves to eat. Though Hatsuko gagged eating bits of lizard and locust, I promised her that tomorrow we would cook the rice and have a proper meal. Thinking of the rice to come and Nakamura waiting for her with an explanation allowed her to swallow. The food quieted our complaining bellies enough that we slept for several hours, then continued on when night fell.

We reached Makabe at dawn the next day and found dozens of other Princess Lily girls. We were overjoyed to reunite with Sachiko and Miyoko. Mitsue stood apart from the others, averting her eyes when Hatsuko glanced her way. We had only a few short minutes before the sun rose and enemy soldiers would be able to see us. I led Hatsuko and the other girls to the main hospital cave. Centuries of rainwater had carved the entrance, a vertical hole in the ground. There would be a safe place to sleep and food waiting for us within its dark depths. Outside the entrance to the cave, wounded soldiers moaned in pain on stretchers. Their comrades who had risked their lives to rescue the fallen begged the guards to let them in.

"You may enter," a guard told the soldiers. "But you must leave the stretchers behind. There is no room for them."

"Don't worry," I assured the brave soldiers who had risked their lives to bring the wounded to safety. "As soon as we are admitted, I will bring help for those men." But when Hatsuko and I stepped forward to enter, two guards blocked our way.

"We are Himeyuri girls," I informed him. The girls behind me nodded. Some of them called out their names or the names of their teachers. But the guard did not move.

This time when I spoke, I used the crisp tone I'd heard Japanese soldiers adopt when they addressed those of lower rank. "Let us in immediately. We work with the hospital as student nurses. We are needed inside. Your superiors will be quite angry with you if you don't admit us and these wounded men."

The guards glanced at each other and muttered, "*Kawaii,*" the Japanese word for "cute." As they laughed, the taller of the two grinned.

Feeling the weight of being responsible now not just for Hatsuko, but for all the other Princess Lily girls who had joined us, I cried out forcefully, "The sun is rising! You must let us in! The bombing is going to start! We will all be killed!"

"No one else is getting in here," the grinning guard said. "This is for hospital staff only."

"But we *are* hospital staff. Do you see this blood?" I pointed to a brown splotch on my collar. "This is from a soldier whose leg I helped amputate. Now let us in so that we can find help and carry these men out here to safety inside."

"No more room. All filled up. There are already so many of you Lily girls down there that they're calling it the Cave of the Virgins."

The shorter guard grunted out a laugh, then ordered, "Move on. No more virgins needed here! But you." The guard pointed to the stretcher bearers. "You soldiers, you can come in." They moved forward, and the guard barked, "Without the stretchers, you idiots. What did I just say? There's no room."

Far behind us, like a train in the distance, the droning of bombers setting off on their deadly mission came once more. I grabbed Hatsuko's hand and shoved my shoulder against the guard to knock him aside and let us in. Instantly his hand closed around my throat. His companion cocked his rifle and pointed it at Hatsuko. The first guard choked me long enough to show that he could kill me if he chose to, then he thrust me out, bawling, "Japanese only! The rest of you, you Okinawans, you are on your own. Now get out of here before I shoot you all!"

But we couldn't move. We were too stunned by this ultimate betrayal. We were being denied shelter, turned out into sure death in the Typhoon of Steel. The able-bodied soldiers shoved their way past us and entered the cave.

An instant later, I was thrown forward onto my face by the percussive impact of a bomb exploding behind us. There was a white flash, and fragments flew past us with a throaty, angry buzz. We screamed as gravel and rocks bludgeoned our backs.

A large stone hit my head with a force that might have been deadly had it not been for *Anmā*'s bonnet. Debris rained down, battering the unshielded, wounded soldiers until their moaning stopped and they lay silent forever. Their comrades who had risked their lives saving them huddled inside the cave and wept.

The instant the barrage stopped, Hatsuko and I clambered to our feet. Mitsue and Miyoko lay motionless on the ground. Sachiko, the fastest runner in our group, writhed in agony, the white of bone and brain showing through the blood that sheeted her face.

Hatsuko and I went to help our friends, our cousin, but a fast-approaching roar stopped us. "More bombers are coming," I said, dragging my sister away. "The next one will kill us!" We joined the few other student nurses who had survived and bolted toward the nearest cave opening we could find. Here too Japanese soldiers lunged at us with bayonets, driving us away.

"Why don't you just kill us right now!" I screamed. "That's what you're doing! You were supposed to protect us! We nursed you! We brought you water! We picked maggots from your wounds!"

The next flight of approaching bombers clouded the sky to the north so completely that I knew we would never survive their devastation. I was commending my soul to our ancestors' care when a Japanese soldier's head popped out of what I thought was a pile of dead brush that had blown against the side of the hill.

"Hurry," he called out in a shrill voice, pushing the camouflage away to reveal the opening to a cave that descended straight down into the earth. The kind soldier pulled us into the cave, and we clambered down into its depths just as the first bombs dropped. Though the hole in the earth was already packed so tightly with other refugees that we all had to stand, we were happy to do so, for none of us would have survived the barrage that roared outside.

"Katsuko?" a voice called out in lull in the shelling. It was Natsuko, searching for her little sister with the rhyming name. In the darkness of the cave, we all picked up the cry and called out for Katsuko. But Katsuko didn't answer. Natsuko, unable to believe what this meant, said, "She was right behind me. She was always right behind me. Someone, please help me find my little sister."

As an explosion that made the earth around us rumble drowned out the rest of her words, my sister found my hand and squeezed with a strength I hadn't felt from her in too long. I clung to it through that long day of destruction. All around us, girls weak from hunger and thirst fainted. Whispers reached us that three girls, wounded by shrapnel and weakened by malaria, had died and that there was not enough room for them to crumple to the earth. We were all packed in so tightly that I too remained upright even when I fell asleep.

At nightfall, though the bombing didn't stop, we flooded out of the cave, driven from safety by thirst, hunger, and the desperate need to relieve ourselves. Since all the other girls had finished off the meager rations of rice they'd been given in Haebaru, Hatsuko and I had to find a private place to cook and eat ours. If we shared what little we had there wouldn't be enough to sustain any of us.

Outside, we rushed away from the cave and eventually found a sheltered spot in what had once been a stable. It had been raining all day, though, and Hatsuko said, "We'll never find anything dry enough to build a fire and cook our rice."

"Don't worry about that," I answered. From around my waist, I untied the tube of money *Anmā* had given me so long ago and used a wad of the bills to light a small fire. It was just large enough to boil the water I had scooped out of a bomb crater in the lid of my mess kit. As we waited for the muddy liquid to boil, I reached into my satchel for our rice. It wasn't there. We emptied every bundle we had and clawed frantically through every scrap they contained. The rice was gone.

"Someone must have stolen it," Hatsuko concluded. Packed in as we had been, I never would have noticed the slither of a thieving hand. We waited for the water to boil and cool; then, because thirst was clawing at our throats, I poured us each a cup of the foul, oily stuff.

I held my cup up. "Here's to the most expensive drink we'll ever drink." Hatsuko didn't laugh at my joke, and I choked down the water in silence.

As we squatted there, I took stock of our situation: We had no food. No clean water. And no safe shelter. The Japanese army had turned us out to die. The ketō would be arriving soon with their flamethrowers. I imagined the flames licking into our hiding place like the tongue of a voracious dragon. I imagined the last sounds I heard on this earth being Hatsuko's tortured cries, and I announced, "We're going home."

"But we will be shot as deserters."

"Hatsuko, the army has deserted us. We have no choice. Everyone here will either surrender or die."

"Death before dishonor."

I wanted to slap her when she said that, but didn't. We weren't having a sisters' spat. There was no longer any winning or losing. There was only living or dying, and I was determined that we would live. "Hatsuko, there is food in our family tomb. Anmā put it there for us. Pork miso. Dried sweet potatoes. Black sugar. And the springs? Remember the springs in the woods behind our house? There will be clean, fresh water. We can drink. Bathe. We're not far, Hatsuko. We can be back in our village in two nights' marching."

"Perhaps Mother and Father will be waiting for us, safe in the tomb."

"It's possible." If anyone could outwit the Japanese and American armies, it was my resourceful mother. How, I wondered, had such a simple countrywoman been able to predict all that would happen? Thinking it would help convince Hatsuko, I added, "You know what Mother always says: 'Life is the treasure.'"

Instead of convincing her, however, *Anmā's* mantra must have reminded Hatsuko of the warrior's code of death before dishonor that Nakamura lived by, and she insisted, "No. I can't. I must find Nakamura."

Again I fought the impulse to slap my sister. I knew that if I did, though, it would only make her more stubborn. Instead, speaking in the flowery way she did with Nakamura, I lured her with this promise: "Nakamura is the reason we must go. Like all the others, he, too, is starving. We must go and fetch food for him. Imagine his delight when you present the crock of *Anmā's* delicious pork miso to him."

In her eyes, I saw the scene she imagined playing out. Nakamura would be on his deathbed, his features even more refined and ennobled by all he'd endured. Hatsuko would cushion his body with hers, helping him to sit up. The first few bites she would feed to him herself. She would snatch him back from the White Dragon of Death. Dazzled by gratitude, he would fix his eyes on hers and their love would be reborn.

"Yes, all right," she agreed.

The way to our village was littered with corpses bloated to two and three times their size. We had covered only a few kilometers when the sight and smell of rotting flesh combined with hunger and thirst made Hatsuko's pace wobbly and uncertain. Unless I found food and water, her energy would continue to dwindle, until she joined the poor souls who'd already given up their lives. That fear drove me to approach the body of a Japanese soldier, lying facedown in a dry ditch. Flies, their blue bellies fat, buzzed around him. I tried to shoo them away, but they wouldn't leave. In the soldier's rucksack I found three hard candies and a tin of food. I was forced to shove his body aside to retrieve the canteen he'd fallen on. His rifle had been smashed by falling rocks, but I was able to remove the bayonet, and I took that with me.

I sucked one of the hard candies, and every sight and sound and smell except for the voluptuous sweetness of barley sugar melting in my mouth faded away. I retraced my path back to Hatsuko, gave her the two candies I had left, and we each took sips from the canteen. The tin, which I opened with the blade of the bayonet, contained squid in oil. Hatsuko and I savored every tentacle of the squid and every drop of its dark oil. The water, candy, and squid gave us the energy to toil on for a few more kilometers before the sun started to rise. Even if it meant stealing from the dead, my sister and I were going home.

· FORTY ·

It is dark outside and a misty drizzle is falling when I get back to the car. In the pink light cast by the SoapLand sign, I see that Jake is asleep. His head rests to one side, nestled against his shoulder. He looks blurry through the wet windshield. All the shops on the street have closed for the night, their shutters lowered. I try to figure out what to tell him, but I haven't even absorbed it all myself. As soon as I open the door, he wakes.

"Hey, how'd it go? You were gone a long time."

"Yeah, he wanted to tell me the story of his life."

"And?"

"And what?"

"Did you get what you needed?"

I show him the list I copied.

"That should work. You okay?"

"It was intense."

"You want to talk about it?"

"I feel like I've already dragged you into more than you bargained for."

"You didn't drag me; the *kami* did. Want to try the best yakitori on the island?"

"I'm not really hungry."

"Then just come with me, because I'm starved. My cousin and her husband have this unbelievable *yatai* over near the Sunabe Seawall."

His cousin's *yatai*, a cross between a noodle cart and a tapas bar, glows as brightly as the red paper lanterns hanging at either end of the seating area, where half a dozen stools are crowded around the counter. As we approach, the owners, a beaming thirtyish couple, greet Jake like a long-lost son. "Jay-koo! Jay-koo! *Hai-sai! Hai-sai!*"

The husband, sautéing mounds of bean sprouts and pork on a griddle that stretches the length of the counter, wears a short white kimono dotted with navy-blue fans over jeans, and sports a soul patch beneath his lower lip. His wife, busy chopping up piles of cabbage and scallions, greets us in happy, fluting Japanese. The heat from the griddle makes her face flush a pretty pink beneath thick bangs and a white kerchief that hides the rest of her hair.

Jake ducks his head in a few swift bows, returning the greetings as he exchanges a volley of Japanese with the couple, who grin and laugh at his every comment. My name, pronounced *Loozoo*, pops out, and they both rain friendly nods and bows my way.

"Luz, I'd like you to meet my cousin Kana." The wife wipes her hand on her apron and extends it over the griddle for me to shake. "And her husband, Matsukichi."

The *yatai* with its luminous openness and welcoming ambience is the perfect antidote to SoapLand's grubby sordidness. All I want to do at this moment is forget everything Vaughn told me.

Kana gestures for us to sit, sit. From a poster advertising Boss Coffee, Tommy Lee Jones's pitted, Easter Island face scowls down at us. He does look like a boss. Certainly no one you'd want to cross. A quilt of business cards, brown as a flurry of moths, is tacked up overhead, covering the ceiling of the *yatai*.

Jake explains, "Matsukichi used to work in Tokyo in equity derivatives."

Matsukichi looks up from the griddle and calls out, "Team lead!"

"And Kana taught Ryukyuan history at Sofia University. But when they had children, they both wanted to come back and raise them as true Okinawans."

"*Uchinānchu! Ichiban!*" Matsukichi calls out, having pieced together that we are talking about his return to Okinawa. "Tokyo no *yasashii*." He waggles his fist, thumb, and little finger out, in the "Hang loose, brah," shaka gesture, and I get that he returned because Tokyo is not as laid-back as his home island.

Matsukichi slides a feast onto the counter in front of us: skewers of yakitori, the grilled meat glistening with tangy sauce; pinwheels of thinly sliced omelette; and bowls of soba topped with pork and vegetables. I recognize in a distant, abstract way that it's delicious, but the SoapLand shocks have tightened my stomach into a hard ball that repels food. Though I try to push the thoughts away, my heart clenches as I imagine the unthinkable hardships that my sweet grandmother endured. Even as images of all she suffered begin to appear in my mind, they are lulled away by an insistent cooing, "*Shi, shi, shi*," and, knowing it is what *Anmā* wants, I am able to eat.

All the happy bantering among Jake, his cousin, and her husband stops dead when a group of Japanese tourists, half a dozen guys in their midtwenties loud and boisterous as drunk frat boys, ducks in under the canvas curtains. They fall silent the instant they see Jake and me. Before they can back out at the sight of a non-Japanese, though, Jake jumps up and waves the newcomers in with a burst of high-volume Japanese.

"Make room for the paying customers," Jake tells me as we quickly vacate our seats, whisking away our trash as we go. Jake's cousin scoops some drinks out of a cooler, pops them into a bag, along with two packaged servings of the deep purple sweet potato cakes I'd seen earlier. With bows all around, we leave Kana and Matsukichi to their customers. Even though only a canvas curtain separates us from the globe of friendliness and warmth, the *yatai* seems a world away the instant we step outside and stroll over to the seawall. On the inland side, the seawall is covered with dazzling graffiti of dancing dragons and singing flowers, big-eyed children and lonesome wizards. The ocean side is reinforced with interlocking clusters of cement jacks the size of picnic tables, meant to break the power of typhoon waves.

"Whenever you feel like it," Jake says, and I know he means whenever I feel like talking about Vaughn. "Or not," he adds, and takes my hand. He curls his arm up until my palm rests on his chest and I can feel his heart beat against it. The moon is even fuller than it was last night, and the air is heavy with the smell and feel of the sea. The darkness is a comfort.

During the day surfers, snorkelers, and divers own the Sunabe Seawall. Church youth groups play volleyball on the narrow beach, and girls lie on bright towels to tan and watch their boyfriends surf. At night, however, the seawall is owned by lonely guys tracking the lights of distant freighters, by solitary drinkers, by couples having intense discussions that end with each one stalking off in opposite directions, and by cats. Yowling, feral cats.

Jake tosses pebbles at a screeching pack until they saunter away, tails twitching lazily, as if they wouldn't have deigned to eat our food even if we'd offered. Out in the water, patches of eerie blue light wobble, marking the spots where night divers are discovering luminescent squid, sleeping manta rays, and clouds of dancing shrimp. Off in the distance,

Naha shimmers through the misty haze like a fairy castle. The wall where we sit is still warm from the day's sun.

Jake rustles around in the bag his cousin gave us and hands me a drink. I can just barely make out the name on the can in the red light cast by the lanterns hung outside the *yatai*. "'Pocari Sweat.'" I pop the tab and take a swig. "Tastes like Gatorade with extra sugar."

"Hey, my cousin could have given us Pepsi Ice Cucumber."

"You're making that up."

"It's as real as Bilk, the new beer milk."

"Beer made out of milk?"

"Very popular. And don't miss the hot new curry soda. Or the soda that tastes like yogurt."

"Your people are sick, Jake."

Jake laughs, finishes his drink, accordions the can into an aluminum puck between his hands, overarms it toward the trash; the can rattles in, and he turns to me. "Were we going to talk?"

"I need to do one thing first."

He looks over, waits for me to tell him what that thing is, and I kiss him.

"Wow. Yeah. Okay. Good first thing to do." He puts his hand behind my neck and pulls me to him. It is velvety when we kiss, more voluptuous than Oxy. All the chattering in my head stops, and the jagged edges melt away. I want to keep kissing him forever. To feed on him like a vampire, because at this moment, for the first time in longer than I can remember, I'm not thinking about Codie, or my grandmother, or my mom; I feel all right. I feel like what I think normal is.

I put my arms around his neck. He is solid within my embrace. I want him to hold me and he does. It seems like I've been traveling a very long time to get to this moment. Like Jake was the destination I've been trying to reach without realizing it. I'm sad to discover that kissing him makes me feel as though I belong somewhere, because the one place I can't belong is with him. I decide that I'm not going to ruin this moment by telling him about my grandmother or Codie or the girl in the cave. I'm going to be normal. I'm going to eat better, get more sleep, exercise. He's going to go back to Christy, but I'm going to be fine. As long as I stop thinking about all this crazy stuff.

Then the *yuta's* curse comes back to me: *Sister cry. Make sick. Sad.*

Angry at that sugar packet–stealing loony-bird *yuta* for planting such sick ideas in my head, angry at her for forcing me on a search that contaminated the best memories of my childhood, angry at Okinawa for being nothing like it was supposed to be, I find Jake's lips again. They are just as soft and warm as before, but this time instead of forgetful ease, panic rises up in me as the comfort I'd found there before slips farther and farther away. I chase it with lips and tongue so frenzied that Jake's hands lift me like an ocean swell and pull me onto his lap. He fumbles with his zipper, tugs at my shorts. Only the shriek of a siren so loud it's like an ice pick in my ear stops us, and we both smash our hands against our ears. The unbearable sound goes on, rising and falling, a warbling wail that haunts *and* hurts. It's the creepy typhoon siren that Vaughn described, and it's even more frightening than he'd said. I expect to see a tsunami wave rising high enough to shadow the moon. I turn a panicked expression to Jake and find that he's laughing and yelling something that's impossible to hear.

The siren cuts off just as Jake is shouting, "DON'T WORRY—" In the sudden silence, we both tentatively take our hands down. Though the siren near us has stopped, others miles away continue the eerie warbling.

"Why are you laughing? That's a typhoon siren, isn't it?"

"Usually, but not tonight. Tonight that just means that it's midnight, that the last day of Obon, Ukui, has started, and the spirits only have twenty-four hours left before they have to go back to their world for another year."

"Well, it scared the shit out of me."

"Come here, girl." Jake opens his arms. I'm leaning back into them when one of the cats returns. A white one with otherworldly blue eyes outlined in black, it jumps onto the seawall, winds figure eights around Jake and me until, drawn by the smell of the dessert, it pounces on the bag. Jake snatches it away and removes the package inside.

The light hits the wrapped pastry that his cousin gave us, and I can see clearly for the first time the logo of the bakery it came from. It is a lily with leaves all the way up to the trumpet-shaped flower bowing its head. It is exactly like the lily on the pin that I stole.

PART III

UKUI THE THIRD AND FINAL DAY

FORTY-ONE

W hat is that?"

"The cake? *Beni imo*," Jake answers. "It's made out of purple sweet potatoes. Very *Uchināanchu*."

"No, the flower on the package."

"Oh, the famous Princess Lily."

"Famous? Why famous?"

"Because of the Princess Lily girls."

"Who were they?"

"High school girls who were forced to be nurses in the Japanese cave hospitals. Why? Luz? Why are you so intense about this?"

It's time. Time to stop just passing through. This assignment, this base, this life. It's time to tell Jake everything. I reach into my pocket and show him the pin.

His eyes narrow as he touches it. "Where did you get this?"

"I saw a girl in the cave. She gave it to me. She was dead." For a moment, he says nothing, and I'm certain I've made a terrible mistake. I brace for him to recoil, to turn back into one of the endless Quasis who've drifted through my life.

Instead he asks an amazing question: "This girl, was she wearing a school uniform? Sailor collar? Tie? The whole nine?"

"How did you know that?"

He takes the brooch, holds it up to catch more of the light. "Back before the war, the few girls who made it into the handful of high schools on the island wore school pins. It was such a huge deal to be picked that they were always buried wearing their pins. Why didn't you show me this before?"

"Because I thought you'd think I was crazy."

He doesn't say anything.

"So? Do you?"

"Think you're crazy? No. Hell, no."

"Why?"

"Why?" He inhales a long breath, looks at me out of the corner of his eye. I recognize the push-pull of trying to decide whether or not to say something as weird as it is true. His verdict goes in my favor, and words he's obviously thought about for a long time tumble out.

"Because this is Okinawa. Because you have to grow up here to truly understand it. Because the rules are different here. Because Americans believe that they can choose their family and relatives and leave them behind whenever they want and that they don't owe anything to the ones who went before. And they're the loneliest, most unhealthy rich people on the planet. And Okinawans believe that once you are part of a family, you are part of it forever, and they are part of you forever, and you owe everything to the ones who went before. And we're the least lonely, longest-lived, not-rich people on the planet. And because, I guess, we all believe what we're taught before we're old enough to ask questions, since it makes us part of the ones we love most. So I may be as deluded as anyone else, but it's what I believe."

"But, Jake? A ghost? I didn't grow up believing in that."

"Listen, on Okinawa, ghosts run our lives. You want a whole list? We honor and placate the dead every day with offerings at the family *butsu-dan*. Families go bankrupt building and maintaining enormous tombs. Twice a year at Shiimii and Obon, the clans gather to weed and sweep the courtyards of their family tombs. Then feast and celebrate there and in their homes with the ancestors. Then there's the Royal Hotel."

"What's that?"

"Giant multimillion-dollar hotel near the ruins of Nakagusuku Castle. When it was started in the seventies, right after the island reverted to Japan, when Okinawa was supposed to turn into Hawaii after a tourism boom hit like a tsunami and vast fortunes were made, the developer was warned that he was building on a sacred site where the medieval castle's tomb had once been. But he scoffed at the warnings and went all in. He put in a swimming pool, a multistory water-slide, even cages for a zoo. He outfitted the rooms with fine furniture, hardwood flooring, and the most expensive tatami mats. But, one after another, his workers got sick with all these mysterious ailments. After two men died, none of the other workers would return to the haunted site, and construction halted. The owner, determined to prove that the stories were superstitious nonsense, spent three nights in this cavernous, empty hotel. After the third night, he was never seen again. Some say he went mad and was institutionalized. Others maintain that he killed himself. Whichever it was, the hotel was abandoned. No Okinawan would go near the place for any amount of money after that. Not even to steal any of the expensive furnishings that have sat there rotting now for forty years. So, yeah, we Okinawans believe. And, apparently, even the U.S. Air Force can't argue with us."

"You mean Murder House?"

"You ever heard of them leaving another base house unoccupied like that? Ever?"

"Have you seen one? A ghost?"

"No, negative spirits, what you call ghosts, only make themselves visible if they die violently or aren't buried right."

"Jake, she held out her hand to me. She gave me the pin. She wanted something."

"Probably to be buried with her *munchū*, her kin group."

"So I'm not on drugs or crazy?"

"I wouldn't go that far."

A bubble of something odd rises in me. It's so unusual that it takes me a second to identify it as hope. Once I do, though, I rush after it, burbling over. "We have to tell someone. Tell the authorities, so they can find out where she belongs."

He doesn't answer.

"Jake? We have to tell someone. You'll back me up, right? The bones in the cave are human. We have to report them."

"It's a little more complicated than that."

I don't want complicated. I want easy. I want this to be over. I want to make peace with the girl in the cave. With Codie. With myself. With Delmar Vaughn's revelations. This might not be the entire answer, but it's a first step, and it's been such a long time since I've even known what direction to go in that when I ask, "What's the problem?" there's a snap in my tone that comes straight from my mom.

"The problem is that you've wandered into the odd historical Bermuda Triangle that Okinawa occupies."

"Jake, it seems kind of obvious: You find human remains, you report them to the police. Done and done."

"Wow. Spoken like a true American. You know what will happen if we report this? I'll tell you. Nothing. That girl's bones will get tossed into a warehouse crammed floor-to-ceiling with the tens of thousands that have already been turned in."

Jake sounds as annoyed as if all those bones were my fault. I blink. Is this the boy who just kissed me with such tenderness only a few moments ago?

Jake shakes his head. "Sorry. Sore spot. It's just that here we are, what? Nearly seventy years after the war, and there's still not an official channel for returning the remains of Okinawans who died in the war to their families. Volunteers have tried to fill the gap. Tried to match DNA samples from families with remains. But DNA testing is expensive, and there really are giant warehouses stuffed with bones. With more still being found every week. This is a tiny island, and more people were killed here than at Hiroshima and Nagasaki combined."

"What? That can't be right. All through school, every time we studied the Second World War, we would always do a whole unit on the atomic bomb. Everyone knows all about the moment that changed history. Mushroom cloud. Instant vaporization. Why would no one have ever even mentioned Okinawa?"

"Good question. We Okinawans have wondered that. A lot. Not to make Hiroshima and Nagasaki any less tragic, but counting all those who died here after the surrender from starvation, disease, and injuries, as much as one-third of the population was killed. All totaled, a quarter of a million people died."

I think of my grandmother. Of orphans being handed out like puppies at a pound.

"For what?" Jake asks. "A war we never wanted? Had no part in starting? A battle Japan knew from the beginning they'd lose? They used us like a human shield, throwing as many bodies as necessary at the invaders to protect their precious homeland. Then, when the war was over, Japan totally shafted us yet again in the so-called peace treaty. Not only did we get twenty-seven years of U.S. military occupation, but they handed over one-fifth of the island to the Pentagon. Most of it prime farmland. Then, after we reverted to Japan in 1971, which was supposed to make us a full Japanese prefecture, which we all dreamed of and protested for, you know what happened?"

I shake my head.

"Jack and shit. With Tokyo's full cooperation, the Pentagon is still essentially running our country." Jake stops. "Sorry, I promised myself that I wouldn't go off on rants like that anymore, but you need to understand some of this backstory so you can see how Okinawa has been trapped in a limbo just like that girl in the cave. Tokyo allocated funds for DNA testing, but all they've actually done so far is 'facilitate information sharing.' Even the Japanese don't understand what a huge psychic wound being separated from our ancestors is for Okinawans."

"So if I report this, the girl will be even more lost than she is now in a cave at the edge of the sea."

"Pretty much."

I hop off the seawall. "I guess then that it's up to us to find out who the girl in the cave is and where she belongs."

· FORTY-TWO ·

I wake up the next morning in the back of the Surfmobile. Jake snores lightly in the front seat. I admire his ability to fall asleep anywhere. The seat is cranked back as far as it can go, giving his head a regal tilt. His dark, shiny hair falls straight back, fanning across the headrest. His snoring is a comforting snuffling that blends nicely with the rustle of a breeze blowing through the high cane of the field we're parked beside. It was way past curfew last night, too late to go back to the base, so Jake managed to find a remote spot up here in the less populated north end of the island where we could sleep for a few hours. He insisted on letting me spread out in the back. Alone. Without putting it into words, we both seemed to agree that anything else would be a kind of desecration of what we had to do.

As soon as it opens, we're going to go to the museum dedicated to the Princess Lily girls. Since so many of the girls died at that site, Jake is certain that their *kami* will be there to guide me. His phone plinks out his *sanshin* ring tone, and he inhales a startled snort, sits up, swivels his head around, surprised to find himself next to a canefield, and glances back at me as he fumbles for his phone. I assume it's Christy. But they always speak in English, and he answers in crisp Japanese, hangs up after a short conversation.

"Was it your family?"

"My dad. They're a drummer short for the Eisā dancing tonight. He told me to find someone to fill in for me at the golf course and to come to the practice field as soon as I can."

"You're an ice dancer?"

"Right. Because I look so good in spandex. No, Eisā dancing. All the villages have teams of dancers and drummers. We practice all year for the island-wide competition in Naha tonight, the Ten Thousand Eisā Dance Parade. Since it's the last night of Obon, we have to escort the dead back to the other world. The team I usually drum with thinks they'll lose if I don't come, so they talked my dad into calling."

"The Ten Thousand Eisā Dance Parade, Jake, you can't miss that. Listen, you've already helped me so much. You should just drop me off at the museum."

"Just drop you off?"

"I've ridden buses and hitched all over this island. I'll be fine."

"No, I don't think so."

Jake takes a shortcut back to the main highway and soon we're creeping through the jungle on a red dirt path. Dense foliage closes in until it scrapes against the windows on either side. High overhead two Cobra attack helicopters bank slowly, returning to the marine base at Futenma. Gray clouds move in, and the choppers are lost. A moment later rain patters against the windshield.

Jake flips on the wipers. The car's suspension groans as we lurch from one rapidly filling pothole to the next. The red dirt is transformed into slick clay that whirs beneath the tires. I am on the verge of questioning whether cars are even supposed to be on what looks like a goat path when a behemoth truck painted in a camouflage pattern hoves into view, crushing the saplings that line either side of the road. A grim-faced marine sits up high behind the flat rectangle of the rain-streaked windshield and glares down at us.

"I guess we're backing up." Jake cranes around to look over his shoulder. Because of some male challenge that passes between him and the driver, Jake backs out faster than he was going when we drove in. He whips into the first road branching off and lets the truck lumber past. The open flatbed has two benches occupied by marines in olive-drab ponchos. The young men, all wearing floppy canvas hats that droop around their faces like wilted petals and funnel water in rivulets off their heads, turn glazed stares our way, too exhausted to do anything more than hang on to the rifles planted between their knees as the truck rocks them from side to side.

"Where did they come from?" I ask.

"The marines lease huge tracts of land around here for jungle maneuvers. They used them a lot during the Vietnam War. Vets said the terrain was worse than the real thing. Like a jungle, but on a roller coaster. All up and down."

When we pull back onto the road, not a twig or a branch scrapes the car; they've all been bulldozed aside by the truck. Once we've made our way to the main highway, we head down south. We drive for more than an hour until I spot the sign that points to the Himeyuri Peace Museum, and we enter what looks like a state park. The parking lot is nearly empty. The rain is still falling steadily enough to keep visitors away.

I start to open my door and Jake asks, "Are you sure about this?"

"Positive. This is my deal. I need to see it through."

"Okay, but I want you to take the car." He holds out his keys. "I can catch a bus easy from here. Also, you're taking my phone." He shoves keys and phone into my bag.

I fish them back out. "That is crazy talk. I am not taking your car *and* your phone." I try to hand Jake back his keys and phone, but he won't take them.

"No, it has to be this way or I won't leave, and the spirits won't be driven back to the next world, and it will pretty much be all your fault."

Behind Jake's easygoing, joking manner, I sense an implacable will. He's like Okinawa, a thin layer of tropical lushness covering a core of limestone.

Of course, I've got my own tough core and tell Jake I'll take his phone, but only if he keeps his car.

He finally agrees, promising to borrow a phone from someone at the practice and check in on me. As I turn away toward the door, Jake pulls me back and kisses me. It's a combination of a good-bye and an I-don't-want-to-leave kiss. Maybe with a little this-has-been-great-I'm-going-back-to-my-girlfriend thrown in.

The rain is little more than a mist when I get out. I don't watch Jake drive away. A side path leads into a heavily wooded area that is quiet and smells of pine. Six-sided stone lanterns, the edges curling up like sultans' shoes, guard the path. Drops collected in the dark green needles plop heavily onto my head.

Green lichen covers the limestone blocks of the stairs everywhere except the spots where it has been scoured away by visitors' feet. A wood railing worn soft by innumerable hands curves gracefully around the winding stairs. At the top, bushes with bulbous branches like a cupped hand full of swollen fingers beg for something from the sky. Farther on, a grove of pines shelters a display dedicated to the kamikaze pilots. Its centerpiece is the portrait of a pilot in his late teens, lying on his stomach on a tatami mat, as he painstakingly writes a farewell letter home the night before his suicide mission.

I emerge onto a grassy field intersected by stone walkways and a broad promenade running between high, zigzagging walks of polished black granite surrounded by dozens of walls inscribed with the names of everyone—soldiers and civilians, Japanese, Okinawan, American— who died in the Battle of Okinawa. I am stunned to see the names of enemies and invaders memorialized, and wonder whether anyone in Washington ever even considered putting the names of the Vietnamese who died on our own Vietnam Wall. The briny scent of the sea leads me to an overlook high atop a ring of black cliffs. Far below, the East China Sea is steely gray in the rain.

The main path winds back into the wooded area, past a succession of monuments. Lonely bouquets lie at their bases. Birds sheltering from the rain cry out to one another with sharp, companionable calls. One monument, a simple granite stone carved with a list of names, has a marker in English that explains that it is dedicated to the native boys, some as young as twelve, who, conscripted by the Japanese Imperial Army to serve as messengers and munitions bearers, perished in even greater numbers than the Okinawan girls had.

Ancient roots worm through the hard-packed earth. Farther on, the thick vegetation gives way once again to broad stone walks. A canopy of branches arches over my head. Ahead, masses of streamers in crayon colors dangle from the trees. As I draw closer, I realize that the streamers are composed of thousands of origami cranes.

The crane streamers wave gently above the serrated mouth of a cave that descends steeply into the craggy ground, a dank, dark hole that exhales the smell of all damp places shut off from the sun. Its rim is edged in black. The monument marking the entrance is written in Japanese. Though I can't understand the characters, a flower chiseled in among them explains everything. The bloom is still closed; its petals have yet to open. The stem, collared in leaves up to the very top, droops, bowing the head of the flower in graceful acceptance of its fate.

The Princess Lily.

A small plaque in English explains that the black patches around the opening are scorch marks left by flamethrowers, grenade explosions. For several minutes I stand motionless as I imagine young girls down there, hiding in the darkness while enemy voices yelled in a foreign language at them from above. The plaque identifies the site as the Cave of the Virgins.

Inside the Himeyuri Peace Museum, maps line the walls of the first room. Arrows swirl across the maps, indicating troop movements and reducing war to two dimensions. Farther on, cases contain artifacts from the lost paradise that the Himeyuri girls grew up in: a simple back loom for weaving banana-fiber cloth, a windup gramophone with a horn-shaped speaker, a lacquerware tea set, a tin of lilac-scented bath powder, books, pens, and, at the very end, a brooch like the one in my pocket that identified these girls as the best of the island's best, the Princess Lily girls.

I follow the polished concrete floor to the next room, where Japanese students—boys in black uniforms; girls in white blouses, plaid skirts, and knee socks—study the testimonies of survivors displayed in glass cases. The room is entirely silent except for the shuffling of feet as the students move from one document to the next.

I turn from the documents and face the re-creation of a section of a hospital cave. The wooden bed planks bolted onto the cave wall in the claustrophobically cramped room seem to exhale the odors of sweat and decay. On a plaque next to the cave, some of the Himeyuri girls' handwritten accounts are translated. The words swirl in front of me, forming images in my mind before I can stop them:

> . . . *a patient with no legs was crawling in the mud.*
> —*16-year-old Sizuko Ōshiro*

> . . . *bloated corpses as large as gasoline drum cans.*
> —*17-year-old Toshi Higa*

> . . . *I could hear maggots eating the rotting flesh.*
> —*15-year-old Tsuneko Kinjō*

> . . . *I can't describe the worst. The worst was indescribable.*
> —*18-year-old Ume Uchida*

The final panel concludes the narrative with: "Only eighteen of the original two hundred and twenty girls survived."

The wall opposite the hospital cave is covered by dozens of black-and-white portraits of the Himeyuri girls who served in the cave hospitals. From a plaque, I learn that these were the last photos taken of the girls right before Shuri was evacuated, and that they only survived because the photographer, who was killed during the bombardment, buried his rolls of film in a metal box that was found when a new road was constructed.

Certain that God, or the universe, or something will provide some sort of clue as to the identity of the girl in the cave, I study the faces of gentle native girls who'd been protected and treasured their whole lives, photographed at a time when they were so convinced that war would be a minor inconvenience that, as the plaque tells me, they carried their schoolbooks with them into the caves. They smile into the camera, looking as if they're in on the best secret ever. As if they can't believe their great good fortune in being Princess Lily girls.

All I can think is, *They're so young.*

I scrutinize the photos, searching for some trait, some feature, that looks familiar. But none of the faces bears the slightest resemblance to the starved and suffering girl who appeared to me in the cave. For the first time, I fully accept Jake's dictate that things are different in Okinawa, and I say a prayer to the *kami*. I ask for their guidance. Then, recalling Jake's advice, I clap my hands softly and whisper, "Please help me find the right girl. Tell me what her name is."

The students close to me exchange looks and move away. I don't care, because when I return my attention to the portraits, one of them jumps out at me. All the other photos depict individual girls, but this one has captured two in the same frame. One rests her hand on the other's shoulder. The taller girl in back has an elegant, long neck, thick braids, and a serene smile. She's the only one of the students not wearing a pin. The shorter girl in front wears her wavy hair in pigtails that flip up just beneath her ears. The beaming smile on her broad, open face mirrors the curve of her perky hairstyle. Though they don't resemble each other, the possessive hand of the older on the shoulder of the younger combined with the younger one's smile of contented security make me so certain that the two girls are sisters that I can feel Codie's hand on my shoulder.

This knowledge, however, doesn't help me in the least. I stare at the rows of white lilies pinned on the left side of all but one of the girls' blouses, placed exactly above their hearts. All of the brooches are identical to the one in my pocket. The pale mother-of-pearl flower heads stand out in sharp contrast against the black of their blouses. And they're all positioned with the blossom drooping inward to the right, toward their hearts. Every girl except the elegant older sister has one. Which means that she is the only student I know for sure is not the girl in the cave. Which leaves me with 219 other candidates. I can't stand the feel of all those girls who've been waiting so long to be reunited with their families staring at me, knowing that the one I've failed so badly is among them.

I rush out of the room and make my way outside to a meditation garden at the back of the museum. An old woman in a kimono sits silently on a bench, staring at a hillside densely planted with flowers, while tears roll down her cheeks. The sun comes out and the orange of the museum's tile roof and the yellows and bright magentas of the flowers beam with a disconcerting gaudiness.

What else can I do except make a report to the authorities? Authorities who will then put the sea-washed bones I tell them about in a warehouse, where the girl with the Princess Lily pin will stay until long after everyone who knew her and has been waiting seven decades to find out what happened to her is dead. I think of Codie sleeping beneath her blanket of red *deigo* tree petals and try to imagine how infinitely more awful it would be if we didn't have even that. Though I ache to believe otherwise, I have to accept the truth: No matter how different the rules are on Okinawa, how much these *kami* of Jake's may or may not be able to intervene in our lives, one rule remains the same: The dead are beyond our help. They are gone forever and ever and ever. We can do nothing for them.

Defeated, I drop onto a stone bench in the shade. The pin in my pocket jabs me. I take it out, study it, and I decide that I'll donate it to the museum. Perhaps they'll make it their mission to identify its owner. Deciding to give the pin away makes me as sad as I was when, without asking me, my mother threw away Codie's old hairbrush that I had saved. The one that still carried her scent and held strands of her hair. I hold the brooch against my own heart, and touch the flower to feel it bending inward toward my sternum, just as the heads of the lilies in all the portraits drooped to the wearer's right. Except that the lily on my chest doesn't face to the right. Though I hold it on my left side, just where all the girls in their portraits had pinned their brooches so that they would curl inward, the one in my hand faces the other way. Outward, to the left. I look down to confirm what my fingers have told me: Yes, this pin is different from all the others.

I rush back into the museum and head straight for the portrait gallery. All the girls' pins do face inward to their right except for the one belonging to the cute girl I took for a little sister. Her lily droops the opposite way, to her left. Pinned over her heart, just like all her classmates, it faces out. Exactly like the one I have in my hand. I find the girl's name on the guide beneath the portraits: Tamiko Kokuba. And the name of her village: Madadayo.

· FORTY-THREE ·

N avigate to Madadayo," I tell the map program on Jake's phone.
I'm standing on the main road with the museum behind me.
The sun is out, and steam rises off the drying road in wisps that smell
of dust and asphalt. I'm trying to get an idea of which way to go, but the
nice lady on the map program keeps telling me that there is no such
place as Madadayo. I try a few more pronunciations with no more luck.
My brain is starting to cook, so I give up and head to a shop across the
highway that rents scuba gear.

Inside, a loud hissing comes from the area where tanks are being
filled with compressed air. Racks of neoprene suits hang like the gaudy
pelts of animals furred in black with neon-colored stripes. A couple
of Japanese vacationers, probably newlyweds—the husband in golf
clothes, his bride wearing a large, droopy hat—sit on a bench trying
on swim fins.

At the counter, an Okinawan woman listens to me repeat the name
of the village several times with a quizzical expression on her face that
finally disappears when she bursts out with the name correctly pronounced, "Ah! Mah-dah-DAY-o!"

She points to a broad-shouldered man filling scuba tanks in the corner and tells me something that I take to mean he knows where Madadayo is. "Yeyo!" she yells at him. The hissing stops, and Yeyo walks over
with a bowlegged gait, his broad, flip-flopped feet gripping the earth.

The woman explains, and he points to me and asks, "Madadayo?"

I dig through my feeble memories of my grandmother speaking
Japanese and answer, "*Onegai shimasu.*"

Yeyo nods and motions for me to follow him outside. A few minutes
later, he flags down a bus, has a lengthy discussion with the driver, then
gestures for me to get on board.

"Madadayo?" I ask.

"Madadayo!" the driver answers with a smile, nodding his head
vigorously.

The bus is filled with housewives holding string bags of groceries on their laps, students with their heads bent over phones and comic books, and old people staring out the windows with peaceful expressions on their faces, as if they are on a holiday that is going perfectly. I sit down next to an elderly man so slender that his belt is cinched up to the last hole and the extra wags down half a foot. He bows, smiles, and asks, "Madadayo?"

"*Hai*, Madadayo," I answer, bobbing my head in a bow, and smiling back.

He grins like I'm his smartest grandchild and, pointing at me, repeats my destination, "Madadayo."

"*Hai, hai!* Madadayo."

He mutters, "Madadayo," to the riders around us, and they all nod in a happy way that tells me not to worry. The route hugs the coastline, rising until we have a view of the ocean that seems to go all the way to China. I settle in, and the miles rock past.

I feel a light pat on my knee and find a serious-faced little girl in a yellow sundress with ties at the shoulder standing in the aisle next to me and holding a piece of paper with Japanese characters written on it in ballpoint pen. The man beside me taps the characters and explains, "Madadayo."

I turn around to face the little girl's mother, who is still holding a pen. I wave the paper in the air and thank her: "*Arigatō gozaimasu*." She nods and the little girl runs away and buries her face in her mother's lap.

A few miles later, Jake's phone announces a message; he has texted me his friend's phone number. I am on the verge of calling him to share the news of my giant discovery at the museum when the bus rocks and hisses to a stop. A cooing like doves in the evening sweeps through the passengers as they call out the stop: "Madadayo." My seatmate taps me lightly on the shoulder and waves his hand, shooing me off. At the front of the bus, I feel how happy everyone is at the success of their group effort to get me to my destination, and I stop to bow and wave good-bye. They wave back and are still waving out the windows when the bus pulls away.

I look toward the ocean far below, which seems as flat and silver as a mirror in the sun. A breeze lifts my hair and cools me down. Next to the highway is a small wooden sign that points to a small road. I pull the paper from my bag and check to make sure that the characters the helpful mother wrote there match the ones on the sign. They do.

The landscape gets more jungly and overgrown the farther I walk down the narrow road. Soon the entire road is shaded by a thick canopy of trees that cools the air beneath. The noise from the highway grows more and more muffled until I can't hear anything but birds and the breeze rustling leaves above my head. No cars pass. I notice horse turds along the road and wonder whether people in Madadayo still use carts.

It's such a peaceful place that I am even able to think about Codie and how this seems exactly like the kind of fun adventure she would have taken me on, without wanting to run back to the ocean cliff and jump off. In fact, it seems like she's with me, and it *is* a fun adventure that we're sharing. I rub my hand against the lily pin and almost break into a run. Excited, I call the number Jake texted me. The owner of the phone answers in Japanese, then passes it to Jake as soon as I speak.

"Lusitania!" he answers. I can barely hear him above the pounding in the background, like thunder with a heavy-metal beat.

"God, Jake, it sounds like it's going to be the Night of Ten Thousand Drummers. On steroids."

"You got that right. Where are you?"

"On my way to Madadayo."

"What's that?"

I tell him about how I figured out the identity of the pin's owner and Jake says, "Awesome, possum."

"Did you really just say that?"

"Maybe I did and maybe I *did.*"

"Jake, have you been drinking?"

"Takes a hella *awamori* to chase the dead back to where they belong. Some of them don't wanna go."

He laughs and I wish I were there with him. Jake is very cute when he's drunk. Hoping that he won't remember the question, the proof that I care, I ask, "Is Christy there?"

"Am I having fun?"

"You seem to be."

"Then that answers your question. She's still up north with her people. Tell me about Madadayo."

"Jake, I wish you could see this place. I'm walking down this narrow road and not another soul has passed me, and it's all shaded and cool. It actually feels enchanted."

"Lots of little hidden parts of Okinawa feel that way."

"I can't wait to find someone related to Tamiko and give them her pin. I hope someone in her family still lives here. They'll know what to do about the bones."

"Great. Good plan. Hey, Luz, seriously, five stars for you. Pretty rare for anyone from the base to care as much as you do."

"I'm not 'anyone from the base.'"

"You're not, Luz. Believe me, you really are not."

I listen to Jake breathe and imagine that he's holding back from saying more because of still being with Christy. That maybe it's possible there's an honorable guy out there. I want to tell him that I appreciate him looking out for me, but someone who sounds half-mad, half-teasing yells at Jake in Japanese, and he says he has to go.

"Jake, I'm going to need you to translate when I get into the village."

"Sure, I'll hang on to Nobu's phone. Call me when you get there, okay?"

"I will."

I stay on the road and soon come to a house with a red-tiled roof. I rehearse saying the girl's name the Japanese way, with the family name first, Kokuba Tamiko. I wish I'd copied the characters down at the museum, but I'm filled with confidence and a feeling that, no matter what, I will end up on the right path; the *kami* are guiding me.

The road widens and ends in a cul-de-sac. Circled around it are more houses with red tile roofs. In a large garden plot, a short woman is bent over, hacking at the roots of a plant until she unearths a large, bushy head of lettuce. It is only when she uses her hand hoe to stand up that she sees me. For a moment she freezes; then she heads my way. She is so short and bowlegged that she looks like Yosemite Sam.

"*Hai-sai mensorei,*" she greets me.

"*Hai-sai,*" I say in return, bowing several times, and smiling big.

She watches me, amused but not overly concerned. I try to guess her age and can't. Even though she doesn't wear glasses or a hearing aid and moves around better than some forty-year-olds I can think of, she seems as old as a sea turtle, and just as calm.

"I'm looking for someone who lives here." I try to pantomime my mission by pointing to myself, then using my fingers to illustrate searching the area. I just end up looking like I'm telling her I can shoot lasers out of my eyes. I hold up my finger to ask her to wait a moment and I dial the number Jake gave me. Not surprisingly, given that he was in the middle of what sounded like a battlefield, he doesn't answer.

Before I can resort to another charade, though, the old lady asks, "Kokuba Tamiko?"

My mouth drops open. I'm so surprised, it takes me a moment to react. The silence fills with the roar of a jet fighter streaking overhead.

"Yes. *Sí, sí,*" I answer, then, shaking away the Spanish that has suddenly crowded into my head, say, "*Hai. Hai!* Kokuba Tamiko." Though I know she can't understand, the English words pour out of me. "How did you know? Are you Kokuba Tamiko?" I point to her, trying to see the pigtailed girl's face in hers.

"Kokuba Tamiko."

I'm certain she's telling me that she's Kokuba Tamiko. Relief at having accomplished my mission floods through me as I reach into my pocket, ready to pull the pin out, return it to her, and figure out how to explain to her about the bones, since they obviously aren't hers. But apparently I have misunderstood, and, leaning on her short hoe, the old woman sets off down the road, waving at me to follow. In spite of rolling from side to side more than moving forward, she marches along at a brisk pace, and soon we are outside the main village on a one-lane dirt road lined by tall bushes with lustrous green leaves and bright yellow flowers at the top that look like hibiscus.

After we walk long enough for sweat to start rolling down in a steady stream from my scalp, the thick bushes stop at a waist-high wall of gnarled gray coral rock, its gate guarded by a pair of fierce *shiisā* dogs. The courtyard inside the wall is shaded by an immense banyan tree. At the center is the first house I've seen on the island with a thatched roof. A long porch lined with sliding doors runs the length of the house. Birds loop in and out of the branches of the tall tree. Pink piglets grunt in a nearby pen. The glossy green leaves of sweet potato vines curl over a neat patch. The golden trunks of a bamboo grove gleam in the woods behind the house. On a distant hillside the last *deigo* tree still in bloom is covered in blossoms so red that the tree appears to be on fire.

It's the coral tree that makes me certain I'm in the right place. I reach out my hand to push the gate back and go in, but the instant I do, the old lady stops me. Scowling and pointing furiously, she makes me stop and read the sign hanging from the gate.

"It's in Japanese," I say, tapping the pretty picture letters.

She counters by stabbing numbers with yen signs next to them and what appear to be hours of operation. I put that together with the sight of plaques posted in front of the pigpen and the stables and a long, open-sided cart with rows of seats, and it dawns on me, "Is this some kind of museum?"

She nods, happy that I'm getting the picture, then rains Japanese down on me. The only word I can pick out of the deluge is "Obon."

"It's closed? For Obon?"

"*Hai! Hai!*" She beams at me.

"Tamiko Kokuba? Here?"

The old lady tilts her head to the side, trying to puzzle out what I'm asking.

I go back to pointing. "Tamiko? Here? In this house?"

She shakes her finger, saying, "*Neh, neh, neh,*" and tries to correct me by first pointing at the house—"Tamiko, *hai!*"—then down at the ground in front of us so that I get the concept of "here." "Tamiko, *neh.*" Point-point. Her eyes stay fastened on her feet as she shakes her head with slow sadness at the fact that Tamiko used to live in that house, but she's not here anymore.

Which I should have known. It's unlikely that, even if Tamiko were one of the eighteen Himeyuri girls who'd survived the Battle of Okinawa, she would still be living in her house anymore. Even on an island where it's normal to be out hoeing up lettuce at an age when most Americans are either dead or acting like it, the odds are against it.

My hand closes around the pin. When I open it in front of the old lady, she gasps, drops the short hoe, covers her open mouth, and looks up at me, her eyes wide. Seeing how moved she is, I want her to have the pin and nudge my hand closer. But she won't take it.

I try calling Jake again to make him explain everything, but he still doesn't answer. So I act out walking along in my big dopey oblivious American way and being stunned to find this pin. I do a whole second act on searching high and low for the owner. I hope that a hand visoring the eyes, peering off into the far horizon is universal for scoping things out. My big finale is placing the pin on the tips of my outstretched hands and bowing to offer it to her.

Her work-gnarled fingers are rough against my palms as she plucks the pin up. It's a relief to have the brooch literally off my hands. The feeling doesn't last long, though, because she reaches up and pins it on me, directly over my heart.

"No, really, it can't be mine. It should be yours." I try to unpin it, but she stops me and does her own bit of improv. Except that hers is like a very expressive dance, a hula, where you know every movement means something and the dancer is telling you an important story, if you only knew what the gestures meant. She lifts her arms above her head to take in the trees and mountains around us and the sky above and makes a graceful wave motion like birds flying through the air that, for some reason, are drawn to me from all directions. Then she repeats a nicer version of my bumpkin walk, of me finding the pin. In her telling, though, the wavy creatures flying through the air all zero in on the spot on the ground where she's pretending the pin is, lift it up like the birds in Cinderella carrying ribbons in their beaks to tie up her hair for the ball, and bring it to me.

I know I'm missing big chunks of what she's actually trying to tell me, but the one thing I'm certain of is that she—and possibly the things flying through the air—*really* wants me to keep the pin. That she believes I was intended to have it. I launch into another goofy charade to express that I understand how much this means. I cup both my hands around the pin so that they make a little echo chamber over my heart, and bow deeply.

The old lady beams, the years fall away, and I see what had been in front of me the whole time: the old woman's beauty. In her day, she must have been stunning. Even now, her eyes are darkly lashed, adorable dimples poke into her full cheeks, and her lips are still plump.

I pat my chest, say, "Luz," and stick my hand out.

She shakes it, pats her chest, and says, "Mitsue."

· FORTY-FOUR ·

Anmā, *she is leaving. Your cousin Mitsue is letting her leave. Shouldn't the kami-sama act through her to help us? Cousin Mitsue is old, but she is still strong. She could do it with her hoe; then we could steal the girl's spirit and enter the next world like your brother did.*

Shi-shi-shi. *Don't fret. All is in motion now. We merely have to be ready to step through the door when it opens.*

Will it open soon?

Yes, it must. Time is running out. It is Ukui tonight, the final night. It is our last chance.

What are you going to do?

Nothing remains to be done except that she must be in the proper place when the time is right.

How do we do that?

It is all in the hands of the kami-sama. *They will do what must be done. Now, we don't have much time, so let me finish my story. I was telling you how I led your aunt back to Madadayo.*

On the last night of our journey, the moon was like a lamp that Anmā had left on to guide us home in the dark. Hatsuko and I followed the road we had walked thousands of times before, yet we did not recognize it. Where once, in the cool shade cast by tall banyan and *deigo* trees, my twin cousins, Shinsei and Uei, and I had had sword fights with branches, not a leaf remained. The hilly field where we had once slid down the slick grass was a naked slope of dust and rock pockmarked by deep bomb craters. Farther on, I searched in vain for the thick hedge of sea hibiscus, always bright with yellow flowers, that led to our house, and found nothing but a desolate path protected by a few blackened branches.

"Are you certain we're going the right way?" Hatsuko asked, almost as if we'd simply made a wrong turn, and if we found the correct path flowers would be blooming along it and the fields on either side of us would be thick with the twisting vines of potato plants and the fragile chartreuse lace of new rice sprouts. As if, over the sound of our labored breathing, we might be able to hear the warble of Grandfather plucking a tune from the strings of his *sanshin*. As if the aroma of Anmā's *gōyā chanpuru* might drift down the lane, welcoming us to a home where they all waited around the table: Mother, Father, our three older brothers, all our aunts, uncles, cousins, even my beloved cousin Chiiko and her baby Little Mouse.

After a long moment, I answered, "Yes, I'm certain." Neither one of us wanted to walk the final steps, to make the last turn in the path before we reached our farm. We stood in the warm night and strained to see and hear what should have been there: fireflies, the glow from our house in the distance, the gurgle of the brook running through the glade, night birds calling songs of love, frogs raising a raucous chorus, our lucky gecko chirping out a happy greeting.

"Come on," Hatsuko urged, taking my hand.

All that was left of our home was the smell of smoke rising from the blackened roof beams. The sliding doors; the thatched palm fronds of the roof; the wood of the veranda; the pig and goat pens; the barn; the books where *Anmā* had kept the accounts; my winter kimono; Hatsuko's brush paintings; the letters our brothers had sent Mother and Father from Manchukuo, the Philippines, Singapore; the photo of the emperor in its box of pale, fragrant *hinoki* wood; all had been reduced to ash. All except for one small item that flashed back the faintest glint of moonlight my way. Fearing that it was what I suspected, I put my foot over it before Hatsuko could notice.

A glimmer of something else buried in the ashes caught her eye instead. Without a word, she stooped to pick up a silver dagger with a loop at its end. It was one of the blades from Father's scissors. I'm certain we both thought of how the long blades had flashed as I snipped at our father's hair, preparing him to do the emperor's bidding, on a day that now seemed so long ago, a day when we believed that victory was inevitable.

"Where's the other blade?" Hatsuko asked, a blank look in her eyes. She dropped to her knees and pawed at the charcoal, not seeming to care how she was blackening her hands, her clothes. "Where is the other blade?" she asked again, but her question had no force. It floated in the silent night as light and airy as dandelion puff about to be blown away forever.

"It must be here somewhere. It was steel. It couldn't have burned. Those were Father's special scissors." Her voice dwindled away bit by bit until it was little more than the whimper of a lost child. I shifted my foot, retrieved the item I'd kept hidden from Hatsuko, slipped it into my pocket, and, as I had learned to do so well, forced myself to think no further of it.

"I know," Hatsuko announced, abruptly standing, holding the silver blade out like a sword. "Father took the other blade with him. To protect Mother when they fled south to safety. With a blade like this he could—"

I shoved my hand over Hatsuko's mouth to silence her and yanked her back down onto the ashes. "Shhh," I breathed in her ear, and we both listened for the sounds I'd heard. From the place where our potato field had once bloomed came voices so strange I doubted they were human.

"*Ketō,*" I whispered.

We listened to the Americans, probably scouts. When the first spoke his voice sounded like the angry shriek of a broken machine. A second was as terrifyingly mechanical as the first. They were true; all the stories we had heard about these raping, devouring, destroying man-beasts were true.

The energy of fear coursed through Hatsuko. In an urgent whisper, she told me, "We have to get the food for Nakamura before they come for us." She sprang into a crouching run and set off for our family tomb hidden in the woods. On our journey to Madadayo we had passed so many tombs that had been blown apart by grenades or shattered into rubble by bombs that I feared what we would find. As we slipped silently through the dense foliage beyond our house, I recalled all the times my mother's extended family had gathered, and how we had complained because the tomb was so far from the main path. When Hatsuko and I reached the tomb and saw that it was still intact, though, we were thankful for the remote location, since that was what had saved it. The heavy stone chiseled into a square had been replaced since I had been there months ago with my mother and my aunts, and once again it blocked the entrance. It took every molecule of strength that Hatsuko and I had between us to move it away.

Inside, we dared to light the wick of a small millet-seed oil lamp. Unlike the smelly, smudgy kerosene lanterns in the caves, the oil was fragrant and didn't fill the air with soot. The gentle light gleamed on the beautifully decorated ceramic urns that held the cleaned bones of our ancestors. Before we proceeded, I asked Hatsuko to join me in offering prayers of thanks to them for guiding and safeguarding us and to beg them to continue helping us.

"We have no time for that," Hatsuko snapped. "We must gather up as much food as we can carry and leave immediately. Before the *Amerikās* come any closer. Oh, here are the crocks of dried sweet potatoes. Here's one of dried bonito fish. Toasted soybeans. Where did Mother bury the pork miso? Nakamura will love our mother's pork miso."

"Hatsuko, you can't be serious."

"Of course I am. That was our plan. That was why I came."

"We made that plan before we knew that Madadayo would be surrounded by *Amerikās*. We can't go back out now. It would be suicide."

"Tamiko, if we *don't* go it will be suicide. Without the food I bring him, my fiancé will die, and then I will have no reason to go on living."

"Hatsuko, listen to me: Nakamura is not your fiancé. He has never spoken to you of marriage."

"Tami-chan, he didn't need to. There are things that pass between a man and a woman that you are too young to understand. Especially when that man is an officer in the Imperial Army fighting for the very survival of our country."

"No, I understand you will give your life for a man who is not worthy of it. A vain and selfish man who betrayed you with your own cousin."

A hard slap stung my cheek. "I forbid you to make any further traitorous remarks that question the honor of a devoted servant of our divine emperor, who stands ready to sacrifice his very life for all we hold dear."

"Hatsuko, stop! Stop spouting such idiocies. There are no spies. There are no gallant officers with shining swords to cut off heads. There is no one here but me. Me and our ancestors. Our Okinawan ancestors. I vowed to *Anmā* that I would protect you, and protect you I will, even if it means I have to knock you out and tie you up."

Hatsuko shook her head, snorted a laugh dismissing my threat, located the patch of freshly dug soil where Mother had buried the crock of pork miso to keep it from spoiling, and began scraping away at it with the silver blade from Father's scissors. When she unearthed the crock and didn't even remove the lid to so much as take a taste of Mother's delicious ginger, brown sugar, and pork mixture, I knew she was serious.

I blocked the exit. "Hatsuko, you can't leave. I promised Mother. We must live, don't you understand? For her. For Father."

"Don't be silly. What are you talking about? Mother and Father will be waiting for us with the other refugees."

"Hatsuko, no," I said gently. "Mother and Father will not be waiting for us." From my pocket, I withdrew what I had found earlier: the mangled remains of Father's spectacles. A few jagged shards of shattered glass still adhered to the frames that had been smashed, so that the spectacles lay out flat as the skin of a dead animal.

Hatsuko set the crock down, held out her hand, and I placed the glasses that Father was never without on her white palm. She stared at the twisted metal as if it were a kanji character that she had yet to learn the meaning of.

I knew she was in shock, and used the moment to explain what had to be done. "We can't leave and go south. The Americans are driving us toward the sea, and once they have all of us penned up with the high black cliffs above the ocean at our backs, there will only be surrender or suicide. So we will remain here until they find us. Then we will surrender, and the soldiers will do with us what soldiers always do with the women of the conquered. But we will live, Hatsuko. For Mother. For Father. For all who have died." I held my open hand out to the bones of our ancestors. "For them. For all of them, we will live." Hatsuko stared back at me as if I were speaking a language she no longer understood. I spoke to her gently, like she was a child with a fever. "This is what must be done, Hat-chan."

She shook her head as though she were waking from a bad dream. "No." She shoved the bits of wire and glass back at me. "No." She repeated the word again as if she could forbid what had already happened. "No. First I will find Nakamura. Then I will find Father and Mother. They will be hungry. They will need the food we will bring them. You can carry the dried sweet potatoes and bonito fish."

"I'm not coming," I said, though she knew that already.

This time when she made to leave, I snatched the silver blade from her hand, knelt at her feet, and pressed the point against the artery thumping beneath my jawbone so hard that blood trickled down my neck. "If you leave, I will kill myself!"

Hatsuko smiled as she took the blade from my hand and slid it into the waistband of her pants. "Life is the treasure," was all she said before taking the crock and slipping out into the dark where demons now ruled.

· FORTY-FIVE ·

"Hey, where are you right now?" Jake asks as soon as I answer his phone.

"Standing on the highway waiting for a bus heading back to the base. Jake, I tried to call you. You won't believe what happened in Madadayo. You have to come back with me to explain everything to a woman I met here who, I'm sure, knew the girl in the cave."

"I will. But right now, want to come meet me in Naha? See my mad *taiko* drumming skills?"

"Sure, but—"

"Just get the forty-six or seventeen bus. It'll take you right into Naha."

"How will I ever find you?"

"Can you get back to Kokusai-dōri?"

"That's a very long street."

"Go to where it crosses Heiwa-dōri, the covered street where we were yesterday. You can watch the parade from there. Maybe you'll even be able to spot me. In any case, just stay there after the parade, and I'll come back and find you."

He hears the uncertainty in my answer and says, "Just get to Kokusai-dōri, okay? Then keep the ocean at your back and the monorail on your left and watch for Heiwa-dōri. Remember? Peace Street? With the entrance marked by that green arch with the white doves on either side?"

"Kokusai-dōri. Heiwa-dōri. I got it."

"You got it, Nahottie."

I smile at him calling me by the slang for an Okinawan hottie and flag down the 17 bus that appears a second later as if by magic.

· FORTY-SIX ·

Hatsuko, who has remained Kokuba Hatsuko all her long, unmarried life, wakes from a nap. The false cheeriness of her room in the Shiawase Nursing Home, with its sunny yellow walls and harshly bright lighting, offends Hatsuko anew. Her longing for the quiet, shadowed austerity of her home in Madadayo is especially painful during the three days of Obon. It is then that she most regrets having allowed her father's brother's grandson, that conniving Tonaki Hideo, to trick her into leaving her home. She is deeply suspicious of the deal he engineered that turned her home, an exact replica of the one destroyed in the war, into a strange sort of zoo. Hideo promised that all would be preserved precisely as it was. That hers was one of the last truly traditional dwellings left on the island, and it needed to be shared with the young. She knows that there is something in it for Hideo and all the greedy Tonakis of her father's birth family who perch like vultures, waiting to wrest complete control of her mother's family's property from her.

Hatsuko rises slowly and remembers other Obons, when she still had a real home to welcome the dead into. Each year on Welcoming Day, she used to rise before dawn to sweep the courtyard of her family tomb so that the spirits within could emerge. Back at her house, she would string lanterns to guide the spirits to her door and place bowls of water on the long veranda so that the returning spirits could wash their feet after their long journey home. Then she would load the family altar with candles, flowers, sugarcane, papayas, and *awamori* until the offerings overflowed onto the floor below.

When the ancestors arrived, Hatsuko would clap and sing along with the spirits, but her smile would be wistful, because those she wanted most never came, since their bones hadn't been recovered. She yearned for her mother to visit so she could apologize and beg her forgiveness, and tell her that she had been right about everything. She'd predicted that the great war would humble Japan and destroy Okinawa, and that was what had happened. *Anmā* predicted that her three sons would die when the sun passed too close to the earth, and when the Second Army transferred all three of Hatsuko's brothers to Hiroshima, that, too, was what happened.

Most of all, Hatsuko ached for Little Guppy with a longing that the passing years only made sharper. Hatsuko knew she had been stupid and blind about many things, but her worst failing was as a big sister; she had failed Tamiko in death even worse than she had in life. Years ago, Hatsuko had gone to the office of the Okinawa Prefecture Department of Welfare and Health where a technician wearing a blue surgical mask and gloves and a name tag that identified her as Reiko had scrubbed a gauze pad over the inside of Hatsuko's cheek. Reiko had promised that if Hatsuko's DNA matched any of the "remains" that had been found, her office would notify her immediately.

For a long while after, Hatsuko waited expectantly for the moment when Tamiko would be returned to her for a proper burial in the family tomb. Hatsuko was buoyed by happiness at the thought that she and Tamiko would be reunited forever in the next life. Then she read an article in the *Ryūkyū Shimpō* about widows of soldiers missing in action staging a protest at the prefectural office because they would be cut off from their husbands forever, since their bones had never been found. The widows were outraged at how little progress had been made in identifying the remains that had been recovered. A photograph taken secretly in the vast government warehouse where unidentified remains were stored accompanied the sad story. It showed shelves filled from floor to ceiling with nothing but the skulls that had been recovered from construction sites. The photo made Hatsuko recall that Reiko, with her single-fold eyelids, long face, and proper Tokyo Japanese, had been from the mainland. As usual, the Japanese government had lied to her, and she gave up hope of finding any help in her search.

In spite of that disappointment, an anticipation that Hatsuko recognized as silly and beyond logic seized her each year as the three days set aside for the return of the departed commenced, and she prayed fervently that this year, her sister's spirit would find its way to her. Each Obon that passed without a visit from her little sister caused Hatsuko's desperation to grow; she had so little time left. Then, three years ago, right after the monsoon rains, Hatsuko had awakened feeling like a puppet whose strings had been cut, barely able to lift an arm or a leg.

While Hatsuko was still recovering and couldn't make her tongue stop betraying the words in her head, Hideo seized upon the opportunity to pack his "auntie" away to this place that had "home" and "happy" in its name, but which was neither. Here Hatsuko knew despair almost as dark as she'd experienced in the Americans' detention camp after the war; her beloved Tami-chan would never find her way to this soulless place.

Every morning the aggressively cheerful activities coordinator would fling her door open without so much as knocking and chirp out, "Hatsuko, the others are waiting for you. Don't be naughty and make the group wait." And every morning, Hatsuko yearned to turn her face to the wall and refuse to ever again leave her bed. That was when she forced herself to recall Onaha Būten, the legendary musician she'd met in the detention camp after the war. Onaha had survived horrors to equal anyone's, yet had somehow summoned the *mabui* to fashion a *sanshin* from an old Spam can so that he could sing and play for his fellow detainees. With Būten's trademark song playing in her head—"Hey, hey, hey, hey, hey. Rise up, come on, rise up! Fall seven times and jump up eight. Let the world know. About our Uchina"— Hatsuko would rise up one more time.

PART IV

UKUI THE LAST NIGHT

The Dead Are Escorted Back to Their World

FORTY-SEVEN

Late on the afternoon of the third and final day of the festival for the dead, Hideo and his wife, Saori, and their two daughters arrive to fetch Hatsuko for the lavish dinner to be held in the Royal Ryukyuan Banquet Hall, where they will bid farewell to the spirits who've returned, and hopefully send them back to their world happy.

Hideo and Saori's daughters are already dressed in their Eisā dance costumes, and the sight of them in the traditional short-sleeved, navy-blue kimonos with closed fans tucked into yellow obis, hair pulled back under polka-dotted kerchiefs, causes Hatsuko's heart to ache with the swell of memory. They wear the same work kimonos that she and Tamiko wore when they were girls and their island was a place out of a fairy tale. The steps the girls practice are the very ones that she and Tamiko danced so long ago, when they escorted the spirits of their ancestors back to the tombs and never seriously believed that they, too, would ever get old and die.

Hatsuko tells Saori that she is not feeling well enough to accompany them. At that the wife heaves a sigh of impatience and reminds her that she was the one who insisted upon inviting her cousin Mitsue. Arrangements have been made. Mitsue is waiting even now to be picked up in Madadayo. Besides, the dinners have already been paid for, and whether they're eaten or not, no money will be refunded. Because the girls beg her, their favorite auntie, to come, Hatsuko acquiesces.

When they arrive at Madadayo and she sees the familiar thatched roof, Hatsuko feels as if she herself is an Obon ghost returning to a home she will never again truly inhabit. Her spirits rise tremendously, though, when Mitsue, still able to hop about like a little bird, comes aboard the van. At dinner, Mitsue encourages her cousin to drink the many toasts to honor the dead that are being imbibed. "We'll be joining them soon," Mitsue says, laughing. "And we don't want any hard feelings when next we meet, now, do we?"

Soon she and Mitsue are leaning together, their cheeks flushed, singing the old ceremonial songs in thin, quavering voices that neither of them recognizes as their own. Because they know they don't have many Obons left, Hatsuko and Mitsue agree to drive into Naha with the family to watch the Eisā dancers from all over the island parade through the streets and alleys, sweeping the dead back where they belong for another year.

In the van, the great-great-nieces make a big fuss over their old aunties. Hatsuko and Mitsue, speaking in the dialect that Hideo and Saori don't understand, agree that the girls are quite sweet, in spite of their horrible parents. The girls' excited chatter combines with the smell of face powder to unloose a flood of memories that washes over the two old women. Hatsuko closes her eyes and Tamiko is again beside her in the cart, swaying back and forth in time to Papaya's rolling gait. They are girls once more, laughing and whispering about which boys they might see that night in the nearby village.

In Naha, Hideo drops his daughters off at the far end of Kokusai-dōri, where dozens of teams of dancers and drummers are assembling for the parade. The rest of them then drive back to park and make their way to the spot Hideo has already picked out for parade viewing. Hatsuko clings to Mitsue, who is so much steadier on her feet, as they follow Hideo through the masses of spectators. People pack the parade route. They perch on the sills of upper-story windows and on rooftops. They pack into alleys and line the steps of outside stairways. A tall man with a news camera on his shoulder, followed by a pretty woman holding a microphone, push their way through the throng. Bar owners send hostesses with trays full of glasses of iced oolong tea and *awamori* into the crowd. Haughty tourists from the mainland stand apart from the common folk. Immense Americans freeze gaggles of their friends in the flashes of their cameras. Hatsuko and Mitsue exchange disapproving glances when the Americans, always eager to flaunt their triumph, rudely hold up Vs for victory each time they are photographed.

The old ladies are buffeted by drunken revelers as they totter along. They search the crowd, but don't see one single familiar face. Even Hideo and his family seem to be strangers, and Hatsuko misses not only the ones who are gone but even the Okinawa she once knew, for it, too, has been lost.

"Aunties," the odious Hideo calls back when Hatsuko and Mitsue fall behind. "You should have asked us to get you wheelchairs."

"I'm fine," Hatsuko barks at the toad. She leans even more heavily on her cane and curses the silly shoes they'd stuck on her feet at the nursing home. Puffy balls of white dough with Velcro closures like a child would wear, the ridiculous shoes force her to shuffle along. *Bare feet!* She'd walked the length and breadth of this island in her bare feet. Potbellied Hideo, trying to look patient and benevolent, wouldn't have lasted one day. With or without shoes.

Hideo makes a sour face and hisses at his wife, "All the places at the front will be taken if we don't hurry. I won't get any good video."

"Let him go on," Mitsue pipes up. "We'll be fine."

"Go ahead then," Saori says to her husband, with an annoyed sigh. "I'll wait for them." Happy to be free, Hideo rushes off. "Save us a spot," Saori calls after her departing husband.

"What is wrong with watching from right here?" Hatsuko asks.

"No, no, this isn't a good spot for video," Saori answers sharply. "Hideo has the place all picked out. He's even told the girls to look our way when they pass."

"How much farther is it?"

"Just up ahead. Right there on Kokusai-dōri."

"Lean on me, cousin," Mitsue says, and Hatsuko, knowing her own legs won't carry her any farther, does just that.

"Thank you," she whispers to Mitsue.

When at last they stop, Hatsuko, breathing heavily, her legs trembling, raises her eyes and sees a lighted green arch with white doves on either end spreading their wings and rising toward the heavens. In the middle is one word. In her own dialect, Hatsuko pronounces it out loud: "Peace."

· FORTY-EIGHT ·

I lean over the riders crammed up against me in the aisle of the crowded bus, and crane to get a view of the place where the sky and the ocean meet. The juncture flutters with a shimmery coral and crimson light as the sun dips into it. The sunset tints the faces of the Okinawans around me as rosy as if we're staring into a fire. All but the last wobbly slice of sun has disappeared into the East China Sea, and the evening is growing dark when the bus hisses to a stop next to dozens of others. I join the crush of excited passengers being disgorged.

Sodden heat still rises from the pavement, but a sea breeze cools the air. Overhead, the monorail shoots around a curve in the lighted track. Behind me, in the distance, a freighter docked in the Naha port is illuminated bright as a fairy castle. The reflections from its lights make blurry columns of aqua and gold in the water. Keeping the freighter at my back and the monorail tracks on my left, I join the throngs surging onto Kokusai-dōri toward the center of the city.

The street has been shut off to traffic, and its wide sidewalks are packed with spectators. I make my way up the broad avenue, dodging around the policemen shoving the crowds back onto the sidewalk. In the dark, nothing about the street looks familiar, until I spot the giant cat with the dead black eyes hanging from the second story of the souvenir shop, waving in his creepy animatronic way. Unfortunately, I can't recall whether the cat was located before or after Heiwa-dōri.

A policeman puts his white-gloved hands on me and pushes like I'm a rider on a Tokyo subway. The crowd is packed so tightly that I can't move. Just as I realize that I'm trapped far from the meeting place, a sound like thunder starts from miles down the street. I feel it low in my gut before I can even identify it as drumming. The distant booming announces that I'm running out of time: The parade has started, the dead are being driven away.

· FORTY-NINE ·

A rumbling explosion startles Hatsuko and she clutches onto Mitsue as her heart flaps within her chest like a trapped bird. She waits for the sky to blaze again with the fires of war and wonders how they will find their way out of this churning mass, so that they can flee to the safety of the caves.

"Auntie," Hideo asks, bending down to look at Hatsuko, "why are you trembling? It is only the drummers. Mitsue, what is wrong with her? Make her close her mouth. People are staring."

"Let them stare," Mitsue snaps. "She needs to rest. We have to get Hatsuko to a quiet spot."

Hatsuko watches the strange man's face contort into speech, but his words are lost in the thunder of the detonations. The other refugees crush in closer. She can feel their fear as the explosion of the Americans' bombs comes closer.

We must head south. We will be safe in the south.

"Tamiko!" She tries to call her little sister's name, but the word is lost between her brain and her mouth. She must find her little sister. This time she won't let her treacherous heart mislead her. This time they won't be separated. This time they will stay together until they are both safe in their family's tomb.

· FIFTY ·

I push hard against the crowd and they push back even harder. The first group of dancers appears in the street. They wear toenail polish–pink kimonos and look like lines of roses dancing beneath the streetlights. The policemen lock arms and force us farther back.

A huge chrysanthemum firework explodes overhead. Its blazing petals light up the street for blocks in either direction, and I catch a glimpse of a green arch and two white doves fluttering up to heaven.

I know which way to go now but am imprisoned by the crowd. I have to get to the green arch so Jake will know I'm there. That I made it. That I'm not just another kid from the base and won't simply vanish one day, never to be seen or thought of again. But I am trapped; I'll never connect with Jake. With anyone. Not even Codie.

A drunk guy in front of me stumbles and falls back, crushing the lily pin on my blouse into my chest until it jabs me hard. I lean in with all my body weight to shove the jerk off me, but he doesn't budge. After a moment's debate, I do what Codie would have done. I take the brooch off and stick the pin in the guy's fat neck. Slapping at the stab like a wasp has bitten him, he whirls around and I slip through. Polite time is over. Whatever it takes, I am going to get to Peace Street in time to meet Jake.

· FIFTY-ONE ·

The mob of refugees, driven mad by fear, is a tall, thick forest locking Hatsuko in place. She is lost. Worse, her little sister is lost. The booms, terrifying and inescapable, come closer. Then flares light up the sky, exposing their positions. They must escape. Hatsuko, overcome by weariness after already marching so long to come this far, can't catch her breath. Sheets of sweat wash down her face even as waves of nausea heave upward. She fears that she will vomit on the refugees around her and fights the urge with every bit of strength she has left. Though she tries to struggle on, her legs have turned rubbery and weak beneath her. She gasps, but the air has become too thick to pull into her lungs. She opens her mouth to scream out her sister's name, but no sound emerges.

Instead, all the frantic people melt away, the tall buildings disappear, the bombing stops, a voluptuous silence encloses Hatsuko, and Tamiko's dear face appears. She is, of course, smiling. And she is dancing. Little Guppy makes her crane-and-pine hand gesture droop comically as she turns her hands into two geese pecking each other. Tamiko doesn't care about being perfect. She cares about making her big sister laugh.

Hatsuko smiles and Tamiko's laughter in return is the only sound in her head. She doesn't hear Mitsue yelling to Hideo. She doesn't hear Hideo, video camera pressed to his eye, order his wife to see what is wrong *now* with the old ladies, that the girls will be passing them in the next group. He has to be ready with the camera. Hatsuko doesn't hear a child scream that an old lady has fallen. There is no sound at all when, in the darkness above Hatsuko, a halo of cell phones lights up to summon an ambulance.

· FIFTY-TWO ·

I use the pin a few more times, though I confine the stabs only to the biggest, most immobile of doofuses. I'm able to take out a few others as they stretch up on tiptoe for a better view simply by pressing my kneecaps against the backs of their overstraightened legs. When they stumble, off balance, I break through the opening they leave. Which is what I've just done when, across the street, in a break in the crowd, I catch a glimpse of a girl I recognize. I'm so certain, not just that I know her, but that she is a dear friend that my hand is up, ready to wave, when I realize that who I think she is, is the girl from the portrait in the museum. I think she is Tamiko Kokuba.

I shake my head and laugh at myself for such skittish suggestibility. A team of dancers passes between us, and I lose sight of the Tamiko look-alike. The dancers wear long jackets of shiny fuchsia and turquoise. Their hair is held back by matching fuchsia headbands. Where the other female teams had swayed in lovely delicate patterns, these girls stomp as ferociously as the boys, and bang just as hard on the small drums they wave above their heads. They dance in their bare feet on pavement that is so hot it steams when boys with buckets running up and down the route splash water onto it. The girls, heads held high, grin into the streetlights as if they don't notice the heat.

At the edge of the Girl Power dance team, behind a cloud of steam, the girl from the portrait appears again. This time, somehow, she's worked her way through the mob lining the street and stands, isolated, at the very front. It's weird how no one crowds in against her. They simply let the girl stand alone. It's even weirder how much she resembles the portrait of Tamiko. She looks about twelve, with her hair in pigtails that flip up just beneath her ears. Her impish smile mirrors the curve of her hair. I can't take my eyes off of her.

Another team of drummers passes between us. Their heads are covered in green cloth wraps. Smart costumes of cobalt blue outlined in white are belted tightly around their waists. They all carry shiny red *taiko* drums big as trash cans that they beat the shit out of with batons to accompany their balls-out singing. They swing the massive drums in powerful arcs as they dance, leaping high in the air. Sweat streams into their faces and bursts off their bare arms with each pounding stroke.

The dancers' black pantaloons tucked into leggings with vertical black and white stripes become bars flashing past as I struggle to catch glimpses of the girl on the other side of the street that I can't help thinking of as Tamiko.

The dancers strike fierce postures, legs high, ankles cocked, as ready to attack as warriors approaching a battle. The pounding of their drums is so loud I can't think. It's like being on the Cyclotron at the state fair and having all your thoughts spun out of you by centrifugal force. Amid all the noise and chaos a clear view of the girl opens up. Just like Tamiko, she has a face as broad and open and happy as a baby frog's that spreads wide as she stares straight at me and smiles, a serene, unhurried smile. She waves in my direction. I'm so certain that she must be waving to someone behind me that I glance around several times. But no one else appears to notice her: She's waving at me. And then she begins beckoning. She wants me to come to her.

· FIFTY-THREE ·

After Mitsue gives the attendant her cousin's information, Hatsuko feels herself being lifted up and tries to tell the stretcher bearers to help Tamiko first; she, too, must have been wounded in the explosion. But the words are flashing silver fish her tongue can't catch. Hatsuko knows it's merely a concussion from the bomb. She'll be herself soon. Meanwhile, whatever it takes, she must not lose her little sister again. She can't. Not after finally finding her. She struggles to rise, but hands force her back down. She feels the comforting boa-constrictor squeeze of a blood-pressure cuff, then the cool disk of a stethoscope on the inside of her elbow. How like the detestable Head Nurse Tanaka to keep such fine tools as these hidden. And an ambulance? Why had they not used this ambulance before? So many were lost who could have been saved.

Feeling like a paper doll floating through the air, Hatsuko is lifted onto a stretcher, then slid into the back of the ambulance. The air-raid sirens shriek. Explosions of red flash in a rhythmic strobing through the vehicle. They speed forward.

· FIFTY-FOUR ·

The girl keeps waving. She gestures with more and more insistence for me to cross the street and come to her. I hold my hands out to indicate the unbroken river of dancers and drummers blocking the street and the police who are even more vigilant than before about stopping anyone from setting one foot onto the asphalt. There's no way I can get across.

I keep shaking my head, certain that I can't be seeing what I think I'm seeing. Yet each time I catch another glimpse of her, the girl resembles the portrait at the museum even more strongly. It's like seeing Tamiko Kokuba come back to life. The obvious explanation is that the girl across the street is her descendant. I don't understand how, though, amid this throng, the girl and I have been able to single each other out. Maybe through some insider Okinawan communications network, Mitsue told her about me. Maybe the girl followed me from Madadayo. Whatever the explanation, I can't wait to give her her ancestor's pin. I stretch my shirt out to show her the pin and act out presenting it to her.

Amazingly, in all the noise and turmoil, the girl seems to know immediately that the pin is for her. She nods with that same odd serenity and gestures with both her hands, as if pulling me toward herself. As if she wanted to embrace me. For a moment, floating in the air above her head, two oddly phosphorescent balls appear. Just as I motion again to the impenetrable wall of policemen, drummers, and dancers between us, though, the street suddenly empties, and all goes silent. Even the siren.

The girl waves for me to hurry up, to grab this chance while I have it. I shove my way into the street, certain I will be pushed back. But the barricade of police arms melts away. I keep my eyes riveted on the girl; if I lose sight of her, I won't ever find her again. Even though I never take my eyes from her, she disappears. The strange orbs, glowing like giant fireflies, appear again. Right below them is the girl. This time, though, the face staring at me from the crowd is the starved face of the girl I found in the cave. I couldn't help her before, couldn't help anyone. But I know now. I know I can save her this time. Save her and make everything all right.

At that moment, the crowd suddenly starts screaming at me; a nearby siren shrieks at full volume; lights whirl. They all conspire to try to stop me. But I won't let them. Not this time. The girl is only a few yards away, then a few feet away. She holds her hand out to me. I hold mine out to her. All I have to do is take her hand, and I know everything will be all right. We reach out to each other. I'm about to touch her outstretched fingers when some goon slams into me so hard that I go flying onto the street. I slide across the pavement, the asphalt shredding the bare shoulder I land on.

I sit up, furious at the idiot who smashed into me, and search the crowd frantically for the girl. Faces strobe past, illuminated in an ambulance's flashing light. I don't understand how the ambulance could have gotten here so quickly. I must have blacked out, and the ambulance is for me. Except that the crowd ignores me as they stare down, shocked, at something out of my sight. The police shove them back, but the spectators crane their necks to keep staring. Most of the women have their hands pressed against open mouths in expressions of horror. I'm certain it's the girl. That she collapsed, possibly died.

I have to get to her. I drag myself up off the hot street. Blood dripping from my scraped shoulder, I shove my way into the crowd and keep shoving until I can see what they're all gawking at.

It's a body sprawled out on the street.

It's Jake.

· FIFTY-FIVE ·

Hatsuko, who has been begging the attendant with his stethoscope on her heart to stop, is delighted when the driver finally slams on his brakes. She has succeeded. She's made them understand that they can't leave without finding her little sister.

Staticky orders from the ambulance dispatcher are broadcast into the back of the ambulance. The attendant barks that they can't transport the person they hit. They have to wait for the police. Dispatch will have to send another unit for the patient they've already got. The dispatcher says all the rules are off. The city is in complete gridlock. No other vehicles can get in; they're the only ones available.

A blast of hot air puffs into the chilly ambulance when the back door is opened. The ambulance rocks beneath Hatsuko as the attendant hops out, then bounces again when another victim of the bombing is loaded aboard. Hatsuko forces her eyes open, but the world is a blur. Still, she is certain that the new patient is Tamiko. She has found her little sister. Finally.

When the doors are slammed shut, she tries to roll over to face Tamiko, but her limbs won't respond. Though Hatsuko lies on the stretcher as still as a stone, her heart flutters wildly; she is desperate for Tamiko to come to her. There is so much she must tell Little Guppy, and so little time left.

· FIFTY-SIX ·

As the ambulance attendants help Jake into the ambulance he tells them something as he points at me. The bleeding from where I gashed my arm has mostly stopped, but Jake convinces them that I need help too. I try to explain that the cuts look a lot worse than they are, but neither of the EMTs has time for a discussion. They've already got a patient on the stretcher, and the old woman needs help a lot more than either Jake or I do. The second EMT hops in back with us, the doors slam, and we speed off as rapidly as the crowd can clear out of our way.

"Jake, how are you?" I ask as the Okinawan EMT shines a penlight into Jake's eyes and orders him to follow its beam.

"Seriously, I'm fine," he answers, after telling the attendant how many fingers he's holding up.

"Seriously, you got hit by an ambulance."

"Bumped is more like it. I was stunned for a minute, but I'm okay now. The real question is, what the hell were you doing sauntering across the street? It was a miracle that my drum team was stopped at that spot right when you ran out in front of an ambulance. An ambulance that had its lights and siren on. What is up with that?" Jake looks at me and waits for an answer. He is still in his Eisā drummer's costume.

I consider lying. But I don't and simply answer, "I saw her. The girl from the cave."

Jake nods, and I'm surprised at how unsurprised he is. "Yeah, I thought it might be something like that. Happens on the last day of Obon. Lot of the dead have too good a time and don't want to go back. Hope someone else chases her back to her world."

The ambulance, blaring its horn to clear the crowd, gains speed. Before I can say anything more, the old woman strapped onto the stretcher a few inches from us opens her eyes and looks around, a confused, haunted expression on her face. She moves her mouth like a fish gasping for oxygen. "Jake, she needs something. What should we do?"

Jake speaks to the attendant, who explains that the old woman is stabilized and they're not supposed to do anything more except transport her to the hospital.

But she clearly needs help. A pair of glasses, their thick, heavy lenses shattered, lies on the stretcher next to her. I realize she can't see and how scared and disoriented she must be. There's so little room between us that I only have to bend forward to enter into her field of vision. Though I'm certain I'm nothing more than a blurry smudge to her, the old lady smiles a smile like angels on Christmas morning when she sees me. But then, as she reaches a trembling hand up, I realize that the smile is not for me. It's for the object that she strokes while exhaling a trembling sigh of relief deeper than any I've ever heard. It's for the lily brooch still pinned on my blouse.

At the hospital, the old woman seems agitated when I have to step away so that the nurses and orderlies who rush out to greet us can transfer her to a gurney. She reaches out her hand to me, and I take it. Though he objects, Jake is ordered to ride in a wheelchair.

The emergency room smells of sweat and vomit and is packed with casualties of the combustion of three days of drinking and close contact with extended family, all coming to a mad crescendo at the Ten Thousand Eisā Dance Parade. We are rushed through the waiting room, back to the examining area. Doctors in white lab coats, nurses in blue scrubs, techs in green whip past, their shoes brushing the floor in a brisk rhythm punctuated by the constant beeping of monitors. A young female physician directs the gurney to be wheeled into a newly vacated examining room. I try to slip away, but the woman only hangs on to my hand more tightly.

Whether they assume we're family, or simply because all the other rooms are full, Jake and I are waved in while the old woman is examined, a heart monitor hooked up, and an IV started. The odors, human and medicinal, combined with the general frenzy of the emergency room act on her like smelling salts under a boxer's nose. She shakes her head and, blinking wildly, struggles as if she were expected to get up and perform vital duties. I hurry over to calm her. She clutches my hand and reaches out again for the lily pin. Her fingers close around it, and words that sound even more foreign to me than Japanese tumble out as if a timer is running and she can't talk fast enough.

I lean in close, stroke her face, and croon, *"Shi-shi-shi."* She relaxes her clawing grip and I pin the lily brooch on her blouse. I place her free hand on the pin, and her face lights up. She grins as if this were part of a secret joke between us and pulls me close. I am enclosed in a cloud of memory and the smells of Pond's cold cream, green tea, and a vinegary body odor. Her voice falls to a whisper as she speaks only to me. I am distressed, confused by the urgency of her feverish monologue that she seems to expect me to understand. Then, from out of the cacophony, a name spoken by a nurse reporting to a doctor about the new patient emerges as clearly as if it were my own: Kokuba Hatsuko. The only Princess Lily girl without a pin. The big sister.

I lean in and listen.

· FIFTY-SEVEN ·

O h, Little Guppy, to see your beautiful face again! My prayers have been answered. The *kami* have returned you to me. Tami-chan, my sweet, my precious little sister, I have waited so long to explain, to beg you for your forgiveness. I should never have abandoned you. Never. The only reason I can give for leaving you alone and unprotected in our family's tomb and for taking the crock of pork miso our mother made to save us is that I was crazed by love. It shames me still to think of how I deserted you. Perhaps, if you know the misfortunes I endured after we parted, you will see that I suffered for my blindness, my ignorance, and for all my failures to be a proper older sister.

"When I walked away from the tomb, Little Guppy, I believed that I could witness nothing worse than what you and I had already seen. But I was wrong. After the Imperial Army collapsed, everyone, soldiers and civilians alike, clawed for life. I saw a Japanese soldier knock an old woman down with the butt of his rifle and steal the shriveled bit of sweet potato she was gnawing on. I saw a starving infant suck the blood streaming from his dying mother's chest. I saw a crazed Japanese soldier molest a dead woman. I saw a father, terrified of the Americans, gather his wife, his mother, his five children around him, then pull the pin on a grenade and turn them all into a cloud of pink dust. I saw a colonel kneel in a field and plunge his sword into his belly and his guts spill out like an overturned basket of eels.

"I forced myself to stop seeing and thought only of reaching Naka-mura before honor compelled him to commit seppuku. For I was cer-tain that he, the proudest of all the emperor's proud soldiers, would surely choose the sword over surrender. Though I was starving, I didn't touch a single bite from our mother's crock. It was all for Nakamura. I would save him and he would love me. If not in this life, then certainly, and forever, in the next.

"The dead were everywhere. They were yellow mud in the rain. When the rain stopped, they shriveled up into mummies in the heat. Adult faces shrank to the size of a child's and turned black. Except for the teeth, which continued to shine in hideous white smiles.

"When I finally reached Makabe the caves were nothing more than scorched holes that stank of flesh turned to charcoal by flamethrow-ers. I gave up all hope then that Nakamura might still be alive. I would have found a way to kill myself, but, upon accepting that I was too late to save the lieutenant, all strength left my starved body, and I sank to the earth. The heavy crock crashed against the rocks and a wave of maggots poured forth. The food was spoiled. Okinawa was spoiled. Life was spoiled.

"I hated the Amerikās for taking my beloved from me and for destroy-ing all that was beautiful on this earth. When the long-nosed giants found me, I no longer cared how they might use me. I hated the enemy so much that even the unearthly blue eyes of the half-naked devils with their red skin marked by frightening tattoos did not scare me. In the moment that they lifted me from the ground in their demon-strong arms, I made a vow that somehow I would discover a way to kill as many of the monsters as I could, so that I would be the most brilliant of shattered jewels when I joined my gallant warrior in a warrior's death.

"In their detention camp, endless rows of tents were staked on a mud flat and surrounded by a double row of barbed-wire fences. I drank only a few sips of water and ate only a few bites of their disgusting, greasy food. Their hamburgers. Their Spam. They both tasted of the slow-acting poison that our teachers had warned us about. My plan was to live only long enough to steal an unguarded weapon and kill as many of the enemy as I could before the poison sent me to a death as honorable as Nakamura's.

"Please, little sister, don't sneer at me. I know now that I was a fool. But then? We were children; we knew only what we had been told. What we had been taught in school.

"Early one morning, when I and the nine other women in my tent were herded out to relieve ourselves, I saw my chance. A guard at the edge of the women's compound had isolated a pretty girl from the country to toy with. He wasn't wearing a shirt and his hairy chest was marked with a tattoo depicting the flesh-eating eagle that they worshiped. The revolver on his hip was ignored as he leaned forward, playing with the terrified girl's hair, pressing his unwanted attentions on her. I advanced quickly toward the demon.

"Unnoticed, I crept up behind him. My hand was reaching out for his gun when the guard spotted someone he knew, straightened up abruptly, and called out to the man, 'Hey, Nocky, get your ass over here.'

"A tall Okinawan man, his head bent low in a servile posture beneath a farmer's conical straw hat that hid his face, rushed over, eager to do the guard's bidding. He wore a ragged kimono belted beneath his potbelly that flapped about his knees as he hurried toward us.

"'Nocky,' the guard said, waving a casual finger at the girl trembling with fear. 'Tell this one that I think she's mighty sweet.'

"Though no proud sword swept out behind the farmer as he bowed lower than even the most obsequious of servants, I recognized the voice that scurried to pander. 'Hai! Hai! Hai! Yes, sir! Right away, sir!'

"For a moment, I couldn't understand why my noble, brave Nakamura, the hero who had sung about death before dishonor and being a jewel shattering into a thousand pieces for the glory of the emperor, had stripped off the uniform of an Imperial officer and disguised himself as a farmer. When he looked up, I thought I had been mistaken, for this wasn't Nakamura's thin, handsome face. This was the face of a man who'd grown fat on the enemy's butter and hamburgers. But it was. It was Nakamura.

"In Japanese he snarled at the girl, 'Do whatever he wants; do you hear me? He will strangle you with his bare hands if you don't. Now, smile. Smile! And don't make trouble or the demons will kill and eat you and all of your family!'

"Her chin quivering, her eyes bright with unshed tears, the girl did lift the corners of her lips as the giant put his arm around her and led her away. But then, bending her head in shame, she didn't see the American guard turn back to Nakamura with surprise lighting his face; the soldier hadn't expected the girl to go with him. He hadn't expected anything. Nor did the girl see Nakamura grin and raise his thumb. Or the guard return the salute and toss him a package of cigarettes marked with the red circle of the rising sun. A package of the Lucky Strikes that we once had believed were proof of America's acceptance of the invincibility of Japan.

"At that instant, as I watched Nakamura greedily hide his booty in the waistband of the stolen kimono, it was as if I had fallen down into one of the caves where we'd hidden. There was no ground beneath my feet as I saw the proof that it had all been lies. All of it. The lice, the young men's shattered bodies, the hunger, the suicides, the death. It had all been for nothing. For lies. It was as though I had been fed nothing but black sugar for years, all the way back to my first day as a Princess Lily girl, when we practiced marching with our sharpened bamboo sticks. All the way back to my first day of grade school, when our Japanese teacher taught us to raise our right arms straight out in front to salute that red circle and pledge with all our silly Okinawan hearts to strive to become worthy to one day be true Japanese. How the thought of being a true Japanese girl had once thrilled me. And how the sweet taste of it that had once been so intoxicating now sickened me.

"Only when his awful prize was safely tucked away did Nakamura notice me. For an instant he forgot and smiled, believing he was greeting one of his admirers, one of the stupid girls in the soot-filled cave who had mooned over him when she wasn't picking lice from her hair. When he saw the shock and contempt on my face, though, he remembered what he had become. The face I had once thought so noble showed its cruel baseness as he snarled, 'Don't look at me like that, darling Hatsuko. You are no Princess Lily anymore.' He pointed to the girl, her slight figure disappearing as the GI led her into the large, dark tent where supplies were stored. 'Believe me, you will do worse than her. Worse than me.'

"'I have already done worse,' I told that villain. 'I abandoned a person of true nobility for the likes of you.'

"Tamiko, until that moment I was under a spell. In the instant that it was broken, I realized what I had done to you. I had left my sister, my *little* sister, alone and unprotected, when you had never been anything but faithful and loving to me.

"I spit in the face I had once thought so handsome, and from that moment on, all I could think of was finding you and returning home, so that I might spend the rest of my life atoning for my selfishness. But, though I begged, no one was permitted to leave the camp. They called us detainees, but we knew that we were prisoners. Each morning from that day on, I was at the gate to greet the latest shipment of newcomers, searching the starvelings for you, for our parents. Though I looked for our brothers, the only Imperial soldiers among the detainees were cowards, like Nakamura, who had disguised themselves as farmers. Unlike Nakamura, however, none of those traitors would meet my gaze. They still had the decency to hang their heads in shame at the humiliation of not having died for the emperor. Knowing the cruelty that they themselves would have shown any enemy prisoner, much less a soldier who disgraced himself by surrendering, they trembled with fear at being discovered.

"Gradually, though, soldiers and civilians alike, we realized our conquerors would treat us all the same. I watched an old farmer ask for one last cigarette before he was crushed to death beneath the treads of the mighty tanks, as the Imperial soldiers had promised. The farmer was stupefied when the guards handed him six cigarettes, tucked two more behind his ears, and gave him a bowl of soup and a pair of boots. Terrified children, new to the camp, still expecting to be eaten, saw other children, plump cheeked and playing games, and began to trust that the red devils' bars of chocolate were not poisoned. Mothers were stunned when the enemy gave their malaria-stricken children quinine as generously as if to their own sons and daughters. I watched a defeated captain burst into tears when an American medic approached with long tweezers that he believed would be used to gouge out his eyes, and instead the American knelt down beside him and tenderly plucked the maggots from his wounds.

"One night in the middle of August, our captors took up their guns and cannons and blasted wildly until the dark sky was filled again with the awful fireworks of tracers and flares. The Imperial soldiers hidden among us screamed that the beasts had fooled us all. That they'd only been holding back for the rampage of revenge that was now about to descend upon us. The next morning, word filtered through the camp that the emperor had surrendered. Many former Imperial soldiers wept, but none of our people shed any tears. We had learned the bitter truth long ago: The emperor for whom we had sacrificed so much had never been our father.

"Oh, dear Tamiko, I dreamed of home every night. Every night, I entered the courtyard of our farm in Madadayo and *Anmā* held her apron over her face to catch the tears of joy as she welcomed me back. Everyone was with her: Father, all four of our brothers, Aunt Junko, Cousin Chiiko, her baby Little Mouse, everyone. Even loyal old Papaya. But you, Tamiko, they all stepped aside when you appeared, for they knew that you were the one I had truly come back for. I woke each morning more certain than ever that my dreams were a vision of what waited for me in Madadayo, and I ached to return and be reunited with you and the rest of our family. Months passed, however, before the Americans finally released me.

"The instant they did, I rushed home, traveling to our village on a smooth new road that connected the north and south of Okinawa for the first time. For longer than I had been alive the Japanese had promised to build such a road; the Americans had made a river of asphalt materialize overnight.

"Tami-chan, you would not have recognized the country I passed through. Runways and roads covered what had been fields and forests. Barracks and command centers had replaced villages and farms. Barbed wire wrapped around the heart of our island. Everywhere I looked, machines even larger than the tanks we feared would be used to crush our bones scraped the earth clean. Worst of all, though, was that the machines had clawed away not only trees and grass, but corpses, skeletons, and the tombs where our ancestors had rested for a thousand years. The tombs that hadn't been obliterated were desecrated. Urns lay broken and scattered in the dust, and with them our connection to the past and the future.

"One morning, before sunrise, I watched as men and women and children were dragged from their beds and forced to leave their homes at gunpoint by American soldiers. The young men who protested as bulldozers obliterated their village, their homes, their lives from the face of the earth were arrested and taken into custody by military police wearing white helmets and white straps across their chests. Unlike you and I, Tami-chan, they must not have seen the movies of the Americans slaughtering the Indians and driving them from their homeland. If they had, they would have known how futile their protests were.

"When I finally reached Madadayo and walked down the narrow lane toward our farm, I held my breath, fearing that it, like so many others, had been bartered away by the Imperial government in the terrible conspiracy between between Tokyo and Washington that saved the mainland and sacrificed Okinawa. But no base had taken the place of our home. No fence locked me out of our property. I stood before the blackened square of earth that had once been the house we grew up in and forced myself not to imagine Father, Mother, and our brothers crowding onto the veranda to welcome me home. Instead, I rushed to the last place where I had seen you, dear sister.

"It was fortunate, indeed, that our family tomb was hidden away, for neither the flamethrowers nor the souvenir hunters, those *Amerikās* who thought that our burial urns were nothing more than mementos to steal, had found it. I called out your name. There was no answer. The square stone blocking the entrance was still ajar and I squeezed in. I feared that I would find your body resting inside, but you were not there. The only evidence of you that I found was hidden behind Great-great-great-grandfather Ryō's urn, where I discovered the air-raid bonnet *Anmā* had made for you. I rejoiced then, certain that you weren't waiting to greet me because, without your padded bonnet, you'd suffered an injury that had wiped out your memory of me and Madadayo. All I had to do was find you and bring you home.

"For months I searched. I traveled from one end of the island to the other. From Kyan to Hedo. Though I believed I had shed all my tears, I wept when I came to the rubble-strewn plot of bare earth that had been Shuri Castle. Only stone fragments remained of our ancient kings' fairy-tale palace. Towering trees that had shaded the nobility of the Ryukyu Islands were blackened stumps. The ancient city was gone, and with it all the centuries of documents, records, and registries. The history of our people had been turned to ash.

"Walking the Americans' ribbon of asphalt, I headed north. As I approached the last of the sixteen detention camps and had still not found you or Mother or Father or any of our aunts and uncles and cousins, I came close to abandoning hope: I was all alone in the world. Even if I'd had a reason to go on living, I had no means. I could either haunt the Americans' trash dumps and scavenge bits of Spam and the sweet beans they left in the discarded cans, or I could return home and wait for the Americans to come and throw me off our land as they'd evicted so many others. I appealed to the kami, I begged Old Jug, to send me a sign that I should go on living. And she did. There, in that last camp, I found our cousin Mitsue. She had not been killed by the bomb blast outside the cave where we were denied entrance after all.

"Her first reaction when she saw me was to hang her head in shame and turn away. But, filled with joy at the sight of someone from our family, I took her in my arms, and soon she, too, was weeping with happiness. We were all each other had left. Over and over, Mitsue begged me to forgive her. I said there was nothing to forgive. If she and Nakamura had found a moment of comfort in the hell we had lived through, then at least he had been good for one thing. The war had twisted us all in ways we could never have imagined. Me worst of all. We determined that we would spend the rest of our lives honoring those who had been taken from us. We returned to Madadayo, where we lived in our family tomb, and prayed for our ancestors' help to survive and to remain on our land when so many others' property had been seized. That is when I found all the precious items our wise mother had hidden there and blessed her for her foresight.

"Mitsue and I built a shack from boxes discarded by the U.S. Army and waited. In short order, a colonel and a representative from the Japanese government came with papers saying that we must leave. Because our property was ideally located high on a cliff facing the East China Sea, it had been appropriated to make way for a giant tower to intercept communications from our new enemies, the communists in China. The man from Tokyo said that we should be honored to be allowed to make this sacrifice; Okinawans could only be protected from such a terrible new threat if we cooperated in our defense.

"The colonel and the Japanese official were surprised by two things. The first was that I spoke English and addressed the colonel directly.

The second was that, because our wise mother, who never trusted the Japanese, had insisted on formally registering our property, I had a copy of our family's *koseki shōhon*. Though most land titles had burned with Shuri, I had the proof that we owned our land, with a seal affixed in Tokyo. Furthermore, I told the gentlemen, I had no quarrel with the Chinese; they weren't my enemies. We had existed peacefully with the Chinese, trading and sharing our cultures, for centuries before Japan invaded. In fact, we had existed peacefully with everyone until the cursed day when the Japanese packed our defenseless island with soldiers and weapons and transformed it into a target. But, I allowed, the Americans could lease a sliver of our land for their tower. If they were willing to pay handsomely for the privilege. Far, far more than the pittance they were giving others when they 'leased' the land they'd taken by force. And, I added, I would require first payment in advance.

"With their money, I hired laborers and rebuilt our house exactly as it had been. That is when I made a most astonishing discovery and one that will make you very happy, little sister. When we dug up the old sweet potato field in order to replant it, you will never guess what we found. The *hōanden* made of *hinoki* wood to contain the emperor's photo that we had always been forbidden to gaze upon.

"I decided that I would look upon the face of the man for whom such unimaginable suffering had been endured. Though my brain had long been free of the delusion that he was a god, my hand still trembled as it touched the brass handle on the front of the wooden display case. I held my breath and opened the small door on the front. A stupid prickle of fear ran through me that the goddess Amaterasu might yet strike me dead for the sacrilege of beholding the image of her descendant.

"Tamiko, I don't know what fearsome lord I thought I would find there, but I didn't expect to see the photo of a small man with weak eyes, a weak, petulant mouth, and ears that poked out like the handles on a jug. A man whose shoulders sagged beneath the weight of all the medals, and badges, sashes, braids, and epaulettes pinned to his uniform. Resting on the table next to him was his hat with what appeared to be a feather duster implanted at its front. He looked like a boy playing soldier. Before the weight of all that had been taken from me by this silly man with his feather-duster hat could crush me with treads heavier than those of any tank, I made my wondrous discovery, the one that will please you.

"Next to the emperor's photo that Father, loyal to the end, had sought to protect was the list he'd begun reading that day of all the students in Madadayo who had been admitted to high school. And guess what, Tami-chan? Your name *was* on that list! The expression we saw on Father's face that morning at breakfast that we took to be disappointment at your rejection was preoccupation; he was consumed with thoughts of the coming war. Tamiko, your name was on the list. You were always a real Princess Lily girl."

· FIFTY-EIGHT ·

After cousin Mitsue had watched the ambulance carrying Hatsuko make its blaring, halting way through the crowd of stumbling drunks, then turn down the first open street and speed away, the wail of its siren warbling like an angry cat, she had rejoiced: It was time to put the plan they had so carefully worked out into action. Today, after more than seventy years, she would finally repay her cousin Hatsuko in full not only for saving her from starvation after the war, but, even more generously, for forgiving her cursed betrayal with Nakamura.

With an authority she'd never accessed before during her long life, Mitsue had ordered Hideo to take her to the hospital; his wife could meet the girls after the parade and wait with them for him to return. Mitsue impressed upon him that his first obligation was to his great-aunt. Hideo had then gestured to the crowd pressing in on them and told Mitsue that her request was impossible; he couldn't possibly leave his family. In answer, Mitsue merely smiled and observed how surprising she found it that he would risk endangering himself and his family by failing to honor someone so close to joining the spirit world.

Overhearing this threat, Saori had hectored her husband. "You have to go. All the Kokuba women are known to be very spiritual. Priestesses, healers, shamans."

"So what?"

"So, they have the ear of the *kami*. We're already dealing with so much. Your setbacks at work. Your headaches. My dizzy spells. Which, by the way, are getting worse. My head is whirling even now. And don't forget the girls' school problems."

Though Hideo had scoffed, "I'm certain that the *kami* aren't responsible for our daughters' poor performance in algebra," he knew that his wife was right. Given what superior students he and Saori both had been, there could be no explanation other than interference from the next world for their daughters' embarrassing marks. Or for his failure to get the regional manager position that had gone to that idiot Ota last month. Another humiliation. Massaging his temples, Hideo surrendered once again to the conspiracy of women plaguing his existence. He told Saori that he would meet her and the girls back at the parking lot after he dropped the old lady off.

On the drive to the hospital, while Hideo fumes and mutters about not getting any of the footage he'd wanted, Mitsue ignores him and meditates in preparation for the fulfillment of her life's most important task. First she has to order her memories. She sorts back through and smooths them over until they form a single stream that flows into this fateful moment.

She starts when Hatsuko found her at the Americans' camp in the far north end of the island, took her in, shared all she had, and never once said a single harsh word about her betrayal. Hatsuko had been changed, and she showed the same generosity to dozens of others. Distant relatives. Former residents of Madadayo. Orphans no one else claimed. She welcomed them all and, sharing her family's land, and the Americans' money, they rebuilt the village and their lives. Once the starving years ended, Mitsue had time to realize that her cousin's forgiveness had come too quickly; she hadn't truly atoned for her sin. It was clear to Mitsue that unless she properly discharged this debt, she would be denied entry to the next world. Therefore, shortly after the Day of Shame, September 8, 1951, when Japan signed the peace treaty that sacrificed one-fifth of Okinawa to the U.S. military, she journeyed to Sefa-utaki to seek true absolution.

At the entrance to the island's most sacred grove, she climbed the steep, slippery steps upward into the dripping green velvet that cloaked the mystery within. Her head bowed and senses alive with the palpable presence of the *kami* humming in the silence about her, Mitsue had entered that hushed and hallowed spot where the *noro* priestesses, once the island's undisputed spiritual leaders, had received their powers. Where for centuries the only men allowed to enter were the ancient kings of the Ryukyuan islands, who left hundreds of horses and thousands of servants waiting when they ascended these very steps to beg the *kami* to bless their reigns.

Pausing in the path trodden by high priestesses and princesses, Mitsue knelt beside a bomb crater that vine and fern had not yet healed. She brushed her fingertips across the wound and was greeted by the dead who gathered there. After honoring them with an offering of a papaya and three American pennies, she continued on her way. At the top of the stairs, she beheld the sacred cleft created by two immense slabs of rock leaning together. Sefa-utaki was a reverse canyon wedged into the side of the black cliff, open to the blue sky above the sea at its far end. Hundreds had gathered beneath its triangle of safety when the Typhoon of Steel raged outside and there they had begged the *kami* to save them. Mitsue dipped her hands into the jugs placed beneath the twin stalactites, Amadayuru Ashikanubi and Shikiyodayuru Amaganubi, that stood sentry beside the opening, and wet them in the drops of heaven's rain that collected there.

Her dripping hands steepled into a form that matched the angle of the rock slabs, Mitsue entered the holy space the slabs formed. At the altar of Chonuhana, she knelt and gazed to the east. With the cathedral of stone framing the fabled ocean view, Mitsue beheld Kudaka Island, floating like a mirage on the horizon between sea and sky. She sent prayers to the goddess Amamikyu, who had created the first Ryukyuans on that holy island where all women from the ages of thirty-one to seventy still served the gods. Mitsue clapped her hands to fully capture the *kami*'s attention and told her story.

"I wronged my cousin grievously by having sex with the man she loved. Nakamura pursued me and, though at first I scorned him, gradually I came to depend upon his attention. Then to crave it. The times we were together in secret when he whispered to me of how I inflamed his desire and he touched me with a gentleness I had all but forgotten were the only moments when I was not tortured by fear and despair and loneliness. The other girls, Hatsuko and the rest, had never known a man's caress. But I had. I knew what I had lost, and for a few blessed moments I could pretend Masaru hadn't died and we were together again. I didn't think it mattered, since I was certain we would all perish on the march to Makabe. I had no feelings for Nakamura. And he had none for me. His love for himself was so great that it left no room for any other. In fact, his self-regard was what gave the lieutenant the confidence to approach me when no one else dared. All the other soldiers were too intimidated by—and I only say this to present the truth—my beauty."

Even as the *kami* guided Mitsue to utter the word "beauty," she understood the penance they desired of her before they would grant absolution. And from that day forward, Mitsue put her great beauty on the shelf like a garment she had outgrown and had no further use for. She stopped wearing a hat and her skin turned dark as old tea. She no longer smiled in a way that dented her cheeks with the dimples of good fortune that men found so fetching. She threw away her Kissupurūfu lipstick. Somehow all these outward measures dimmed Mitsue's radiance enough that, for the first time in her memory, heads did not automatically turn toward her like flowers seeking the light. Though she missed being admired by men, Mitsue found it a small enough price to pay to honor her cousin's magnanimity.

Over the years, more and more surviving relatives and residents of Madadayo or their descendants returned to their village. Hatsuko continued to welcome them all. Even her father's once-grand relatives wormed their way in, though they were worthless at anything other than calligraphy and numbers. Still, with Hatsuko guiding them, they rebuilt Madadayo just as it had been on the day before the sea had gone gray with warships. Mitsue devoted her life to helping Hatsuko prepare for her sister's return, which, as time passed, they both came to understand would have to be as a spirit.

Working side by side every day for years, then decades, Hatsuko and Mitsue grew as close as a pair of Mandarin ducks, one never going anywhere without the other, until the stroke that the scheming Hideo had used as a pretext to shuffle Hatsuko off to that unbearable nursing home. Though Mitsue tried to convince her old friend to return to Madadayo with her, Hatsuko knew that she could no longer care for herself. Besides, with the minutes lasting for an eternity and the days, weeks, and months disappearing in two blinks, it wasn't worth the trouble while she lived. No, it was what was to happen to her after she died that concerned Hatsuko. And on that score, she left very clear, very insistent instructions with her cousin. Instructions that Mitsue was now determined to carry out. If only the toad Hideo could get them to the hospital in time.

"This is impossible," Hideo spits out when he finds that the hospital lot is already crammed full not just with parked cars, but with vehicles slowly orbiting in search of a space to snap up. "I'll never get a spot."

"Don't worry, Hideo-san," Mitsue suggests, making her voice the birdlike chirp of supplication that weak men like him so enjoy. "You can just let me out, and I'll go by myself."

Hideo doesn't even make a pretense of objecting. Happy to be relieved of his burden, he pulls up beneath the portico leading into the emergency room, and asks in a perfunctory way, "You have my number?"

"Oh, yes, yes," Mitsue hastens to answer.

"Call if there's a problem. Tell dear Hatsuko that I did everything I possibly could to come visit. Make sure she knows that."

"Don't worry," Mitsue assures him. "Your great-aunt won't go to the next world bearing you any hard feelings for not looking after her tonight."

He nods and Mitsue hides a smile, thinking of all the other offenses that Hideo has committed before this night that Hatsuko will most certainly recall when accounts are taken.

"I must get back and pick up my family."

"Oh, yes, yes, of course, your family," Mitsue chimes in a soothing way that disguises the contempt she feels for this silly man's puny, isolated idea of what a family is.

"We'll return for you and my aunt as soon as we can."

"Please take your time. We'll be fine." Mitsue must hide how delighted she is to be rid of the unpleasant little man; what she must do this night will be so much easier without him. Right before alighting from the van, Mitsue turns to Hideo and says with as much cheerful innocence as she can pretend, "Just two old ladies in a hospital. What could be safer?"

Hideo gives a grunt of something approximating agreement, Mitsue gets out, slides the van door shut, and he drives off without so much as a glance back.

Mitsue's tread is brisk and determined as she marches into the hospital. She asks the attendant on duty to direct her to Kokuba Hatsuko. As she makes her way through the crowded waiting room, her lips stretch into a smile so wide that her dimples make a rare appearance.

· FIFTY-NINE ·

Jake and I are both happy to be overlooked in the chaos as a room is readied for Hatsuko who, exhausted by speaking and overcome by the medication she's been given, sleeps on one side of me while Jake sits on the other. I stare into his eyes, searching for half-remembered conditions like "fixed gaze" and "pupils of unequal size."

As I study it, Jake's face goes slack; his eyes unfocus and roll wildly. "Who are you?" he asks. "Where am I? What is this place? Is it snack time? When's recess?"

"Jake? What is it? What's wrong?" I am about to call out for help when he laughs. I slug his biceps. "You jerk."

"Luz, seriously, I'm fine. Or will be as soon as they let us out of here."

"You're like a military kid."

"How's that?"

"Can't stand to be fussed over. The center of attention."

"Is that a military kid thing?"

"In my family it is."

Hatsuko mutters in her sleep, and Jake and I tense as we wait for her breathing to fall back into a regular rhythm. We listen to the steady beat of the monitor, until we're certain that, for the moment, Hatsuko is all right. Then, whispering as if she can hear me, I tell Jake who she is and what I learned at the museum and in Madadayo.

"The girl in the cave?"

"No, her sister." I tell him about the trip to Madadayo. About the portraits in the museum. I point to the lily brooch. "That's her sister's pin. She recognized it. Isn't that amazing? Isn't the whole thing amazing?"

Jake shrugs. "Kind of amazing. Kind of not."

"How can it not be amazing?"

"First of all, Okinawa is tiny. Once we knew the Princess Lily part, we were, at most, another day away from finding her. Second of all, the *kami* wanted you to find her."

"Did she say that? Hatsuko? When she was talking to me?"

"I couldn't make out a lot of what she was saying. She was mostly muttering, and when she did speak up, it was in Okinawan. I've been trying to learn *Uchināguchi,* but not even us *Uchinānchu* speak it much anymore. It sure seemed like she expected you to understand, though."

I glance up at Jake and lose track of what I was about to say. All I can manage to focus on is how much I like his face. I like it way, *way* too much. Finally I say, "You saved my life."

"Not really. That ambulance was barely crawling along. And I fell more than it hit me."

"No, you did. You saved my life." When I say it the second time, we both know that I don't mean the ambulance or the shove. Or not just them.

Jake doesn't answer, just takes my hand, brushes off the bits of road grit still clinging there, brings it to his lips, and kisses every one of my fingernails. Then, his tone serious, he says, "Luz, I need to tell you something."

The elephant in the room is finally going to be named, and that name will be Christy. Every molecule in my body wants to jump up, to leave, to stop whatever blow-off speech Jake has queued up. Instead, I blurt out, "No worries. It's not a problem. We had fun. Whatever."

"God, Luz, just let me talk, okay?" The sounds around us—a couple of drunks fighting in the waiting area, the descending wail of an ambulance as it pulls up outside, the symphony of beeps—all rise in volume to fill the silence that I desperately don't want to end. Jake keeps holding my hand, molding it between his. His skin color, that apple-jelly gold, is a tanner version of my own. On him I see how exquisite it is. He doesn't want to say what he has to say any more than I want to hear it, and it's a long time before he starts again. "Christy and I have been together a long time—"

The jangle of the curtain being whipped back along its metal track stops Jake. The instant I see who it is, I jump to my feet and bow. Then, while trying to figure out why she is grinning like someone walking into her own surprise party, I greet the beautiful old woman from Madadayo: "*Hai-sai*, Mitsue-san."

· SIXTY ·

Mitsue laughs, delighted to see the strange American who had come to Madadayo here in the hospital caring for her cousin. How clever the *kami* are to use a *hāfu* to do their work! she thinks. And to even provide an interpreter in the form of a handsome Okinawan boy. Mitsue tells him that she has come to bring Hatsuko home.

"No, she can't be moved," the boy responds in Japanese softened by his *Uchinānchu* accent.

"Yes, she can. We will use the wheelchair you're sitting in. You don't seem to need it."

"I don't, but she has to stay here. They're trying to find a room for her right now."

"Her room is waiting for her back in her home in Madadayo. That is where she wants to be. It was all decided in advance." With that, Mitsue holds up a document written in Hatsuko's elegant calligraphy, and witnessed, registered, and sealed by all the proper authorities.

The *hāfu* girl asks what's happening and the boy explains. "She wants to take her home."

"Is that a good idea?"

"No, they're working to get her admitted right now."

The boy tells Mitsue this, and she asks, "Why? Hatsuko is dying. If she stays here, the doctors will attach her to machines that will force her worn-out body to do what it should no longer be forced to do. And for what? To make her last days a misery? Worst of all, if she remains here, she will be cremated as the law requires now, and then my cousin will be denied what she wants most: a proper Okinawan funeral."

The boy has no answer.

"That is why she wrote this." Mitsue holds up the document that

Hatsuko had gone over so many times with her. "All her instructions are very clear. Now up! Get up!"

The boy, startled by how fierce the gentle old woman has become, stands, and pushes the wheelchair to her. Mitsue leans over Hatsuko and whispers in her old friend's ear, "It's time, dear cousin."

Hatsuko's eyes flutter open.

"She's ready," Mitsue tells the boy, who has come to understand the part he must play. He gathers Hatsuko's whisper of a body in his arms and settles her into the wheelchair with a delicacy that causes the *hāfu* girl's eyes to go soft with longing.

As he pushes the chair out through the waiting area, Mitsue tells the boy, "If you're still here when an angry man with a nervous wife arrives, tell him that his great-aunt has been taken home. You might also mention that she has removed him as the executor of her estate and has deeded all her property directly to the Okinawan Heritage Society."

"I think we're leaving now too."

"That's just as well. He's quite unpleasant and bound to become more so."

Though the boy begs her to allow him to run and fetch his car to drive them home, Mitsue insists upon taking a cab. The boy selects a comfortable taxi for them and helps tuck Hatsuko into the backseat, where she can lie down with her head in Mitsue's lap, and the two women set off for Madadayo, for home.

· SIXTY-ONE ·

Jake and I drive a long time without saying anything, and the smells of Okinawa at night fill the car with their own conversation. It is one I've never heard correctly before. Instead of sickly sweet, the night simply smells green, humid and blossoming and full of life re-creating itself.

The red glow from Kadena's twenty-four thousand feet of runways comes into view. It feels like a fire burning in the hearth, welcoming me home. Runway lights are home. My home. The home I grew up with. Just like they were home for my mother. What she grew up with. They're what we were given, and, no matter how many times we move, how the bases and states and countries switch around, runway lights will always be what feels like home to us.

I want the coming-home feeling to go on. I don't want it wrecked by what Jake has to tell me. I'm exhausted and I know that's why my eyes fill when I think about how everything will end tomorrow. Tomorrow Christy comes back. Tomorrow my mom comes back. My mission has been accomplished. I try to come up with another reason for sticking around.

As we approach the gate, Jake says, "There was one thing Hatsuko kept saying."

"There was?"

"Yeah, she kept repeating it over while she stared really hard at you. I guess I caught it because it's something my mom says all the time. *Nuchi du takara.*"

"*Nuchi du takara,*" I repeat, as if the strange words will straighten themselves out if I put them in my mouth.

"Life is the treasure."

"'Life is the treasure.' That's what she was saying to me?"

"Yeah, really emphatically too."

"*Nuchi du takara,*" I say, remembering the words then and how Hatsuko had spoken them more as a command than as a statement.

"That saying pulled Okinawans through some tough times. Some *really* tough times." Jake says in a way that makes me know he's talking about my tough times and about me making it through. He pulls into our carport, kills the engine, starts off, "Luz—"

I stop him. "Jake, don't, okay? I understand. You're with Christy. You were with her when I met you. Can we just leave it like this?"

"Luz—"

"No, Jake, I have to live here." The instant I say it, "have to live," I know it's true. "I have to be a real part of this"—I stumble over the word that is as right as it is corny—"community. I can't start off screwing everything up. Whatever it was, it's over."

Before he can answer, I'm out of the car. I don't look back, don't even hesitate until I'm inside the apartment. I lock the door behind me and go to the back patio, where there's a view of the runway. I sit out in the dense air and think about Hatsuko's message for me, life is the treasure, and about making it through tough times. The more I concentrate on those words, the stronger the sense of Codie being present grows, until I remember that making it through tough times, *really* tough times, is what Codie and I have always done. I stare at the runway in the distance so long that the glowing trident of red and gold lights feels like home again.

· SIXTY-TWO ·

The cool air of dawn brings Hatsuko the indispensable scent of the sea and the fragrance of sixty years of incense burned at the *butsudan,* mixed with the fresh smell of the *igusa* straw tatami beneath her. Now that she rests on her own futon she is ready. She knows that her final journey has begun when she hears again the chickens clucking and pecking about for tasty bugs. Goats bleating out their impatience to be fed. Pigs grunting as they root through cooling mud for the bits of sweet potato Mother has thrown out. Missing is the mooing of the cows, since they have all been requisitioned by the Imperial Army.

The groaning of wood against leather signals Papaya's arrival, carrying a cartload of night soil. The leathery leaves of the tall sea hibiscus that line the narrow path slap against the cart as she makes her way out to the fields. A rustling in the thatched roof high overhead is followed by a series of happy chirps, and Hatsuko imagines the gecko that brought luck to her family puffing up the sac at his throat into a lovely pink bubble.

When their old rooster Kobo crows to announce her last day on earth, Hatsuko has only one regret: She never found Tamiko's remains. Her sister's earthbound spirit came to her last night only long enough for her to explain and be forgiven but not to learn where Tamiko's bones are buried, which means that Tamiko will not be waiting for her in the next realm. She touches the lily pin on her chest and tells Mitsue, "Please make sure that no one removes this pin."

"Of course."

"Good," she says, then speaks her final words, "I will see you again soon, my dearest friend." A short while later, Kokuba Hatsuko leaves this world as easily as a boat slipping its moorings.

With her cousin's last breath set free, Mitsue goes to work. It has been nearly half a century since she was part of a true Okinawan funeral, but with Hatsuko's instructions to guide her, she calls in the five selected female relatives. Together they bathe Hatsuko, cut her fingernails, toenails, and hair, and wrap the clippings in fine rice paper to be buried with her. They dress her in the kimono Hatsuko had purchased for this day. Mitsue smiles when she sees that the kimono is printed in bright *bingata* style with images of her favorite animal, the Okinawan rail, a flightless bird being driven to extinction by the foreign invaders, mongooses, and cats. She fastens the lily pin to the front of her cousin's kimono. As the backs of her fingers brush against the washboard ridges of her cousin's motionless chest, the *kami* cause her to recall the *hāfu* girl trying to give her the lily pin. As is so often the case with the ways of the *kami*, she doesn't understand why they put the girl in her heart. All that is clear is what must be done.

When they're finished, Mitsue dispatches her helpers to notify everyone in Madadayo. There is only one outsider who must be told the news. The *kami* have made their mysterious wishes known. Mitsue begins making the calls that will connect her to the American girl.

· SIXTY-THREE ·

When my phone rings early the next morning, I'm surprised to see Jake's name appear and assume that he's slipping in one final communication before he returns to Christy. Before I can tell him I am serious and not to call anymore, he says, "Mitsue just called."

"Mitsue? From Madadayo? How did she even get your number?"

"At the hospital she recognized from my uniform what team I dance with and called the center where we practice. They gave her my number."

"Wow, that's random."

"No, that's Okinawa. There aren't six degrees of separation between any of us. More like two. Three at the most. Anyway, Mitsue wanted me to let you know that Hatsuko is gone."

"Oh." I don't know what to say and settle on, "Thanks for telling me."

"She wants you to come to the funeral."

"Me? Why?"

"She said you'd know why. She made me promise that I'd make sure you were there. It's today. In Madadayo. An hour before sunset. I'd take you myself but—"

"It's fine, Jake. No worries. I'll figure it out."

"Luz—"

"Jake, really, can you not talk about this? I understand. You and Christy. I get it. I always knew you were together. Seriously, don't stress."

"And, Luz, seriously, shut up, okay? It's not that simple. I just wanted to tell you that I have obligations. To her. To our families. We've all known one another for a long time. I know this is probably hard for you to understand, but it means that I have to do this the right way. And that will take time. Do you trust me?"

I think about the question, and answer, "I do," because, surprisingly, it's the truth. As I hang up, Jake's message, "She said you'd know why," echoes in my mind, because Mitsue is right; I just don't know how I'm going to accomplish what I now know I have to do. Not with my mom coming home. All I'm sure of is that I need her, and I need her car.

The first step is, obviously, cleaning her room. The havoc I find there seems unfamiliar, as if an entirely different person had wreaked it. I return the photo of Delmar Vaughn and the envelope with *"yuta"* written on it to their hiding spot. I pack the socks back into tight balls, make the bed with hospital corners crisp enough to cut yourself on, and hang all the uniforms up with the perfect amount of space between each one. Somehow, as I return my mom's room to its original state of immaculate order, the confusion in my mind gets sorted out too and a plan emerges, complete with all the lies I'll need to tell to implement it.

In the storage area at the end of the carport, I drag out our battered olive-drab footlocker with the broken brass latches and sweat-curled leather grips. "Overholt, Eugene, Airman 2nd Class E-3," is stenciled in white on the dented metal top. Next to the name of the man I will still always think of as my grandfather is glued the tattered, browned remnants of a shipping label with the destination typed at the bottom: Kadena Air Base. We once had a tiny key to open the brass lock, but it disappeared long ago, so my mom popped it open with a kitchen knife and we filled it with our stuff.

Glued inside the top of the lid are the magazine photos my grandfather pasted there before he shipped out on his first trip away from Missouri: Clint Eastwood in a poncho and a flat cowboy hat with a thin cigar clenched between his front teeth. Elvis and Priscilla getting married. Raquel Welch in a fur bikini. A red Dodge Charger. I wonder for a moment about what kind of a badass Eugene had dreamed of being. Whether Delmar Vaughn or the U.S. Air Force stole those dreams. Or if Okinawa and my grandmother were the most badass things that were ever, under any circumstances, going to happen to E-3 Overholt.

I take out the divider on top. Underneath it are report cards: mine, Codie's. Finger paintings. Crayon drawings. Locks of hair and impossibly tiny baby teeth in Ziploc bags with either Codie's or my name Sharpied on them. Albums with bright color photos show Codie and me blowing out birthday candles; sitting under Christmas trees unwrapping presents; standing in front of a base house, squinting into the sun, holding up Easter baskets. I uncover a plaster-of-paris handprint with Codie's name written into the plaster when it was still wet. I fit my hand over the print and cover it entirely with just my palm. It was my grandmother, my *anmā*, who must have saved all the memorabilia from mine and Codie's childhood, since the mementos end around the time she died.

Pulling myself out of this memory dive, I dig back in and find what I'm looking for: the kimonos *Anmā* made for Codie and me for Girls' Day and shipped to us when we were stationed in Germany. We'd been disappointed because the kimonos weren't made of bright fabric with pink cherry blossoms and blue Mount Fujis printed on it. Instead, she'd taken apart one of her drab old kimonos from Okinawa and made the dull, dark indigo fabric printed with a subtle pattern of white cross-hatchings into our kimonos.

Though we thought the kimonos were dreary, we both loved the soft lining that *Anmā* had sewn in so we could wear them in cold, snowy Germany. She had made that lining by piecing together squares from our old baby blankets and it was a patchwork of blue and pink kittens chasing balls of yarn, baby Donald Ducks and baby Mickey Mouses playing badminton, rows of pink elephants holding one another's tails, and storks in mailmen's uniforms flying through the air dangling happy babies in slings from their long, pointed beaks. She'd made the blankets before Codie and I were born, and they captured a whole cartoon world of happy expectancy. *Anmā* had even sewn little pockets into the lining. Sometimes we flipped the kimonos inside out to show the pastel patchwork. But we liked having the soft flannel menagerie cuddled against our skin too much to do that very often.

I neatly snip out a large square of the lining from Codie's kimono so that it again looks like a blanket waiting to receive a child about to be born. I carefully place one of Codie's curls and a baby tooth inside the little pocket, wrap it all into a tight bundle, and stuff it inside a red-and-green, holly-bedecked gift bag left over from Christmas, then set out for the runway to meet my mom's flight. As I cut through the ravine, sweeping spiderwebs radiant with early morning light out of the way, I rehearse all the lies I will need to tell my mom in order to do what I have to do, what the *kami* want me to do.

· SIXTY-FOUR ·

Throughout the long day Mitsue receives the visits of representatives from each of the households in Madadayo. Every visitor presses into her hand an envelope containing small offerings of money to help defray entombment expenses. As noon approaches, kinsmen are dispatched to clear the brush and weeds along the path to the family tomb and in the courtyard in front of it. The men remove the stone slab closing the tomb and leave fresh mud to seal it after the funeral. Inside the house, women cook. On the long veranda, several of the oldest male relatives, the ones who still know how, fold squares of paper into the flowers and birds that will be needed at the ceremony.

Hatsuko had not wanted a Buddhist priest to be summoned to chant a service, since that had never been the custom in her family. Her mother and her sisters had always insisted on the pure, the old ways as they were practiced before Buddhism and Shinto invaded. So visitors simply come, one by one, to weep and bid farewell to the woman who'd given them back their lives after the war. After the final mourner, Hatsuko's body is placed in the coffin she'd had made years before, and her knees are drawn up to her chest so that she might return to the womb of the earth in the correct manner.

As the shadow of the banyan tree spreads long across the courtyard, and a cooling breeze from the East China Sea brings the scent of the ocean, the villagers gather in the place where their ancestors had once assembled to hear Hatsuko's father read out the wishes of the emperor. As Hatsuko had asked, the village priestesses have donned their white robes and wait to carry out the ceremonies she has prescribed. The procession to the tomb is about to begin when two strangers arrive.

Mitsue, delighted that the *kami* had succeeded in relaying her invitation through the drummer, greets the *hāfu* girl, who arrives with her mother, also a *hāfu*, but one who looks so *Uchinānchu* that Mitsue understands the spirits' special interest in her daughter. Mitsue and the others are pleased that the mother, though a soldier with a soldier's rigid bearing, speaks their dialect in an enchanting way, like a child, a well-mannered child who was taught the respectful ways to address her elders. When she introduces herself as Gena, the villagers whisper among themselves, impressed that the soldier's mother had given her a name that means "silvery" in Japanese. They theorize that Silvery's mother must have been at one with the *kami* to know that her daughter was going to be a warrior and wear bits of silver on a uniform. Silvery's daughter, though, has an unpronounceable name that puzzles them until someone who spent years cutting cane in the Philippines tells them it means "light." Whereupon Mitsue announces that the name

Light is even more prescient than Silvery for a remarkable girl who would become an agent of the *kami*.

As Silvery speaks, Mitsue is overcome by the feeling that she knows this woman soldier. Or, at the very least, that she reminds her strongly of someone she knows but can't quite recall. Mitsue is still trying to place the frustratingly elusive memory when Silvery tells the gathered villagers that she is sorry for intruding; it was her daughter's crazy idea. Mitsue rushes to assure her that she and her daughter are very welcome. That, in fact, she went to a great deal of trouble to invite Light. Her daughter is an exceptional young woman, she adds. One clearly blessed by the *kami*.

All eyes turn to the special girl Light as the others beam an approval that needs no translation. Their attention makes Light and her mother nervous. Silvery, who appears unused to hearing her daughter praised and, seeming not to believe that they are truly wanted, continues apologizing. Consulting frequently with a dictionary on her phone, Silvery explains in the babyish way so at odds with her crisp, bluish-gray camouflage uniform that her older daughter was killed recently and that Light has taken her sister's death very hard. She says that Light insisted on coming here today because the online grief counselor who is mentoring her through the stages of grief had ordered her to come. None of the villagers know what an "online grief counselor" is. Silvery consults the dictionary on her phone several times and pieces together a translation.

"My daughter's 'death guide,'" she tries, "her 'spirit teacher' told her to come."

Light looks uneasily from her mother to the villagers, and only relaxes when, after a few seconds' delay while they absorb the words, they begin muttering, "*Un, un,*" and bobbing their heads in enthusiastic agreement. "Death guide?" "Spirit teacher?" Of course, she must mean *yuta*.

Silvery explains that this death guide had ordered Light to come today, saying that it would help her to accept her sister's death. That it would give her closure. Here Silvery illustrates the strange English word by touching the tips of her forefingers and thumbs together, making a circle. The villagers nod their heads with even greater enthusiasm, understanding Silvery's "closure" symbol immediately. They agree it is the perfect way to represent the obligation of helping a dead relative complete her long journey to that other realm.

Silvery then points to the green-and-red bag her daughter is clutching and, rolling her eyes to indicate that she realizes how foolish it is, explains that Light insisted that they stop on the way to Madadayo, so that she could scramble down one of those steep black cliffs all the way to the beach below. Alone. Light wouldn't let her come. Silvery tells them that she waited at the top of the cliffs for more than an hour while her daughter was down on the beach. Silvery asks them to understand that Light has been through a hard time, but she seems to be coming out of it, and that's the reason she is indulging this obvious misinterpretation of Ryukyuan ways. Poor Light, Silvery continues, believes that whatever she collected on the beach is required as some sort of offering. She asks Mitsue to please try to understand when Light presents her with . . . Silvery stops to consult her dictionary again and, shaking her head at the inadequacy of her translation, and finally finishes with "old wood of the sea."

Mitsue and the villagers wave off her apologies. Who among them has not consulted a *yuta*? And then performed whatever task, no matter how outlandish, that she prescribed? Really, there is nothing to understand. The grandmothers who see their granddaughters in this girl who is both bereaved and favored of the gods, are the first to open their arms to her and wrap her in hugs. It takes several stunned moments for Light to believe in the novelty of being accepted so immediately and so completely by a new group. But as she breathes in the wet hay smell of green tea and Pond's cold cream coming from the old women, she relaxes with a deep sigh into their embrace. Light borrows her mother's phone dictionary and, laboriously plucking out the words, gestures to the assembled and says, "Everyone. Here. Madadayo. My grandmother."

The villagers put their hands close to their faces and clap gentle claps of delight.

With all the apologies and explanations out of the way, Mitsue declares it time, and the procession begins. At the edge of the village, they stop short just before reaching the gate of a house where a young boy is recovering from a bout of pleurisy. A rope of rice straw is quickly fashioned and placed at the gate to prevent Hatsuko's spirit from taking the sick boy with her. Outside of Madadayo, they wind their way through the open fields. The breeze has stopped and not a puff of wind rustles the crops. Clouds hang like shimmering layers of mica that the setting sun shines sideways beams through. Red-bellied lizards dart out of the tall *susuki* grass, their silver tails wiggling calligraphy into the dry dust. The sweet potato vines glow in the focused light, their leaves so bright it hurts to look at them. Acacia trees shaggy with yellow flowers canopy the path. The mourners march in silence, their only accompaniment the lamentations of the cicadas droning out the grief of all creatures who must leave this green and gentle place.

When the trail narrows and enters into the cool, permanent dark of the thicket of red pines, the priestesses in white lead the way. The woods are cool and smell of resin. Light leaves her mother's side and allows all the mourners to pass her by until Mitsue, in the rear, reaches her. She signals to the old woman to hang back and they let the others go ahead, watching as the priestesses disappear in the dark. When the last mourner has been swallowed up in the folds of deep green, Light removes a package from her Christmas bag and hands it to Mitsue. Mitsue unwraps the soft pastel flannel and finds sea-washed bones light as balsa wood.

Mitsue strokes the bones, whispers, "Tamiko," on a long exhalation, and presses her cousin Hatsuko's lost sister to her chest. Her friend's prayers have been answered.

The mourners are already kneeling when Mitsue and Light join them in the courtyard enclosed by a rock wall ringing the tomb. As the priestesses say the prayers and set forth the offerings Hatsuko has stipulated, the mourners of Madadayo weep. The smell of black Okinawan incense returns them to the golden time before the war, when they and Hatsuko were young and they ran together through the sugarcane fields and into the shadowed woods where they shared all the secrets of a mysterious world. They remember Hatsuko's sister, Little Guppy, always trailing her about like a baby duckling, and how the happy girl's round cheeks would turn red in the cold as they stood in the winter wind blowing up the black cliff high above the East China Sea and sang the old song of farewell that saw off so many young men and women leaving their poverty-stricken island for Hawaii, Peru, Los Angeles, Brazil, the mainland.

Go, my lucky child
On the ship of good fortune,
And return, tethered
By a golden thread.

After all the prayers and paper birds and flowers have been offered, the coffin is carried into the tomb. Mitsue places a tray holding Hatsuko's favorite teacup, rice bowl, her set of chopsticks, and teapot on top of the coffin. In the center of the tray, at a spot she estimates to be directly about Hatsuko's heart, Mitsue nestles the flannel-wrapped bundle, gives it one last pat, and bids farewell to the cousin who was a sister to her for seven decades.

As the rock slab is replaced, Mitsue's tears are ones of relief, because she has finally discharged her solemn duty. When the men reseal the tomb, though, sorrow descends, for she realizes that never again will she have anyone to share her life with. Whom will she discuss all the exciting news of the past few days with? Mitsue now can only guess what Hatsuko would make of the American girl, Light, who was silent and almost detached until the moment when Mitsue carried the flannel-wrapped bundle into the tomb. Why, she wants to ask her old friend, did seeing that cloth, a worn baby blanket bright with ducks and elephants, disappear forever cause the girl to collapse in the wrenching sobs of the freshly bereaved? And what would her dear cousin have to say about the mother, Silvery, who did not immediately take her grieving child into her arms but waited until that child turned to her? And how would Hatsuko have described the expression that crossed the soldier's tight face when she finally did fully embrace her daughter? Would her old friend agree that the look seemed to be one of wonder? As if, until that moment, Silvery had never properly held her own child? And then why, after her mother whispered something in her ear, did an identical look of wonder cross the daughter's face? It is puzzling. But then, the *Amerikās* are a puzzling people.

But what Mitsue wishes most that she could confer with Hatsuko about is what happened next: Holding her only remaining child, Silvery smiled. And when she did, Mitsue knew exactly who Light's mother reminded her of: Aunt Junko and cousin Chiiko, for she has the same gap between her front teeth as they did. The same gap that even Chiiko's sweet girl Little Mouse did. But it's not just that gap; Silvery simply looks like one of Aunt Junko's daughters. Mitsue is certain that Hatsuko would scoff and say that such a connection is impossible: Junko's daughter, Chiiko, died in the war and Chiiko's daughter, Little Mouse, was never heard of again. Hatsuko would remind her that, after the war, they themselves had searched for a gap-toothed toddler in all the camps. And, besides, look at Light. No gap there. Only neat, straight teeth. Still, Mitsue thinks, watching the two visitors, mother and daughter, as they walk side by side away from the tomb back through the dark woods to Madadayo. Still.

It is nearing twilight when the funeral party exits the tunnel of green and emerges into the open fields. A wild, piercing cry high overhead stops the group. They search the sky until, in the waning rays of the evening sun, they spot a crested serpent eagle as it rises from the tallest branches of an ancient Ryukyuan pine. A band of white borders the majestic spread of the eagle's wings. The wing tips extend out beyond the white like dark fingers raking the sky as it glides silently from its perch, then wheels in the sky and heads west. The mask around the bird's eyes turns to gold as it faces the sun. With one mighty stroke, the bird soars on, out toward the Pacific Ocean. No one can recall the last time they saw such a bird, once so plentiful in their youth, and they all watch until the eagle disappears from view.

· SIXTY-FIVE ·

It's a little weird, though not totally unexpected, that Jake ignores me when school starts a week later. Ignore, though, that isn't the right word, since I can feel a spot on my back heating up like there's a laser aimed at it from where he stands at the edge of the crowd gathered on the front lawn of Kadena High School, staring at me. Christy and the rest of the Smokinawans are with him.

"What a man-whore," Jacey hisses into my ear.

"Naw, it's not like that," I tell her.

"Like what?" Kirby, his arm draped over Jacey's shoulder, asks.

"Nothing."

"Spit it out, Cabooskie. You want me to put the hurt on Furusato for you? Because I will. Someone disrespects my girls, I'ma cut a bitch. You know I will."

"Thanks, Kirbs." Even though he's kidding, Kirby does actually have a nice protective streak that Jacey brings out. I can even see the possibility that he'll grow up into a decent man.

An honor guard of Rotzees in khaki uniforms with white webbed belts crossing their chests marches out. The instant the first notes of "The Star-Spangled Banner" play over the school's loudspeaker system, we all shut up, freeze, slap our right hands over our hearts, and watch our country's flag being raised. Right beside it, on a flagpole precisely the same height, the crimson bull's-eye of Japan's rising sun ascends. DaQuane and Wynn, red eyed and reeking of pot, slip in next to us and sing out, loud and proud.

Instead of singing, I look away from both flags, stare at the clouds, white and high as Marie Antoinette's wig, and think about my mom. It's been different since she came back. Actually, things were exactly the same as before when I met her at the flight line. She was surprised to see me for about two seconds, then asked if I was in trouble with SF, needed to go into rehab, or was pregnant. No, nothing really changed until the funeral. Until I caught the last glimpse I would ever have of those cut-up squares of baby blanket that had stroked Codie's skin going into the tomb forever. That's when I lost it. When I surrendered. When, amazingly, my mom stepped up to catch me as I fell and whispered the most astonishing thing to me: "Your sister did not die outside the perimeter. She was inside the wire. She died instantly. Being a good soldier. Your sister was a good soldier, Luz."

Because I understood then that the same question that had haunted me had also tortured her, and that she'd volunteered to go to the Sandbox so she could get answers for both of us, I said, "So are you, Mom. You're a good soldier." That's when I laid my grudge against her down.

So now we're careful around each other. And when she's not, when she's a jerk, which she and I will both always be entirely capable of being, I think about my mom as a baby, a newborn whose skin color made her father feel like the butt of a false friend's joke. Baby Gena must have been just one color betrayal too many for Eugene Overholt, since she came along about the time that he was figuring out that his beloved air force had also done him wrong. That the supposedly harmless rainbow herbicides—agents Purple, Pink, and Orange—were killing him deader than any Charlie in the Mekong Delta could have.

And my sweet little grandmother? *Anmā*? I think a lot about her too. An ex–Koza bar girl, steeped in the belief that her entire purpose in life was to bear away a family's shame in silence, what chance did she ever have to be the mother her daughter needed? I remember *Anmā* doing the best she could, dancing in secret with me and Codie, finding rare solace in the feel, the smell of her granddaughters' dark curls, the ones that reminded her of being crazy in love with another man who wasn't worthy of her, and my heart aches thinking of the damaged daughter these two damaged humans raised. A daughter who only found her true home in the military. Who was so genuinely devoted to the U.S. Air Force that she passed it on to her own daughter, believing, truly believing, that it was the most treasured legacy she had.

Once I accept that all of them, even my screwed-up mom, were just trying to do the best they knew how, I have no choice but to do the same. I even use military time now, just because it makes my mom happy. Makes her feel like the world is under control and has its shit wrapped up tight, the way it's supposed to be. Which, I guess, is what we all want.

O'er the lah-hand of the WEED and the HOMO. Of. The.
Buh-rave.

Kirby, DaQuane, and Wynn yell out their version of the last line of "The Star-Spangled Banner." The instant the anthem ends, the "on" switch is flipped, and all us military kids are reanimated again. At precisely 0815 hours, the bell rings and the doors open. Another first day at a new school starts, and Jacey and I surge up the steps together. We consulted on our first-day outfits. Even went to the BX together to see whether there was anything not terminally lame. There wasn't. So she's wearing the pink top I loaned her that looks amazing with her coloring, and I've got on a great pair of skinny jeans that shrank and she can't wear anymore. Codie and I used to do the same thing, trade back and forth. I thought it was only a sister thing. Turns out it's not.

Our fellow brats eddy around us, the boisterous ones, the shy ones. The ones who've been on the Rock for a while and know the lay of the land, the ones who just PCS'd in. The Post Princesses. The Gung Hos. The strangers who'll sit beside us in class and play with us on teams. The kids who'll become our best friends or our archnemeses. The ones with whom we'll keep in touch for a few years, then not recall who stopped writing. The ones who won't remember sitting next to us in geometry. The ones who'll tell us at the reunion in twenty years that they had the biggest crush on us. The ones who will look us up after their children are grown and they've retired and have time to wonder what it would have been like to have grown up with the same friends. The ones who will want to connect with their childhoods, who they once were, and will settle for sharing the name of a base, the name of a teacher we both had, the name of a maid who might have worked for both our families. It won't even matter all that much that we were on that base, had that teacher, that maid, at different times and never really knew each other. It's a connection. It's a true thing from our childhoods, and we shared it.

I'll meet new people this year, my last at a dependent school, and the first thing we'll ask one another is, "Where have you been stationed?" If our bases overlap we'll talk about how great the French fries were at that one snack bar by the pool or how there was that bakery right next to the base and the smell of baking bread would drive us crazy. I'll send them all Christmas cards. I'll keep in touch. I won't be the one who stops answering, because it turns out that friends are like the Velveteen Rabbit: They're all Quasis if you don't believe in them enough to make them real.

At the top of the stairs, me and my brat brothers and sisters funnel into the crowded hall and start looking for our first classes. I have calculus on the second floor. As I head for the stairs, I catch Jake scanning the crowd. When his gaze falls on me, the one he was searching for, he stops looking around, and tugs down the collar of his shirt enough to show me that he's wearing Codie's opal necklace. It makes me happy that he recovered it from the shrine. He touches the opal, but doesn't give me a sexy smile or mouth the word "pretty" or do any of those flirty, playa things. He just closes his shirt and hides the gem's pale radiance next to his heart.

I don't know exactly what will happen with Jake and me. Maybe nothing will. Whatever does or doesn't happen, though, I'm certain that the most important thing already has. I'm certain that Jake Furusato will never forget me.

· SIXTY-SIX ·

My mother, *Anmā*, Kokuba Tamiko, Little Guppy, killed herself so that I could exist. Now that we have been released, I understand why. In the forty-nine days after we are delivered to our family's tomb, yet before we complete our journey to the next world, the entire story is made known to me. Even the saddest parts, which Mother had never allowed me to share. Even the parts that took place after Aunt Hatsuko left our family's tomb and, carrying my grandmother's crock of pork miso, went in search of the unworthy Nakamura.

I see everything that happened after the sisters were parted. I see how, in the days after Hatsuko's departure, my mother was tortured by visions of what would befall her feckless sister without her, the one with her broad Okinawan feet firmly planted on the earth. And so *Anmā* left our family's tomb, where ten generations of ancestors guarded her, where she would have been safe and grown fat eating my grandmother's dried sweet potatoes and bonito, and went into a world that was now ruled by demons. She left to save a life that she thought was her sister's but was not. The life she saved was mine.

I see the colors she saw in the weeks before I came to be. The sea was still the blue of jewels. The sky was still the blue of softness. But there were no greens. There was only endless brown and black. The bleak colors swirled and formed into charred stumps, mud, potholes, and rotting corpses. My mother knew then that her sister, so much more refined and delicate than she, could not possibly have survived, and she gave up her search. She no longer wanted to live in a world without green, without her sister. The *mabui* left her body and, bereft of her spirit, Mother could no longer go on. Little Guppy lay down beside the bombed-out remnants of a stone wall built to protect a family from typhoons. But the family and their house were gone; nothing but ash and the stink of decay remained. That is where my mother prepared to die.

Nearly starved, dehydrated, weak as a kitten, she was close to death when my father found her. He was a Japanese private who covered her mouth and called out the emperor's name as he finished. When he was through using her, the soldier, instead of taking his hand away and letting *Anmā* go, pressed it down harder, as though she were the cause of his and Japan's disgrace. He pressed with both hands until her nose and mouth were covered. At the realization that he was killing her, my mother's spirit returned with a raging fury determined that no mainland bully was going to take another thing from her. Certainly not her life. Little Guppy bit down on the lump of flesh at the base of the private's thumb so hard that she severed the tendon, causing the finger to droop from his hand, forever unusable. She escaped while he howled in pain.

Anmā met the second of my fathers as she squatted beside a stream and washed away the soldier's blood from her face and her own from the inside of her thighs. This father was an Okinawan boy barely older than she. He spoke to her in their language and begged for forgiveness and wept as he did what he did. *Anmā*, squashed against the earth, reached out a hand, found a rock, and left that father unconscious.

Anmā met the last of my fathers when a typhoon descended on the island. When the howling winds hurled uprooted trees, sections of chain-link fence, and rusted truck doors sideways through the air, *Anmā* sought protection in an abandoned tomb. In the dark, she didn't realize that the tomb already had an occupant. He was an American giant with a long nose and goat eyes. She could no more have resisted a monster nearly three times her size than she could have battled the typhoon raging outside. When it was over, he scurried away when a fraught calm descended as the eye of the storm passed over.

Though there was no one else in the tomb, as the ferocity of the typhoon's second act howled outside, *Anmā* realized that she was no longer alone. She knew I was with her. The giant had forgotten his pack of food. Inside the box, she found caramels, thick crackers, a package with four cigarettes, a tin with a key that peeled back the skin like an apple to reveal a rectangle of pink meat, and powders, one a bitter dark brown that dissolved on the tongue, the other yellow and salty with a vague taste of chicken fat. More than food, though, *Anmā* needed water, and, with many prayers of apologies, she emptied one of the oldest burial urns of its contents and placed it outside to collect rain. She quickly gathered enough to quench her thirst, then made herself eat and drink as much as her shrunken stomach could hold, while she whispered to me, "*Nuchi du takara. Nuchi du takara.*"

Anmā remained alive for me. Later, when she felt me flip and frolic within her, she rejoiced. Hundreds, thousands of other girls chose differently. Especially the ones raped by the invaders. Those girls drank tea brewed from camphor wood leaves, had cones of mugwort burned on their bellies, or ate the fruit of the sago palm to kill the unwanted child they carried. Or themselves. Many no longer cared which. Others took their newborns to the sea and let the waves carry their shame away. *Anmā*, though, she loved me from the first second that I existed within her. She ceased mourning for all who had been lost. I was her consolation, her companion and hope on a hard road. I was her family.

The retreating Japanese army drove us farther and farther south, until at last we refugees came to the sea. We huddled by the thousands on the beach in the shade of the high cliffs. There we waited, trapped by the ocean in front of us and impenetrable thickets of Devil's Claw bushes with thorns cruel as barbed wire on either side. Japanese soldiers perched like black crows on the cliffs above us yelled down threats that they would kill anyone who might shame them by surrendering. They made good on their promise when five of our group waded into the water and tried to swim to the American ships that surrounded us. When the steady waves lifted the swimmers up, the Japanese soldiers shot them, one after another.

The heat was monstrous. There was no water. As the sun rose, the shade receded, and the killing rays stalked us across the blistering sand as relentlessly as a hunter his prey. *Anmā* had saved one of the Americans' thick crackers, and so that I might survive, she tried to eat it. She chewed but couldn't swallow. She opened her parched mouth and the crumbs, dry as sand, fell out. From that moment on, I lost the strength to move within her and was still. *Anmā* knew that unless she did something, we both would die violent deaths that would condemn us to haunt this terrible place forever. That we would never be released to join our ancestors. The only way to avoid such imprisonment was suicide.

On the last day, a girl of five, driven mad by thirst, ran into the waves and drank salt water. She died that night, convulsed in agonizing seizures. While all attention was on the dying child and her wailing mother, *Anmā* crept away from the group and entered the thicket of Devil's Claw bushes.

The thorns slashed at her like a thousand knives. Blood twisted down her arms and legs and dried there in black streaks, but she pressed on. By inching forward and ignoring the pain, *Anmā* made a tortoise's progress toward escape. She had fought her way halfway through the thorned maze when she heard a roaring and smelled kerosene: The Americans had come with their flamethrowers and were burning the thicket. Shrieks tore the black air as flames ignited others hidden in the bushes. The fires encircled us. Searing waves of heat washed over us. *Anmā* coughed and her hand came away covered in blood. We were now certain to die a death so terrible that our souls would be trapped in this hellish place forever. *Anmā* clapped her hands to catch the attention of the *kami*, especially Old Jug, and prayed as the burning air smelling of human flesh being roasted singed her lungs and the flames drew closer.

The *kami* directed her to climb. Though she barely had enough strength left to walk, she obeyed and climbed. My mother clawed her way to the winding trail, away from the beach, and climbed. Up the black cliff. Up above the black smoke. Higher and higher she went, until the blazing thicket was only an ember and the ocean a dark shimmer far below us.

At the top of the cliff, the ten thousand souls who had already killed themselves—whether forced or willing—rose up and greeted us. *Anmā* took a few moments to bid farewell to the island she had so loved, before she stepped into the arms of the waiting spirits. We fell then into the long, dark dream that is ending now. Thanks to the ceremonies Mitsue and others performed, my mother and I have completed our journey to the next world. We are *kami-sama*.

For the first time, I have senses and they all come alive. I feel a cool, soft breeze against my skin. I smell for the first time, and the scents of lily and pineapple fill my nostrils. A *sanshin* plays in the distance and, up close, right next to my ear, I hear the sound of my mother's heartbeat. I open my eyes. My first sight is the lapis lazuli air shimmering around me. The second is my mother's face. It is a good face.

She asks me, "Child, why do you stay here with your mother?" I try to remember how I arrived in this perfect place, to snatch back bits and pieces of the long time of the dark dream from before, but they are already disappearing like rain puddles drying in the sun, and we have always been here. She pushes me from her lap. "Go. Run and play."

I have always been a strong, healthy boy, and my twin cousins, my best friends, Shinsei and Uei, who call out for me to join them, have always been waiting for me. I run off on my fast, sturdy legs and everything is just as it was in *Anmā's* memories. We pluck the straightest boughs we can find from a screw pine tree to make fine samurai swords and fight a fierce battle. We trap banana spiders bigger than a man's hand and have a race. We slide down a hill of sweet-smelling *susuki* grass and never worry that *habu* vipers might be hiding beneath the silvery blades.

When I look back, *Anmā* is wearing the uniform of the schoolgirl she once was and now will be forever, and she is running toward the house where she grew up, where her sister, my aunt Hatsuko, holds her arms open wide in welcome. My aunt says, "Little Guppy, my Little Guppy," over and over. They hold each other's faces in their hands and weep. Every tear traps a sad memory, and when all are shed, the sadness has evaporated and the sisters take their places on the long veranda of the house where they grew up.

In the courtyard, beneath the vast roof of a banyan tree, all 2,046 ancestors from ten generations back gather to feast on pigs' ears in vinegar, sweet potato in green-tea sauce, stir-fried bitter melon, and pork stewed in squid's ink washed down with cold wheat tea sweetened with black sugar for the children and millet brandy for the adults. My legendary great-great-great-grandfather Ryō plucks tunes from his *sanshin*. Everyone claps as Cousin Zenko and Uncle Shima dance their clumsy dances. My uncle Ichirō, Forest Orchid Boy, laughs as his lover, Nobuko, puts the panama hat she has woven on their child's head.

The timid dwarf deer, drawn by our merriment, tiptoe out of the for-

est. Emerald frogs, long-haired mice, and clouds of orchid-leaf butter-
flies also join us. A chartreuse-spotted monkey lizard skitters across
my foot. Suddenly I recall the most important question and run back
to the veranda to ask it before it slips away forever from my memory.

"*Anmā*, when will I be born?"

"What? Don't say that. Don't talk about leaving when we have only
finally gotten here. Go. Play with your cousins."

"No, little sister," Aunt Hatsuko interrupts, "the child is right."

"Right? To ask to leave paradise? To suffer as we suffered?"

"And to taste desire like a shiny coin in your mouth? And to work
until the blood sings in his muscles? And to breathe the breaths exhaled
by his own child?"

"How much of that did we have?"

"Enough, sister. Enough. We had life; we had the treasure."

"No, I can't allow it. There is too much pain. I won't see my child
suffer."

"It is not for you to decide. The *kami* have already spoken through him."

"But aren't we *kami* now?"

"Sister, it is the child's turn."

"But whom will he be born to? How will it be arranged?"

"I know who will arrange it."

"Who?"

"Cousin Chiiko."

"Aunt Junko's daughter? My second mother who carried me everywhere on her back? Did she survive the war?"

"Oh, no, she was hanged by the Japanese a short time after you left
for Shuri. The Japanese claimed she was a spy, because she screamed at
the soldiers quartered in her house and whacked them with her broom
after they killed and roasted her last chicken."

Anmā laughs. "Just like Aunt Junko. She would say anything to
anyone. Remember how Father used to say it was because of the gap
between their front teeth? How that opening let all the foolish words
in their heads spill out?"

"See, she's just over there."

"What happened to her children?"

"They're here as well. After she was hanged, all her children were
orphaned, since their father never returned from Manchukuo."

"Even Little Mouse? Kazumi, the sweetest baby anyone ever saw?"

"She was the only one who survived the war."

"You can't possibly be thinking of her to be my son's mother."

"No, of course not. Don't be silly. Little Mouse died quite some time ago, an old woman, alone in a foreign country, never knowing who her mother was. It is Mouse's granddaughter who might be a perfect mother for your son. I actually met the young woman. A remarkable girl. Favored by the *kami*. She reminded me of you. Why, I've even met the young man who will be the father. I promise you, sister, you couldn't do any better. Shall we speak to Chiiko and Little Mouse about arranging it? They're over there with Aunt Junko."

"I will speak to her, Hat-chan, but that is all. I make no promises."

"Oh, when did my Little Guppy become so serious? Come along."

My mother and Aunt Hatsuko go to join their aunt Junko and cousin Chiiko. Junko and Chiiko are eating salted *gōyā* melon seeds and spitting the hulls out between the gaps in their front teeth. With their free hands, they both pat and stroke the young woman sitting between them, who must be Chiiko's orphaned daughter, once the happy toddler Little Mouse. Little Mouse's back is to me, but she is dressed like an American, wearing a tight pink sweater that hugs her waist. The women put their heads together, and I know that they are arranging with Mouse for me to be born to her granddaughter.

Aunt Hatsuko points toward me, and Mouse in her pink sweater turns around. She has a kind face, a good face for a great-grandmother. Her black hair rises into a bubble held back from her broad forehead by a shiny band of ribbon. Her eyes are thickly lined, and on her lips is a pink so pale it is almost white. When she smiles, a gap between her front teeth, just like her mother's and her grandmother's, is revealed.

As I wonder what her granddaughter, the one who will be my mother, is like, a curly-haired young woman dressed in an American military uniform enters the courtyard and is welcomed into our family. The young woman wears a crisp blue blouse decorated with colorful rectangles over her heart. On her shoulders are silver chevrons as perfect as a bird's wings rising in flight. In her hand she carries a patchwork square of soft fabric in pretty pastel colors that would be ideal for wrapping a baby in. Obviously I won't be that baby, and this young woman won't be my mother, since she is no longer among the living.

Mouse gathers the girl into her arms, buries her face in the cushion of dark curls on the young woman's head, and kisses every one. It is made known to me that it is this young woman's sister whom they are thinking of to be my mother. I like the looks of her enough to believe that, when the time is right, her sister will make a suitable mother.

With that decided, I run off after my cousins. At the top of a gentle hill, I pause and look back down. The women on the veranda are lost in conversation. Aunt Hatsuko tells my mother that she was a Princess Lily girl all along, that her name *was* on the list that their father never finished reading. At this, my mother gives a deep sigh that releases her final breath of earth air, the last bit of sadness tethering her to the world of the living. A moment later, the two sisters, laughing about how fat and greasy Nakamura ended up becoming, tilt so far over toward each other that the pins on their chests touch, the drooping head of one flower touching the drooping head of the other. From where I stand, at the moment that the two lilies meet it looks as if together they form one complete heart.

A screw pine sword slashes the air next to my ear, and then makes a wobbly stab at my belly. I whirl around, hoist my weapon, and chase after my cousins, pelting them with rotten loquats as I run up the hill, into the shimmering air.

ACKNOWLEDGMENTS

This novel began in 1970 when I was an Air Force dependent strolling around the vast green fairways of a golf course at Kadena Air Base, and I wondered, Why, on this tiny island where everyone off base is so cramped together, do we get all this space to play a game? The list of those who helped me find answers to that question is long. First among them is Steve Rabson, professor emeritus of East Asian Studies at Brown University and a gift sent by the *kami* to help me get it right. His writing about Okinawa and his impeccable translations of the island's literature and poetry, particularly the short story collection he coedited, *Southern Exposure: Modern Japanese Literature from Okinawa*, were essential.

Of the hundreds of sources I used, I have to single out several extraordinary first-person narratives: *A Princess Lily of the Ryukus* by Jo Nobuko Martin and *The Girl with the White Flag* by Tomiko Higa are deeply moving accounts by native girls who survived the horrors of the Battle of Okinawa. *From Okinawa to the Americas* by Hana Yamagawa provided a rare glimpse into island life before the war. The work of the legendary Chalmers Johnson, starting with *Okinawa: Cold War Island*, was of great help to me in appreciating the unique role Okinawa plays in the American empire.

For educating me about contemporary Okinawa, I'd like to thank Tomoe Yokoda and James Matej of the Okinawan Cultural Association of Texas; Christy Nogra, currently stationed at Kadena; and my eleventh-hour hero, Jim Kassebaum, chief marketing officer for Marine Corps Community Services Okinawa, who told me what I needed to know about Kadena Air Base as it is today. Another gift sent by the *kami* was the performer and scholar Byron Fija, whose dedication to keeping the Okinawan language alive inspires me.

Muchisimas gracias to my talented friend Christy Krames for transforming the geography of my imagination into maps as artful as they are accurate.

I thank my indispensable readers for their insights and expertise: Carol Dawson, who, through all the iterations, kept asking the crucial questions; Mary Edwards Wertsch, friend and author who wrote our people's handbook, *Military Brats;* Kathleen Orillion and Carol Flake, always generous, always intuitive; Nancy Mims, who infused the work with an artist's empathy; Stephen Harrigan and Elizabeth Crook, who never fail to provide wise counsel; and Tiffany Yates-Martin, who continues to be the coolest copy editor. Ever. Special dollops of gratitude go to my sisters and best readers, Martha and Kay Bird, brave and noble brats who, along with brothers John, Tom, and Steve, were the bubble of air that kept me alive through all the moves.

For the fifth time in a row, I am the luckiest author around to have the privilege of working with the paragons of publishing at Alfred A. Knopf: Kim Thornton, Annie Eggers, Christine Gillespie, Gabriele Wilson, Kathleen Fridella, Peggy Samedi, and Maggie Hinders. I am grateful for your talent, taste, enthusiasm, and dedication. I can never truly thank my editor, the magnificent Ann Close, for the imperceptible magic she always works which, somehow, transforms impossible messes into books. The radiant spirit of Nina Bourne hovers around all of you.

For always, from the very beginning, having my back, here's to you, Kristine Dahl.

And to Gabriel and George. You are my hometown.

For readers interested in learning more about the Land of Constant Courtesy, I recommend starting with *Okinawa: The History of an Island People* by George Kerr.